PART
& PARCEL

A SIDEWINDER STORY

ABIGAIL
ROUX

D1003008

RIPTIDE
PUBLISHING

Riptide Publishing
PO Box 1537
Burnsville, NC 28714
www.riptidepublishing.com

Part & Parcel (A Sidewinder Story)

Cover art: L.C. Chase, lcchase.com/design.htm
Editor: Rachel Haimowitz
Layout: L.C. Chase, lcchase.com/design.htm

ISBN: 978-1-62649-369-8

First edition
December, 2015

Also available in ebook:
ISBN: 978-1-62649-368-1

PART
& PARCEL

A SIDEWINDER STORY

ABIGAIL
ROUX

RIPTIDE
PUBLISHING

There are only two kinds of people that understand Marines: Marines and the enemy. Everyone else has a second-hand opinion.

Gen. William Thornson, U.S. Army

TABLE OF CONTENTS

CHAPTER ONE

1999

Lights flashed. People screamed in the distance. Nick's back hit the ground, and it was all blue sky and smoke. His body was cold when it should have been hot, going colder by the second. The sounds faded, and then the light, and there was peace for a while. Just sweet peace.

When Nick woke, pain flooded him like he'd never felt before. He jerked, fighting for breath, clawing at whatever was burning inside his right arm.

"Hold him down!" someone yelled. "Jesus Christ! Hold him!"

"Irish," someone breathed close to his ear. A smooth voice, one that meant safety and home. "Irish, it's Six. You got to be calm, bud."

Nick immediately tried to still himself. If Ty was telling him to calm, it meant his panicking was a threat to someone. Where were they? Were they still out in the field? Were they prisoners again? Pain burned through him. He gritted his teeth and fumbled around for Ty's hand, desperate for something—anything—to ground him.

"Six." Nick gasped, barely recognizing his own voice.

Ty's fingers were hot in Nick's hands, but Ty's grip was unwavering. "We've got you."

"Who the fuck let this bag run out?" someone else shouted. Nick belatedly recognized Kelly's voice, and damn, he sounded pissed. "Get out of the fucking way! You can't do your job, I'll do it for you!"

Ty's face swam into Nick's flickering field of view. He had Nick's hand in both of his, holding Nick's fingers close to his face the way they'd held each other every night in captivity. Nick clung to him, breathing hard, trying not to beg for help.

"You're okay. Hold on, Irish."

Nick stared into his eyes, clutching at him until cold began to soak into his arm. It climbed through his veins, cloying, cloudy, seeping into every part of him and pushing out the heat and pain.

"That's it, bud," Ty whispered. He petted Nick's face, thumb resting against Nick's cheekbone. "You're okay. It's all okay."

Nick closed his eyes, trusting Ty to be telling him the truth.

When he woke again, it was to a much more pleasant world. The pain was just a distant whisper at the edges of his being, and the panic had left him with Ty's assurances. He turned his head, squinting against the bright lights. He could hear someone sweeping, accompanied by the tinkle of broken glass and the rustle of plastic. And of course the beeps and whirring of monitors that he knew all too well.

"O'Flaherty?" Kelly said carefully. His voice was a whisper, as if he wasn't sure that Nick was really conscious and didn't want to wake him if he wasn't.

Nick turned his head to find Kelly sitting on the other side of his bed, a tentative smile on his face. "Hey, Doc."

Kelly set aside the book he'd been reading and scooted his chair closer. He rested one elbow on the edge of the bed, giving Nick a small smile. "Welcome back, Staff Sergeant."

"The others?"

"All okay. You were the only casualty."

"What'd I lose?"

"Your pride," another voice answered. It took Nick far too long to focus on the man who'd come up behind Kelly. Elias Sanchez bent closer, as if he realized Nick couldn't see him. "Not only did you get yourself shot, but you also lost our bet."

"Bullshit," Nick grunted, closing his eyes again.

Eli and Kelly both chuckled at him. Eli tapped Kelly on the shoulder. "Six needs you for his report. I got this."

Kelly gave Eli his chair, offering Nick a gentle pat on the chest. "I'll come check on you when we're done." He pointed at the machinery, shooting Eli a look he probably didn't think Nick would notice. "Watch his pain. If it tops again, he'll do even more damage to himself."

The sweeping sound stopped for a moment. "If he's going to fucking trash my MedBay again, we'll tie him down."

"Come near him with those restraints and I'll fucking kill you," Kelly snarled.

Eli squeezed Kelly's shoulder. "Doc."

"Nobody fucking ties him down," Kelly growled, pointing one long finger at whoever had been given the task of cleaning up whatever mess Nick had made in his earlier rampage.

Eli waved Kelly away, and Kelly left them with one last look at Nick. Nick watched him go with a frown. He wasn't sure why Kelly was so opposed to the restraints. Hell, last time he'd been injured Nick had asked them to restrain him because he'd almost killed the corpsman who'd been there to administer a blood test and had woken Nick too abruptly. The restraints were just to keep everyone safe, including Nick.

"Why's he angry?" Nick asked Eli.

"You been talking in your sleep," Eli said with a reassuring smile. It didn't reach his eyes, though, and from the sadness in them Nick knew immediately what he must have been saying. Heat flushed across his cheeks. "None of us knew how much all that shit stuck with you and Grady. You never talk about it, so we figured you were okay. But you called out for Ty a couple times, so they had him come in here. You were . . . begging." Eli winced and lowered his head.

Nick fought hard to swallow, forcing himself to keep looking at Eli so Eli wouldn't know he was ashamed of it.

"Grady said he has the same dreams, told us a little about what you were probably dreaming."

"Oh," Nick said weakly, his eyes going unfocused because it was just too much effort otherwise.

"Doc didn't take it too well. Hell, none of us did."

Nick recalled the flash of anger in Kelly's normally placid gray eyes and shivered.

"Hey Lucky, you ever need to talk that shit out, I got you. You know that, right?"

Nick met his eyes and nodded, earning himself a gentle pat on the head as Eli leaned closer. Nick stared at Eli for a few seconds, trying to remember what had happened *this time* after he'd been hit. It was all a haze of fire and drugs.

Eli began to grin, his dark eyes finally sparkling. "First person to get hurt this tour, that was the deal."

"No."

"Deal's a deal, *papá.*" He reached into the pocket of his uniform and withdrew a black permanent marker. "It's for your own good."

"Oh God," Nick grunted, and he could only give a long-suffering sigh as Eli began a Sharpie doodle on his forearm. "If you draw a dick on me . . ."

"Would I do that?" Eli asked without looking up from his work. "I been practicing that Celtic knot stuff you showed me. This is going to be classy as shit."

Nick couldn't help his smile as he closed his eyes, relaxing as Eli's familiar presence filled him with warmth and safety. "*You're* classy as shit."

"Oohrah!"

February 22, 2013

Nick stepped over the body of the man he'd just killed and reached for the car Ty and Zane were trapped inside. He'd seen the NIA agents closing in on the squad car, and he'd moved as fast as his ruined knee allowed to get to them. The relief when he reached for the door locks was the first good thing he'd felt in weeks.

And then someone grabbed him from behind.

"No!" Ty cried. He banged on the glass, struggling with the handle. "No!"

A knife drove into Nick's side before he could react. His eyes were locked on Ty's, everything moving in slow motion, the streets of Miami morphing into a desert with streaks of military lightning overhead. The attacker twisted the knife to bring Miami and the real world crashing back down on him, and Nick screamed.

Ty echoed it with an anguished cry and threw himself against the opposite window, slamming his fist into the already cracked glass over and over as Nick sank to his knees. He bowed his head, losing sight of his friend, losing sight of everything. He was still being held around the neck by the man with the knife, and Nick's mind raced for a way to free himself. His attacker yanked the knife out of Nick's side and plunged it in again, wrenching another scream from Nick. He arched his back, eyes squeezed shut as tears streaked down his face. His fingers grazed the KA-BAR he'd stashed in his boot, and he gasped for one last lungful of air.

He flipped the knife in his palm and jammed it into the killer's throat, then folded over and desperately grasped for the wound at his side to stanch the bleeding. Black SUVs were drawing near, full of more NIA agents with guns and knives who no doubt wanted to ask Ty and Zane some very pointed questions.

If the rest of Sidewinder was going to help them, they would have reached Nick by now. They'd obviously been held up in battle or, God forbid, hadn't made it out alive. Nick was on his own, Ty and Zane's lives in his bloody hands.

Nick began crawling for the cruiser, keeping low as the rattle of gunfire from further down the street got closer. His fingers reached the gun he had dropped during his tussle. There was so much blood, he didn't know if he'd be able to grip the damn thing. He collapsed in the debris, holding on to the handle of the knife in his side and crying out in agony. It would be easy to give up. It would stop hurting if he just gave up.

He met Ty's eyes through the glass of the police cruiser. He would never make it to the door. There was only one way to get Ty and Zane out of that car, and as they stared at each other, Ty seemed to read his mind. Nick reached out with a trembling, bloody hand and aimed the gun as Ty and Zane ducked out of sight.

The shot was excruciating. Nick seemed to feel every last inch of his broken body as the aftershock tore through him. When he came back to his senses, Ty was grasping at him, tugging him, trying to help him up. Nick tried to get to his feet, but he couldn't even feel them. He reached out for the other man nearby for extra support, surprised to see Eli there in the middle of Miami. But his hand passed right through him: there was nothing there but shadow, and Nick collapsed in Ty's arms.

Ty fell to his knees again, holding Nick to him. Nothing hurt anymore. Nothing.

Nick stared up at the sky. It was the color Kelly's eyes could sometimes turn. Kelly . . . he hadn't been able to say good-bye. He wouldn't be able to. This was it.

He focused on Ty, nodding in acceptance. This was it. "Okay."

"It's okay," Ty whispered. His fingers tightened in Nick's shirt, cradling him in his lap. "We'll get you all patched up and you'll be fine. Zane, help me!"

Nick tried to speak, tried to tell Ty this was the end, that it was okay. The gunfire was closer, and Ty hunched defensively.

"Run, Ty," Nick managed to get out.

"We're not leaving you here," Ty snarled. He was angry, but Nick understood. They'd been angry at Elias Sanchez for dying on them, too.

Nick struggled for more words. He hadn't given his life for Ty and Zane just to see them die with him in the street. "I'm already dead, babe. Go."

"No!"

Nick couldn't keep his eyes open any longer. They fell shut against his will, Ty's face against the cheerful sunshine and the silhouette of Eli standing over him and grinning the last things he saw. "See you on the other side, brother."

March 2, 2013

Kelly didn't sleep much lately, and when he did, his dreams were full of terror and pain. He woke up every time thinking he'd lost Nick, confused and unsure of what was real and what merely was his deepest fear haunting him. He woke up exhausted, and scared to drift back off for fear that the man sleeping in the hospital bed next to him wouldn't be there when he woke next.

The last time he'd slept had been for about three hours that morning. He'd curled up on the uncomfortable recliner, too spent to fight sleep any longer, and left the other guys to keep vigil at Nick's bedside. Zane Garrett had been there when Kelly awoke, sitting in a wheelchair, peacefully reading a book at Nick's side and occasionally talking to Nick about what he was reading. Kelly had sat and watched them for a few minutes, sadness engulfing him despite assurances from the doctors that Nick would wake at any time.

He hoped Nick could hear them. He hoped Nick knew that they were all there with him, each of them trying to make up for the fact that they'd left Nick behind, alone in the street with his life bleeding out of him.

Kelly sat by the bed now, paying little attention to the sounds of the machines monitoring Nick's status. Owen Johns was curled on the tiny bench under the window that passed as a couch, snoring softly. They were all exhausted and still recovering from their own injuries, but no one would leave, so they were taking shifts. The others had all gone for lunch at Kelly's insistence. He appreciated them being there, and he knew they needed to be there as much for their sake as for his or Nick's. They all loved Nick. They all thought they'd lost him when they'd left him behind. They all deserved to be there when Nick woke. But Kelly needed a little time alone. Time to be alone with himself, with his thoughts and fears and hopes. Time to be alone with Nick, who had yet to wake four full days after nearly bleeding out in the street.

Owen being asleep on the other side of the room didn't bother Kelly. At least he didn't have to pay him any attention, and could instead focus on Nick. His friend. His lover. His would-be fiancé who'd never truly proposed.

Kelly smiled sadly. He held Nick's hand in both of his and traced the tip of his finger over scars and bruises. Nick's hands had paid for all the damage he'd done to the people trying to hurt them. Kelly's chest swelled with pride and pain. He flipped Nick's hand over, following the life line on Nick's palm. Nick had a knife scar on the back of his hand, and it trailed from his wrist up toward the webbing between his thumb and forefinger, connecting almost perfectly with his life line. Together, they almost encircled his entire hand.

Kelly had always joked about Nick's scars meaning he'd live forever. Now he wasn't sure it was all that funny.

He could hear Nick's laugh in his mind, though. See the way his eyes crinkled when he grinned. It was so real and so close it seemed like he could reach out and touch. But he might never see or hear Nick's laughter again, and Kelly wasn't handling it very well.

He sighed heavily as his finger trailed along the scar, his vision blurring with tears and exhaustion. Nick's fingers twitched, giving the illusion that he was brushing Kelly's hand affectionately.

Kelly quirked his lips, trying not to be upset by it.

Nick would wake up. He wasn't dying. He would come back to them, full of laughter and joy, just like he always did.

"Hey, Doc."

Kelly's head shot up at that simple, hoarse whisper, his eyes wide, his heart suddenly racing.

Nick was staring at him.

Kelly pushed to his feet, sending his chair screeching back. Owen leapt up at the noise, crouching, prepared for battle. "What?" he cried.

Kelly leaned over Nick, reaching for his face. When his fingers touched Nick's skin, Nick's eyes fluttered closed.

"No, no, Nicko, stay awake," Kelly begged. He felt Owen moving but couldn't tear his attention away from Nick's face to see what he was doing.

Nick opened his eyes again. They were clear and green, but had faded like when Nick didn't feel well. "Are you okay?" Nick asked him.

Kelly held his breath for a moment, trying to think through the elation to find a response. He finally huffed a laugh and nodded, pressing his forehead to Nick's cheek. "Welcome back."

"Where's Eli?" Nick asked, his eyes closed, his voice tortured from days without speaking.

Kelly's heart stuttered, and he glanced up to meet Owen's eyes. Owen's mouth moved, but no sound came out. He finally swallowed hard and nodded. "I'll go get Six."

Kelly returned his attention to Nick, running his fingers through Nick's hair. "Eli's gone, bud," he whispered.

Nick's forehead furrowed and he squeezed his eyes tight. Then he took in a deep breath and opened them again. "That's right."

The relief that flooded through Kelly was bittersweet. Where had Nick been for the last few days, lost in his memories?

"What day is it?" Nick asked, his voice so rough it was almost painful to listen to. "Did I miss Opening Day?"

Kelly laughed, knowing he was dangerously close to hysterical now that the weight of worry had been lifted. He hugged Nick closer, smooshing his face against Nick's. Nick's hand settled carefully on Kelly's back.

"No, you didn't miss it," Kelly finally managed. "Still lots of time."

"Well, that's a relief," Nick whispered as his fingers curled into Kelly's shirt.

His breathing was more labored against Kelly's cheek, and his grip on Kelly's back began to tighten, his nails digging in. The beeping of his monitors, which had faded into background noise for Kelly about two days ago, began to encroach on his awareness, beeping going faster, a warning Kelly knew all too well.

Kelly pushed away from Nick just before the machines went into a full-blown panic and Nick twisted on the bed, writhing and gasping. Kelly shoved his chair aside, sending it toppling sideways, as he ran for the door to call for help.

He should have known a gentle reunion wasn't Nick's style.

March 4, 2013

It was early March in Boston, and Kelly's fellow mourners were forced to brave a brisk wind as they gathered in the cemetery. Many in the crowd were in uniform, shined and pressed and stoic as befitted the funeral of a retired member of the Boston Police Department.

Kelly had to squint against the sun to see the small crowd around them. The wind ripped at his lapels, ruffled his hair, and made his eyes water. He wasn't the only one. Several of those around him were fighting the stiff breeze, using handkerchiefs and sunglasses to fend it off.

He turned his eyes back toward the coffin as it was lowered into the ground. Nick's four sisters, only two of whom Kelly had actually met, stood together, singing a beautiful version of "The Parting Glass." The youngest one got choked up before the second verse and wasn't able to continue. She stood with her head lowered, tears streaming down her cheeks, as her sisters continued the song. Watching her, Kelly couldn't really feel anything. No empathy, no sadness. Nothing.

Nick moved beside him, jostling his shoulder as he stepped out of line from the others. He was relying heavily on a cane, but something about his perfectly pressed uniform contrasted with the limp and gave him a gravitas that he probably wouldn't care to lend intentionally to Brian O'Flaherty's funeral.

Nick took his youngest sister by the arm, straightening her up without a word. She buried her face in his chest, holding to him as he sang the next verse with them.

Kelly shivered at the way Nick's eyes never strayed to the coffin, how he stared right over the crowd and sang to help his sisters say farewell to a man who didn't deserve it.

Kelly was still watching Nick when the song ended. He was still watching him when the crowd began to disperse. Nick stood alone as his sisters moved away to throw dirt into the grave. Kelly frowned worriedly when Nick didn't follow them, and he counted to five before he stood and joined Nick.

"You okay?" Kelly whispered. He took Nick's elbow, standing close enough that Nick leaned against him with a huff.

"I'll be fine," Nick grumbled. He snickered and met Kelly's eyes. "She moved away on me and I realized I was stuck without someone to lean on."

Kelly scowled. Nick's condition was no fucking laughing matter, but Nick kept on making jokes out of it. It was his way of coping, but Kelly wasn't laughing. He wound his arm around Nick's waist, and Nick wrapped an arm around Kelly's shoulders, using the cane and putting a lot of weight on Kelly as they moved together toward the line of waiting vehicles. Nick had chosen to ride in his own car rather than join the family in the procession.

"Nicholas," a woman called from behind them. Kelly glanced over his shoulder to find Nick's mother there. She'd remained mostly stoic throughout her husband's service. In fact, the only person who'd seemed especially upset over Brian's passing had been their youngest daughter, Nessa. She was only a year or two out of high school—Kelly couldn't quite remember how old she was—and she was inconsolable over the loss of her father.

Kelly had fought to find sympathy for her. But that girl had known a very different father than Nick had known.

"Ma'am," Nick said without turning around. He had his head lowered, his arm still around Kelly's neck, but tightening as he tensed.

"You're coming, aren't you?"

Kelly shook his head. "He's done too much already. I have to get him home."

"He only had one father," she snapped, hard eyes on Kelly.

"I'll see you there," Nick said over his shoulder, his fingers tightening on Kelly's jacket before Kelly could respond.

His mother moved away, giving Kelly another look that told him exactly what she thought of the fact that her only son had a *boyfriend*.

"How the hell did two such horrible people come up with something amazing like you?" Kelly snarled.

"Murphy's Law," Nick grunted as they continued on toward his Range Rover. "We'll stay long enough for people to see my face. Then we're done."

"Okay," Kelly whispered, wondering how the hell Nick had spent his entire life like this, doing what was expected of him to appease people who treated him horribly. It was brand-new insight into Nick's otherworldly stores of patience. Kelly hugged him closer, and Nick hissed and stumbled a little. "Sorry! Shit, I keep forgetting about the stitches!"

"It's okay," Nick said, his voice strained as they reached the car. He lifted his jacket out to peer at his side, where just ten days ago an attacker had stabbed him. Twice. There was blood on his otherwise pristine white shirt. "Hey! Looks like an excuse not to stay too long at a sorry-your-shitty-dad-died party, huh?"

Kelly rolled his eyes and helped Nick into the car.

"You okay?" Kelly asked yet again as they sat in the dim back corner of a bar several blocks from Nick's childhood home. It was his father's local watering hole, where the mourners had come to pay their last respects after the coffin had been lowered into the ground.

Nick shook his head, staring at the full glass of whiskey in front of him. He hadn't taken a sip. It was a drink meant to honor his father's memory, and he intended to let it sit there. How many times had he been sent to this tavern to find his father and tell him it was time to come home? How many times had he been shouted out of this bar and run home, praying he'd get there before his dad did?

He tapped two fingers on the table, rattling the drink. "Let's go home, huh?"

Kelly didn't question him; he merely nodded and pushed his chair back to stand. He helped Nick get to his feet, handing him his cane and offering his arm. It'd been mere days since Nick had been released from the hospital in Miami. Kelly had been with him every second of his recovery, and this routine was one they'd repeated at least five times a day since Nick had woken. He appreciated Kelly being there, but for the first time in their long history of fighting side by side, Nick was ashamed of needing help. Kelly wasn't a corpsman anymore, he was Nick's boyfriend.

When Kelly had called his sister Kat to let her know that Nick was alive, Kat had told them about Brian. He was dying, in the hospital with mere days to live. Nick hadn't made it home in time, nor had he especially tried to, and he knew without a doubt that his mother would never forgive him.

Nick was having a hard time pretending to be the grieving son.

He leaned on Kelly as they threaded their way through the small crowd, spared from the obligation of saying good-bye or shaking hands with his late father's friends. Everyone knew what he'd been through, everyone knew he probably still should have been at home in bed, if not in the hospital. Everyone knew he was still weak.

Nick fucking hated it.

"Nicky," a man in uniform said as Nick and Kelly neared the front door. Nick stopped, and Kelly discreetly stepped away so Nick wasn't leaning on him as he faced the man. "How are you, son?"

Nick gave a curt nod in answer. He was at least five inches taller than the man, but he remembered having to crane his neck to see his face when he stood in their living room waiting for Nick's father to go to work.

"I was surprised to see you out there."

Nick didn't respond. He merely stared, waiting.

His silence apparently made his father's old partner nervous, because the man continued talking, his words faster and his fidgeting more pronounced. "Everyone knows what you tried to do for your daddy. Even if that liver didn't take, you gave him one more year. Him dying wasn't your fault, Nicky."

Nick made a clicking noise with his tongue and stood a little straighter. "I know," he said, voice just as flat as his expression.

He turned before the man could say more, reaching for Kelly's arm as they made their way out of the pub.

"Wasn't your fault," Kelly grumbled under his breath. "Why the fuck do any of these asshats think you'd be sitting around blaming yourself because your dad's body rejected a piece of liver you risked your life donating?"

"Because *they* think it's my fault," Nick said blithely, his head down to watch his steps on the uneven sidewalk.

"You don't really think that, do you?" Kelly asked, sounding half-horrified and half-insulted.

"I know it. That was my dad's partner. They worked together for thirty years. He responded to a domestic disturbance call at my house one night when I was about ten. Wrote the report up and everything. Disturbance caused by fall down the stairs."

Kelly slowed and glanced over his shoulder.

"My dad's friends all know that if I could kill people with the power of my mind, my dad would have been the first to go."

Kelly snorted angrily. "What, they think you filled your liver with hate before you gave it to him?"

Nick chuckled, shaking his head as he continued to stare devotedly at the ground. He tightened his grip on Kelly's arm, and Kelly moved closer to him as they walked toward the car.

"Maybe I did," Nick murmured after a few seconds of silence.

"Nick."

"I'd be okay with it," he admitted. He slowed as the pain in his knee swelled, and he had to stand there for a moment with his eyes closed, waiting for it to pass. He'd eventually need surgery to repair the damage that had been done by a vicious kick. The orthopedist wanted him fully healed from his other injuries first, though, and so he was left to limp around and live on painkillers until then.

For a man who'd spent his entire life being active and relying on his dominant physical capabilities day in and day out, it was possibly the most frustrating state of being he could imagine.

"Okay?" Kelly whispered.

Nick took a deep breath, gazing at Kelly.

Kelly raised an eyebrow, a smile playing at the corners of his mouth. "What?"

"I love you," Nick said, but the words came out a whisper, as if the mere thought had stolen them before they could form.

Kelly grinned a little wider and slid his arm around Nick's waist again, squeezing him as they continued on toward the car.

CHAPTER TWO

April 4, 2013

Nick was on the couch watching a baseball game, but by the fifth inning, he got stiff and sore and lost interest because the Sox were playing like shit and it was only the third game of the season. After using the head and then limping back to the sofa, he gave up on appearances, took a pain pill, slumped down on the sofa in a cocoon of blankets, and tossed his feet up on the coffee table, trying to ease the ache in his body.

It wasn't helping. Nothing was helping. He closed his eyes, taking a deep breath to try to keep his mind from running in circles like it had been day in and day out since he's gotten home from Miami.

He needed to do something with his hands. He needed to do something with his *mind*. Kelly had been adamant lately that he not overtax himself, and Nick had been following orders. He knew he wasn't right yet, physically or mentally. He'd nearly died in the street in Miami, and that was going to take more than a month or two to get over.

He glanced around the *Fiddler*, mentally making a list of the things he needed to do. She still had holes in her. In the doors to the salon, in the door to the main cabin. The bunks belowdecks were still in shambles as well, and Nick was tired of fighting with his stupid insurance company about it. She deserved to be made whole again as soon as he was physically able.

Hell, maybe putting her right again would help put *him* right again too.

It would have to wait until he wasn't hurting and drugged, though. He couldn't even concentrate on baseball. He stared at another stupid fucking erectile dysfunction commercial, shaking his head and sneering at the screen. His attention wavered to the shelves hidden in the compartments beside the TV, and he scowled. He hadn't looked in that compartment in a long time, not since the incident with the CIA when he'd been terrified that they'd shot up the box he kept hidden in there.

He pushed himself off the couch, the blanket still over his head and dragging behind him as he trudged over to the cabinet. He stared at the handle, preparing himself for what was inside, then he jerked it open and grabbed the beat-up old cardboard storage box on the top shelf.

He clutched it to his chest as he returned to his spot on the couch, wincing when he flopped too hard onto the cushions and jarred all his sore parts.

The box fell to the floor, settling between his bare feet. He hung his head as he stared at the lid, the blanket heavy over his head. What the hell was he thinking? He hadn't opened this box since the day Elias Sanchez's mother had handed it to him in the middle of Arlington Cemetery; why the hell did he think *now* was a good time to do this?

No. He knew why. Eli had been talking to him ever since the knife had slid into his side. His life had flashed before his eyes: a frenzied, terrified montage of all the time he'd wasted and the precious things he'd lost. And Eli had been there with him in the street, staying behind when he'd begged the others to go and save themselves.

Eli had stayed with him.

Nick took a deep, steadying breath, then gingerly pulled the lid off the box and set it on the couch beside him.

Nick O,

If you're reading this letter right now, I guess that means I kicked it. I always kind of figured your crazy ass would go first, down in a blaze of glory or some bullshit. I finally beat you to something.

I'm writing this from a hospital bed. You probably remember the day, you were just here with me. Hell, I think you might still be here, hitting on that male nurse out there (you're not as subtle as you used to be, bro). You spent hours here, cheering me up, telling me stories from the old days, sitting with me when I fell asleep and waiting until I woke up again.

I love you, brother. I realized today that I never tell you enough, but I love you. I keep thinking about how goddamned pure your friendship is, and I love you.

As I'm writing this, you and Grady aren't speaking to each other and you haven't for almost a year. Johns is off doing his thing in California, wearing fancy suits and too busy to return our calls. Doc is still in some sort of fugue state, building that damn cabin he won't let any of us help him with. And I'm pretty sure I have enough evidence to convict Digger of three bank robberies in Louisiana.

It breaks my heart, papá. We were so fucking solid. Now, the team is all but dead.

All those people trying to kill Sidewinder over the years, and it was us that did it in the end. When I get out of this place, I'm going to fucking fix it. And you're the linchpin, bro, you're the one who holds us together. I got to fix you first.

But since I intend to write a new one of these every couple years, I guess I died pretty fucking young, huh? I'm hoping I just forgot to keep writing them and you're like ninety years old right now and we escaped from our old folks' home together and ran away on the Fiddler. *Although, your poor fucking leg, bro. I don't know if I should hope that you're ninety or not.*

Maybe I didn't get a chance to fix it. Maybe I couldn't.

I know what it'd do to me if I lost one of you this soon. We were supposed to grow old together. We were supposed to go off on the Fiddler *and disappear into the sunset together. I'd be a fucking wreck if I lost that. But you and me, we got something the others don't have. Losing you would hit me harder than any of them, and I'm not ashamed to tell you that. I don't care if you tell them that. They know it. I'm fucking tearing up again just thinking about it, and I swear to God if you put me through that shit I'll resurrect you just to beat your ass.*

I don't know how I died, but I'm betting odds are you went out with me. Back to back, brother to brother, just like we always talked about. Because that's the kind of man you are.

But if you couldn't be there with me, and you're reading this, I'm sorry. I know you're hurting. I know you're hurting even more because the others are all scattered and there's no one for you to lean on. So, in the words of my best friend Nick fucking O'Flaherty, "I'm going to do you a favor, son, and you're going to love me for it."

The game was approaching its end and Nick still had his blanket wrapped over his head like ET, staring sightlessly at the screen, still numb from the words he'd read, when he heard Kelly board the *Fiddler*. He muted the television and nudged the cardboard box under the coffee table with his foot, but he didn't try moving otherwise as Kelly stepped into the salon with an armful of groceries.

"Need help?" Nick asked him.

"No, this is all there is," Kelly said as he deftly closed the door behind him with his foot, balancing a canvas bag full of groceries in each hand. He gave Nick a snort as he walked by. He didn't comment on Nick's blanket. It was probably too common a sight lately to warrant it.

Nick worried at his lower lip with his teeth as he tracked Kelly through the salon and into the galley. He had to crane his neck to watch Kelly putting groceries up, and his blanket fell away from his head.

"How's your game?" Kelly asked as he pulled things out of the bags and laid them out on the counters.

"Eh." Nick clicked the TV off, still peering behind him.

Kelly glanced up, his brow deeply furrowed. "You okay?"

"I'm good. Think I sat here too long, but I'm fine."

Kelly put away the last items that required refrigeration, and left the rest on the counter in favor of moving back in front of Nick with his hands on his hips. He was scowling now, and Nick shifted self-consciously.

"What'd I do?" Nick asked him.

"You tell me."

"I'm being good. I haven't moved. Much."

Kelly's expression turned skeptical, and he stepped around the coffee table and put a knee on the couch next to Nick, leaning over him. Nick watched him raptly, suddenly breathless as Kelly's fingers slid against his cheek. But what he'd thought was going to be a gentle caress—something too few and far between since his injury—was simply Kelly's fingers pressing against the pulse point at his neck.

Nick held his breath as he gazed up at Kelly, who had his head lowered, his eyes unfocused and a frown on his face. He was mentally calculating Nick's pulse rate; that was the expression he'd always worn, from the very first day they'd met, when he was doctoring someone. That familiarity didn't keep Nick from watching him longingly, though.

Kelly's frown deepened, and he raised his head to meet Nick's eyes. They stared at each other for long seconds, and Kelly's shoulders relaxed, his thumb grazing the point of Nick's chin and sliding gently toward his lips. The fingers he'd pressed against Nick's pulse curled, and when his thumb brushed Nick's lip, Nick's eyes fluttered closed. He didn't realize it, though, until Kelly pulled his hand away.

Nick grabbed for him, managing to snag his hand before he could stand. Kelly's eyes widened, and they found themselves staring at each other again as Nick held Kelly's hand and Kelly knelt awkwardly next to him.

Nick pressed Kelly's hand to his heart. "Sit with me?"

"You okay?" Kelly asked as he eased down beside Nick. His hand was warm through Nick's thin T-shirt.

"Yeah," Nick whispered. He slid his hand up Kelly's arm, staring into his storm-tossed eyes.

"You sure? Your heart's racing." Kelly moved his fingers up like he was going to check Nick's pulse again.

Nick licked his lips, nodding jerkily. "That's because I'm nervous," he practically gasped.

Kelly stared, unblinking, unflinching. His thumb rested against Nick's chin again, and his eyes followed its progress as he slid it up the line of Nick's jaw to his cheekbone.

It seemed like forever to Nick, like it took Kelly *hours* to move. It seemed like he held his breath for so long that his lungs burned, that his body screamed for him to do something, *anything*, to relieve the pressure building.

It wasn't until Kelly finally met his eyes again, when his fingers finally tightened against the back of Nick's neck, when he finally leaned closer, that Nick sucked in a breath. A moment later Kelly's lips were on his, warm and gentle and familiar.

Nick didn't dare move, didn't dare make a sound beyond the involuntary whimper that escaped his parted lips once Kelly pulled back. He was left with his eyes closed and his breath stolen, grasping Kelly harder so he wouldn't move away.

Kelly brushed his nose against Nick's, and then his lips met Nick's again and he shifted like he might climb into Nick's lap. Nick tightened his grip on Kelly's forearm, and Kelly moaned quietly against his lips.

"I miss you," Nick whispered between gentle kisses.

Kelly pressed his forehead to Nick's, leaning his body against Nick's shoulder. "Asshole," he grunted.

Nick ducked his head, but Kelly put a hand on his shoulder and shoved off of him, raising up and slinging one leg over Nick's lap. Nick gripped Kelly's hips to remind him to be careful as Kelly straddled him, both hands resting on Nick's shoulders, his head cocked. Nick swallowed hard, flushing with a heady mixture of nerves and adrenaline and desire as Kelly pushed his blanket off his shoulders with a smirk.

"How's your heart rate?" Kelly asked wryly.

Nick was embarrassingly out of breath, but he managed a smile. "Racing."

Kelly rewarded him with a crooked grin. "Mine too."

Nick sat up straighter, wincing, still staring into Kelly's shadowed eyes as his fingers wandered under Kelly's shirt to graze over his ribs. Kelly leaned closer to brush his nose against Nick's.

"What have you done?" Kelly asked, dropping his voice to a seductive whisper.

Nick sucked in a deep breath, holding it as he tried to find a good answer that wouldn't get him yelled at. When he finally let it gust out,

Kelly rolled his eyes and sat back, pursing his lips and nodding as if he'd known Nick had been up to no good.

"I told you to sit," Kelly huffed. "I told you not to move. I told you to rest."

"I know, but—"

"Nick!"

Nick practically growled as he rested his head on the back of the couch and flopped his hands to the cushions. It was like being in the Marines and having to report to his corpsman all over again. "It's been over four weeks, Kels."

"You know if you overwork yourself it'll set back your recovery."

"I was looking for Seymour," Nick said, his voice a bit more caustic than he'd meant for it to be.

Kelly sat back, eyes gone wide. "You have him?"

Nick's attention strayed to the coffee table, and Kelly glanced over his shoulder, where he could no doubt see Seymour on the table, along with the envelope full of letters Nick had found in the top of the cardboard box full of Eli's things. The box itself was now sitting beneath the glass top.

Kelly leaned back, his lithe body twisting and straining against Nick as he plucked up the sock monkey. "I can't believe you found him. Where was he?"

Nick found it hard to swallow, and he licked his lips to stall as his eyes strayed to the envelope again. "It's the stuff Eli's mom gave me," he said, voice gone hoarse as he thought about the letter he'd read. "I . . . I just had this sudden need to go through it, I don't know."

Kelly sat back on Nick's thighs, cocking his head and frowning at the ragged sock monkey in his hands. Seymour was about twenty inches tall, with a scraggly tail, gangly arms and legs, and big ears that had more often than not been used as handles. He had at one time sported white, green, and orange stripes, with a little blue-and-green beanie and blue puffs for buttons, but the colors were faded and dirty and the button puffs were long gone.

Kelly had always been vaguely disturbed by the look on Seymour's face, especially after they'd had to sew up his left eye, but Eli had loved him and carried him with him wherever they went, including into battle. He'd stick him in his back pocket or his pack, depending on where they were. When the monkey had taken a piece of shrapnel to the eye—and saved Eli's ass in the process—Eli had ordered a purple heart ribbon to sew onto his beanie so everyone would know Seymour was a combat veteran.

They'd taken pictures of him at landmarks around the world, sometimes risking life and limb and jail time to position him. It had always been their understanding that Seymour was to continue traveling even after Eli's death, until he had seen the world.

"Seymour," Nick grumbled affectionately.

"Huh?"

"EZ was always so proud of the pun. Seymour needs to *see more.*"

Kelly blinked at him, then looked back at the sock monkey. "Oh my God."

Nick chuckled, then bit his lip when Kelly glared at him. "Did that just hit you?"

"Yes. Shut up."

Nick was grinning when he took Seymour from Kelly, but his smile fell quickly as he brushed his fingers over Seymour's face.

"Nick?"

"He wanted me to have that stuff, and I . . . I should have gone through it years ago."

"Nick," Kelly said on a sigh.

Nick shifted under him, sliding his hands to Kelly's hips. "I don't know how he was so ready. He knew exactly what needed to go where. Why was he ready? If I hadn't woken up? The only thing I would have left behind for you is a boat with a bunch of holes in her that I was too stubborn to fix."

Kelly's hand came to rest on Nick's cheek, and he leaned closer. "Nick."

Nick just shook his head.

"How long have you been—"

"Why was he ready?" Nick asked again, and he realized his fingers were digging into Kelly's skin.

Kelly brought his other hand up, cupping Nick's face. He knew Nick was always grounded by touch, and two hands on his face was the best way to calm him. "Babe. Jesus, how long have you been lingering on this? Why haven't you said anything?"

Nick shook his head, his eyes going unfocused.

"What brought this on? What am I missing?"

Nick cleared his throat once, then did it again. He nodded his head toward the big manila envelope on the table. "That."

Kelly glanced over his shoulder again, the edges of confusion lining his face. He grabbed the envelope from the table. "What is this?"

"I found it in Eli's stuff. Right on top, waiting for me."

Kelly was scowling when he turned the envelope over, resting more weight on Nick's thighs. Nick's knee was killing him, but he wasn't about to ask Kelly to move.

"What's in it?" Kelly asked.

"Letters. A bunch of sealed letters, all numbered like we're supposed to open them in order. Fucking Sanchez," Nick gritted out, his voice wavering. He'd only made it through the first page of the letter he'd found in the outer envelope with his name on it. "The fucker knew she'd give me that shit. He left me a letter in there, taped to that package."

Kelly's brow furrowed and his eyes narrowed as he grabbed the package and turned it over to see the envelope taped to the front. He pulled the letter out of it and unfolded it. Nick watched him with extreme trepidation. He'd found himself tearing up as he'd read it, which was why he hadn't finished it. He wasn't typically a crier. He'd been stone-faced at Sanchez's funeral, the shoulder the rest of them had broken down and cried on. But halfway into that handwritten letter he'd been using his blanket cocoon to wipe his face, so he'd stopped and put the letter back, waiting until he had a little more support to read it.

But even having Kelly here with him didn't make it better. Kelly read the first page as Nick studiously stared at anything *but* him.

Sure enough, a few seconds in and Kelly's eyes were glistening. When he lowered the page, he laughed shakily. "He was a piece of work," he said, a hitch in his voice. He wiped at his eyes, like he was trying to make sure they were still dry. "That's a dirty trick to play on his buddies. What's the rest of it say?"

"I don't know, I couldn't get past the first page." Nick gave a helpless shrug. "I could hear his voice in my head when I read it."

Kelly stared at him long enough that Nick started to fight the urge to fidget.

"I miss him too," Kelly finally said.

"I should have done it years ago. I should have patched the *Fiddler* years ago."

"She still floats," Kelly whispered.

Nick didn't hear him, though. "I should have . . . there's so much I should have done so much earlier." Nick had to swallow as he gazed into Kelly's eyes. "I should have told you I loved you so many more times than I have."

They sat that way for what seemed like forever, with Kelly's eyes reflecting as much turmoil as a New England squall, with Nick's stomach tumbling and his breath getting harder and harder to catch. Nick finally had to lower his head, not wanting to meet Kelly's piercing gaze any longer.

"Irish," Kelly whispered. "He wouldn't have wanted you to hurt. He had his mother give you these things because this was what he loved enough to drag around with him everywhere he went. And he wanted you to have the things he loved. These should be happy things, not . . . penance. Why are you even doing this right now?"

"I don't know, I just . . . I've been thinking about him a lot lately."

"You shouldn't have to do this alone," Kelly said as he folded the letter up. "I'll help you. If you'll let me. But not now."

"Why not now?"

"You're not recovered enough for Eli's shenanigans. Doctor's orders."

"Right," Nick said, turning his head to try to hide his bitterness. "Doctor's orders."

"Hey," Kelly grunted, tapping Nick's chest. "Once I'm convinced you're able, we'll pull them back out, okay?"

Nick nodded, forcing himself to meet Kelly's eyes again. They stared at each other, the silence falling heavy between them.

"I'm sorry, Nicko." Kelly set the package aside and took Nick's face in both hands again, leaning closer.

Nick frowned. "For what?"

"I didn't realize it, but the past couple weeks, I haven't been treating you as . . ."

Nick licked his lips, unable to fight the nervous gesture and unable to avert his eyes since Kelly had his face trapped.

"As my boyfriend," Kelly finished with a wince. He sat back, slumping in Nick's lap and moving his hands down Nick's chest and under his shirt. His fingers grazed though the fine hair on Nick's chest. Nick shivered—from the touch and the sentiment.

He forced himself to ask the question he already knew the answer to. "What have you been seeing if not that?"

"My teammate. My friend." Kelly winced. "My patient."

Nick gave a curt nod and lowered his head, the wound in his side throbbing for some reason. He couldn't help the blush that he felt creeping across his face, either. It burned hot as he thought of the past month of his recovery and how damn weak and helpless he'd been. Of course Kelly was seeing him as a patient and not his boyfriend; it wasn't exactly easy to woo someone when they had to help you up and down the stairs to go to bed or take a shower or any number of other things that had just been too hard for Nick to accomplish on his own.

It was especially hard to woo someone when you hadn't been capable of having sex in *weeks*. If it wasn't Nick's physical condition getting in the way, it was his mental condition, and if it wasn't one or both of those, it was all the medication flowing through him that made him so fucking tired. Nick closed his eyes, fighting the embarrassment and pain when he thought of how Kelly must see him now.

Kelly placed the tip of his finger under Nick's chin and forced Nick to look up again. "Don't be ashamed, babe," he said, his words just as warm as his touch. "Most men would have died after what happened to you. Wouldn't have even held out long enough to get in an ambulance. But you didn't give up. You kept fighting even when your body had nothing left to fight with. Don't you ever be ashamed of still being alive. Or for needing help while you get better."

Nick found it difficult to swallow past the lump forming in his throat. He managed it as Kelly held his gaze, smiling softly. Kelly took his face in both hands again, then curled to press his lips to Nick's.

"This is the last time I'll check your pulse without a compelling reason," Kelly murmured against Nick's lips. "Starting today, you're not my patient anymore. No more doctor's orders, I promise."

He leaned back, resting more of his weight on Nick's thighs. He licked his lips slowly, and a familiar light entered his eyes, as if he was plotting. Nick knew that look. He both loved and dreaded that look.

"What?" Nick asked.

"Nicholas," Kelly said with a sigh. "Will you go to dinner with me?"

"What?"

"A date. We've never actually been on a real date. Will you go on a date with me?"

Nick blinked rapidly, his mouth falling open.

"We'll get dressed up, go to a fancy restaurant. Your *favorite* restaurant. I'll wine and dine you. And you can turn on that famous O'Flaherty charm to try to get me in bed."

Nick's fingers tightened on Kelly's waist. "*Try?*"

Kelly shrugged, quirking an eyebrow in silent challenge.

"We could just . . . go to bed now."

Kelly shook his head, pursing his lips disapprovingly. "Huh-uh. I need some romance. You're good at romance, and I want some."

He trailed his fingers down Nick's neck, tracing out along his collarbones. Kelly followed the progress of his fingers with his eyes, biting his lip when he got out to Nick's shoulder and slid his hand over Nick's biceps. He shook his head slightly, as if he might not be aware he was doing it, as he dug his fingers into Nick's muscle. Nick may have been recovering, and he may have been miserable and weak and in pain, but his upper arms had been taking the brunt of the duty and they were in impressive shape.

"Kels?" Nick didn't dare speak above a whisper and break whatever spell had been cast.

Kelly tore his attention away from where he was tracing Nick's arm, and met Nick's eyes. "I'd like to see you as my boyfriend again," Kelly admitted, a rare hint of color rising to his cheeks. "Instead of a teammate or a patient."

Nick fought for a shaky breath, only letting it out when Kelly leaned closer. He straightened and caught Kelly's lips with his own, managing the briefest tease of a kiss before Kelly pulled away.

He put a finger on Nick's lips and dismounted, looming over Nick with a smirk. "I never put out before the first date. Now, go get pretty for our dinner," he said as he walked away. "And pack a bag!"

Kelly was fighting the urge to fiddle with his tie when he stepped into the restaurant. He'd left Nick on the *Fiddler* after gathering an overnight bag of clothing, including his best suit, and made his way to the Liberty, the only hotel in Boston he was familiar with. He'd chosen it because he knew Nick loved the place, though, and tonight was just as much about him seducing his boyfriend as it was about Nick seducing him.

The restaurant had been of Nick's choosing, and looking around the place, Kelly was getting the impression that tonight was going to cost a pretty penny if they ordered more than tap water. When the hell did O'Flaherty get such fucking expensive tastes?

"Name, sir?" the hostess asked.

Kelly cleared his throat, fingers grazing his tie as he stepped forward. "Nick O'Flaherty," he said, and he was shocked by the butterflies in his stomach. He might have been taking this date thing a little too seriously, but that was the whole point.

His heart had broken right in two when Nick had asked him to sit with him, when he'd admitted that he was nervous for Kelly to be touching him. When he'd said "Doctor's orders" with the same distaste he said "New York Yankees." How had Kelly let Nick's recovery loom that large between them? It wasn't worth analyzing now, and there were a dozen ways to go about course-correcting. But this one seemed like the most fun.

He'd never seen Nick's full-court press. Nick hadn't needed it to convince Kelly to sleep with him, or to commit to him. Kelly was looking forward to it.

The hostess led him through a maze of tiny, intimate tables toward the center of the main floor, where Nick was sitting straight and tall, watching him with a smile. Nick stood when they approached the table, buttoning his suit jacket. Kelly gave the hostess a nod, then stepped toward Nick with a grin.

"Wow," he said, giving Nick a full-body once-over. Despite the weeks of recovery and issues, Nick had been rehabbing with the work ethic of a Marine, and it showed. He took Kelly's elbow, holding on to him gently as he leaned in and pressed a chaste kiss to Kelly's cheek. Kelly's eyes fluttered closed. Holy God, Nick smelled good tonight.

"You look great," Nick told him, his lips tantalizingly close to the shell of Kelly's ear. His fingers glided over the lapel of Kelly's jacket, coming up to adjust the knot of Kelly's tie. His eyes never left Kelly's, and his lips quirked into a smirk. "Tie looks amazing with your eyes."

"Thanks," Kelly breathed, staring until Nick stepped back and gestured to the vacant seat.

As soon as they'd both settled in, a waiter approached the table, and their first official date was in full swing. Kelly managed to take it seriously right up until the dessert menu was laid at his elbow.

He shook his head and grunted. "Okay, seriously. Let's get the check and head back to my room."

Nick quirked an eyebrow and shifted his shoulders, laying one hand on the table. "And skip dessert?"

"Nicko," Kelly grunted. "You earned me on my knees just with the cut of that suit, okay."

A gentleman at the table beside them coughed loudly and gave Kelly a disapproving glance. Kelly eyed him briefly before returning his attention to his companion. Nick had covered his mouth with his palm, his elbow resting on the table.

"What?" Kelly asked him.

Nick shook his head. "If you want to go, we can. But the crème brûlée here is really good."

Kelly narrowed his eyes. Nick snaked his hand across the tiny tabletop, and Kelly laid his in its path. Nick twined their fingers together, a serene smile gracing his handsome face.

Kelly realized he was shaking his head fondly. "And you accuse *me* of being able to get whatever I want with a smile."

"You can," Nick said softly. His thumb brushed over Kelly's. "I'd give you anything you wanted. Smile or not."

Kelly squeezed his hand hard. "Only thing I want is you, babe."

Nick had been right. The crème brûlée was truly fantastic. And when the check came, they had the most realistic first-date moment of the night as they awkwardly tried to figure out who would pay. Nick finally won out and slid his credit card into the leather folder, then he took Kelly's hand in his and leaned forward, kissing Kelly's knuckles.

"I'm glad we did this," he said, rubbing his lips over Kelly's fingers again.

"Can I tell you a secret?" Kelly waited until Nick was looking into his eyes. "I was nervous. When I was getting ready, I was so nervous I thought I was going to throw up. I couldn't even get my tie tied right."

Nick chuckled, worrying at his lower lip with his teeth. "I wasn't."

"No?"

Nick shook his head. "Tonight I know what I'm supposed to do. I know my place again."

Kelly frowned hard. "Your place? The hell does that mean?"

"No, no, let me get through. Since waking up, all these weeks recovering, it was hard to know what I was to you."

"Dude."

"I don't mean it bad, just let me explain," Nick said, voice still calm and smooth. "You'll always be the Doc first and foremost, and that's what you fell back on when I woke up in the hospital. And you got me through this just like every time before. But we just . . . we don't have a playbook for this. We were already kind of winging the boyfriend thing. And I know how you feel about lies and hiding things and . . . I know how much it hurt you, me lying. Keeping things from you. God! Pretending I didn't remember asking you to marry me. I haven't earned forgiveness for any of that."

"You don't have to earn it," Kelly blurted. "I gave it freely. You know I don't fucking hold grudges."

"I know."

Nick had obviously been fighting hard to maintain eye contact, and his fingers fidgeted with Kelly's as he powered through his discomfort. He finally lowered his gaze, though, and Kelly could almost see him gearing up for something big.

"Nick?"

"It's just . . . at what point do I recover enough for you to stop being the Doc and start . . ." Nick trailed off, taking an uneven breath as he looked back up at Kelly. "No one would blame you, Kels. If you slipped back into corpsman mode and just stayed there, after this. I have no right to call you mine. Not anymore."

Kelly's heart squeezed painfully as he realized what Nick was trying to do: to give Kelly an out. He clutched Nick's hand harder, leaning closer with a sympathetic frown. "You're probably right," he said gently. "No one would blame me if I walked away now. Not even you."

Nick hummed through a weak smile, the sound low and rumbling in the undercurrent of the restaurant.

Kelly kissed Nick's fingers, shaking his head. "But I'm not going to do that, and we both know why. So how about you say that word again for me?"

Kelly could see the relief washing through Nick just as clearly as if it were an ocean wave. His grip on Kelly's hand tightened and he closed his eyes, releasing a pent-up breath. "What word?" he asked, smiling tentatively when he opened his eyes again.

"You know which one," Kelly said, dropping his voice to a growl.

Nick gazed at him for a few seconds, his entire demeanor relaxing when he offered a soft, "Mine."

Kelly's heart skipped a beat, and goose bumps rose on his arms, just like always. "I love the way you say that word."

"Thank you for letting me keep saying it."

The waiter placed their folder on the corner of the table and thanked them for dining with him tonight, but Kelly couldn't pull his eyes from Nick's to respond to the man.

Nick smiled slowly and threw Kelly a wink before releasing his hand and glancing at the waiter with a murmur of thanks. He retrieved his credit card and signed the receipt, then gave Kelly a nod and pushed back in his chair. Kelly moved quickly so he could help Nick if he needed it.

He'd recovered faster than most people would have, mostly because he'd been in peak condition before the incident in Miami and had made it into an ambulance in time.

Unfortunately, the stab wounds hadn't been his only injury; he'd suffered a vicious kick to his knee as well, and was still awaiting surgery to address the damage. The only silver lining from that, according to Nick, was the handicapped parking permit and the cane he carried. He had several, but his favorite—and the one he was using tonight—was an antique, which may well have been the sole reason Nick favored it, and was made of ebony that shone after Nick oiled it down. The handle was engraved silver, so worn from use and age that it was impossible to tell what the engraving had been.

Nick plucked the cane from the back of his chair, nodding for Kelly to lead the way to the door. Kelly fought not to look over his shoulder to check Nick's progress. Nick was a big boy who could traverse a restaurant unsupervised, he was closer to healthy than the hospital bed, and Kelly wasn't the Doc tonight. When they got to the door, though, Kelly turned and held out his arm for Nick to take, and they stepped out into the warm evening together, arms entwined. Nick was relying heavily on the cane as they began to stroll.

"You didn't take your pain pills today, did you?" Kelly asked.

Nick shook his head and jutted out his chin. "Not since this afternoon. I wanted to be clearheaded tonight. And avoid other side effects, too."

Kelly snorted, warmth spreading through him. "In that case . . ." He halted and turning toward the street, raising his hand. "We'll splurge on a cab."

Nick hooked the handle of the cane around Kelly's wrist and tugged, spinning Kelly back to face him. Kelly could only blink, wide-eyed, as Nick stepped into his space, using the cane to keep Kelly planted right where he was. Nick nudged his nose against Kelly's, tilting his head to one side, then the other, like he was trying to determine the optimum angle of attack.

Kelly held his breath, his blood thrumming, his ears buzzing. He parted his mouth, dragging his lower lip over Nick's, gasping quietly when Nick's beard brushed the sensitive edge of his lip.

Nick kissed him. His hand splayed at the small of Kelly's back. His breath caught on Kelly's lips. Kelly moaned and grasped at Nick's bulky shoulders, his fingers glancing over the soft, expensive material of Nick's suit jacket as he tried to find purchase.

Nick kept the kiss safe for public consumption, his tongue and teeth merely offering a promise of what was to come. When they parted, Kelly wavered forward, seeking more. Nick chuckled, the sound traveling through Kelly to raise goose bumps all over his skin yet again.

"You smell good," Kelly whispered. When the summer breeze had calmed and lost the faint hint of food and the sea, Kelly caught the unfamiliar scent of whatever was on Nick. "Is that new?"

Nick hummed an affirmative and kissed Kelly again.

"What is it?"

"Absinthe. Thought I'd try something new since I was charged with romancing you."

"I like it." Kelly nodded, meeting Nick's shadowed eyes. Then he grinned slowly, and Nick mirrored the expression. "My place or yours?"

Nick took Kelly's chin in his fingers. "I realize this isn't really a first date kind of thing to say, but ... I love you."

"My place, then, it's closer," Kelly said in a rush, and then turned to hail a cab as Nick chuckled behind him.

Kelly's body was buzzing with excitement and nerves by the time they made their way down the hall to their room in the Liberty. He was expelling the energy by bouncing up on his toes with every few steps because Nick seemed unhurried, leaning on his ebony cane and casting Kelly the occasional smirk.

"When you said you got a room I thought you were joking," Nick said as Kelly fished his key out of his suit pocket.

Kelly merely shrugged, then shoved the door open and stepped aside, holding it for Nick to enter first. "I thought it would be neat," he said, kicking his toe against the door and then dragging it across the carpet. "Romantic and ... stuff."

Nick patted his belly as he walked by. "The first time we were ever together was in a hotel."

"Which first time?" Kelly asked wryly.

Nick turned to face him, head cocked, leaning his weight on the cane. Kelly's smile fell as he stared into Nick's eyes. Their *first* first time in a hotel room had been back in their Jacksonville days, accompanied by an adventurous young lady with a uniform kink. Their second first, though, that had been just them. Nick had come home for forty-eight-hours special liberty during his last deployment, and he and Kelly had spent most of those forty-eight hours together in a hotel room in Baltimore, learning every inch of each other's bodies and talking about trying to do this for real when Nick came home.

What Kelly hadn't realized at the time, and what he hadn't really thought much about since learning it, was that the first time they'd had sex during those two days, Nick had just received orders that would turn their lives upside down: orders to kill a man his friends had trusted, even loved. He'd been struggling with that secret even then, and it had colored all his actions since. Almost their entire relationship had been built on the promises they'd made each other during a time when Nick had been keeping the biggest, most dangerous secret of his life.

And Nick had been paying for it ever since. So had Kelly, in a way.

Kelly cleared his throat, rubbing his palms along his thighs. Nick moved in his peripheral vision, and Kelly raised his head to see Nick carefully setting his cane aside and shrugging out of his suit coat.

"Come here, Kels," Nick murmured as he removed his cuff links.

Kelly pushed away the unsavory memories, hopefully never to be thought of again. He tossed his suit jacket aside and started on the buttons of his shirt, approaching Nick with a lascivious lick of his lips.

Nick batted his hands away from the buttons and finished the task for him as they met each other's eyes. Nick was grinning as he bunched Kelly's shirt in both hands and pulled him closer, but there was something missing in his expression, replaced by pain he was trying to hide.

"Did you bring your pills?" Kelly asked quietly.

Nick nodded and pulled their bodies flush. "I'll take them later. We both know the night'll be over when I do."

Kelly clucked his tongue, but Nick kissed him before he could argue. He pulled him closer, encircling him in strong arms, humming against Kelly's lips and sliding his fingers under Kelly's belt. Kelly melted into his embrace. His hands found their way into Nick's hair, clutching at his short curls, and he knew as soon as Nick made the slightest of moves that he'd be on his back and begging.

It had been so long. Too long.

"Nick," Kelly breathed, shocked by how eager and needy he sounded.

"I know," Nick gasped. His cheeks were flushed and he was staring at Kelly like he could devour him. He nudged Kelly toward the bed, his voice choked. "Get out of those fucking clothes."

Kelly fumbled with his belt as Nick carefully rid himself of his own suit. His hands slowed, though, as his eyes strayed to Nick's movements, to the defined muscles and fresh scars revealed as Nick undressed. Kelly didn't manage to do anything but watch him disrobe before Nick had him in his arms again, and Kelly didn't care that he was still fully clothed. His fingers dug into Nick's ribs, glancing over the ugly, raised scar on his torso as he pulled at him. He held Nick tightly, helping take a little weight off his knee as they stumbled the last few steps and fell into the bed together. Nick wound up on top, powerful muscles and the bulk of his weight working to restrain Kelly as he kissed him.

Kelly curled around him, pulling at his hair, relieved to have his legs wrapped around Nick after weeks—hell, *months*—of only being able to hold on to him at night as they slept. It wasn't that Nick hadn't wanted it since he'd begun to recover, it was that he'd deemed his own body's reactions too unpredictable to make it fun, since the painkillers deadened *all* the senses, including the pleasurable ones.

Nick's hand found its way into Kelly's hair, grip tightening almost to the point of pain, and he delved his tongue into Kelly's mouth, flicking the tip over Kelly's, drawing moans from them both. Nick was hard against Kelly's cock, and Kelly shimmied so Nick could feel it.

Nick broke the kiss with a gasp. He pushed up onto his elbow, and Kelly was dismayed to see him grimacing.

Kelly tried to reach for him, but Nick still had him pinned. "Your knee?" Kelly asked.

Nick nodded and pushed up, his weight on his hands and his one good leg. He glanced up at the headboard like he was gauging how far he'd need to crawl to get Kelly into the center of the bed. Kelly gazed up at him. At the hard line of his jaw hidden under his scruff that he refused to shave. At the scar along his collarbone where a bullet had grazed him in the line of duty years ago and he'd called Kelly from the hospital, drugged to his eyeballs, to tell him to take care of his *Fiddler* if he died. At the light reflecting off his beautiful green eyes and revealing depths to them, fathomless depths, that could only be seen by someone who'd witnessed the many ways in which Nicholas O'Flaherty could sacrifice himself for someone he loved.

"Nick," Kelly found himself whispering. He didn't even realize he'd spoken until Nick looked back down at him, eyes alight, sending a shiver through Kelly's body. Kelly slid his free fingers down Nick's cheekbone. "God, you're fucking beautiful."

Nick smiled, the laugh lines around his eyes crinkling, the warmth turning his eyes a brand-new shade of green. He bent and kissed Kelly carefully.

Kelly arched his back, shoving his groin against Nick's pointedly before wrapping his free arm around Nick's neck. "Roll."

Nick gathered him up in his arms and flipped them obediently, kissing Kelly long and hard as they readjusted their positions. Kelly rutted against him, wishing he'd managed to get his suit pants off before they started this.

Nick slung one foot over the backs of Kelly's thighs. "I'm sorry. I thought I could deal with it long enough to make it," he admitted.

Kelly kissed him so he wouldn't have to try to keep explaining. Nick's warm fingers spread over Kelly's spine as their bodies pressed tight. Nick pulled his other leg up, squeezing his thighs against Kelly's hips and then sliding his foot against Kelly's calf, wrapping around him in a way he so rarely did even when his body was completely healthy. Kelly rolled his hips, settling between Nick's legs as the kiss grew more heated.

"You feel good there," Nick gasped against Kelly's lips. Nick's fingertips were at the small of Kelly's back, fumbling at the thick leather of Kelly's belt like he was trying to secure a handhold on a vertical climb.

"I've fucking missed this," Kelly growled, kissing at Nick's neck and chest.

Nick let his good knee fall to the side, giving Kelly room to get closer.

Kelly pushed from his knee, aiming closer for a kiss, but he wound up driving his hips against Nick harder than he'd intended, dragging the shaft of his hard cock against Nick's groin. Kelly gasped as a jolt of pleasure blazed through him. Nick's mouth fell open and he squeezed his eyes shut, back arching. He hadn't made a sound, and Kelly couldn't tell if the wince was because it had felt good or if he'd hurt him.

"Sorry." Kelly slid his fingers into Nick's hair.

When Nick opened his eyes to meet Kelly's, the dim lights caught the spark in them. Kelly realized he was gaping as they stared at each other, their breaths coming in staccato bursts, their heartbeats pounding in time with each other's.

"Felt good," Nick huffed. The answer had been almost immediate, but to Kelly it felt that time was slowing. Maybe even reversing.

He continued to stare, continued to pet Nick's hair, continued the rhythmic rocking of his hips that felt so damn good.

"Kels," Nick grunted, and he pushed his legs together hard, squeezing Kelly's hips between his thighs.

Kelly shook himself from the spell and looked down to where their chests were pressed together, where Kelly's unbuttoned shirt was caught between them and the buttons were digging in. "Sorry. God, I'm a little nervous, babe. Like this is our first time or some shit."

Nick worked his fingers loose from Kelly's belt and reached for Kelly's face with both hands. "Me too," he confessed. He smiled gently, and something about it eased the butterflies in Kelly's belly. Then Nick licked his lips, and the infamously nervous gesture from his boyfriend immediately ratcheted up and amplified the tumbling again. "Kels," Nick started, but he hesitated long enough for Kelly to find a whole new level of anxiety.

"We should have just fucked on the *Fiddler* like you wanted to," Kelly said in a rush. "This is way too much pressure to put on both of us, what the hell was I thinking? Thinking this would be a good idea?" He pushed away from Nick, breaking Nick's hold, sat back on his haunches and shook his head as he stared at the fancy fucking headboard of their fancy fucking hotel room. "Haven't had sex since before you almost died, it's obviously stressful for both of us, why the fuck did I think, 'Hey, let's pretend we're on a date' would take the pressure *off*? Why do you let me plan shit?"

Nick snorted. When Kelly returned his attention to Nick's face, Nick was watching him fondly, a crooked smile on his lips, his body relaxed. He slowly straightened out his bad leg, pushing his knee in so that it grazed Kelly's hip on its way past him. Kelly realized he was kneeling between Nick's splayed legs, and his cock jumped as he let his eyes stray down Nick's naked body.

"It was a good idea, babe," Nick said.

"But you're nervous. And I'm nervous."

"I know. But I'm not nervous because of performance pressure or whatever the fuck you're freaking out about. Come back here." He reached for Kelly, barely able to touch the tips of his fingers to Kelly's exposed chest.

Kelly huffed as he struggled out of his shirt and tossed it over the end of the bed. He leaned over again, both hands propped on either side of Nick, and he was peripherally aware of Nick's bent knee pushing out to the side again. Nick slid his hands up Kelly's arms and onto his chest, then trailed his fingers down and around until he'd encircled Kelly in a hug as Kelly carefully rested his weight on him.

"I was nervous because . . ." Nick's eyes darted back and forth as he looked into Kelly's. "I want to ask you to do something for me, but I don't want you to feel like you have to if you don't want it."

"You know I'd do anything for you." Kelly kissed Nick to emphasize his sincerity.

"I know, babe," Nick forced his eyes open after the kiss. "But this is for you."

Kelly straightened up. He realized he was frowning, and he tried to school his expression a little better. "Okay."

Nick's hands turned gentle on Kelly's back, barely a caress as he stuck his fingers back under Kelly's belt. "Will you top me?" Nick asked, unblinking as he gazed at Kelly.

Kelly's mouth fell open, and he would have sworn that his heart skipped a beat or five. "Top you?"

Nick nodded. "Means you'd do the fucking."

"Yeah, I know what it means."

"See, it didn't look like you knew—"

"Nick!" Kelly pushed up again, but this time Nick didn't let him get away. He locked his fingers at Kelly's spine, and Kelly was forced to lie back over him, their bodies rubbing, Kelly's cock enjoying every second of it.

"If you don't want to it's okay," Nick continued. "I just . . . thought . . ." He cleared his throat and pressed his lips together as he held Kelly's gaze, obviously trying not to display how nervous he still was. "Thought it would be easier."

Kelly was torn between wanting to allay his nerves, and enjoying the rare show of insecurity. Even during his recovery, when Nick had been so vulnerable, he'd rarely been unsure like this. It was charming. Every fiber of Kelly's being wanted to wrap him up and cuddle him.

Kelly traced the tip of his forefinger along Nick's forehead, then down his temple and jawline.

"I'd be inside you?" he asked softly.

When Nick's lips parted on a gasp, Kelly slid his thumb over Nick's bottom lip.

Nick's eyes fluttered shut. "Yeah," he breathed.

Kelly couldn't resist the opportunity to take Nick's bottom lip between his, using the tip of his tongue to taste, taking his sweet time. Nick's knee came to rest against Kelly's hip, and Kelly automatically reached back to squeeze behind Nick's thigh.

Nick was breathing hard beneath him, and Kelly realized his own breath was hard to come by.

"Do you want to?" Nick whispered, and though he was trying desperately to keep his tone neutral, Kelly knew him too well to miss the hope and desire behind the tremor in his words.

"*God*, yes."

Nick nodded, probably searching for words but unable to find any. He pulled his other knee back up, squeezed Kelly between his thighs.

Kelly hummed and dove into another kiss. Adrenaline raced through him at the thought that he could slide into Nick, feel Nick's body wrapping around his in every possible way, look into those phenomenal green eyes of his as they made love.

Kelly wasn't about to make him ask again. He took Nick's hand in his own and pressed it hard into the mattress, then kissed him hungrily, sucking on his tongue, biting at it, scraping his teeth over Nick's lip. He moved them both until he had Nick in the center of the bed, and he took one last lascivious kiss before pushing away from him.

"One second," he grunted, and then scooted off the end of the bed to ditch the rest of his suit.

Nick watched him, propped on his elbows, smiling fondly.

"How long have you been thinking about this?" Kelly asked as he struggled with his shoes.

Nick hummed, the sound coming from deep in his chest. "I'm not sure. I should have brought it up earlier, but I was . . ."

Kelly tossed his shoes aside. He shoved his pants down, then kicked out of them. "Nervous?"

Nick winced, rocking his knee back and forth.

Kelly watched him for a few seconds, his stomach tumbling. He was more nervous now than he had been the first time Nick had fucked him. He felt like a teenager on prom night.

"But fuck, it's not like we haven't spent the last year playing with a drawer full of dildos, Kels," Nick said wryly.

"Dude."

Nick clucked his tongue and stretched out, raising one knee in invitation. "Where'd you hide the lube in this place?"

Kelly narrowed his eyes and bent over the bed. He dragged his hand up Nick's leg, then bent to kiss the inside of Nick's thigh before crawling toward him and resting one knee between his legs, testing the position. Nick splayed his leg, giving Kelly room.

Kelly met his eyes, and when he moved to touch him, his fingers trembled. He took a deep breath, then grabbed the back of Nick's thigh and pulled to seat it against his hip, right against the six-shooter tattoo that Nick loved so much.

Kelly stretched out, coming to within a breath of Nick's face as he reached toward the pillows. Nick's entire body was taut beneath him, his hands trailing over Kelly's skin. He was watching Kelly raptly, not seeming to realize he was tracing the dream catcher inked into Kelly's rib cage.

Kelly kissed him as he got his fingers on the lube he'd stashed at the head of the bed.

"Always prepared," Nick said, smirking even as Kelly stole another kiss.

"I wasn't sure how tonight was going to play out," Kelly admitted. "There's some in the bathroom, too. And between the cushions of the couch."

Nick chuckled, his smile bringing out the hint of dimples hidden beneath his beard and lighting his eyes. His fingers were gentle on Kelly's ribs.

"There's even some in the Rover," Kelly continued. "All over the *Fiddler*. I basically stashed lube all over Boston in the hopes of getting laid tonight."

Nick was still laughing, but it faded into a more somber smile. "I'm sorry it's been so long," he whispered, and his eyes fluttered closed as Kelly drew closer for another kiss.

"Sex isn't the reason I'm here, Nicko." Kelly kissed him over and over as he let more of his weight rest on Nick. "You don't have to apologize for needing time."

Nick licked his lips, shifting under him. They kissed one last time before Kelly began making his way down Nick's body. His chin, his neck, nipping at his collarbone and the smooth skin that contrasted with the scruff of his beard. Kelly scraped his teeth over Nick's chest and licked at a nipple, then sucked on it because he knew it'd make Nick writhe. Nick dug his fingers into Kelly's hair, his body contorting. His heart was racing under Kelly's lips when Kelly kissed his chest. Kelly wasn't sure entirely why, but Nick's nerves were beginning to turn him on even more. It felt like Nick was handing something over to him. Not just his body. His trust. Control. Wading into waters they'd never ventured into, and he wanted to go there with Kelly.

Kelly pushed to all fours, his cock jumping when his hips dragged against the insides of Nick's thighs. Nick held out his hand, and Kelly squeezed lube into his palm, then put some into his own and tossed the bottle toward the pillows. Despite the actions being familiar, the nerves still tumbled through him.

"Come here and kiss me before we both punk out of this," Nick said in exasperation.

Kelly smirked because that was exactly what he'd been about to do. When he bent over Nick, Nick hooked one leg over Kelly's hip. Kelly moaned into the kiss when Nick's lubed palm wrapped around his cock.

Nick coated him liberally, obviously taking pleasure in the slide of his palm over Kelly's cock. Kelly panted into the kiss as Nick jacked him slowly. If it felt this good with Nick's fingers around him and that leg draped over him, how amazing would it be to slide inside him and have him wrap around Kelly as they fucked?

"Yeah, Nick," Kelly grunted, biting at Nick's lip and thrusting into his hand. Nick responded with a muffled hum.

Kelly reached between them, fumbling a little before Nick's fingers found his and guided him between his legs. Nick hitched his foot higher onto Kelly's back, squeezing Kelly and sliding their cocks together as Kelly carefully pushed one finger inside him, then another.

This wasn't entirely new for either of them. Nick enjoyed having something inside him almost as much as Kelly did; from rimming to dildos to having two of Kelly's fingers inside him while they fucked, Nick could take whatever Kelly dished out. Nick's slick hand cupped Kelly's balls as Kelly slid a third finger into him.

They kissed a little more desperately as Nick's noises grew more obscene. They pushed closer until their noses were in the way, using more tongue and more teeth, moaning with every exhalation and breathing harshly through their noses because they both refused to part for air.

"Babe," Kelly finally croaked, twisting his fingers inside Nick and reveling in the way Nick's breath caught.

Nick could only whisper his name.

Kelly withdrew slowly, wrenching a groan and a gasp from Nick. Kelly's cock was absolutely pulsing with need, and he was getting light-headed with the desire to shove into Nick's body and just take him.

He was so nervous he could barely think. It wasn't just that it was his first time, it was his first time with Nick. And what if it was Nick's first time too? What if it went badly? Oh God . . .

Nick huffed a breath against his lips, and suddenly Kelly's nerves settled. Their noses and foreheads were pressed together, their eyes closed. Every breath was shared, every groan close enough to vibrate their lips.

"You sure?" Kelly hissed.

Nick nodded. "Go slow, okay? At first."

"Promise," Kelly managed.

Nick pulled both knees up, squeezing at Kelly's ribs before placing the heel of one foot on the small of Kelly's back. Kelly pushed onto his elbows. Nick couldn't seem to catch his breath as they locked eyes. Hell, neither could Kelly. Kelly wondered if Nick's knee was up to this, but then he shook it off. Nick would tell him if he was hurting, and Kelly wasn't the Doc tonight. Nick grinned slowly, and Kelly kissed him hard. The head of his cock pressed at Nick's ass.

Kelly took Nick's hand in his and held it to the mattress above their heads. Nick's fingers gripped him tight, his knuckles turning white. Kelly bowed his back, nuzzling against Nick's neck, forcing his face up under his chin to place his lips against Nick's pulse point. He rotated his hips, loving the way Nick's thighs felt against him, then pushed forward to work the head of his cock into Nick.

It was agonizingly slow.

The desperate, wanton moan that escaped Nick's lips made Kelly's blood run hot. The way Nick's body moved beneath his was intoxicating. Everything tightened, from the fingers grasping at Kelly's to the muscles that fought Kelly's entry. Kelly waited for his next breath, fighting the dizzying rush of lust and adrenaline, but when he realized that he simply wouldn't be able to catch his breath at all, he stole a hungry kiss.

Nick rolled his hips, helping Kelly sink deeper. Kelly pressed his face to Nick's cheek and groped for his other hand as he rocked into him.

"Fuck!" Nick finally managed to get out. His head was tilted back, his lips parted and his eyes squeezed shut.

Kelly nuzzled his forehead against Nick's temple. "Okay?"

It took Nick a few attempts to answer. He couldn't catch his breath, and he couldn't seem to stop writhing as Kelly moved inside him. But he finally gritted out, "Feels good. You feel good."

Kelly let Nick's hands go so he wouldn't feel trapped, and slid both arms under Nick's shoulders, holding him tight and kissing him languorously. He sank deep, as deep as he could get, searching for the right angle to hit Nick's prostate. He'd learned a lot of tricks with Nick O'Flaherty as his teacher.

"Oh God, Nick." Kelly's words were nearly lost in Nick's mouth as they kissed. Nick's only response was to gasp his name.

Kelly's fingers dug into Kelly's shoulder blades, and Nick's hand found its way up into Kelly's hair again. Kelly finally propped himself on his elbows, his hips still rolling, his muscles straining as he got a chance to look down into Nick's eyes. He didn't take his eyes off Nick's, and Nick didn't blink.

Nick bit his lip, then grinned. "Harder, Kels."

Kelly picked up the pace, driving deeper with each thrust, fucking Nick until the headboard banged against the wall. Nick stretched to brace one hand against the wall, locking his elbow to stop the noise. Kelly kissed his chin.

"You're so fucking tight, babe. Jesus Christ."

"Don't stop," Nick gritted out. Kelly tried to reach between them so he could jack Nick off as they fucked, but Nick hooked his ankles together at the small of Kelly's back and squeezed, making it impossible.

"I'm going to come," Kelly warned. "I want to feel you first. Feel you come."

Nick groaned in response, his eyes falling shut as he bucked his hips to meet Kelly's thrusts. "Come inside me, babe. Come on."

Nick sure as fuck didn't have to ask twice. Kelly redoubled his efforts, thrusts deliberate so he'd be sure to feel every tantalizing slide of his cock into Nick's body, dragging his belly against Nick's cock with every slow thrust into him. Nick cried out his name, grinding his hips up, moving with Kelly's rhythm. He was using the friction from Kelly's belly to get himself off, and Kelly could feel his muscles tensing, feel him getting closer and closer to release.

God, he wanted to know what it felt like being inside him when Nick came.

He held off as long as he could, but he couldn't think of anything except Nick's tight, warm body wrapped around him, about the trust it took to ask for this, about the devotion in Nick's eyes when he begged Kelly . . . begged him to fill him full of cum, begged him for harder, begged him for more.

"A little more," Nick told him, his voice gone rough. "God, just wreck me, Kels!"

"Fuck!" Kelly gasped the word over and over until he had no more breath to speak. He was working them both into a sweat, their bodies entwining with practiced eased; even with their roles switched they knew how to move against each other.

Nick arched his back, bucking his hips like he was trying to throw Kelly off. He laid his hands above his head, and Kelly immediately reached for them, twining their fingers together, pressing him down. Nick's entire body was trembling, taut and racked with pleasure. He moaned long and loud, the sound desperate and heated and almost resembling Kelly's name.

"Oh fuck, babe," Kelly hissed, and he gave up on trying to stave off his orgasm. "Fuck yes!"

Nick tried pushing back at Kelly's hands, but Kelly was coming inside him and every muscle in his body fought to maintain the ground he'd won. He fucked him through the climax, fucked him until Nick could do nothing but squeeze his fingers and moan his name and wrap his legs tighter around him, fucked him until both their bodies were trembling and the headboard was banging along with the increasingly ruthless rhythm, fucked him until the entire room was filled with the scents of sweat and sex and that intoxicating absinthe cologne.

Kelly buried his face in Nick's neck and cried out for him—for mercy—but he kept moving, kept shooting off inside him, kept holding him down and grinding his body against Nick's cock until the friction was too much for Nick. His muscles spasmed, his cum spurting between them as he struggled against Kelly's hold and graced Kelly's ears with the most sinful moans Kelly had ever heard. Kelly moved one hand to grip Nick's hair, and Nick took advantage of his newfound freedom by dragging his fingernails down Kelly's back. Kelly gritted his teeth, but all he could think of was filling Nick full of cum so he could watch it run out of him.

He was still grasping at Nick long seconds later. He was still stretched out on top of him, too, with Nick's legs wound around him and his one free hand still clutching at Kelly's shoulder. They were both still breathing hard, and Nick's eyes were closed. Kelly released his hand slowly, not surprised when his fingers ached as he flexed them.

Nick opened one eye to peer up at him.

"Okay?" Kelly asked, his voice ragged.

Nick huffed and closed his eye again. He nodded, and Kelly lowered himself just enough to kiss him. Nick shifted his hips, and they both gasped into the kiss.

"Oh God," Nick whimpered. He grasped at Kelly's hip, digging his fingers into Kelly's ass to keep him from moving again. "No, no, no."

"Relax. Kiss me," Kelly murmured, echoing the words Nick had used their first time together. He kissed Nick again, keeping it gentle and soothing to distract him. Nick still groaned against his lips, his body tense as Kelly carefully pulled out of him. Kelly wound up on his hands and knees, forehead pressed to Nick's, breaths at a premium as he tried to slow his heart. "Okay?"

Nick nodded, eyes still closed. "Yeah."

"Did you come?" Kelly asked, even though he knew the answer. Nick nodded again, trying to catch his breath. "If you hadn't I was going to make sure my tongue was in your ass when you did."

Nick groaned and knocked his good knee against Kelly's hip. "Jesus, you get dirtier every time we fuck."

Kelly chuckled at that, but he soon realized that he had no idea what to say now. He knelt there in awkward silence for a few more seconds, then stole one more kiss and rolled off Nick, splaying beside him in the king-size bed.

After a full minute had passed, both of them still breathing hard, the silence stretching into unusual territory, Nick's fingers found Kelly's between their bodies and grasped them.

Kelly glanced at him. Nick still had his eyes closed, his tongue touched to his upper teeth.

"Nicko?" Kelly rolled onto his side, placing a hand on Nick's chest and kissing his shoulder.

"That was good, Doc," Nick rumbled, and the pitch of his voice sent a thrill up Kelly's spine.

He turned his head, and Kelly stretched to kiss him. Nick cradled the back of Kelly's head, and even through the distraction of the kiss and the afterglow of a pretty amazing orgasm, Kelly could feel the tremor in Nick's hand. Whether it was from pain or not didn't really matter. Kelly knew how to fix it.

"I'll get your pills." He sat up, patting Nick's belly, then trudged toward the door for the overnight bag he'd packed for them both because he knew Nick wouldn't take him seriously and pack his own. He realized he was frowning as he rummaged through it. When his hand landed on Nick's travel pill container, he was still frowning. After what they'd just done, he really shouldn't be frowning.

Nick was now stretched out across the bed like a cat on a warm rug, and when Kelly glanced at him, at powerful muscles, at skin covered in scars and ink, at auburn waves and the beard Nick was still afraid to shave because his hands were unsteady, and those incredible green eyes that could bore their way into Kelly's soul, every part of Kelly's body screamed for him to pounce Nick's ass and do that again.

"You okay?" Nick asked when he found Kelly staring.

Kelly bit his lip. "You want some water?"

Nick nodded, and Kelly turned to the bathroom to get a glass of water and a damp rag to clean off with. He made quick work of the mess on his belly, and even managed to get most of the lube off without resorting to getting in the shower like he usually had to. Then he grabbed a fresh hand towel, wet it, and brought it out to Nick, who was watching him like a hawk, a frown flirting over his expression.

"What's up with this?" Nick asked, and he waved a hand over Kelly's face when Kelly handed him the glass of water and his pills.

Kelly couldn't help but smile. Nick always knew when something was off with him, and he usually knew when to push and when to let Kelly work through his moods himself.

He climbed into the bed and stretched out sideways next to Nick, propping himself on his elbow, waiting until Nick downed his pills.

"Was that the first time you'd ever done that?" Kelly asked.

Nick's lips twitched. It wasn't quite a smile, but it wasn't really a frown either. He took another sip of water, swallowing hard. "No."

Kelly nodded. He didn't want to examine why he was relieved by that, but he kind of wished he'd asked earlier so he wouldn't have been so fucking nervous.

"It was the second time," Nick added, taking another drink to cover his smirk.

Kelly's eyes widened and sought out Nick's, and Nick swallowed his water and laughed at him.

"Why is that funny?" Kelly asked.

"You look kind of terrified right now."

"I do not."

"Do too." Nick downed the rest of his water and tossed the empty glass toward the sofa, then rolled so he was facing Kelly. He placed a hand on Kelly's hip, his fingers gentle as he stroked along the dream catcher tattoo. "What's on your mind?"

"The first time," Kelly said hesitantly. "Was it . . . not . . ."

"It was fine," Nick answered quickly, meeting Kelly's eyes. He smiled again, which went a long way toward making Kelly believe him. "It wasn't fun, though. It got less fun as it happened, which is why I was so fucking nervous, I guess. When I said slow down, he didn't, and I never trusted him after that. It was . . . pretty much the end of him and me. But I'm sorry, I should have been able to separate that from you. I know you."

"Don't apologize, babe."

Nick shrugged, sighing heavily. "I know you."

"Don't." Kelly petted Nick's cheek. "It's okay."

"It just . . . it wasn't something I'd ever wanted to do again."

Kelly pursed his lips, chewing on the inside of his cheek.

"Not until you."

Kelly stared into his eyes, not trying to think of anything to say. There was nothing he *could* say that would be more effective than listening. He edged closer, letting Nick wrap his arms around him, sliding his leg between Nick's knees, and resting his head against Nick's chest.

"I love you, Kelly."

Kelly took a deep breath and sighed it out slowly, kissing Nick's chest, eyes drifting shut as Nick held him close. After a few seconds he realized that Nick was holding his breath and his heart was racing. He raised his head to meet Nick's eyes, searching for a hint as to why.

Nick was silent, letting him look.

"What's wrong?" Kelly asked.

Nick shook his head, smiling sadly.

"What?"

When Nick spoke, his voice had gone hoarse. "It's just . . . someday I hope you'll say it back again."

CHAPTER THREE

April 8, 2013

Nick navigated the Rover through the throngs of airport traffic. His phone beeped, and a glance told him that Ty Grady had retrieved his suitcase from baggage claim and was heading outside to wait for him. Nick didn't bother responding, since he was coming up on the arrivals now.

It didn't take him long to spot Ty, standing with his bag over his shoulder, phone in hand. He pulled as close as he could and unlocked the doors, not bothering to get out since his knee was still iffy and Ty could handle his own damn bag.

Ty tossed it into the back and slid into the passenger seat. He knocked his shoulder into Nick's getting in, grinning like the proverbial cat who ate the canary.

"Hey, bud," Nick greeted, submitting to an awkward, sideways, one-armed hug. "How was the flight?"

Ty shrugged and buckled his seat belt. "Nothing exciting."

"I'll take nothing exciting for the rest of our lives," Nick said as pulled back out into traffic, glancing at Ty again. "Have you let Zane know you landed?"

Ty rolled his eyes, nodding as he settled into the seat and tossed one foot up on the dash. "Yes, Mother. One fucking time I forget, and trust me, I'll never do it again."

Nick was chuckling, shaking his head.

"Where's Doc," Ty asked, glancing into the backseat pointedly.

Nick's smile fell and he cleared his throat, wincing. "He went home for a while."

Ty was silent, and Nick could feel his eyes on him.

"What?" Nick grunted.

"I know he went home for a while. You told me that much on the phone. I guess more pointedly I'm asking, why?"

Nick sighed, glancing in his rearview mirror. "We had a fight."

"I didn't think you two were capable of fighting."

"Neither did we."

Ty grunted, turning a little in the seat. "You're either super upset or super drugged. You haven't even yelled at me for having my foot on the dash."

"That's 'cause I don't really give a shit if your foot's on the dash."

"Super drugged, then?"

"Shut up."

Ty snorted and slid his aviators down his nose so Nick could see him narrowing his eyes.

"I'll tell you about it between innings," Nick offered.

"Irish," Ty said softly, and his voice had lost the teasing note. He took his sunglasses off. "Are you okay?"

"Yeah," Nick said with an almost careless shrug. "It was a stupid fight, and once we realized it was stupid, we tried to figure out why it was stupid. We decided it was partly cabin fever. Kelly'd been stuck taking care of me for so long, so we figured a little time apart would do us both good."

"Been there," Ty mumbled.

"You and Garrett doing okay?"

"Yeah, we're solid. He even told me I'm allowed to drink this week, as long as I don't wind up on the news for doing something stupid."

"Yeah, we'll mix alcohol and my painkillers and see who goes into shock first."

Ty laughed, the sound clear as a bell and somehow soothing to Nick's aching soul. "It'd be just like Tijuana that one time," he said, and they shared a groan at the memory. After a few thoughtful seconds passed, Ty asked, "What time is the game?"

"Day game, starts at one. I thought we'd head straight to Fenway; we can soak in the opening day shenanigans."

Ty was grinning when Nick glanced over at him. "Sox and Orioles on Opening Day right after we both barely live through something," he mused, reaching up to press the button that would open the sunroof. The sunshine streamed in, along with a salty breeze that smelled of spring, and Ty turned his face up to meet it. "Fate."

He put his fingers through the sunroof, basking in the warmth on his face. His evil cackle was music to Nick's ears.

Several hours later they'd made their way through traffic and the noontime excitement that was Fenway on the Red Sox home opener. It was the seventh game of the season, and the Sox were four and two. Boston was buzzing.

Nick was buzzing too, but not exactly with excitement. Every time he let his mind drift, it immediately went to Kelly and made his heart ache like he was physically sick. He'd spent the last couple days keeping as busy as he possibly could, or taking enough of his painkillers that he didn't feel or think about anything. It was an unhealthy spiral, but at least he knew it.

He'd told Ty as much on the phone two nights ago, and that was how they'd wound up here together, just the two of them. He hadn't asked Ty to come stay with him for the week. But he hadn't needed to ask.

Ty was a step ahead of him as they made their way to the front-row seats Kelly had managed to acquire for the home opener, giant plastic souvenir cups of beer in each hand. It was only a couple of flights of stairs, but to Nick it looked daunting. Ty was letting him hold on to his shoulder, even though Nick knew Ty was still supposed to be in a sling after blowing up half of Miami.

When they got to their seats, Ty was grinning like the Cheshire Cat, the field reflecting in his aviators. He helped Nick get settled, both of them laughing at how grumbly and creaky they were.

"Tell you what, Irish, I never thought either of us would be this old," Ty said as he hefted one foot up on the wall in front of them.

"That makes two of us." Nick slouched with a grimace. "Do you know what you'd do with your favorite belongings if you died?"

"What?"

"I was just . . . I finally got out that box of Eli's stuff, the one his mom gave me. His whole life boiled down to just one box of his favorite things, sitting on a shelf on the *Fiddler*. And I've been fucking fixating on it for days now."

He glanced at Ty when Ty didn't answer, only to find Ty gazing off into the distance, a frown marring his features, nodding to some unheard rhythm. He finally shook his head. "I don't know what I would put in a box like that," he admitted.

"Me either."

"What's in it?"

Nick swallowed hard. "I don't know. I got as far as Seymour and a stack of letters he wrote before it got too hard."

"Oh God, Seymour." Ty grinned as his eyes lit up. "I'd forgotten about him!"

"You want to go through it with me?"

"Yeah," Ty said immediately, tapping Nick's knee with his fist. "Yeah, I'd like that."

Nick nodded and shifted around to get more comfortable, situating his cane between his legs as he crossed one foot over the other.

"That the cane Sanchez gave you when you got hit with the shrapnel?" Ty asked. Their elbows brushed as they both got settled, but it was once again a familiar feeling. For a while there, Nick's relationship with Ty had been stilted and awkward. The relief he'd felt when they'd begun to straighten things out couldn't be measured in words.

Nick tapped the toe of his boot with the cane. "Yeah."

"Does Doc know what you can do with that thing?" Ty asked carefully.

Nick shrugged, wincing as he gazed at the outfield and the bright green grass. "I don't know. Why?"

"He wasn't around when you took that shrapnel. He never saw you with the cane."

"What's your point, Tyler?" Nick asked, smiling to soften the blow of his question. He didn't fucking want to talk about Kelly, but he also knew Ty was here to help him. Ty couldn't really do a lot for him if they never talked about Kelly.

Ty shifted in his seat. "I don't know. Just think he'd like to know what you can do with it."

"Why?"

"'Cause it's hot."

Nick barked a laugh, and Ty smirked.

"Seriously, you should show him. That'll solve your sex problems." He took a drink from his cup of beer. "Solved mine a couple times back in the day."

"Ty."

"What? We're being honest with each other, right? I'm just saying. Had a massive, massive crush on you the first, like, two . . . three years. Five. Five years."

Nick rolled his eyes, surprised to find that he was blushing as Ty chuckled into his cup. He swiped a hand over his mouth, shaking his head. "Kelly and I don't have sex problems. None that can be fixed with a cane, anyway."

"If you say so. How'd you get it through security?"

"People don't fucking check canes and slings and shit. Speaking of, where the hell is that sling Garrett told me you had to wear?"

"I lost it."

Nick tilted his head to look at Ty over the top of his sunglasses.

Ty gave him an innocent shrug. "On the plane. Legit. What?"

"You better have a spare to be wearing when I send you home."

Ty chuckled and sat back, looking out at the Green Monster. Nick watched his profile for a few moments. He knew Ty was keeping something to himself.

"What's on your mind, Six?" he asked softly.

Ty sighed, his shoulders slumping and a small smile flitting over his lips, like he was relieved to have been called out on holding back. "Been waiting to read you in until you were doing better." Ty met his eyes pointedly. "You doing better?"

"Yeah, what is it?"

"When Zane and I got back home after the cartel shit in Miami, there was a . . . welcome package waiting for us."

Nick's entire body went stiff and cold, his heart beating in his throat, fluttering so fast it made him light-headed.

"Nick?" Ty's voice came from somewhere far away. His hand on Nick's shoulder was warm, though, and Nick closed his eyes and let Ty's touch pull him back from that feeling of drowning before it could go too far.

Nick sat forward, swallowing hard. "What kind of welcome package?" he croaked.

"Not like that," Ty said in a rush. His hazel eyes were wide, and he was leaning close to Nick, his hand on the back of Nick's neck. He shifted to wrap his arm around Nick's shoulders, patting him like he was trying to calm him.

Nick licked his lips, preparing to tell Ty that he wasn't about to fucking panic or something, but he was breathing fast and his ears were ringing and yeah, he'd been about to panic. He concentrated on Ty's touch, closing his eyes and lifting his face to the sun. He took a deep breath.

"You okay?" Ty asked gently.

"Hold on."

"Jesus, dude," he heard Ty muttering as he took several deep, even breaths. The weight of Ty's hand on him, the smell of the sunshine and grass, and the rhythm of breathing in through his nose, out through his mouth all helped to push back the panic, and he finally opened his eyes again.

He nodded at Ty. "That's unpleasant."

"That happen a lot?"

"No, first time. Go on."

"Sorry." Ty's hand didn't leave Nick's shoulder. "It was an actual welcome packet, not a bomb."

Nick gave a curt nod. "From the Company?"

"Yeah."

"That's not much better than a bomb."

"No, it's okay. They're not putting us in the field. We're just support. An outpost."

Nick scowled at him. Ty was grinning, his eyes shining like Nick hadn't seen in quite a while. Nick gave him a long-suffering sigh.

"They're rebuilding the bookstore," Ty went on, beaming. "Replacing everything we lost in the explosion. And they're installing all kinds of Company-issue shit, Irish, it's going to be fucking amazing. You'll geek out over it just like Zane has, I promise."

Nick brought a hand up to rub at the bridge of his nose, grimacing as he recognized the light in Ty's eyes.

"They tricked out the basement. They're even putting a little elevator in, with one of those cage doors that close."

"Do you fit in it?" Nick asked, smiling along with Ty's enthusiasm despite his misgivings over the whole thing.

"I will admit it's coffin-sized. But cool nonetheless."

"Ty."

Ty gave him a mischievous smirk. "We'll run the bookstore day to day, and the back room is only for . . . special deliveries."

Nick sighed heavily.

Ty was grinning like a shark. "All the fun stuff comes through the back door."

Nick rolled his eyes, fighting valiantly not to smile and give Ty the satisfaction. Ty was snickering, though, and he jostled Nick with his elbow, patting his arm and then squeezing it.

"I've missed you, Irish," Ty said with relish. Nick turned his head, and when their eyes met, Ty's smile faded into a more somber expression. "I'm sorry I left you behind."

"You *didn't*. If you had moved me with that knife in me, it would have killed me. You know that as well as I do."

Ty adjusted his arm around Nick's shoulders, squeezing him hard. Nick slumped a little more, resting into Ty's embrace. They sat that way through all the pregame festivities, Ty's arm warm and heavy around Nick's shoulders, like a familiar blanket wrapped around him after a day in the cold.

Despite all the things they'd been through, together and apart, over the last couple years, this felt like old times. The easy camaraderie that Nick and Ty had enjoyed from the moment they'd met on that bus to Parris Island was back. And for the first time in twenty years, they could share every last part of themselves without the fear of secrets or the dull ache of distant longing coloring anything they said.

Nick savored every second of it.

When the national anthem was announced, Ty helped Nick stand, his hand gentle on Nick's elbow. They faced the flag blowing in the spring breeze, and as if they were one entity, they each snapped into a smart salute.

When it was over and they were settling back into their seats, the stadium buzzing with excitement around them, an older man who'd been sitting a few seats down reached across the young boy who sat between him and Nick, and touched Nick's arm to get his attention.

Nick flinched, then glanced at the man and the boy.

"My grandson and me wanted to thank you boys for your service," the man said, his voice solemn. He held out his gnarled hand, and it trembled as Nick looked at it.

Nick took it, shaking it dazedly. "Thank you," he managed. "And thank you for yours."

The man nodded, then instructed his grandson to do the same as he shook Ty's hand as well. The boy, who was anywhere between eight and twelve maybe—Nick had no idea how to tell the age of children—gave Nick a sideways glance as he tentatively shook Nick's hand. Then he turned to his grandfather and hissed a question. He probably thought he was being discreet, but Nick heard him loud and clear: "How'd they know you were a soldier, Pop?"

The old man just smiled as he tossed a piece of popcorn into his mouth. "It's just something you know."

Nick tore his attention away from the pair and glanced at Ty, frowning. Ty winked at him, grinning as he sank down in his seat and got comfortable again.

Nick took a deep, steadying breath. He didn't deserve handshakes from veterans at a baseball game. Just like he didn't deserve to hear Kelly say "I love you." He'd lost the right to both those privileges and he wasn't sure it was possible to earn it back.

"Hey." Ty's voice was sharp in Nick's ear. "I know that look. That's your 'I'm a horrible sociopathic serial killer' look."

Nick jerked, meeting Ty's eyes.

"Knock it off, Irish. We're goddamn heroes." Ty nudged him with his elbow. "Go O's."

"Not in this house," Nick growled, and he jabbed Ty's foot with the end of his cane, smiling when Ty howled.

April 15, 2013

"Hey," Owen said as soon as Skype loaded. He was wearing a suit and tie, an expensive one, and it was a little odd considering that Kelly was used to him in jeans and a T-shirt. His face was washed out, and Kelly turned the computer until the sun no longer obscured half of the screen. He wondered how long he'd last in the glare on the deck before retreating back inside.

"How's it going?" he asked.

"Pretty good. Got another raise, few extra weeks of vacation. I think they're realizing the benefits of keeping me around even if I do occasionally disappear and get blown up on company time. How's Lucky?"

Kelly winced. "He's in Boston."

Owen scowled and leaned closer to his laptop's camera. He was in his office, which was stark and modern with wide windows that showed San Diego behind him. "Where are *you*?"

"Colorado."

"Why?"

Kelly shrugged and winced harder. "Let's just say he's doing well enough to need some space."

Owen frowned at him for so long that Kelly tapped at his keyboard to see if the program had frozen.

"You two have a fight?"

"Little bit. That's not why I came home, though!" Kelly was quick to add. "We had a fight, and it was so fucking dumb. We both just stopped mid-yelling and realized we were like caged dogs or something, fighting because we could."

"Want to talk about it?"

"Kind of? Are you busy?"

"It's my lunch break," Owen said, and then waved a bowl in front of the camera. "Tell me about it."

"Okay. Well, Nick wasn't really handling any of it well, you know? The recovery, and then his dad went and fucking died on him, and he's just not the same *Nick*. I guess it throws me off. I'm not used to seeing something that can shake him. So I guess I kind of went into Doc mode. And last week he seemed more miserable than normal, and he said something that made me realize I was treating him like a recovering Marine."

"He *is* a recovering Marine." Owen raised a forkful of what appeared to be salad.

"Yeah, but he's also my boyfriend."

"Weird," Owen muttered around his mouthful of food, eyes on his bowl as he pushed things around with a plastic fork. "Yeah, no, I get it. You were being the Doc instead of a boyfriend. That's not surprising, considering how many times you've nursed one of us through a recovery, though, dude."

"That's what Nick said too. That's not why we fought."

"Okay, so we're getting the long version?"

Kelly snorted and propped one foot on his chair. Damn it, watching Owen eat was making him hungry. He retrieved a pack of cigarettes from the side table and slid one out. Owen waited patiently as he lit up.

"We had a date night kind of thing to see if we could rewire ourselves to think romance instead of teammates," Kelly said, smoke accompanying his words. "I got a hotel room, we got ready separately and all that. It was kind of fun."

"You guys have never done that. I mean shit, you lived together for five years before you ever thought about dating; it's kind of a different dynamic."

"Yeah. It went pretty well. It was fun. And Nick is a smooth motherfucker on a date, I've never really gotten the full effect before." Kelly took another drag as Owen shook his head. "We went back to the hotel at the end of the night. Had a . . . really nice evening."

"Thank you for the euphemism," Owen grumbled. "Are you saying you got into a fight on date night?"

"Basically."

"Before or after the sex?"

"After. Like, right after. Like, still naked after."

"There goes the euphemism." Owen pushed his bowl away, scrubbing his hands over his face.

"Sorry. I can't really tell this story without the sex part."

Owen was smiling crookedly when he looked back at the screen. "It's okay. I'm getting used to it. What kind of fight was it?"

"Well, the entire time, I mean it was a good night, okay? I'll leave it at that for details. But after, I couldn't shake this feeling that something was just off. Like, I should have been thrilled with what happened, you know? But something..."

"Just hit me with the dick talk, I can take it," Owen groaned.

"You can take the dick?" Kelly deadpanned.

Owen stared at the camera, and Kelly fought hard not to grin. He finally lost and snorted, unable to pull a straight face to match Owen's.

"Okay, see, Nick is usually the one doing the fucking."

Kelly waited for Owen to tell him to keep going before he went into more detail. Owen had been the one with the most issues to work through when he'd found out that not one, but *three* of his former Force Recon teammates were bisexual. He waved his finger through the air, nodding.

Kelly took a deep breath. "But that night, he asked me do it. First time ever. That's just not like him, you know?"

"I can imagine, man. Lucky doesn't strike me as the type to let someone fuck him."

"Yeah. So I did, and it was... it was *good*. But after..."

Owen was still nodding, waiting for Kelly to work through it on his own. Kelly sighed and slumped his shoulders, taking another deep drag of his cigarette.

"After, we were in bed, and he told me he loved me. And... I thought..." Kelly's eyes began to lose focus as he stared off into the woods over the top of his computer. He snapped his attention back and sighed. "We were laying there with each other, and I could tell that something was wrong. He was holding his breath, you know? Like he was waiting for something. And when I asked him what was wrong, he gave me that... you know that smile Nick has? Where he knows he's about to take a hit, or he's about to lose something that he loves, but he still tries to give you that smile so you'll think everything's going to be okay?"

"I know exactly what you're talking about."

"He gave me that smile. And then he said... he said, 'Someday I hope you'll say it back again.' Like..."

"Say what?" Owen asked, scowling.

"I love you!" Kelly shouted, growing frustrated all over again, just like he had that night in Nick's arms. "I hadn't said 'I love you' back to him!"

Owen's eyebrows jumped, and he sat back a little. "Oh."

"I would have put money on it, thinking I had. I mean, he *knows* I love him, okay? And when I asked him what the hell he was talking about, he said I hadn't told him I loved him since before Miami happened. Since the last time we'd had sex, which was before I left for that last adventure trek I was on when Liam Bell showed up and shit hit the fan."

Owen winced, and Kelly could tell he was trying hard to remain neutral. "Was he right?" he asked carefully.

Kelly blushed hotly and ducked his head, running his finger over his toes as he adjusted in his chair. He pulled his knee closer to his chest, holding his foot in his hand and placing his cigarette in his mouth again. "That's what we argued about," he said around the cigarette. "I realized he *was* right, though. I hadn't said it back in a long time. At first, when all the secrets came out and we were in the middle of the cartel bullshit with Ty and Zane, I was so fucking angry at him. And it's hard to say I love you when you're pissed, okay. But he knows I love him. And when I asked him why the fuck he hadn't said something to me about it, he said he thought he had to earn it back. He thought I wasn't saying it because I was still angry with him for keeping secrets."

"Well . . . you are," Owen pointed out.

"I know I am," Kelly snapped. "He was keeping some pretty big fucking secrets from me, okay?"

"I know, Doc."

Kelly barely heard him through the creeping anger, though. "He promised me I'd be his partner in crime, okay? But then I find out he's pretending he doesn't even remember proposing to me because he's being blackmailed by some dumbass rogue NSA agent. Fucking Liam Bell."

"I know, Doc."

"And! And then he tells me that he'd performed a government-sanctioned hit on Ty's favorite creepy uncle—straight-up murdered the dude right under my nose—all because creepy uncle was a little too creepy for Uncle Sam."

Owen seemed to know that Kelly wasn't paying any attention to him now, but he kept trying. "Doc. Kelly."

"And he didn't even tell me of his own free will! Oh no, no, I hear about it from *Ty*, and why? Because Nick can't talk right now, Nick's handcuffed to the damn bed because he went and confessed to murder and stuff after stabbing himself for sympathy! He can keep it from me for an entire year of fucking me, but one puppy-dog look from Ty and he's spilling his guts out. Literally!"

"Yeah . . . Doc, I was there."

"Fucking fooled *me* just like everyone else! Lied to me like I was his mother! That's not the kind of secret you keep from someone while you're asking them to marry you!"

"Doc, are you more upset that he murdered Richard Burns, or that he did it without you knowing and helping?"

Kelly scowled as Owen's questions finally broke through the cloud of rage, but he didn't really have to contemplate the answer for very long. "The second one," he admitted. "He knows I would have helped him. I've told him dozens of times, I'm with him no matter what."

"That's sweet and kind of psychotic," Owen mumbled. "Okay, back on track."

Kelly huffed and nodded. "Bottom line, he thought I was punishing him. That I was withholding declarations of love as some sort of penance for what he did." Kelly's heart ached just thinking about it, what Nick had been going through, suffering silently with his guilt and pain because he thought that was what Kelly wanted him to do. He cleared his throat and ducked his head, tapping the ashes from his cigarette.

"I can see how that would be upsetting," Owen said evenly. "For you *and* for him. That was the fight?"

"Yeah," Kelly said, not looking up.

"And that was why you got the weird feeling off him, because he was bending over backward trying to gain forgiveness. Like Nick does."

Kelly squeezed his eyes closed. He hated that Nick had even considered the idea that he needed to regain anything from Kelly, hated that he might have asked Kelly to top him as some sort of *offering* and not because he'd wanted it. He hated Nick for it, and he hated himself for being so fucking blind to his own behavior and to Nick's. He finally forced himself to meet Owen's eyes again. "I felt like shit when I realized it. And you know how Nick is, he was just . . . anything he could say to make it better. I finally screamed at him, I didn't want him to make it up to me, I just wanted him to be *him* again."

"Ouch," Owen whispered.

Kelly nodded, his chest twisting uncomfortably. "And the look in his eyes when I said that? Johns, it was like I fucking punched him in the gut. He just . . . withered. All the fight in him is gone."

"Well hell, Doc, what do you want from the man? All the fight in him is gone because he used it all."

"I know. I fucking hate myself for saying that to him." Kelly bit his lip and sighed, waiting for Owen to give him advice or a verdict or *anything*. His cigarette was almost gone when he put it between his lips.

"How'd you end up in Colorado?" Owen finally asked.

Kelly shrugged. "We both just stopped in the middle of it, like . . . you know, what the hell are we doing here? Nick told me it wasn't fair to me that this was happening, that he wanted me to take a week or two and do whatever I wanted. And he wanted a week or two to himself to do the same. And it sounded like a good idea at the time." Kelly sighed and stared off at the quiet woods.

"This was a week ago?"

"Roughly, yeah."

"Have you talked to him since you left?"

Kelly shook his head.

"Did you call me because you needed to vent, or because you want advice?"

"Advice, please."

"Okay. Get your head out of your ass and call your boyfriend."

Kelly snorted.

"You *know* Nick, Doc. You know that if he thinks he's lost something, he'll let it go. If you told him he wasn't *him* anymore, that you might not be able to forgive him for what he did, he'll take that as contract terminated and he'll let you go without a peep of complaint, thinking that's what you want. If you're waiting for him to call you or come to you and tell you he needs you back, you're going to be waiting just like Ty did that year they didn't speak. That's just not who Nick is."

Kelly's insides roiled. He smashed his cigarette out in the dish on the table, trying not to hyperventilate at the mere thought of it. "You're right," he croaked. "Jesus, I hadn't thought of that."

"I'm pretty sure Ty's still in Boston right now, you could ping him, get some inside info."

"Ty's in Boston?"

"Yeah. He went up to go to the home opener with Nick last week. He stayed all week so he could catch the marathon, too. You didn't know? I just figured you were all there together."

Kelly shook his head. "I was supposed to go with Nick to Opening Day. He was so worried about it when he woke up in Miami, I got him tickets. Thought it'd be . . . I missed it, though."

Owen pursed his lips, nodding but refusing to comment.

Kelly ran his hand over his face. "I miss him. And I feel stupid for fighting with him."

"One little fight in two years, I think you're doing pretty well."

Kelly snorted. He didn't point out that they'd only spent about one third of that time together, and it was hardly a little fight. It didn't matter. "I'll call him right now."

"Good plan."

"Thanks, babe. I appreciate it."

"Anytime, Doc. When you get this shit sorted, you and Nick come out to see us. I want you guys to meet Riley before I fuck it up," Owen said with a grin.

Kelly barked a laugh. "We'll plan something solid when I get back to Boston."

"Copy. Talk later, Doc."

"See you, boss," Kelly said fondly, and Owen ended the Skype session.

Kelly was left sitting in the sun with a lot to ponder, his phone burning a hole in his pocket as he thought about Nick, so many fucking miles away.

After a few minutes to let everything sink in, he pulled out his phone and dialed Nick.

Butterflies began to flutter through his chest and belly as the phone rang. It made him grin. Plenty of people had caused him butterflies over the years, but Nick . . . Nick was different. Nick was the only one who could instill those anticipatory nerves so long after their first kiss. Kelly was going to make sure he never took that for granted again.

"Doc?" Nick answered after a few rings, and Kelly sat up straighter, frowning at Nick's winded voice, at the chaotic noise in the background.

"Nick?"

"Listen, I love you!" Nick blurted, breathless and panicked. "Neither of us are hurt, babe, but I got to go. We're trying to make it home."

"What? Why—"

"I got to go!" Nick shouted, and Kelly could hear the distinct sound of sirens before Nick abruptly ended the call.

Kelly sat frozen, the phone still to his ear, eyes unblinking and heart racing. What the hell had Nick and Ty gotten themselves into *now*?

He finally shook himself into moving, exiting out of Skype and pulling up his internet browser, doing a quick search for Boston to see if the news would bring up anything that might give him a clue.

Two minutes later, Kelly was staring in horror at dozens of reports about a bombing at the Boston Marathon.

"Oh God, Nicko," he whispered as he clicked through the details. Had Nick and Ty gone down to see the marathon like Ty had mentioned to Owen? They'd both run it a couple times when they were younger, and Nick had often volunteered to work the marathon and parades before he made detective.

Kelly shook his head, cursing Nick for not giving him more information. He was calculating how long it would take him to get there if he bought a plane ticket right this second when his phone buzzed in his clenched fist.

He fumbled with it getting it to his ear. "Nick?"

"Hey," Nick answered, and he sounded much calmer now. "I'm sorry."

"Are you okay?"

"Yeah, we're on the *Fiddler*. You saw what happened?"

"Yeah, what the hell, dude?"

"I don't know. Look, I know you're probably about to buy plane tickets, but hold off, okay?"

Kelly snorted and glanced at his computer, where he had indeed been about to press the purchase button.

"There's uh . . . it's not official yet, but I'm pretty sure it will be soon, some sort of curfew while they hunt these guys."

Kelly's heart leapt into his throat. "You're not . . . you're not getting involved, are you?"

Nick was silent for an uncomfortably long moment, and Kelly's stomach churned faster and faster as he waited. He knew how Nick felt about Boston; he would die to protect that city, and this sort of attack was exactly the type of thing that would hit Nick right in heart. It didn't matter that he could barely walk; Nick would go to war.

"No," Nick finally answered, voice gone flat.

Kelly breathed out a loud sigh of relief. "Ty's there with you?"

"Yeah. He's on the phone with Garrett."

"As long as you're not alone," Kelly said. "I should have been there."

"Kels . . ." Nick's voice dropped to an intimate murmur. "Don't, okay? You're not here because we both agreed it was the best thing. I don't . . . there's nothing I can do here, and Boston is about to become a scary place for a while. Ty and I are going to drive out of the city so we don't have to deal with the TSA. He's taking the Rover on to Baltimore, I'm going to tag along to Providence, then . . . I mean, if it's okay, I'm going to come to you. Unless . . . I mean, I can go on to Baltimore with Ty, if you—"

Kelly was nodding vigorously. "Of course it's okay. Just get here safe," he said before Nick could complete his ridiculous suggestion. "Let me know when to come get you."

"You got it."

"Nick," Kelly said urgently, sensing that Nick was about to end the call. "I love you."

Nick inhaled sharply, then huffed into the phone. "Foundations of gunpowder, right? Just like you told me," he said bitterly.

"Nick," Kelly whispered as his chest squeezed.

"I know. I love you, too. I'll see you soon."

Kelly stared at the phone for a long time after the call ended. He was still staring at it when a text message popped up, telling him Nick's flight details. He had about eight hours to get his shit together and get to Denver. He lurched out of his chair and headed inside to find pants.

When Nick found Kelly at the airport, he couldn't move fast enough to get to him. Kelly quite obviously thought about leaping at Nick when they got closer, but thankfully he kept their greeting to a less-than-gentle hug instead. Nick held on to him almost desperately, long after Kelly's arms around his neck loosened, refusing to let go for fear that Kelly would give him that *look* and tell him they needed to talk. Nick had been dreading a call or Skype message from Kelly all week saying they needed to *talk*, but it would be so much worse in person.

"I'm glad you're okay," Kelly whispered into his ear.

Nick kissed Kelly's neck, holding him tighter as relief and even more nerves flooded him. "I'm sorry we fought. Sorry for what I said."

Kelly patted the back of his head. "We'll figure it out."

"I was afraid you'd tell me to go to Baltimore," Nick admitted, flushing at how fucking stupid and needy he sounded. Kelly had always been comfortable and familiar for him. He'd never felt awkward around him, even when they'd first met during a SERE course at Fort Rucker and huddled for warmth covered in camo paint during the resistance and escape training. This uncertainty he was suffering with now, the feeling that—for the first time since he'd laid eyes on Kelly Abbott—he might not be wanted, was nearly crippling.

Kelly's fingers threaded through his hair, and Nick squeezed a grunt out of him.

"We'll fix this." Kelly's voice was unwavering, his body firm against Nick's. He gently extricated himself from Nick's grasp, taking

Nick's face in his hands. He was smiling, warmth shining in his moonlight-blue eyes. "It might take us some time, but we'll fix this."

Nick could only nod. The relief was too much for words.

Kelly gave him a last pat on the cheek, then made to take his suitcase off him, but Nick stopped him and unzipped it, digging in it to find his cane first.

"Why didn't you take that with you on the plane? Didn't you have to walk a bunch?"

"Yeah, but this wouldn't go through security," Nick said, raising the ebony cane before leaning on it as they made their way toward the exits.

"What? Why?"

Nick grinned and bit his lip as he watched Kelly in his peripheral vision.

Kelly leaned forward to see Nick's expression, then rolled his eyes, turning away in feigned disgust. "Oh my God, what kind of cane is that? Is it a gun? A sword?"

Nick snickered. "I wondered how long you'd go before you got curious."

"You're such a fucking nerd."

Nick was still grinning when Kelly slid his hand into one of Nick's back pockets, and they made their way to where he'd parked his truck.

Nick told him about that morning as they drove, how Ty had tried to convince him to go see the marathon. Nick had resisted, mainly because his knee had been killing him and the traffic and crowds were a nightmare.

They'd compromised by going out for brunch, then intended to head toward the marathon for nostalgia's sake. They'd never made it there, though. Both Nick and Ty knew enough about a city under attack to know that if they couldn't actively help, they should get the hell out, so they'd made their way back to the *Fiddler*, fielding panicked calls from Zane, Hagan, two of Nick's sisters, and finally Kelly.

Kelly kept apologizing for not calling sooner, and Nick kept telling him to stop. "I mean, hell, you just got a TV two years ago, I know you never watch the news."

Kelly reached across the bench seat and took Nick's hand, and he didn't let it go. Nick studied his profile, and even after Kelly felt eyes on him and glanced sideways to catch him staring, he didn't look away.

Kelly squeezed his hand. "What are you doing?"

"Leering."

Kelly quirked an eyebrow and grinned lopsidedly. "You see something you like?"

"No," Nick answered, exhaustion making his tone detached and almost clinical.

Kelly glanced at him again, eyebrows going higher, a smile still playing at his lips. "You see something you love?" he teased.

Nick found himself grinning, and they drove on in comfortable silence without him even needing to answer. He fought sleep the rest of the drive to the cabin, and was actually nodding off when they hit the long gravel drive.

"You been sleeping okay?" Kelly asked with a warm smile as he navigated the truck up the driveway.

Nick shifted until he was leaning against the door, watching Kelly. "Okay," he murmured. "Ty bunked with me a few nights."

Kelly snorted. "For him or for you?"

"Both. Seems neither of us do well alone."

Kelly nodded. Nick and Ty had always done that, especially after traumatic periods like the one they'd barely lived through in Miami. They slept huddled together like puppies, often back to back, to stave off nightmares and help their minds heal faster. Kelly knew them both well enough that he didn't even bat an eyelash at it.

How many people could Nick date who would just nod in understanding after learning he'd spent a few nights cuddling with his best friend? Not too damn many, that was for sure.

"I'm sorry about what I said on the phone," Nick said. "I know you meant what you said; I shouldn't have been pissy about it."

"It's okay," Kelly broke in, his gentle smile never faltering. "I'm the one who said I was afraid we couldn't survive without chaos, and . . . I'm making it a self-fulfilling prophecy right now. It's a dick move, to put that on you, make you worry about all this trouble that keeps finding us, and then when we hit a calm in the storm I can't even get my head out of my ass long enough to fucking tell you I love you. I deserved to be called on it."

Nick shook his head, but Kelly was still smiling, and he didn't give Nick a chance to argue. "I can say it when your life's not in danger too," he claimed, throwing Nick a wink. "I love you."

"I've missed you," Nick said.

Kelly didn't take his eyes off the driveway, but the smile pulled at his lips. "We'll fix that, too."

A few hours later, they'd gotten Nick's things up into the bedroom of Kelly's cabin, eaten a light dinner, and headed up to the loft. Kelly was already in bed when Nick limped out of the bathroom, drying his hair with a towel and shivering in the cool breeze coming from the open balcony doors.

Kelly put his book away and slipped a pair of reading glasses off, folding them up and setting them on the book.

Nick paused, staring at the glasses in consternation.

"You okay?" Kelly asked, yanking Nick's attention back to him.

"When'd you start wearing reading glasses?" Nick blurted.

Kelly glanced at the bedside table, a blush creeping up his cheeks. "I've had them for a while. Couple years."

"Are you serious?" Nick said, his voice cracking in dismay.

Kelly snorted and bit his lip, obviously trying not to laugh outright. "I don't think I've ever worn them around you. We always have so little time together . . ."

Nick moved toward the bed, his knee aching as he crawled in beside Kelly. He waited a beat as Kelly watched him expectantly. "They look good on you."

Kelly seemed relieved, his lips twitching and his shoulders relaxing as he gave Nick a small smile. "Yeah?"

Nick didn't answer, instead soaking up every little detail of Kelly's face, thinking back on the last week without him and how bereft he had felt each night.

Kelly's smile grew, "I'm not wearing my reading glasses during sex."

"Never say never," Nick grumbled as he settled under the covers and fluffed his pillow.

Kelly laughed as he stretched to flick the lamp off, filling the loft with moonlight. A moment later, he carefully scooted into Nick's arms. Nick held his breath as Kelly's hands slid over him, as he rested his head on Nick's shoulder and settled against him. His hand hovered over the healing knife wounds on Nick's side, and then he placed his palm against Nick's skin, his thumb grazing part of the scar.

Nick released his breath in a shaky puff, and he closed his arms around Kelly and turned into him, burying his nose in Kelly's hair and closing his eyes. "I missed the way you smell."

"Irish," Kelly grunted against Nick's neck. "Let's not do this shit again, okay? Next time just open your fucking mouth and talk to me instead of keeping it all bottled up. And I can do better at being a boyfriend instead of a doc."

"Deal," Nick whispered.

Kelly tilted his face toward Nick's, and Nick kissed him. He tugged him closer, his fingers finding bare skin, warmth stealing over him. Kelly shoved at him and rolled on top of him, still kissing him as he tossed his leg over Nick and straddled him. He pushed up onto his elbows and rubbed his nose against Nick's.

"First thing in the morning, I want to sit down and talk this out, okay?" he said, his eyes searching Nick's. "No more of this hanging over us."

"Yeah," Nick managed as he gazed into Kelly's eyes.

"First thing."

Nick nodded obediently. He settled his hands on Kelly's hips, delighted to realize that, despite the painkillers he'd taken when they'd reached the cabin, Kelly's proximity and what he did to Nick was stronger tonight than the dulling effects of the drugs. From the look in Kelly's eyes, he noticed it too.

"And until morning?" Nick asked almost breathlessly.

Kelly hummed, and the sound sent a thrill through Nick. Kelly brushed his nose against Nick's, his lips tantalizingly close to Nick's as he spoke. "I think we can find something to occupy us." He leaned even closer, aiming for a kiss.

Nick brought his hand up and smacked his palm over Kelly's mouth. Kelly grunted questioningly.

"Can we occupy us with the reading glasses on?" Nick asked, barely managing to get the words out without laughing.

The muffled exclamation that came out around his palm was almost certainly a curse, and Nick chuckled when Kelly grabbed his wrist and pinned it to the mattress. His laugh morphed into a groan.

"Really," Kelly grumbled.

"So hot," Nick teased.

"Okay." Kelly gave him a tiny, unsatisfactory kiss before he rolled and flopped onto his back.

"What?" Nick grunted. "What are we doing?"

"Nothing."

"Aw, but Kels!"

"Nope, ruined it."

Nick chased after him, rolling and taking Kelly into his arms as they both struggled not to laugh. He kissed the back of Kelly's bare shoulder, working his way up Kelly's neck as he pulled their bodies flush. Kelly shimmied his hips and pushed back into Nick, groaning as he rubbed his ass against Nick's hard cock.

"You sure it's ruined?" Nick whispered against Kelly's ear.

Kelly's hand settled on his hip, and he turned his head to look over his shoulder. Nick propped himself on his elbow, watching him with a curious frown. The mood had shifted imperceptibly, and Kelly was no longer smiling.

"What?" Nick asked with sudden dread.

Kelly shook his head. "It's been a long time, babe."

"Are you . . . do we need to wait?"

Kelly winced, shifting nervously. "It's just that the drawer's empty."

Nick's eyes darted to the bedside drawer where Kelly had always stored his condoms, lube, and a pocket *Kama Sutra* that had been meant as a prank but had gotten some mileage over the years. "*Empty* empty?"

"I mean, there's still a bunch of condoms in there," Kelly said in a rush. "They're probably expired. But no lube."

Nick grunted. In his haste to pack this afternoon, he certainly hadn't tossed any into his bag. It had been weeks since he had fucked Kelly; there was no way he'd think of doing it without lubricant of some sort.

He clucked his tongue, one eyebrow raised. "Been busy this week, huh?" he teased, and bent to press a kiss to Kelly's chest.

"The lube and the iPad full of videos got a workout, okay, don't judge me." Kelly grasped at Nick's hair, his fingers curling.

Nick hummed as he continued kissing his way down Kelly's body. He tugged Kelly to lay flat and positioned himself so he was putting all his weight on his hip instead of his knees. He brushed his lips over Kelly's taut muscles, licking his way down his ribs. "Good thing your boyfriend is industrious," Nick said against the six-shooter tattooed on Kelly's hip bone.

Kelly barked a laugh. "That's a big word for someone with their mouth about to be full."

Kelly wasn't quite awake as he stumbled around the kitchen, gathering breakfast foods in the hope that Nick might feel like fixing it when he woke. He hadn't been grocery shopping in the last few days because he'd been expecting to head back to Boston soon. So he'd gotten up early with every intention of going shopping, but as he'd been making a list of what they needed, he'd discovered his travel toiletry kit in the downstairs bathroom, complete with a brand-new bottle of KY.

Shopping could wait until this afternoon as long as there was enough food for Nick to work his magic with for breakfast.

He was scrambling around in the lower cabinets, trying to find Nick some tea, when he heard a thump from upstairs. He bumped his head on the top of the cabinet he'd been scrounging in, and it knocked him to his knees. He withdrew his head and shoulders, rubbing his head and cussing up a storm.

"You okay?" he called. He held his breath waiting for a reply, still vigorously rubbing his head to ease the sting.

"Yeah," Nick finally called back. "Can you give me a hand when you get a chance?"

Kelly took the steps two at a time and found Nick sitting on the edge of the bed, shoulders slumped. He pointed toward the bathroom, where his cane rested against the armoire beside the door.

"I got cocky last night, forgot how fucking sore I am in the morning."

"You were definitely cocky last night," Kelly reminded as he retrieved the cane for him.

"So were you."

Kelly snickered. His fingers searched the silver head of the cane for some sort of hidden switch or button since Nick had confirmed that this particular cane was hiding something.

"Want me to show you how to do it?" Nick asked.

"No," Kelly grunted. He turned it over, unable to find anything that might indicate the cane was anything other than just a cane, and then he shoved it in Nick's hands. "Yes."

Nick smiled gently. He showed Kelly a small button under the handle, hidden amidst the engraving where the shaft met the silver. Then he pushed at Kelly's belly, moving him out of the way. He clicked the button, and a five-inch blade deployed from the tip of the cane with a melodramatic *clink*.

Kelly huffed as he looked from the cane to Nick's sparkling eyes. "There's a word for what you are."

"Awesome?"

"Not the word I was thinking of."

Nick shrugged as he returned the blade to its hiding spot. He stood with a wince and a grunt, and Kelly took an impulsive step toward him to hug him. Nick froze in surprise, his arms out to the side and his body tense. Then he relaxed and wrapped his arms around Kelly, resting his chin on Kelly's shoulder.

"Of all the stupid fucking things we've done over the years, I think fighting right after I almost lost you has to be the stupidest," Kelly grumbled against Nick's shoulder.

Nick's hands tightened on Kelly's back. He was nodding against Kelly's cheek.

Kelly held him for a few long moments, then pulled away and offered Nick a gentle smile. He let Nick move past him toward the bathroom, but instead of going back downstairs he perched on the side of the bed, waiting for Nick to come back out. When Nick did, he seemed surprised to see Kelly still there. Kelly grinned mischievously.

"What?" Nick asked guardedly.

Kelly held up the bottle of lube he'd found. "Talk first or fuck first?"

Nick huffed a laugh and shook his head as he limped closer. Kelly was glad to see that signature O'Flaherty smirk back on Nick's face. It had been sorely missed since Sidewinder's last deployment. He stood and pulled Nick closer, turning them until Nick's back was to the bed, and then he gave him a gentle shove. Nick sat with a grunt. Kelly took his cane and rested it against the table, then settled beside him, leaning their shoulders together.

"Talk first," Nick finally answered, his voice a rumble that slid down Kelly's spine. Nick held his hand out, resting it on his knee, and Kelly took the invitation and clasped their fingers together.

"I'm sorry I treated you like I did," Kelly offered.

Nick was already shaking his head before Kelly could finish. "We all fall back on our training. And it's your nature to take care of the people you love."

"It's yours too, you know."

Nick pressed his lips together tight.

"That's all you were doing. You got to stop punishing yourself."

"Yeah." Nick didn't sound too confident, though.

"You know I love you, right? You knew the whole time. Right?"

"Of course I did," Nick mumbled, looking pained.

"And you know I would never, ever want you to feel guilty for anything you've done, even if it was something that made me angry."

Nick closed his eyes closed and turned his head away.

"Nicko, you punish yourself enough. You've got the fucking market cornered on Catholic guilt. You can be confident, for the rest of our lives, that I'll never want to punish you."

Nick forced himself to meet Kelly's eyes again, a blush creeping across his cheeks. "I'm sorry. I was being stupid, I know. I just can't quite get a handle on myself yet. I don't . . . I don't feel like I'm me."

Kelly squeezed his hand. "I know. But look, I get why you thought it. I probably would have too. Your mind is not that fucked up, understand? You were right."

Nick nodded jerkily.

"And I'm here, okay? I'm here to help you find that handle on yourself again. I'm here until you feel like *you* again and then some."

Nick's grip on Kelly's fingers tightened. "Thank you," he whispered.

"I didn't call you yesterday morning because of the bombing," Kelly blurted.

Nick was silent, his entire body still.

"I called you because I missed you and I was going to ask you to either let me come to Boston, or for you to come here. I didn't even know there had been an attack when I called."

Nick glanced around the room uncomfortably, then back at Kelly. "I know, Kels. You told me all this yesterday."

"Yeah, but did you hear me?" Kelly asked as he shifted to face Nick, his fingers trailing down Nick's arm. "At the airport you said you were afraid I'd tell you to go to Baltimore with Ty."

Nick paled, nodding jerkily.

Kelly sighed. "How can you be so fucking stupid when you're like the smartest person I've ever known? Aside from maybe Johns, which is why I called him for advice when I needed it."

Nick ran his fingers across Kelly's cheekbone, his eyes tracing Kelly's face. "Advice about what?"

"You. Us. Logically, you know that I would never fucking tell you to go to Ty, or Owen, or Digger, or anyone, before I would have you come to me. And that was true before we started fucking. But something inside you is just *broken* when it comes to your heart." He tapped Nick's chest.

Nick blinked a few times, looking away from Kelly as the last hints of color drained from his face.

"You just can't believe that I would love you unconditionally, that I could love you the same way you love me. Can you?"

Nick swallowed hard, and he released Kelly's hand so he could put his palm to his chest. He seemed to be struggling for breath, and Kelly belatedly recognized that Nick was fighting to stay calm. What the hell was this, a panic attack? Since when did *talking with Kelly* kick Nick into a panic attack?

"Nick." Kelly said, voice calm but urgent. He hopped to his feet and moved in front of Nick, hesitating a moment before he took Nick's face between his hands.

During their service, each of the Sidewinder boys had had different ways of panicking, and each of them had had different ways of being calmed. Eli or Digger, you didn't fucking touch them unless you wanted to die. Owen needed air and he needed to walk, so you let him pace as much as he could until he'd calmed himself. Ty, you just gave him somewhere to hide until he could work through the feeling, and Kelly's rare bouts were handled in much the same way. But Nick needed grounding, needed a gentle touch and gentle words to let him know he wasn't alone. If he didn't get it, he often tried to fight his way through to the other side, and people wound up getting hurt.

"Irish, it's okay," Kelly cooed, brushing his palm against Nick's cheek like he was petting a dog. "It's okay, Nicko, breathe. Oh, babe, I'm sorry. It's okay."

Nick closed his eyes, letting Kelly's touch and voice settle him just like they always had. He gasped for air, struggling to breathe in through his nose and out through his mouth. Kelly bent closer to him, his hands still on Nick's face, waiting for Nick to come back to him.

Nick finally forced his eyes open, meeting Kelly's.

"I'm sorry, that was harsh." Kelly brushed his hand over Nick's bottom lip. "That was too harsh."

"It's okay," Nick managed. "I'm sorry."

"Babe," Kelly whispered, and the soothing pitch of his voice seemed to cut right through the remnants of Nick's mental spiral. Nick was meeting his gaze again, his expression calming, his green eyes clear. "You want to do this later?"

Nick shook his head, taking one of Kelly's wrists in gentle fingers and pulling his hand away from his face. "Go on."

"It was harsh," Kelly repeated as he straightened. "But it's true, isn't it?"

"I guess," Nick rasped.

"I know how you love me. I know it with all my heart. And you have to know somewhere in there that I love you the same way. I love you with everything I am. I do."

"But I . . ."

"If you fucking tell me that you don't deserve it, I'm going to make you bleed."

Nick blinked slowly, and Kelly huffed at him.

"I lied to you," Nick said, and he tried to lower his head but Kelly's hands coming up to his cheeks again stopped him, forcing him to maintain eye contact.

"I know. And yeah, it hurt me. But it also fucking tore you apart to do it. I *know* you. You didn't lie because you wanted to, because you thought it was fun. You didn't do it for any kind of personal gain, you did it to keep me safe. To keep Ty and Zane safe. Hell, to keep *yourself* safe. I saw how miserable that lie made you for a year, even if I didn't know at the time what was causing it. I knew you weren't happy. You did it with a literal gun to your head. Are you really so fucking blind to the gray areas of the world that you think that doesn't make a difference?"

Nick stared into his eyes, and Kelly hoped Nick could see the fire that was kindling deep inside him, that Nick was letting the words sink in. If there was anything that Kelly was willing to fight for, it was Nick. Even if that fight was against the man himself.

"I love that your heart is so good," Kelly said. "I love it about you. But you're not that naïve, babe, you're not. Why do you insist on ruining the good things you have as penance for shit you can't control?"

Nick licked his lips, and the color drained from his face again. "Am I ruining *this*?"

Kelly's heart stuttered, and his anger and determination were replaced by stark fear. "No, I didn't mean that," he said quickly. "I'm . . . I'm sorry, that was . . . Fuck! I'm trying to tough love you into forgiving yourself and I'm not very good at the tough love thing, okay?" He stood up, gulping in a deep breath. Great, now *he* was the one about to panic. He laughed nervously and ran his hand through his hair.

Nick reached for Kelly's forearm, tugging him closer. He was gazing up at him adoringly when he cupped Kelly's face with one palm. "You're right," he said, as if the words had surprised him. "I'm wallowing. I've never done that before."

Kelly sighed and wrapped his fingers around Nick's wrist, running his other hand over Nick's hair. "It's okay to wallow. Just . . . please come back to me soon. I never realized I needed you to be you as badly as I do, okay? But I do. I need you to be you so I can be me."

Nick was silent, and Kelly got lost in tracing Nick's features for a moment. Then he darted in and kissed him, trying to get that surprised gasp Nick sometimes gave when Kelly caught him off guard.

He smiled against Nick's lips when he was rewarded with one, and he reached for Nick's shoulder to push him back to the bed.

Nick went along with it, laying out amidst the messy sheets, his hands gentle and searching, clutching at Kelly's hips, sliding up Kelly's shirt. He kissed Kelly until Kelly straddled him and sat up to readjust his position, but Nick planted his hands on Kelly's chest when he tried to bend over for another kiss.

"You okay?" Kelly asked, head cocked.

"Move in with me."

Kelly tilted his head the other way, not sure he'd heard correctly. "What?"

"You heard me. Up 'til now we've had reasons to be apart. Good reasons. But now they're all gone, and there's nothing keeping us from being together all the time. Nothing but us."

Kelly's chest fluttered, and he pressed a hand there to settle it. "You want me to move to Boston?"

"No."

"No?"

"I mean, yes. Yes," Nick stuttered. "But no, I . . . I want us to be *together*. I don't want you to leave your cabin. You love it here, you built this place by yourself. This is your home. And . . . it's my home, too."

"You're saying you want to move here? You want to get rid of the *Fiddler*?"

"N-not . . . no. I can't get rid of her, she's . . . she's been through too much to abandon her. I . . ."

"Nick. We can't bring the *Fiddler* here."

Nick snorted and closed his eyes, and it was obvious that he was nervous and fumbling to get what was in his head to come out of his lips in the right order. Kelly would never admit that he enjoyed it when Nick fumbled, but it was so rare and so charming that he'd taken advantage of it on every single occasion from the day they'd met and would probably continue to do so until the day they died.

Nick shook his head, taking a deep breath. "I just mean, I want for us to be together no matter where it is. We could spend summers here and then take the *Fiddler* down the coast and spend winters somewhere warm, like the Keys or the Caribbean."

Kelly leaned closer. "What about Boston?"

Nick's expression softened, and he reached for Kelly, his fingers gliding down the side of Kelly's face. "If Boston doesn't fit in our plans, then I'll say good-bye to her. She doesn't need me anymore anyway."

Kelly bit his lip, his gaze dropping to watch his fingers trace over Nick's bare chest. The sadness in Nick's eyes was too much for him to see. "You're wrong there. And I don't want that."

"What do you want?" Nick asked.

"You. Let's just wing it. We'll stay in one place until we need new scenery, and then we'll fly to another, or road trip, or take the *Fiddler* on a cruise around the fucking world. We don't have to plan anything, Nicko, we don't need any patterns. We're at endgame right now. The only thing waiting anymore is us."

Nick stared at him, silent and stunned. He slowly reached with his other hand, grasping the back of Kelly's neck, and Kelly leaned down to press a gentle kiss to his lips. Nick's hold on him tightened and the kiss grew more heated. When Kelly finally sat up some minutes later, they were both breathless. He started trying to get out of his shirt as Nick's hands dragged down his body.

"How's your knee?" Kelly asked as Nick sat up to chase another kiss.

"What knee?"

Kelly was snickering when he asked, "Can I ride you?"

Nick nodded and kissed him messily, his strong hands gripping at Kelly's hair and the back of his shirt as Kelly rolled his hips against Nick's hardening cock.

"Okay, good talk," Kelly grunted, and Nick helped him push his shirt over his head.

CHAPTER FOUR

May 31, 2013

They wound up staying in Colorado for almost two months, long enough for Nick to finally have his knee surgically repaired and get through enough rehab that the steps on the *Fiddler* wouldn't be much of an issue when they returned to Boston. They took a week at the end of May to head for Baltimore, where Ty and Zane were celebrating Ty's birthday with the grand opening of their new bookstore, which Kelly was distraught to learn was a front operation for the CIA.

He refused to listen to details, and instead raged for an hour as Ty tried to calm him. Nick sat grinning in a corner the entire time, reading and sipping from a bottle of Yoo-hoo he'd pilfered from Zane's stash in the back of the store.

Ty failed spectacularly at calming Kelly, of course. Ty and Zane were still involved in a life that might get them killed, and Kelly wasn't fucking having it. It took Nick all night to talk him down. He convinced Kelly, after a lot of discussion and some physical persuasion, that Ty and Zane were just support operators, that they'd never be involved in anything that might kill them again, and therefore that they'd never drag Kelly and Nick into anything ever again either.

Kelly would believe it when he saw it, but he certainly wasn't going to give *Nick* grief over it. Nick was no longer Ty's keeper.

They left Baltimore a week later, and Kelly was content in the relative safety and happiness of his friends.

They went on to Boston from there, and they spent the last day of May systematically cleaning out the *Fiddler* and preparing her for the summer.

Nick's mission was to make room for Kelly's things, and while Kelly hadn't really thought he was serious, he was surprised to see that Nick really was clearing out half of his possessions to make room for Kelly to truly to move in.

"We'll store what I don't want to get rid of and then move it to the cabin later," he said with a shrug as he headed back down to collect another box full of things to give away, trash, or store. They were really doing this.

Nick was almost six weeks out of knee surgery and was walking much better, and to his admitted dismay he'd been able to mostly get rid of the cane. He was well enough, though, to go up and down the stairs and carry heavy boxes, and sometimes when he got really excited or distracted, he didn't even limp. Kelly watched the stairwell for a few moments, a smile on his face. When Nick committed to something, he committed with everything he had.

They were really doing this.

He returned his attention to the stuff on the table in front of him. Stacks of papers, books, and old case files that may or may not have been legal for Nick to have kept on the yacht. Nick took unsolved mysteries personally, and Kelly had no doubt at all that Nick had absconded with copies of the files on cases where answers had eluded him to continue puzzling them out.

But now Nick was done with the Boston Police Department. He would never be a detective again; even if his heart and mind were still in it—and Kelly suspected they were—his body was not. The Boston PD had come calling, offering him a bump to lieutenant so he could hide his injuries behind a desk. Nick had turned them down. But when Kelly had tried to put some of those old case files in the trash pile, Nick had quietly moved them to the storage pile.

Kelly grabbed the last handful of trash folders from the coffee table and stood. Something slipped from one of the supposedly empty folders and tapped across the table. He peered over the stack, scowling at the mini SD card he'd dropped.

He clucked his tongue and thumped the files back down, plucking the SD card up and turning it over. There was no telling what was on the thing, or why it had been in a stack of papers Nick had already earmarked for recycling. It was tiny, so it was possible Nick hadn't known it was mixed up in this stuff.

Kelly ambled through the galley to the banquette where his laptop was sitting, and he slid into the bench seat and powered the Mac on. He'd take a glimpse at the contents, and if anything was on it, he'd just have Nick look it over when he was done with whatever he'd been cursing at down in their cabin for the last couple minutes.

When he found the converter for the mini SD card and pulled up the files, it appeared there were only a handful of videos on it. They weren't named or dated, merely labeled with numbers, so Kelly clicked on the first one to get an idea of whether this was personal or work stuff.

The video popped up, and Kelly sat back, wide-eyed, when the first few seconds showed Nick in the main cabin of the *Fiddler*, standing at the side of the neatly made bed, tanned and shirtless and barefoot, smirking at the camera as he unbuttoned his jeans.

Kelly grinned and reached for the volume to turn it up. He didn't remember making this particular sex tape, but he hadn't necessarily been sober during all of them. It was always entertaining to relive one of their exploits, and this little gem apparently had *five* videos on it, all of them at least twenty minutes long.

"Are you fucking recording this?" Nick asked as Kelly ratcheted up the volume. Kelly's cock stirred appreciatively at the growl of Nick's voice, at the predatory look in his eyes as he stared almost directly into the camera.

The camera jittered as it was set on a hard surface and left there, aimed at the bed. "For posterity, O'Flaherty, come on."

Kelly's body flushed with ice and his stomach flipped at the sound of the voice. It wasn't him talking. The man moved toward Nick and into the view of the camera, shedding his last stitch of clothing as he drew closer to Nick. The guy was about Nick's height, with jet-black hair and a beard. He was fit and well-defined, with a body type that spoke of manual labor and real strength, not just hours on a machine in a gym.

This wasn't a video of Kelly and Nick fucking. It was of Nick and someone else.

Kelly's heart hammered in his throat, and he felt light-headed, his entire body tingling and his eyes burning because he was neglecting the need to blink.

The video rolled on, the naked stranger reaching for Nick's jeans and tugging at him. The way Nick looked at him . . . the way they touched with familiar brushes of their fingertips . . . this was not a recording of their first time together. And there were four more of these videos on this card.

"You are a sight for sore eyes, babe," Nick growled, right before they kissed passionately.

Nick's hands swept down the man's back, and the guy melted into him, like he knew Nick was about to turn on that dominant switch of his.

Kelly jerked and he reached for the keyboard to stop it. But he couldn't. He was analyzing the details of the footage almost against his will. The video was relatively recent; he could tell by the décor of the cabin, the style of Nick's hair, and the definition in his broad shoulders. It was before Nick's last brush with death, though, because his ribs were free of the scar that should have marred him where he'd taken the knife in the fight in Miami.

Kelly realized with the slow burning shame of jealousy that his first thought, his first *clear* thought, was to wonder if this was before he and Nick had committed to each other, or after.

They'd spent the entirety of their relationship thus far in what was essentially a long-distance arrangement. Kelly had never questioned Nick's fidelity, he'd never had a reason to. But he realized with something like a wrecking ball to the gut that if either of them had ever wanted to step out, to set up a video camera and record themselves fucking some stranger in one of the beds they shared when they were together, they'd both had all the opportunity in the world to do so.

Kelly's stomach churned as he watched Nick manhandle this guy into the very same bed he and Nick had slept in last night. After a few more minutes of sitting, stunned, Kelly was subjected to the sight and sound of his boyfriend fucking this stranger. He wanted to look away, but he couldn't. He heard Nick whisper the guy's name. Aidan.

"The fireman." Kelly swallowed hard, shaking his head. This was the guy Nick had been casually seeing when he and Kelly had acted on their attraction in Colorado. This was the guy Nick had given up to be with Kelly.

Kelly's eyes began to lose focus. This had to be from before. Nick wasn't the kind of guy to step out, he never had been and he never would be. But telling himself that didn't help the swirl of nausea in Kelly's gut, the spike of jealousy, or the odd dose of being turned on from the moans of pleasure emitting from the laptop. He knew what Nick was doing to this guy. He knew *intimately*.

He heard a noise on the steps to his side, but he was still too traumatized to move. He merely sat there, staring at the laptop as the passionate sounds of two men fucking filled the pilothouse.

"Are you watching porn up here?" Nick asked incredulously, a hint of exasperated laughter in his voice as he thumped a box down on the top step and shoved it away from the staircase. "You're supposed to be working!"

Kelly ripped his attention from the laptop. Nick was grinning, but as soon as Kelly met his eyes, his expression morphed into one of alarm. His smile dropped, his eyes widened, and his shoulders tensed as he pulled himself to his full height.

"Are you okay?"

"Why?" Kelly croaked.

"What's wrong," Nick asked as he stepped closer. "What happened? What are you doing?"

Kelly stared into Nick's green eyes, trying to wipe the image of the video from his mind and tell himself that Nick would *never* hurt him.

"I . . ." Kelly was at a loss for words, though. He looked back at the laptop screen, shaking his head.

Nick slid into the banquette beside him, turning the laptop so he could see the screen. It took a few seconds of watching and listening for Nick to realize that he was seeing himself and Aidan. "Jesus, Kels. What the fuck?"

"I found an SD card in a file."

"Kelly!"

"Needed to check what was on it."

Nick stopped the video, then shoved the laptop away from them. "That was Aidan," he said quickly, turning in the bench so he was facing Kelly. "He liked to use his phone . . . That was the guy I—"

"I know," Kelly said, but he realized the words hadn't quite come out.

"Kelly," Nick said sharply. "Babe, that was before us."

Kelly shook his head, clearing his throat, and then nodded.

Nick's hand landed on his shoulder and shook him, turning him so he was forced to face Nick. "Kelly," he said forcefully. "Look at me. Talk to me."

"It just . . . I wasn't prepared for what I was seeing."

Nick ducked his head, maintaining eye contact when Kelly tried to look away. "Kels. Tell me what . . . Do I need to fix this? What do you want me to do?"

Kelly shut his eyes tightly. "No," he said, trying to smile and meet Nick's eyes. His mind flashed back to the look of possessive lust he'd seen in those eyes when Nick had watched Aidan move, and he tried to shake it off. All he managed to do was replay in his mind the moment that Nick had breached Aidan and they'd both moaned as they wrapped around each other. And there were four more videos just like that one. Kelly shook his head violently. "It's in the past. It just caught me off guard."

They sat together in the banquette, eyes locked, the laptop casting Nick's skin in a bluish glow. Kelly's eyes strayed to the screen, where the video was paused with Nick's muscular shoulders strained as he held his former lover to the bed, where another man's legs were wrapped around him.

Nick slammed the laptop closed and yanked out the SD card.

Kelly's stomach turned and he scooted away from Nick, escaping from the other end of the banquette to stand and pace away.

"Kelly?"

"I need some air."

"Doc, wait." Nick scrambled to the edge of the bench seat and grabbed for Kelly's hand. His grip was gentle, his eyes pleading.

Kelly grunted. "I just need some air, okay?"

"I'm sorry this upset you, babe. I had no idea it even existed. I didn't know he saved them."

"It's not that," Kelly groaned. He squeezed Nick's hand, knowing it wasn't fair to push him away when he'd done literally nothing wrong.

Nick sat on the edge of the bench seat, holding Kelly's fingers carefully, watching him with a mixture of fear and hope. Kelly *hated* that Nick looked sick and nervous right now. He hated that Nick was probably ready to do whatever Kelly asked right now to make amends for something that wasn't even wrong. They'd both been with people in the past. Hell, Kelly had watched Nick have sex with women before, live, right there in the room with him. They'd even shared one night with the same woman: Kelly's first experience with another man anywhere near him in a sexual way, and it had been with Nick.

It wasn't the sex that was upsetting him. Not really. Sure, Kelly wasn't thrilled to have the mental image of Nick with another man in the very same sheets they had on their bed right now, but he knew himself well enough to know that a part of him was a little turned on by it too.

"It's just . . . I thought it was of us at first," he managed to say. "And then it wasn't my voice talking to you. And it wasn't me you were touching. And my first thought was . . . my first thought was, 'When did this happen?' And I hate that I thought that at all."

Nick huffed out a gust of air like Kelly had jabbed him in the stomach. His grip on Kelly's fingers loosened more. "You know I'd never do that, right?"

Kelly nodded jerkily. "I know. A year ago, I don't think I would have even had the thought. But you know . . . I always *knew* I could tell when you were lying, Irish. And I *knew* you would never lie to me in the first place. And I *knew* you would never, ever hurt me. And the past year, everything that's happened? We both *know* I was wrong."

Nick blanched as Kelly met his gaze, the spark of life seeping from his eyes until they were more gray than green. His hand dropped away from Kelly's, and when he blinked he was no longer meeting Kelly's eyes.

Kelly's heart ached, and his stomach turned. He pressed a hand to the old bullet wound in his chest to make it stop tingling. He despised the moments Nick's vivacious spirit drained from him, but they'd always been honest with each other. Now was no time to stop that, even if it hurt. It would hurt less later. "I guess it bothers me more than I wanted to admit. More than I realized, I mean. But I'm working through it. And this is *not* your fault."

Nick's lips were pressed tight together, and he merely nodded without risking looking into Kelly's eyes again.

Kelly reached for him, but he stopped himself before his fingers could make contact with Nick's cheek. He balled his hand into a fist and tucked it against his side instead.

"I need some air," he whispered, and he moved toward the salon doors before he could be sick.

CHAPTER FIVE

Kelly flopped down the steps from the flybridge, a scowl on his sunburned face. He'd worked through his issues with a cigarette and a beer and then another cigarette, and though he knew he wouldn't be getting the image of Nick and another man out of his mind anytime soon, running away from the problem wasn't going to help him. He and Nick had learned their lesson already about not communicating. Kelly wasn't about to let this little blip erase all the progress they'd made, and he felt a little more relaxed already from his time alone to think about it.

He had discovered in the past year that it was best for him to walk away and calm down before getting into any sort of fight with Nick, especially since his first instinct was to be physical, and that was certainly the last method of arguing Nick ever used.

He opened his mouth to call out for Nick, then snapped it shut when he saw his boyfriend sitting on the couch in the salon, surrounded by bits and bobs, a letter in one hand, the other hand shielding his eyes as he read it.

"Nick?" Kelly called as he edged toward him. "What are you doing?"

Nick looked up. His eyes were red-rimmed and he wasn't even trying to play off the fact that he'd been sitting there with tears in his eyes.

"Oh God, what is it?" Kelly blurted.

Nick waved the papers in his hand. "I tried the letters again."

"What?"

"Fucking Sanchez," Nick gritted out, his voice wavering. "I was trying to . . . I don't know. Stay out of your hair."

"And you thought reading that letter again would help?"

Nick shrugged and glanced around at all the possessions he'd pulled out of Sanchez's box. He looked lost and alone, and Kelly moved to sit beside him, sliding his arm around Nick's shoulders. It was just as much for his own comfort as Nick's, though.

Kelly picked up the oversized manila envelope with Nick's name scrawled on it. He knew from before that it contained the letter Nick had been reading. But he hadn't looked at it very hard the first time Nick had dragged this stuff out. Inside he found more letters. "What the hell did he do, write a letter to everyone he knew?"

Nick laughed shakily and shrugged. Kelly pulled one of the envelopes out. It was sealed, with a number on the front in Eli's handwriting. Kelly scowled and extracted a few more. They were all numbered.

"What are we supposed to do with these?"

Nick took a deep breath, then picked up the second page of the letter and read it out loud.

"I have instructions for you, and you have to follow them like a good little Marine or I'm going to haunt your Irish ass." Nick rested his head in one hand, closing his eyes. It took him several seconds to regain his voice. "Step number one is to finish reading this fucking letter so you don't fuck up any of the other steps."

Nick and Kelly shared a glance. "He knew us so well," Kelly said.

Nick nodded. "I may be dead," he read with a hitch in his voice. "But I'm going to force you boys to love each other again. And it starts right here, right now. So take a week off work. Get your boots on. Prepare to be loved from beyond the grave."

Nick had to stop reading. Kelly took the letter and scanned it, trying to find the spot where Nick had trailed off.

"Do you remember the trip we took after we were discharged?" Kelly read. "Remember it. How the fuck could we forget it? That was the end of us."

December 9, 2002

Kelly fought through the hazy rush of panic and adrenaline that always came with waking up in a strange place. He wound up tossing the sheets off his body, crawling over his bedmate, and rolling gracelessly to the ground.

The floor shook with his impact. Table lamps rattled. Someone groaned.

Kelly sat up and pressed his back to the table behind him, hand groping for a weapon, eyes wild as he looked around. It was obviously a hotel room, and a nice one at that. It most definitely was not the hotel in which he'd closed his eyes. "Where the hell am I?"

A face appeared over the edge of one of the beds, and Kelly's blurry vision saw it like someone peering down from a cloud. "Doc, you got to calm down," Eli said.

Kelly's chest heaved with the remnants of panic and confusion. He blinked at Eli, mouth hanging open. Eli rolled over, disappearing from Kelly's view. A moment later, Ty sat up and swung his legs over the edge of the bed Kelly had just bailed out of.

"Dude, you crushed my ribs."

Kelly looked down at himself, straightening with a wince as the newly stitched wound in his side pulled. It was healing already. Kelly put his hand over it and gave the room another desperate once over. "What happened?"

"Which time?" Ty asked, laughing. It turned into a cough and he doubled over, holding his ribs. "Oh God, I think they're really broken."

Ty stood, revealing a bruise spreading across his rib cage. "I didn't do that, you need to get those looked at."

"Corpsman up," Ty called.

Kelly shook his head, hand returning to his side. "Who stitched this?"

"I did," Ty answered with a huff. "It's good work."

"Where are we?" Kelly asked again.

"This is the softest pillow I've ever had," Digger said.

"That's my ass, man," Eli told him, voice muffled like he had his face in the mattress. "You sleep sideways."

"I don't care, this is nice."

"Shut up!" Owen called. From the sound of it, the three of them were sharing a bed. How the hell had all three of them fit into a queen-sized bed? "That better be a gun sticking into my hip, man."

Kelly swallowed hard, blinking to focus his vision. "Where's Irish, is he okay?"

Ty nodded, then looked over his shoulder at the other side of the bed Kelly had bailed from. "Irish. Hey, Irish!" He tossed a pillow toward the head of the bed.

"No," Nick grunted in response.

Kelly sat there for a time, breathing heavily, trying to remember how they'd all wound up here together, sleeping in puppy piles in a strange hotel. He finally shoved himself to his knees and crawled back to the bed before using it to climb to his feet. He wobbled when he stood, putting his hands out to steady himself.

"Holy God," he muttered. He looked to the side, out the floor to ceiling windows. "Oh Jesus, is that the Empire State Building?"

Ty stood and trudged over to stand beside him, wavering as he blinked at the window. "Are we stateside?"

"Are we alive?" Owen countered. "I don't feel alive."

Nick slid out of the bed and shuffled to the window, his shoulder bumping into Kelly's as they both looked down at the streets of New York City far below.

"Are you freaking out?" Nick asked Kelly under his breath.

"Yes! Join me!"

Nick snorted and wrapped an arm around Kelly as he waved a hand at the scene outside their window. "Welcome to civilian life, Doc."

Kelly turned to the others, eyes going wider. They were all in various stages of sitting up. Ty was still standing behind them, weaving from side to side like he was trying to keep his balance on a ship. He shook his head, looking sick.

Eli was sitting with the sheets pooled around his lap, rubbing his eyes with the heel of his hand. "*Ay Dios mío, dame fuerza.*"

Kelly raised both eyebrows.

"I don't remember anything right now," Eli said. "Did you say we're stateside?"

"We're in DC," Digger told them. "At least . . . I thought we were."

"What are we doing in DC?" Owen asked, raising his head finally.

"What is the Empire State Building doing in DC?" Ty cried.

Kelly looked out the window again. He could see his own reflection in the glass, bearded and shaggy from the missions they'd been running, bruises everywhere, including one on his cheek that looked like he'd been sucker punched.

The memory was slowly returning.

They'd been discharged and sent home without a word of explanation. As soon as they'd landed in DC, Nick and Eli had started drinking to numb the pain of "losing the only thing they'd ever given a shit about." The rest of them had soon followed suit.

He didn't know how they'd wound up in New York City, but now that he was remembering why they'd been trying to find oblivion in a bottle, he sort of wished they'd tried harder.

"Civilian life," he muttered, echoing Nick's bitter words. He glanced to the side, where Ty was crawling back into bed and stuffing his head under a pillow. "What the hell are we supposed to do with civilian life?"

Everyone was so silent, Kelly could hear Eli breathing from all the way across the room. No one would meet his eyes.

"Rob banks?" Digger finally suggested.

"No!" Nick and Owen both barked.

Nick sat on the end of the bed nearest Kelly, hanging his head. Kelly stared at him, his stomach tumbling at the mere thought that they were done. What the hell were they supposed to do if they weren't a team anymore?

"This is the end, isn't it?" Kelly asked quietly. "Sidewinder no longer exists."

Eli shook his head and the others grumbled quietly. But Nick shot off the bed again, fast enough that it made Kelly's tender head spin, and Kelly flinched when Nick advanced on him. He chucked a pillow at Kelly's face, and Kelly had to duck away from it and from him. He backed up until his bare back hit the window, and he gasped when Nick kept coming, shocked by the vehemence.

"Don't ever fucking say that again," Nick snarled, his finger pointed in Kelly's face, eyes blazing and teeth gritted. "Not where I can fucking hear you," he growled before he stalked off toward the door.

Kelly watched him go, eyes wide, wounded by the anger and the threat.

"Bro," Eli called as he scrambled off the bed to go after Nick. "Yo, Rico, wait up!" He glanced at Kelly and shook his head as Kelly shrugged at him, and the others sat in silence, staring at each other uncomfortably as Eli ran after Nick.

"He took that better than I thought he would," Ty finally offered from beneath his pillow.

May 31, 2013

"I'd forgotten about that morning," Kelly said. "Or maybe blocked it out. God, you were so angry."

"You deserved it." Nick was hanging his head, his eyes closed, his fingers splayed through his hair.

"You're right," Kelly said quietly. His own memory of that last trip with his boys was bittersweet at best. It wasn't the last time all six of them had been together, not by any stretch of the imagination. But it had been the end of Sidewinder. The end of the best thing he'd ever been a part of. And Kelly had been the main catalyst of that end. He'd seen a town in Colorado as they'd been driving through, and he'd fallen in love with it. Weeks later, when they'd still been holding on to the last gasps of their time together, when they'd still been on that road trip and traveling and having fun and being *a team*, Kelly had decided it was time to go, said good-bye to them, and retreated to that little town.

His decision to leave had ended Sidewinder. And he'd never forgiven himself. He doubted the others had ever forgiven him either.

Kelly looked from the letter to Nick again, and he slid his hand over Nick's back, letting it rest on his spine. "Nicko," he whispered.

Nick cleared his throat. He wouldn't look at Kelly, instead concentrating on the letter he held. He started to read again, speaking Eli's words for him. "Of all the things we did together, of all the times we had, that trip was my favorite. It's the time I remember in the dark, when the dreams are too sad and the scars hurt too much. Because it was everything good about the best time of our lives, and we *all* need to remember it. Together. And that's why I'm writing this letter. Because you boys need to remember Sidewinder the way I remember us. The way we were when we threw all our seabags into the back of Ty's Bronco and set off across the country with zero idea of what we were doing."

Nick stopped to swallow, and he coughed quietly. "Jesus, we were crazy."

"Were?" Kelly asked with a smirk.

Nick snorted.

"What's the rest say?"

"Step number two won't be easy," Nick read. "But there's a reason I'm giving this task to you, Rico. You have to call each of the other guys and make them meet you at my gravestone. Without telling them why. So buck up, buttercup, this might get tricky."

CHAPTER SIX

Kelly lay in bed, staring sightlessly through the dark. He was restless but also bone-tired, so he couldn't even get up the energy to fidget. His heart ached, and Nick's warmth next to him seemed to be making it worse instead of better.

Nick was just as restless, but he'd fallen victim to his pain pills and drifted off into what seemed like a torturous sleep. He was tossing and turning, murmuring in languages Kelly recognized but didn't know how to translate. Every now and then, Nick would gasp and his entire body would tense, leaving Kelly bracing for impact. It hadn't come yet, though, so Kelly was left to ponder the day.

And it had been a hellish day.

After reading Eli's instructions, Nick had quietly gotten up and excused himself. He'd taken a few minutes for himself, then come back to tell Kelly he wanted to do this. He *needed* to do this. Kelly had said he wasn't strong enough yet, and Nick had merely nodded and disappeared down the stairs without another peep.

The fact that he hadn't argued, hadn't fought for it, worried Kelly more than the fact that he wanted to do it in the first place.

He tossed his head, huffing loudly and squeezing his eyes closed. If he could just get his mind to stop whirring for a few minutes, he'd be able to find sleep. He rolled the other way, reaching carefully across the crumpled sheets to press the tips of his fingers to Nick's back. Nick tensed with the touch, and Kelly withdrew his hand. What the hell was he doing? Just because he couldn't sleep didn't mean he had the right to wake Nick as well. It was rare enough for Nick to be able to sleep at all lately; he deserved it, even if it was laced with bad dreams.

Kelly was haunted by the look he'd seen in Nick's eyes when they'd read Eli's letter that afternoon, surrounded by all of Eli's favorite things. It almost overrode the heartache from watching that video of Nick and a stranger, together in this bed . . . in these sheets.

Kelly rolled to his back again, giving his head a violent shake as if he could actually rid himself of the images. He'd rather think about Eli's letters than *that*.

Kelly had expected Nick to drop everything right then and get on the phone to the other guys to tell them about Eli's letters. But Nick had asked Kelly first. Asked him for his opinion. Hell, asked him for permission. But Nick had been through enough in the last year, and Eli was dead. He could wait until Nick was stronger.

And judging by the occasional whimper coming from Nick as he slept, he wasn't strong enough now. He just wasn't fucking strong enough for this.

Kelly peered at Nick through the darkness. He'd gone still and quiet since Kelly had touched him, curled on his side with his back to Kelly. No more murmurs, no more soft breaths or gasps. He was so still . . .

He wasn't even breathing.

Kelly jerked, heart pounding as he frantically flashed back through the previous times in their lives he'd found Nick not breathing. He grasped for Nick's shoulder, tugging him flat. "Irish?"

Nick rolled and pounced so fast that Kelly had no time to switch gears from panicking to defending himself. By the time he realized what had happened—that Nick had been playing possum—Nick had him pinned to the mattress with a knife at his throat.

"Nick," Kelly gasped.

Nick hissed at him, shushing him. Then he said something that might have been Dari, which told Kelly *where* Nick thought he was, if not when. He wasn't sure, though, and all he could really hear was his blood rushing through his ears anyway.

"O'Flaherty," Kelly tried. When he spoke, the movement of his jaw pressed his skin against the blade, drawing blood. He raised his chin, but Nick pressed harder into him. "Nick. It's Doc."

The faint smell of blood reached Kelly's nose, and his body went cold. He knew what Nick could and would do to him, what they could do to each other, if this went wrong. He went still, praying that Nick would snap out of it in time, that the scent of blood wouldn't trigger whatever Nick had been trying to bury since he'd returned from his last deployment.

Nick's breaths were harsh against his face, his body coiled and hard and ready for battle. The blade wasn't cool, meaning that wherever Nick had been hiding it, he'd been holding on to it long enough to warm the steel.

Slowly he began to relax against Kelly. The knife let up, leaving a burning line behind that began to trickle down the side of Kelly's neck. Kelly didn't dare move, though, not yet.

"Doc," Nick gasped.

Kelly puffed a breath. It was the only sound he dared to make. He felt Nick shifting over him. A moment later, he heard the knife thump to the ground beside the bed.

"Oh God," Nick grunted.

Kelly breathed out slowly, almost light-headed from the rush of relief.

"Are you okay?" Nick asked shakily.

"Yeah." Kelly managed a nervous laugh. "Yeah, sure. Terrified and a little turned on. You know . . . typical Friday night."

"I'm sorry. I thought . . . I . . ."

Nick placed a hand on Kelly's chest, patting him like he meant to soothe him, or perhaps to assure himself that Kelly was okay. Kelly reached for him, trying to make contact in order to ground Nick until he could reach the lamp switch. His fingers grazed against Nick's bearded cheek, and he touched him carefully.

Nick grabbed his wrist, squeezing it hard enough to make Kelly wince, and slammed it against the mattress, then straddled Kelly's thighs.

Kelly couldn't see him, but he could sure as hell feel him. He tensed again, preparing to defend himself, violently if he needed to. He'd never seen Nick snap out of it and then fall back in like this. His free hand fumbled for the bedside table, for the light switch or something—anything—heavy enough to do damage. He didn't want to hurt Nick, but he didn't want to fucking die, either.

Then Nick pressed him into the mattress and kissed him, forcing his knee between Kelly's splayed legs, rolling his hips to rub his hardening cock against Kelly's as he bit and sucked at Kelly's lip. It only took Kelly a few seconds to catch up, and when he did, he wrapped his arms around Nick, returning the fervent kisses with just as much hunger.

"Kisses are so much better than knives," he murmured into Nick's mouth. "Just . . . so you know."

Nick hummed against his lips, hooked a hand under Kelly's knee, and lifted it so he could rut against his ass. "Did I hurt you?"

Kelly shook his head. "Not hurt."

"I'm sorry," Nick whispered, then kissed him again, tongue and teeth turning it into anything but apologetic.

The angle of Kelly's leg was almost at critical mass, and he began struggling to try to get it free. He was still returning the kisses enthusiastically, moaning with every nip of Nick's teeth, with every demanding push of his hips.

He bucked his hips when Nick pulled him too far and pain shot down his cold hamstring. Kelly brought his free hand up and twisted it into Nick's hair, yanking hard enough to hurt him. Nick winced, jerking his head up with a gasp. They remained that way for long, tense seconds, staring into the darkness, trying to see each other, unable to do anything but feel and hear. Kelly's breaths were ragged, and his body raged like a wildfire everywhere Nick had touched him. A trickle of blood made its way down his throat toward his hairline.

Nick's breathing was as loud as the waves against the hull, his body taut as a bowstring waiting to be plucked.

"What?" Kelly finally snapped.

Nick answered with a wordless grunt as he pressed their bodies flush again, bearing down on Kelly's arm with one hand and letting go of Kelly's leg with the other. He dragged his teeth over Kelly's collarbone and neck instead, his hand roaming up Kelly's rib cage at an alarmingly leisurely pace. Kelly groaned and writhed beneath him, his eyes rolling up before they closed completely. A moan slipped unbidden from between his lips.

Nick kissed him again, obviously spurred on by the sound. Before the kiss had ended, Nick had his fingers at Kelly's throat, the pads resting under Kelly's jawbone, just where he liked them. Kelly could feel the blood smearing against the paper-thin cut under his jaw.

"Oh God, babe." Kelly's voice was harsh and needy, and Nick's cock twitched against his ass when he spoke. Nick loved it when he begged. And Kelly loved it when Nick made him *want* to beg.

"God's not here," Nick snarled into his ear.

Nick let go of Kelly's neck and bunched his fingers in Kelly's hair, yanking his head back. His lips moved over Kelly's face, finally resting against his temple. "Roll the fuck over, babe."

Kelly was trying to do it before he even had a chance to think it through. He twisted his hips, pushing off with one foot even as he was still submitting to Nick's lips on his. Nick's tongue was in his mouth, sucking, licking, forcing Kelly to kiss him back or be lost to it.

Kelly's shoulders were still flat on the bed, but he'd managed to turn his hips as far as they could possibly go with Nick holding him down like he was. He gave his arm a tug, trying to loosen Nick's hold so he could turn over like he'd been instructed. Nick's fingers tightened over his wrist. He let go of Kelly's hair, though, and reached under the pillow above Kelly's head, his entire body sliding up Kelly's, his abs pushing into Kelly's, his hard cock dragging against Kelly's ass cheek.

"Let me turn," Kelly grunted, giving his arm another pointed tug. "On my knees."

He felt Nick shake his head. The bottle of lube that they kept under their pillows had enough left in it for tonight. Kelly heard the top pop open.

"Yeah, babe," he gasped, his heart speeding at the mere thought of Nick fucking him in this mood. "Please, Nicko. Please."

Nick didn't let Kelly's wrist go, and Kelly didn't blame him. If he got free, he would probably ruin whatever plan Nick had by jacking himself off to the thought of how fucking green Nick's eyes must be. He started fumbling around for the lamp instead, knocking over things on the table, whimpering in desperation because the sudden desire to see Nick's eyes was almost a physical need.

Two of Nick's slick fingers slid into Kelly, then twisted, spreading him apart. Kelly cried out and tried to move his hips for better access, but Nick had one of Kelly's legs trapped between his knees. Kelly raised his free leg, pulling his knee up toward his chin. He wrapped his free hand around it, but almost immediately lay out again on his back, reaching for the table.

"Yeah, yeah," Nick breathed, and he delved into another kiss as he grabbed Kelly's calf and shoved it up and over his shoulder.

Kelly knocked over his glass of water, and it shattered when it hit the floor. Nick grunted and trapped Kelly's other hand, yanking it behind his back, almost like he would when arresting a suspect who'd been fighting. Kelly had no limbs under his own control right now—he was all twisted around on his side with his ass in the air, his leg over Nick's shoulder, and both hands held down. It was a beautiful restraining job. Kelly had seen Nick do it several times while sparring, using his broad shoulders and dense muscles, his deceptive flexibility that came with them, to his advantage.

Kelly closed his eyes, breathing out shakily. Nick's cock pushed at his ass, and Kelly tilted his hips upward to help the entry. Nick didn't need help, though. He shoved into Kelly, grunting and gasping as he worked in deeper with every roll of his hips.

"Oh," Kelly managed, and the word was so quiet and so pitiful, he wasn't even sure what he'd been going for there, but all he knew now was the shaft of Nick's cock spreading him wide, the head of Nick's cock boring into him.

Nick didn't let up once he'd sunk himself deep inside him. He released Kelly's other hand, though, using his body weight to keep Kelly down as he thrust into him. "Roll over," he ordered again, a little more breathless this time.

Kelly pushed his heel against the mattress and reached for the headboard, trying to move, to break Nick's hold so he could roll to his belly. Nick picked up his pace, ripping a cry from Kelly as he writhed and pleaded for more.

He kept trying to turn, but Nick's hold was unbreakable. "Babe," he pleaded. "Nick. I can't roll if you don't let me go."

"Then fucking get creative," Nick snarled before he bit down on Kelly's collarbone and pulled down on Kelly's shoulder. He was moving his knees, bringing them in closer to Kelly's ass. He was either going for better leverage or a new angle, and Kelly redoubled his efforts at rolling over. Whatever Nick had in mind next, he wanted to be a part of it. He needed to be on his knees. Needed it.

He struggled to get there, and with every movement of his body, Nick was making the most obscene noises. Groaning and huffing, grunts that trailed off into the tiniest of whimpers that swept over Kelly's body and raised goose bumps all over his skin. He bit Kelly's lip, keeping it between his teeth as he shoved his cock all the way in. He rolled his hips, spreading Kelly wide, laying him bare as they kissed.

Cries and pleas for mercy followed, but each one fell on deaf ears as Nick maintained his punishing rhythm. Kelly grabbed at Nick with his one free hand, twisting in his hair, scratching down his arm, groping for Nick's hip so he could feel the sinuous movements.

He was still trying to turn one way or the other, but Nick had him in what amounted to a wrestler's hold. Kelly didn't remember this move from his high school wrestling team, though.

Nick pulled Kelly's captive arm down toward their bodies. His other hand found a handful of Kelly's hair, and Kelly cried out when he gripped it too hard and yanked Kelly's head back. He almost immediately let go, though, and when he trailed his fingers down Kelly's face and across his lips, his touches were gentle, reverent. He slipped his thumb across Kelly's lower lip, cradling Kelly's head in one large palm.

"Nick," Kelly gasped.

Nick kissed him, slowing his rhythm until his thrusts were so slow that Kelly could feel every inch of his cock slipping into him. Kelly writhed, not even sure what he was seeking. Nick pressed their lips together so gently they were barely even real kisses.

"More," Kelly blurted. He reached for Nick, gouging his fingernails down Nick's back to spur him on, bucking his hips. He almost succeeded in turning, using the leverage from his leg over Nick's shoulder, but then Nick pushed up onto his knees, lifting Kelly's lower half completely off the bed, leaving Kelly to scramble for something to grasp onto.

Nick sank deeper into him as he repositioned him, though Kelly hadn't thought that was possible. He let out an outraged howl, his body bowing, every piece of him trembling and burning and *screaming* for release. Nick leaned over him, still holding his ass off the bed, still entangled with his legs so he couldn't get away. Kelly begged for mercy in whispered words that he wasn't sure were coming out.

"Say it again," Nick ordered in a threadbare voice.

"Please," Kelly whispered.

Nick leaned back and handily dismantled all that hard work Kelly had done to roll over. He wrapped Kelly's legs around his waist, his hands gentle and then rough, caressing and then gripping hard. He laid Kelly out in front of him, then slipped his hands under Kelly's shoulders to hold him close.

He turned his face against Kelly's, their cheeks brushing, his lips grazing Kelly's ear. "Say it again."

Kelly whimpered as he tried to get away, tried to get closer, tried to make Nick fuck him harder, tried to make it end. His hands were splayed against Nick's back, the raised ridges of scars under his palms, the irregular pattern of a tattoo inked a little too deep disrupting the smooth skin under Kelly's palms. He trembled under Kelly's touch.

"Please," Kelly shouted. Nick rolled his hips pointedly, the swollen head of his cock massaging Kelly's prostate.

He pressed his lips to Kelly's, the tips of their noses resting together. "I love you," he gasped, never letting up on the rhythm of his thrusts, refusing to grant Kelly a moment of respite as his words and caresses turned tender.

"Nick." The name might as well have been a prayer on Kelly's lips. "Oh God, please. I love you. I love you. Please!"

Nick kissed him to silence him, and moments later Kelly was coming, struggling to move as Nick clamped down on him, grasping at Nick and pleading for mercy, crying out his name over and over until his voice was even more abused than his body.

It seemed to go on forever, until Kelly was seeing stars, until he couldn't breathe anything but the scent of Nick's body, until Nick's moans of his name filled his ears, until *Nick* was all he knew.

Kelly's body was still aflame, the ache settling bone deep by the time Nick carefully pulled out. They both moaned, breaths coming at a premium, each other's names mingling between them as Nick rolled off Kelly and took Kelly with him.

They faced each other in the darkness, Kelly's leg resting on Nick's hip, neither of them capable of speaking yet. After a few torturous seconds of silence, Nick rolled away from him, his body straining under Kelly's leg. Then the light on Nick's side of the bed flipped on, searing right through Kelly's retinas.

"Oh, you dickbag," Kelly muttered, trying to shield his eyes and turning his head away from the measly light of the forty-watt bulb in that stupid fucking lamp.

"Sorry," Nick murmured as he rolled back to face Kelly. He was reaching for Kelly's face, and he pushed at Kelly's jaw, making him tilt his head up.

His fingers were gentle on Kelly's neck and chin, but Kelly was frowning as he stared into Nick's eyes. They weren't bright, shining green like he'd imagined.

"What are you doing?" Kelly asked, keeping his voice to a whisper because speaking any louder felt wrong.

"You've got blood all over you," Nick told him, tearing his eyes away from Kelly's neck to meet his eyes. "I cut you."

Kelly nodded and reached to press three fingers to the throbbing area he thought was the source of the blood.

"Why didn't you say something?"

Kelly pursed his lips and shook his head, looking down at the blood on his fingers and then back to Nick. "It's nothing. I've bled more than this shaving when the water's choppy."

Nick didn't look convinced. His eyes strayed back to the cut.

"Nick. You just smeared it everywhere with your hand, it's really not bad." Kelly took Nick's hand and turned it over to show him.

He realized his mistake too late as he watched the color drain from Nick's already ashen countenance.

"Babe," Kelly whispered carefully.

Nick tore his attention away from his bloody hand and met Kelly's eyes. He licked his lips and nodded jerkily. "I'll get a cloth to clean it up," he croaked, and began to roll away.

Kelly grabbed for him, digging his fingers into Nick's hard triceps to stop him. "I'll get it. Baby. Nick. It's okay. It happened, you fought it off, and I'm okay. Please stay with me. Don't run."

"I wasn't—"

"*Yes*," Kelly hissed. He closed his eyes in a bid for calm. "You were."

His stomach tumbled as they both remained where they were, wrapped together, still breathless and sweaty, cum still slick between them. He scooted a little closer, placing his palm on Nick's cheek. He kissed him on the very tip of his nose, earning a little snort of amusement from his stoic boyfriend.

"What was that all about?" Kelly finally whispered, moving his lips against Nick's.

Nick's eyes fluttered closed, and a flush began to spread high on his cheeks. His fingers dug into Kelly's rib cage. "I was . . . lost."

Kelly nodded. "I understand."

"But then it was you under me," Nick continued in a rush. "And I had to hurry in case *that* was really the dream, and I'd wake up in the sand before I could have you."

Kelly realized he was holding his breath, his mouth ajar and his eyes squeezed tightly shut. When Nick shifted in his arms and pressed their lips together, Kelly slid his arm under Nick's head so he could hold him better. He wrapped him up in a hug, kissing him gently over and over as Nick gripped his thigh and wrapped Kelly's leg over his hip. He held on to Kelly like he might still be dreaming, afraid to let him go.

"Nicko," Kelly finally whispered. Nick squeezed him tighter, shoving his face against Kelly's chest. Kelly spoke against his unruly auburn hair. "You were right, babe. Eli's talking to us. To you."

Nick's breath was hot against Kelly's skin.

"I think . . . I think you need to listen to him."

Nick pulled back to meet his eyes, his breath stuttering.

"You were right," Kelly whispered, running his hand through Nick's hair. "You need to do it."

"This is Grady," Ty Grady answered on the third ring. Even though he was supposed to be retired from the FBI and doing cupcake jobs for the CIA, Ty still hadn't shaken the habit of answering the phone as if someone was calling to tell him about a murder.

"Hey, Tyler," Nick said with a smile, trying to cover his nerves by closing his eyes as he spoke. "How's it going?"

"Irish? You okay?"

"Yeah, I'm fine. Everything's fine. Don't panic."

"Don't panic is what people say when they're panicking!"

"I'm not panicking!" Nick insisted. "No one's panicking."

"Well I am now!"

Nick had to laugh, and Ty huffed. Nick was silent for a few seconds, just listening to the soft breaths of his best friend on the phone. It spoke to the last couple years of their lives that a phone call from a friend immediately caused concern. That was something they'd both agreed to work on when Ty had been visiting Boston last month.

"I need to call more often, huh?" Nick asked, still smiling.

"Or how about getting your ass on a plane and coming to see me again, huh? I have a surprise."

"Yeah, Zane sent me a text message about your kittens, dude."

"That asshole! I told him not to tell you until you came back here!"

"He asked me to come steal them and make it look like a ransom job."

"Wow. Dude. Wow." Ty muttered and thumped around for a few seconds as Nick listened with a gentle smile.

"Send me pictures, then," Nick finally groaned.

"I'll have to find them first; I'm teaching them evasion techniques and . . . they're really good at it."

"You're putting your kittens through SERE training?" Nick asked flatly.

"Yeah, want to help me?"

"Kind of," Nick admitted with a laugh.

"Irish. Come on, man, you're killing me here. Please tell me you're calling to invite me to come back to Boston."

Nick closed his eyes again, smiling despite the overwhelming feeling that he was still a pretty shitty friend. Ty's trip to Boston in April had been the first time in years that it had felt like old times together. He was happy to learn he wasn't the only one pining for a second round. "Yeah," he finally said. "Yeah, I am. But I need you and maybe Garrett to do me a favor before you come."

"A favor," Ty repeated. His voice had gone flat, and without the benefit of his facial expressions, it was impossible to gauge Ty's mood. "You even have to ask, man? Anything."

Nick licked his lips, trying again to press down the bubbling of nerves making their way toward his chest.

He'd fucked up royally with Ty. Ty had forgiven him for everything he'd done, able to see past the actions and into Nick's soul just like always. Nick had nearly given his life for Ty's, but he still felt the weight of penance on his shoulders. Now, these letters from Eli might give him a chance to lift the rest of that weight, and he'd do anything for that chance. Literally anything.

"Nick?"

"I need you to meet me in DC in a week."

"What? Why?"

Nick closed his eyes again and sighed shakily. "I can't tell you."

Ty was silent, and for a moment Nick thought he'd lost him. "Promise me you're not in trouble," Ty finally demanded.

Nick snorted and shook his head. "I promise."

"Okay. Where do I go, we meet at the airport?"

"No. I need you to meet me at Eli's grave."

Ty was silent again, and Nick's entire body tumbled with nerves as he waited for Ty to speak again.

"I'll be there," Ty finally said. "I don't know if Zane can come, but I'll be there."

"Thank you," Nick said in relief. "I'll see you then, brother."

"Yeah." Ty sounded just as nervous as Nick felt. "Hey," he added before Nick could say good-bye. "You still mean that, right? Brother?"

Nick swallowed hard, realizing he was nodding vigorously as he clutched at his phone. "With everything I am."

"Good," Ty whispered. "I'll see you in a week."

Ty ended the call without further chat, and Nick's heart was racing when he set the phone down. He sat on the flybridge, staring at the phone.

"You okay?" Kelly asked him when he thumped up the steps.

Nick turned to meet his eyes, wincing. "Yeah. Ty's on board."

"Seriously? That was fast."

"You could at least fake having a little faith in my abilities," Nick said, flopping back onto the bench seat and throwing his arm over his eyes a little too dramatically.

It made Kelly snort, though, and he came over and sat, sliding himself under Nick so Nick's head was in his lap, patting Nick's belly when he settled in. "Don't rest yet, babe. One down. Two to go."

Nick groaned and lifted his phone again, hitting the next number in his speed dial. He looked up at Kelly, studying him from below as the phone rang. "God, you're beautiful," he whispered.

Kelly winked at him, smirking.

"Owen Johns," Owen answered. He sounded like he was holding his phone between his cheek and his shoulder. If Nick knew Owen, and he did, he was probably fixing his silk tie in front of a mirror.

Nick sat up so Kelly couldn't distract him. "It's O'Flaherty, bud, you busy?"

"Irish?" Owen asked with a frown in his voice. "No, I'm getting ready for a meeting, what's wrong?"

Nick gave that a small smile. Owen was always ready to come to the rescue. Hell, that's what Sidewinder did. "I need you to do something for me. No questions asked."

"You know I'll do it if it's possible," Owen promised. "What is it? Are you okay?"

"I'm fine. No one's in danger, it's not life or death, I promise. Promise. But I'll be in DC in a week and I want you there."

"DC. We're talking about Washington?"

"That's the one."

"How long will you need me there?"

"A week. More if you want to sightsee after."

Owen inhaled noisily. "After what?"

"Can't tell you, bud."

Owen laughed bitterly. Yeah, he probably knew that story. Second verse, same as the first. "Do I need a weapon?"

"Nope," Nick said, trying to interject a little more cheer into his tone. "Just bring yourself. Hell, bring your girl if you want to, let us all meet her. I have no doubt Ty will show up with his kittens. If you can't make it, we'll wait until you can."

"Who's we? Besides Six and his kittens?"

"Me and Kelly. Ty and maybe Zane. I'm about to call D and ask him too."

Owen was quiet long enough that Nick had to check that the call was still connected. Owen worked for Caliburn Technologies, a powerful security company based in San Diego; he traveled all over the world, and if his suits weren't tailored to the tune of a thousand dollars or more, he was slumming it for the day. He had access to all kinds of resources, but the only thing Nick was asking for was him. It was probably throwing Owen off as he tried to figure out what the hell was going on.

"This isn't another surprise wedding, is it?" Owen finally asked.

The words hit Nick unexpectedly and he flinched, tossing a surreptitious glance across the flybridge, where Kelly was opening a beer bottle on the edge of a table. They weren't exactly at the marrying stage right now, despite how desperately Nick wanted to spend the rest of his life with Kelly. He'd kept too many secrets, hurt too many people. Hurt Kelly. He had a lot of making up to do before he could ask Kelly to marry him again. He shook his head. "No."

"You okay, brother?" Owen asked softly.

"I promise," Nick told him again, sadness and a smile warring in his voice. "Can you make it?"

"Yeah. Yeah, I'll be there. Where do I meet you?"

Nick inhaled noisily. "Here's the thing."

"Yo!" Digger shouted when he finally got his phone to his ear.

"Yo, yourself," Nick said, grinning despite how he was still reeling from the first two calls. "Turn your motor off, bud, I need to talk to you."

"Rico!" Digger cried. "Long time, bubba. What's down?"

Nick snorted. Digger and Nick kept pace, talking at least once a week. And while Digger seemed content down in his bayou, there was a hint of something missing from his voice since Miami that Nick had all but given up on. It was good to detect that tiny bit of sadistic glee in his laugh again.

"What are you doing?" Nick asked suspiciously.

"Not a damn thing."

"Never mind. I didn't ask," Nick insisted as he put his hand over his eyes.

"Why, who you been talking to?"

"Don't incriminate me with details."

"Don't ask questions you don't want answers to then!"

"You're right, I'm sorry!"

Nick could hear Digger laughing.

"Are you still confined to the States?" Nick asked.

"No, I'm clear to roam. Why?"

"Want to go on an adventure?"

"Oh yeah, baby, where we going?" Digger cried. Nick could tell that he'd hopped to his feet.

"Washington, DC. Go buy your tickets for next week. One way."

"I'll be there with motherfucking bells on, baby. What's our target?"

Nick laughed again, harder this time. "No target. Just a little favor we're doing for a friend."

"No target?" Digger asked, and Nick imagined his shoulders slumping.

"No target," Nick insisted. "No guns. No tactical gear. No nothing but your fine ass in a plane."

"What friend is this?" Digger asked warily. "You boys the only friends I got I'll still do favors for."

"You know him. Haven't seen him in a while," Nick answered, his voice taking on a more solemn note. "Trust me, you won't regret the trip."

"I trust you," Digger assured him. "That's where the bullet hole in my ass cheek came from."

"Yeah, but you still get people to kiss it, so you're welcome."

"True that!"

Nick grinned. "See you in a week. We'll pick you up at the airport."

"See you, brother!"

Kelly sat down beside Nick as he ended the call, and handed him a beer. Nick gave him a grateful smile and rested his arm on the back of the couch for Kelly to lean against.

"You did that easier than I thought you would," Kelly told him.

Nick nodded. "I figured Johns would be the harder sell, but he barely questioned it."

Owen had been the hardest to convince when Nick and Kelly had started a relationship. And when Ty had come out to the group years before, Owen had stormed off in a fit of rage. It had taken him months to forgive Ty for lying to them. Nick suspected there was also a little homophobia going on there, or at least some confusion over it. So when Nick and Kelly had started up, they'd kept it from the others until they were sure there was something permanent between them. When Owen had found out, he'd tried his best to be accepting and supportive, but Owen didn't do accepting and supportive very well on a good day.

He was doing the best he could, though, Nick had to give him that. It was more than a lot of people tried. Still, it was hard for anyone to keep in constant touch with Owen. It wasn't a malicious or angry absence. It was just a man who was busy and forgot to keep up.

Digger was a little different. All you had to do was promise him the chance to maim something or set it on fire, and he was yours for the weekend.

"We all thought we lost you, Nick," Kelly said quietly, drawing Nick out of his reverie. "I think they'd do anything you asked them right now."

Nick swallowed hard, torn over whether to answer or just . . . carry on and ignore the pain in his chest. "I couldn't tell D what we were doing," he said, deciding to ignore Kelly's words. "I'll tell him at the airport."

"I figured Ty would give you more trouble," Kelly told him as he got comfortable against Nick. "Secrets and lies and all that shit."

Nick swallowed hard, flushing. Secrets and lies. He gave Kelly a quick glance, trying to gauge whether it was a pointed comment or just Kelly being straightforward like usual. His fingers strayed to the ragged scar in his side as he took a sip from his beer.

When he looked up again, Kelly was watching him, sitting sideways on the seat next to him. "No one blames you, you know?"

"I do," Nick whispered.

"We almost lost you. But hell, I'm starting to feel like we did anyway."

Nick flinched, closing his eyes.

Kelly's hand settled on his knee, squeezing gently. "We love you. All of us. Maybe Eli's giving you a chance to fucking remember that, huh?"

Nick pulled Kelly closer, sighing as he stared at the pile of letters on the table in front of them.

They had read the rest of Eli's first letter. All the envelopes were numbered, and they were not to be opened until the appropriate moment. At the end of the letter, Eli informed Nick that when he had everyone standing in the graveyard, he was to open the letter numbered 1. Each subsequent letter would tell them what to do or where to go.

"You don't even want to peek at them?" Kelly wheedled.

"I really do," Nick said with a smirk. "But I also don't want Eli haunting my Irish ass, so I'm following the rules and so are you."

Kelly laughed. "Fair enough."

Nick pulled him closer, kissing him on the cheek. Kelly was still smiling when he turned his head and met Nick's lips with his own. Nick wasn't sure why or how he had managed to procure this type of love and loyalty, but he was going to make sure he did everything in his power to return it.

He slid his hand against Kelly's cheek, gliding down to grip the side of his neck and hold him there as they kissed. Kelly shifted so he could stretch and put his beer bottle on the table, then grabbed Nick's shoulder and pulled himself to straddle Nick's lap.

Nick moaned when Kelly leaned against his shoulders and kissed him again.

"Not even a day into your mission and you got snagged by a honeypot," Kelly teased between kisses.

"If you're a honeypot, then this was one hell of a long con," Nick said, then reached around and slid his hands into Kelly's back pockets. "Bravo."

"So . . . I guess we need to pack," Kelly finally said. He was still trailing kisses along Nick's neck, and his words tickled the tender skin there.

"Don't be hasty, now," Nick murmured, holding Kelly tighter and tilting his head to the side to give Kelly more room.

Kelly just laughed at him, kissing him one last time before sitting up. "Don't get distracted. We have work to do."

Nick nodded and took in a deep breath. His eyes strayed to the thin line just under the curve of Kelly's jaw. It was healing already because the knife Nick had used had been so sharp. It was more of a paper cut than anything, but looking at it made Nick's stomach tumble, made his throat constrict. He took in a shaky breath, eyes riveted as he slid his thumb under the cut.

"Babe," Kelly said quietly. The amusement was gone from his voice, the laughter fading along with the light in his eyes. He took Nick's hand in his and pushed it down. "Hey. Stop it."

"I'm sorry," Nick murmured as he forced himself to meet Kelly's eyes. "I don't even know where I got the knife."

"Nick," Kelly grunted, his shoulders slumping. He leaned his head back, staring over Nick at the bay. Nick had to look away from him. He hated the look in Kelly's eyes, the one that betrayed his frustration and impatience.

Nick knew his mind was fucked up. He was trying, desperately trying, to get it back on track. His biggest fear right now, aside from worrying that he was going to slit Kelly's throat in the middle of a dream, was that Kelly would get fed up with him again and not stick around long enough for Nick to be able to get it together.

"I'm sorry."

"Stop saying that. Stop being sorry. Jesus, be a cocky asshole for a day."

"Okay," Nick whispered.

Kelly patted his cheek, still looking annoyed.

Nick fumbled around on the seat beside him, picking up the last page of Eli's letter. He cleared his throat, glancing up at Kelly again carefully.

Kelly rested his weight on Nick's thighs and raised one eyebrow at the page. "What?"

"He gave us a packing list," Nick told him.

"Seriously?" His smile returned, and Nick was stunned by the way that simple gesture could light Kelly's eyes, make the gray and blue swirl together as the sun caught them. "What's on it?"

Nick handed him the page. "I'm going to email it to each of the guys with the other info. Let them panic a little over why we need climbing gear, a tiny leprechaun hat, and a video camera all on the same trip."

"Tiny leprechaun hat," Kelly repeated. He took the list and looked it over, his eyes growing wider. "Where the hell are we supposed to get one of those?"

Nick bit his lip, trying not to smile. "I've got a bunch in a box downstairs."

"Seriously?"

"Yeah, I collected them every year after the St. Paddy's parade."

Kelly barked a laugh, setting the letter aside to put both hands on Nick's shoulders again. "What for?"

"For . . . reasons."

Kelly was still laughing when he kissed Nick again.

CHAPTER SEVEN

Ty and Zane were the last to join the group waiting at Arlington Cemetery. Zane had no idea what was going on, why they'd been asked to drop everything to come to DC, or what had prompted Ty to go to a party store last night and buy two tiny leprechaun hats before the trip. He hadn't asked questions, though, even when Ty had tossed his seabag, the leprechaun hats, the kittens, and *Zane* into the Mustang that morning to make the drive. He'd learned years ago that asking questions when Sidewinders were involved was an exercise in futility.

He shouldn't have been surprised to find the entire team there waiting for them, but he was anyway. Whatever help Nick needed in Washington required everyone, and the last time they'd all been together, they had destroyed a Colombian cartel in Miami.

It was kind of a big deal.

"Oh God, we're going to die," Zane muttered as he and Ty approached the others.

Ty walked right up to Nick and threw his arms around Nick's neck. Nick stumbled with the weight, his eyes widening in shock. Then he returned the bear hug fervently, even though they'd both seen each other just weeks ago. It made Zane smile to see them happy. He almost wondered what they would be like now that they'd rediscovered just how much they meant to each other.

Ty gave the other guys each an enthusiastic hug of their own, and Zane followed, shaking everyone's hands.

Owen gripped him hard and patted him on the arm. "Garrett. Good to see you again," he said, and he sounded sincere. It was a real change from the first few times they'd greeted one another with nothing but a cold nod.

Digger was his usual, exuberant self, and he gave a round of powerful hugs all around, picking Ty up off the ground and setting him back down. He did the same to Zane, much to Zane's dismay. Kelly was all smiles, as usual. Kelly was always smiling. Even when he'd had tears tracking down his face as he'd watched his team head back to deployment without him, he'd had a smile on. Zane lingered over their greeting, hugging Kelly just a little tighter than the others. "Good to see you again, Doc."

"You too, Garrett. I'm glad you could make it. Nick's super excited to talk to you about something he found."

"Yeah?" Zane asked, grinning.

"Yeah, I don't know, he starts on zombies and conspiracies and I check out. He'll talk to you about it."

Zane snorted. "Can't wait."

"Okay, we're all here now," Owen said once the greetings were over with. "What the hell is going on?"

Nick nodded, not saying anything as he set his stuff on the ground and knelt in front of Elias Sanchez's grave to dig around in his pack. Zane winced at the look on Nick's face. His knee was obviously not in any kind of shape for him to be kneeling like that. Kelly had to take his elbow to help him stand back up, and he was noticeably in pain from the exertion. Everyone, including Zane, studiously ignored it.

He focused on the fresh flowers and a couple of trinkets on Sanchez's grave instead. This wasn't the first time he'd been here; Ty made the trip every year. He felt bad suddenly that they hadn't brought something this time. Even as he was thinking it, Ty moved past him and knelt to set something on the ground next to the flowers. Zane strained to see over his shoulder, and realized it was a Bronco emblem that Ty was pushing into the grass.

Zane had to smile fondly as Ty stood back up and met his eyes. Ty gave him a melancholy smile, and they both returned their attention to Nick.

Nick had an envelope in one hand and several sheets of folded paper in the other. He held up the papers, seeming to steel himself before trying to speak. "After Eli's funeral, his mom gave me a box of his stuff."

Zane glanced around at the others, who were all still and silent. Zane had never met Elias Sanchez. He'd been killed in the weeks before Zane and Ty had been partnered together. They'd worked the case, hunting the serial killer who had taken Eli's life. Zane had never fully realized how important Eli was to Ty and the rest of Sidewinder until much later, though. He'd seen them cry over the man, and these Recon Marines weren't the type to waste tears.

Nick worked his jaw, taking a moment before continuing. "I couldn't go through it. I was afraid to, so I left it on my boat all this time."

He glanced to Kelly, who gave him a calming smile and a nod.

"During my recovery I was stuck on the *Fiddler*. A lot. I finally got up the nerve to go through Eli's box, and while I was looking for that old sock puppet of his, I found this packet of letters instead. This was the first one. It's um . . . it's a little hard to read, but if you guys want to see it . . . he explains this better than I can."

Owen immediately held out his hand for it. Nick gave it to him, licking his lips in a rare show of nerves.

Owen started reading it out loud, but after a few sentences he got choked up and had to stop. He read the rest to himself, his eyes welling by the time he got to the second page. He finished with a watery laugh and handed it to Ty. Then he wiped his eyes and stepped closer to Nick, giving him a wordless hug. Nick rested his chin on Owen's shoulder, gripping him hard and murmuring something to him that Zane couldn't hear.

Zane watched in morbid fascination for a few seconds, struck dumb by the amount of emotion being openly displayed by two men who were notoriously good at hiding such things. Then he and Digger read the letter over Ty's shoulders. By the time he was done, he understood the urgency of Nick's call to arms, and he understood the tears and the sadness and the need to meet at Eli's grave. He even understood the tiny leprechaun hats.

"Eli knew you'd get us here," Ty said to Nick, smiling sadly. Nick returned the smile with weak one. "Now I get why you wouldn't let me read this when we went through his box."

"I'm sorry," Nick said with a wince.

"No, Irish, it's fine. You did what he told you to do."

"So what do we do now?" Digger asked shakily.

"Once we're all together, we open the next letter." Nick glanced around at everyone, his handsome face perhaps as solemn as Zane had ever seen it. "Everybody in?"

"EZ's talking to us, man," Digger said. "I'm listening."

"Me too," Owen and Ty both said.

"Before we read that letter, though," Kelly said, and he rummaged in Nick's bag for a second before pulling out a ragged orange-and-green sock monkey. He held it up. "Seymour needs to see more."

After a moment of silence, Digger smacked his forehead with his palm. "Damn!"

"Yeah, it took me ten years, too," Kelly mumbled.

Zane watched with a confused smile as Ty and Kelly arranged the sock monkey so he'd sit by himself on Eli's gravestone.

Nick edged closer to him, giving him a self-conscious smile and a nod. "Thanks for bringing Six out to play, Garrett."

Zane shook his head. "Once you see what he's got in that Mustang, you might change your tune."

Nick snorted.

"What are they doing?" Zane asked with a nod toward the sock monkey.

"He's Eli's." Nick's voice was distant and somber. "He's had his picture taken at landmarks and special places all over the world. And this . . ." Nick looked around Arlington Cemetery and fought to swallow. His eyes were back on Eli's headstone when Kelly took a picture of Seymour with his phone. "Doesn't get much more special than this."

There are going to be some rules for this trip. You will follow these rules. Don't make me Swayze the shit out of you.

1. No sex. No hooking up. This is about us, and I can't have any of you getting all distracted. You can go out and blow off steam, but it

*can't be for chasing tail. This rule is unbendable. I don't care if you're all
married with eight kids. I don't care if you're married to each other. No.
Sex. Full stop.*

*2. No one abandons the mission. I know you got lives to get back to,
so if you need to leave for work or for an emergency, do it. But everyone
goes with you. When it's done, you get back on the road where you pulled
off. I don't give a shit.*

*3. You're going to hit some casinos on your route. No one is allowed
to touch the dice except Digger and O'Flaherty. The rest of you are
bad luck.*

*4. I'm going to come back to this and add rule number four, I
thought these up while I was going to sleep and I've forgotten what four
was, but it was very important.*

*5. Lastly, no matter how much you hate this, no matter how
annoying it is, no matter how much pain you're in, remember Rule Five.
EZ loves you.*

*Now that you're all together, you're going to need to get Johns's big-ass
black credit card. Go buy some plane tickets to Denver, Colorado. When
you land, I want you to go to baggage claim, stare at the little devil in the
suitcase that always makes Nick uneasy. Do it long enough that he starts
cursing because that shit's funny. Then go rent a car.*

*You're going to need the car for 14 days. Tell them you're dropping it
off in Las Vegas, NV.*

And get lots of insurance on it.

Once you're in the rental agency waiting, you can open the next letter.

Kelly settled his bag under the seat in front of him and fumbled
around for his seat belt. His knuckles brushed Nick's hip and Nick
glanced sideways at him, smirking.

"Sorry," Kelly offered, trying to sound as insincere as he could. He
pushed his shoulder into Nick, jostling them both. "We could join
the Mile High Club on this flight, you know."

"I'm a member in good standing," Nick said flippantly as he
turned the page of the book he was reading on his iPad. "And it's
against the rules."

Kelly huffed and snapped his seat belt closed. "Did Eli know you were bi?"

Nick looked up quickly, one eyebrow raised. He glanced sideways at Kelly carefully. Kelly heard movement behind them, and almost in tandem, Owen and Digger both propped their elbows on the back of the seat and peered over to join the conversation. Kelly and Nick both craned their heads to look at them, and Nick rolled his eyes as he turned back around.

"In his letter to you, he said you were probably off flirting with the male nurse," Kelly told Nick. "Did he know?"

"Yeah," Nick said, looking devotedly at his book.

"Did you tell him?" Owen asked. He had both arms crossed over the seat back, his chin resting on his wrist. "How long did he know?"

Nick shook his head and turned his iPad off, stuffing it in the seat back. "He ran into me one night in Wilmington, when we were all still stationed at Lejeune. Saw me with a guy I was . . . kind of serious with."

Kelly turned in his seat to see Nick's face better. He was staring wistfully at the back of the seat in front of him.

"He came up to me in the club, said hello, introduced himself to the guy I was with. Never even fucking blinked. Like it was something he saw every day." Nick shook his head, smiling. "I'll never forget how fucking scared I was. And he just gave me a wink and told me I was fine. Kept on going like always."

"Why didn't you tell the rest of us?" Kelly asked, voice going softer.

Nick's wry smile was barely there, and then it was gone again. He met Kelly's eyes, then looked back at Owen and Digger. "I don't even know anymore," he said, voice full of regret.

Digger reached over the back of the seat and patted Nick on the head. Then he disappeared again, and Kelly heard the clicking sound of his seat belt. Owen remained, chin on his arm, looking down at Nick thoughtfully.

"All in good time, right?" Owen said gently.

Nick gave him a slight nod and a smile, and Owen winked before sitting back down. Kelly took Nick's arm, squeezing him.

"You're okay," he whispered to him, and Nick leaned into him to steal a kiss.

A second later, someone knelt in the aisle beside Kelly and patted his knee, interrupting the kiss.

"Hey," Kelly grunted to Ty, frowning in confusion as the man grinned up at him.

"Switch places with me," Ty requested.

Kelly glanced a few rows back at the top of Zane's head and Ty's vacant seat beside him. "What? Why?"

"Just for takeoff. I need to talk to Irish."

Kelly and Nick shared a glance, and Nick shrugged. Kelly rolled his eyes and unbuckled, moving past Ty in the tight space and letting him have his seat. He made his way to Zane's row and sat, grumbling to himself as he buckled up.

"What's he doing?" he asked Zane.

Zane sighed heavily, flipping through a magazine he appeared to have fished out of the front pocket. "I don't know, he was fine and then he just hopped up and darted away."

"Huh."

"Like living with a nervous Chihuahua," Zane mumbled. There was a soft mew from the cat carrier at his feet that seemed to agree.

Kelly nearly choked trying not to laugh. He leaned sideways so he could see up the few rows to where Nick and Ty sat, their heads bowed together. Ty laughed, and through the cracks of the seats, Kelly saw Nick cover his face with one hand.

A slow smile spread over Kelly's face, and he made himself comfortable, resting his head on the seat behind him. "Just like old times."

It only took Nick ten seconds to start complaining as they stood beneath the little stone gargoyle in the baggage claim of the Denver airport. "Who puts creepy-ass suitcase demons in an airport—do they *want* me to be afraid of my luggage?" was Zane's favorite complaint. They piled into the shuttle that would take them to the rental agencies, with Zane handling his and Ty's suitcases so Ty could hold the kitten carrier and keep them calm.

Fifteen minutes after getting off the shuttle, Zane was still standing in the rental car line, wondering how in the hell he kept getting himself into these situations and weighing the good and the bad of being officially adopted by Sidewinder. He'd been flattered at first to be accepted by Ty's former brothers-in-arms, but now he wasn't sure it was a great development.

Sidewinder was bunched together in the waiting area, huddled around Kelly as he read the second letter of Eli's instructions. Zane glanced over his shoulder at them, smiling despite himself.

He sure as hell hoped Elias Sanchez knew what he was doing.

Ty glanced up like he'd felt Zane's eyes on him, and he smiled and winked. Zane had to look away before he found himself grinning again. Ty was sitting with the cat carrier between his feet, cooing at Jiminy and Cricket to keep them calm. Zane had tried to talk him into kenneling them, but Ty had argued that they were still too young, too feral, too uncomfortable with strangers. And he was right, damn him. So they needed a vehicle large enough for six men, six bags, two kittens, and one very bossy letter-writing ghost.

When Zane got to the counter, he asked for a Chevy Suburban.

Nick joined him as he was filling out the rental information.

"Ty told me to list you as the main driver," Zane told him without looking up.

"Good," Nick grunted as he got his license out. "Don't put Digger on there. Or Kelly."

"Got it," Zane said with a slow grin, keeping his attention on the forms.

"Or Ty, for that matter," Nick added, causing Zane to snort and chuckle.

"Got it," he drawled out again, finishing up the form and handing it back to the agent. He turned to look Nick over, taking a deep breath. "How are you?"

Nick looked up, eyes wide like Zane had surprised him with the question. "I'm good."

"Really?"

Nick licked his lips slowly, glancing over his shoulder at the others. He looked solemn when he turned back to Zane. "Not . . . yet."

Zane didn't really know what to say to an honest answer, so he settled for a nod that left the silence between them awkward. Zane was almost glad for the interruption when Ty joined them, the letter in his hand.

"You put Nick as the main driver?"

"Just like you told me to," Zane answered with an exasperated roll of his eyes.

"Eli says Nick has to drive every other day. No one else can do it." Ty handed Nick the letter so he could read it for himself.

After scanning it, Nick mumbled almost to himself. "He doesn't say why."

"I'm sure he has his reasons," Ty said with a careless shrug. He was watching Nick carefully as he spoke, and he waited a few seconds before adding, "He's sending us to Wyoming."

"What?" Zane asked flatly.

"Yellowstone?" Nick asked as he shoved his wallet back into his jeans and handed the letter back to Ty.

Ty nodded, grinning.

"Oh God."

"What's wrong with Yellowstone?" Zane asked. "I've always wanted to go there."

"Nothing, it's fantastic. We camped there for a few days, back on this road trip Eli's having us retrace," Ty explained. "We were stalked by a herd of bored teenagers on vacation with their families. For the entire three days we were there."

Zane snorted before he could stop himself, and he tried to school his expression into a sympathetic frown. "I bet the six of you, ten or eleven years ago, were quite the hormone bait. Y'all were what, twenty-six to twenty-eight?"

Nick and Ty shared a glance that Zane couldn't quite decipher, both of them smirking.

Zane rolled his eyes. "Please tell me there was never any underage dabbling."

"We vetted everyone," Nick assured him with an insulted glare. "Gross," he added as he walked away.

Ty watched him head back to the group, then turned to Zane with a wide grin and leaned his elbow against the counter. "I wish you'd known him a decade ago."

"Oh yeah? Why is that?"

"Think you would have liked him," Ty said in a lower tone, his eyes turning melancholy.

Zane glanced at Ty with a confused frown as he took a stack of papers from the counter agent. He and Nick hadn't exactly been friends at first sight, but they'd come to an understanding and had actually become quite close. "I like Nick, baby. We get along fine."

Ty seemed sad as he stared off across the waiting area. "You don't know the Nick we did." He waited a moment, watching as Nick and Digger argued over something Digger was trying to stick into Nick's pack. Something flammable, no doubt. A hopeful, mischievous smile tugged at Ty's lips. "Not yet, anyway."

Zane's eyes strayed to Nick and the others as Ty's meaning sank in. It was painfully obvious, and had been for some time, that Nick wasn't okay, and he hadn't been okay since his last deployment. He'd even admitted as much to Zane one night as they'd sat together, but at the time Zane hadn't known him well enough to be alarmed. Looking back, Zane often wondered how things would have turned out if he had simply pressed Nick for an explanation that night, if he had offered his friend an ear and a shoulder to lean on.

They found out eventually, in a bloodbath of fire and alphabet agencies, why Nick's last deployment had shaken him. Nick had been tapped by the NIA to carry out an assassination of a deputy assistant director of the FBI who also happened to be Ty's mentor and the man who'd pulled Ty and Eli into the Bureau years ago. Nick had killed him right under their noses, operating so dark that even Kelly hadn't sniffed him out. The whole thing had come out when Nick had confessed to Ty under extreme duress, and it had culminated in the operation that had nearly taken Nick's life in Miami.

Thinking back on all of it, Zane supposed Ty was right; he'd never really known any of Sidewinder before that. There was nothing Zane could say or do to help Nick, of course, but he was holding out hope that maybe Elias Sanchez and his letters could.

He nudged Ty's elbow instead of commenting. "Go get him back, he has to sign this stuff since he's driving."

"What about me?"

"What about you?"

Ty slid the papers toward him. "Don't I need to sign too?"

Zane pulled the papers away from him. "No."

"Did Irish tell you not to put me as a driver?"

Zane cleared his throat. "I have the right to remain silent."

"Put me on there," Ty demanded. He smacked Zane's ass before he headed off, and Zane watched him go in bemusement.

"Your week's going to be interesting," the counter agent commented as she clicked away at her computer.

Zane snorted. "You have no idea."

With six big men in the Chevy Suburban they had all piled into, and a suitcase for each of them, they had to set up the third row seat. Bags and stuff were shoved into the floorboards and in the uncomfortable center seats. Seymour had a prime seat up front. The kittens were let loose so they wouldn't cry the entire drive, and Nick got assurances from everyone in the vehicle that they wouldn't be allowed to get near his feet as he drove.

Nick couldn't quite get a handle on why Eli would peg him for taking half the driving. He knew why the others would want him to drive, if given the choice: He'd always done most of the driving. With as many courses as he'd been through—between the Marines, the Boston PD, and Paddy Whelan's most talented getaway drivers—he was actually qualified to be a stunt driver if he felt the need to die in a fiery crash. Everyone felt better with him behind the wheel, especially on tricky roads. He would have been driving for most of the trip anyway, so Nick was having a hard time figuring out why Eli had insisted.

No matter why, he was sitting in the driver's seat, waiting for everyone to get settled and buckled.

"We're not going to try to make it to Yellowstone tonight, are we?" Kelly asked from the third row seat. "That's a long way to drive after a long day."

Nick glanced in the rearview mirror. Kelly and Digger had offered to sit in the back, saying they were the shortest and needed the least leg room. Nick suspected they were plotting back there where the grown-ups couldn't supervise them, but their logic was too sound to object.

He gave Kelly a fond smile, and Kelly returned it with a wink.

Ty looked up from struggling with his seat belt, and met Nick's eyes in the mirror. "What's halfway?"

Nick shrugged.

"Probably Rock Springs," Zane offered. He had been given the passenger seat simply because he needed the legroom. He had his phone out, scowling as he tried to set the directions up.

"How long is that drive?" Nick asked. "To Rock Springs?"

"Five hours."

Nick grunted and slid his hands over the wheel, looking over the Chevy, familiarizing himself with the vehicle. "Let's get going then," he said, and he started the Suburban with another glance in the mirror.

"What's his name?" Owen asked, and Nick felt his feet on the center console, nudging at Nick's elbow. He glared at Owen's shoes, and Owen slowly slid them to the floorboard again.

"Whose name?" Zane asked, turning in his seat to face Owen.

"Rental cars always get a name," Ty explained.

"Of course they do," Zane mumbled as he turned back around and buckled his seat belt. "Does your Mustang have a name?"

"No," Ty grunted.

Zane glanced up and met Nick's eyes, scowling. "But you name the rental cars."

"It's best if you don't try to make logic out of most of the things you'll be seeing this week," Nick advised.

"Understood."

"Where are the kitties?" Digger asked as Nick threw the SUV into reverse.

"They're . . . in SERE training," Ty answered, his voice muffled.

"Tyler, you get eyes on those animals right now," Nick barked. He was answered with two inquiring mews from somewhere in the far back.

"Got 'em!" Digger said happily. "Wait."

"Got 'em," Owen added, sounding positively despondent about it. "Well. Had 'em."

"Who's in charge of music?" Kelly asked.

"Not you," Owen said immediately.

Digger laughed. "That's stone cold."

Nick and Zane shared a long-suffering glance and sigh.

"No one's in charge of music," Nick said as he held up his phone. "We'll put Pandora on so no one fucking loses their shit, deal?"

There were faint sounds of agreement from the back. Nick pulled up the streaming music app and started it on a random song, then plugged it into the car so it would play through the speakers.

His elbow was nudged again, and he turned to glare at Owen, but one of the kittens was sitting on the console instead. It was the little orange one, and he blinked at Nick with big blue eyes.

"Which one are you?" Nick asked the animal.

Ty leaned forward. "That's Jiminy. He likes shoulders."

As if on cue, Jiminy put one front paw on Nick's arm, his claws out, preparing to clamber up to Nick's shoulder.

Nick put his finger on the kitten's nose. "Stand down, Marine."

The kitten mewed in response, and Ty plucked him off the console.

Nick was just barely out of the rental company's parking lot when Ty shoved his face between the two front seats. "The letter says we're supposed to open the next one before we stop for the night."

"Oh God," Nick grumbled. He shifted in the seat, trying to get comfortable, messing with the seat controls once he got to the first stoplight.

"I know," Ty said with a grin.

"What?" Zane asked, the dread in his voice almost palpable.

"If he wants us to read the next set of instructions before we find lodging for the night . . ." Nick started.

Ty chimed in almost gleefully to finish the thought. "Means he's going to make us sleep somewhere specific."

"What, like, he wants us to camp or something?" Zane asked.

Nick groaned quietly. "I guess we'll find out."

CHAPTER EIGHT

*I*t's a long drive from Denver to Yellowstone, boys, so unless you're all still as fucking crazy as we were at twenty-five or someone gives Six some 5-hour Energy, my guess is you'll be stopping halfway.

If I'm wrong and you made it to Yellowstone, go ahead and open the next letter.

But I ain't wrong 'cause I'm never wrong, and I'm guessing you're in Nowhere, Wyoming, right now, looking for a place to sleep. Find a local directory and hunt down the third cheapest, scariest motel in the area. Third from the bottom. You have one pass 'cause I know if Johns or O'Flaherty sees a roach they'll be out of there, and I don't want you sleeping in filth. I just want you remembering what it was like before we had a choice.

See, we stopped making our own choices at seventeen. We were told where to sleep, what to eat, when to do a chin-up, when we could go get laid, where to go, how to get there, and who to kill. In the brief moments when we did have a choice, we didn't really. We were held hostage by our ideals, our loyalty, and our bank accounts. We didn't have a choice where we slept, so we put all our ability to choose in each other. We chose each other.

So check for bedbugs first. And then fucking remember why we chose each other. Once you get to Old Faithful, open the next letter.

"I'm going to fucking kill him," Owen muttered as he stared at the ill-lit façade of the Motel 8 in Rock Springs, Wyoming. "It's not even a fucking Motel 6, dude."

Nick had to bite his lip hard to keep from agreeing with him. He was also trying not to laugh. "Okay, so . . . bring in only what you need. Just in case we have to burn our clothes later," he ordered as he grabbed his pack and eased it over his shoulder.

The others grumbled and snickered in equal amounts as they got out of the Suburban. The night was cool, and Nick welcomed the relief from the blazing summer sun as they made their way across the parking lot to the overhang that sheltered the lobby door.

Kelly appeared at his side, sliding his hand into Nick's back pocket. "Doing okay?"

Nick gave him a smile and a nod, sliding his arm over Kelly's shoulders. It felt natural to walk that way, wrapped around each other. The drive itself hadn't been too bad, but it had certainly been a long day. Starting the morning in Boston, flying to DC and gearing up for that emotional meeting, then the flight to Colorado, and finally the five-hour drive, during which Owen had repeatedly threatened to murder everyone in the car. Nick wasn't just tired, he was fucking exhausted, and all he wanted was to crawl into bed with Kelly and recharge his batteries.

He wouldn't have minded crawling into Kelly tonight either, but it was against the rules, and he was determined to follow those.

No matter how frustrating they might be.

They were lagging behind the others by the time they entered the lobby. It was vacant, which wasn't surprising this time of night. Owen leaned over the counter to see into the back office. They left him to handle it so he could take his murderous tendencies out on something besides them, and Ty came up to Nick and Kelly, one eyebrow raised.

"Sleeping arrangements?"

"Three rooms?" Kelly suggested. "At fifty bucks a pop, I think we can afford to splurge."

"Not really what Eli was going for," Nick said as he watched Owen speak to a bleary-eyed night clerk.

"Are we seriously following his instructions to the letter?" Kelly asked with a laugh. His grin fell when Nick met his eyes, though.

"What are we doing out here if we're not going to follow them?" Nick snapped.

"You're right," Kelly said immediately, holding up a hand to appease him. "You're right."

They were all silent, and Nick could feel their eyes on him as he studiously tried to ignore the attention. He finally cleared his throat and gave Kelly an apologetic sideways glance. "Three rooms," he said with a shrug. "Makes sense."

"You sure?"

Nick nodded. "First floor so I can avoid the steps."

Kelly stared at him for a few uncomfortable seconds, then moved away to join Owen at the counter.

"Hey," Ty said as he stepped closer to Nick.

Zane wandered away, hands stuffed in his pockets, whistling like he was trying to show he wasn't interested in overhearing.

"You two fighting?" Ty asked Nick.

"What?"

"Doc. There's some tension there, it's kind of weird."

Nick blinked at him, feeling stupid. "Really?"

Ty raised both eyebrows and leaned a little closer, searching Nick's eyes for something.

"We're good," Nick insisted.

Ty backed away a step, still scowling but looking like he believed it.

Nick winced and glanced over his shoulder at Kelly. "I guess it's just weird not being able to touch him. Or . . . talk to him."

"What do you mean?" Ty asked.

"It's like we're speaking different languages lately. He can't hear me. I can't hear him."

"Well," Ty said softly, looking over his shoulder. "You two have always figured it out."

Nick lowered his head, nodding. They always figured it out.

Ty grunted, and when Nick looked back at him, Ty was frowning harder, watching Zane as he wandered around the kitschy lobby. They shared a wry glance.

"Tonight's going to suck," Ty muttered as he turned away.

They wound up being able to get two rooms on the ground floor, and one on the second. Digger and Owen took the upper room because it had two double beds instead of one queen, and Owen tossed Ty and Nick the other sets of keys as they trudged up the shaky iron steps. The keys were actual keys, with little vintage plastic tags that were probably as old as Nick was. Nick snorted, a smirk playing over his lips.

"Eli would have loved this place," Ty grumbled as they walked to their rooms in the moonlight.

Nick let his smile break free as he ran his thumb over the plastic. Ty was right, Eli would have loved it. They said good-night to Ty and Zane, and they could hear Digger and Owen talking near the railing right above them. Digger leaned over far enough that Nick could see him outlined against the night sky.

"What up, Romeo?" he called softly.

"Go to sleep, Juliet," Kelly whispered in return, his grin bright enough to rival the moon. Nick stared at him as he handed the key to him, and Kelly let his fingers linger on Nick's when he took it. That simple touch and that enchanting smile were like torture for Nick, knowing he couldn't do more than pull Kelly to him and kiss him.

Kelly read his mind, and he tugged Nick to him with a smirk. The kiss was gentle, and Nick's eyes fluttered closed as Kelly took charge of it.

"You two never gonna make it all week," Digger observed from above. By the time they both looked up, he was gone.

Kelly took Nick's hand and held on as he unlocked the door. The room wasn't as bad as Nick had expected it to be. It seemed clean, anyway, and that was all he asked for. They were both coming out of their clothes almost before the door had latched, and it was only the habit of expecting trouble in the middle of the night that made Nick retain his boxers when he finally settled into the bed.

The light in the bathroom switched off, and Kelly prowled out into the bedroom, eyes on Nick, a smirk flirting over his lips. "Are we really not having sex on this trip?"

Nick snorted. At least they would both be on the same frustrated page the whole week. "We go without sex for weeks at a time when we're apart."

"When we're apart, being the key phrase there."

"I know," Nick assured him. He leaned against the flimsy headboard, absently rubbing at his sore quad muscle. All the walking and flying and driving were a little more than his surgically repaired knee was ready for.

"I've got something for that," Kelly told him, and he bent to search in his bag.

"If you come up with lube, I'm going to cry," Nick warned him.

Kelly laughed as he continued searching, and it pulled a grin out of Nick. He loved Kelly's laugh, possibly more than he loved his smile.

"You realize Eli won't know if we break the rules, right?" Kelly said as he tossed his medical kit on the end of the bed and crawled in beside Nick.

"Yeah, he will," Nick said quietly.

Kelly searched his eyes for a second, dropping the teasing. He finally nodded as if he understood Nick's determination. "Okay, babe," he whispered. He pulled a tin of homemade something out of his bag and twisted the top off.

"What is that?" Nick demanded. He'd submitted to a tin of homemade something one time years ago that Ty had sworn was magic, and he'd spent the next week peeling his skin off in strips.

"Emu oil," Kelly said, turning the little tin so Nick could see the label. It looked like it had been printed in someone's basement.

"Oh, *fuck* no," Nick blurted, and he reached for the edge of the bed to get away.

Kelly pounced and wrapped him up from behind, dragging him into the middle of the bed and holding him down. "I've used this on you before, it's fine!"

"Emu oil!" Nick cried as he lay flat on his back and stared up at Kelly with wide eyes. "Is it made out of real emus?"

"I . . . I assume so, yes."

"Gross. Gross!"

"It's all I have with me for sore muscles!"

"I'd rather have sore muscles than emu oil!"

Kelly was laughing hard enough that he could barely respond. He held up the little tin and shook his head as he composed himself. "Just let me try some, I need to know if it works well enough to buy more."

"Why would you buy *more*? Those poor fucking emus!"

Kelly hung his head and wheezed, bracing himself on Nick's belly. "Oh my God."

"This is worse than the itching lotion you tried to jizz all over me!"

Kelly was still trying to catch his breath, but he did manage to swipe two fingers through the emu oil and spread it over Nick's quad muscle as Nick tried to get away.

Nick cried out in horror.

"Now are you going to let me rub it in, or are you going to get it all over your princess fingers?" Kelly asked.

"This is horrible," Nick muttered, and he covered his eyes. Kelly's hands were warm and skillful when he started spreading the emu oil over Nick's thigh, but that wasn't enough to distract Nick from what he was using them to spread. "This is the worst thing a bird has ever done to me."

"Shame, since you've always treated cocks so well," Kelly said, his voice trembling.

Nick peered at him from between his fingers. Kelly's brow was furrowed in concentration as he worked the oil in. His long fingers were strong and talented, and soon enough Nick had forgotten his horror and was concentrating on Kelly instead. When Kelly looked up and met Nick's eyes with a wink, warmth stole through Nick's body.

Kelly's hands snuck a little higher, pushing under Nick's boxers, his fingers just grazing over the juncture of Nick's thigh and hip before he slid one hand down the inside of Nick's thigh.

"Babe," Nick whispered, shifting his hips and closing his eyes as his body reacted. "This is mean."

Kelly bent, tugging at the elastic band of the boxers, and he kissed Nick's hip. "When are we going to get some ink right here?" he asked, tracing Nick's hip bone with one finger. He bent to kiss it again, and when he spoke his lips moved against Nick's skin. "I think I'd like a target to aim for."

Nick breathed out slowly and grabbed a handful of Kelly's hair. Kelly raised his head and met Nick's eyes.

"The rules?" Kelly prompted gently.

"Come here," Nick demanded shakily, and Kelly crawled up his body to lie over him and kiss him. His skillful seduction meant Nick was ready for whatever Kelly wanted, and their hard cocks rubbed together through the thin material of their boxers. Nick wrapped his arms around Kelly, deepening the kiss.

He was about to roll them over when music began to blare. They both jumped, Kelly rolling off Nick and to his knees, Nick shooting straight up and into a sitting position to give the room a wild-eyed once over.

"What the fuck?" Kelly gasped.

"Is that your phone?" Nick asked.

"My phone's dead. Is it yours?"

"Must be, but I don't have that song on it and I lost service an hour into Wyoming."

They sat and listened to the music, and Nick soon recognized it as a salsa song from the late '90s. It had been one of Eli's favorites.

He clambered out of bed and searched through his jeans pockets for his phone, and when he found it, sure enough, it was blasting a song from the Pandora app they'd been running in the car.

"I thought Pandora required service and stuff," Kelly said, giving Nick's phone a wary look.

"It does. Looks like I picked up the network again. I must have left it running when we lost service in the car."

They stared at each other, and at the phone. Nick opened up the Pandora app, silencing it. He closed out the app to make sure it wouldn't malfunction again, then put his phone on silent so they'd be assured of no more shocks.

"That was super weird," Kelly finally blurted.

Nick nodded, still frowning at his phone.

"Sounded like the kind of stuff Sanchez listened to," Kelly added.

Nick hummed. "Interesting timing, too."

"Does that mean no rule-breaking?" Kelly asked, shoulders slumping.

Nick nodded furtively. "He told me he'd haunt my Irish ass."

"Motherfucking Sanchez!" Kelly rolled his eyes and flopped onto his back.

Nick laughed, albeit uncomfortably, and then he set the phone aside and turned out all the lights, crawling in next to Kelly. He felt guilty, but he wasn't sure if it was coming from his adherence to the rules and *not* fucking his boyfriend like they both so obviously wanted, or from the fact that he'd almost broken those rules less than twenty-four hours into the trip. The phone going off and the music choice from Pandora were a little spooky to him, too. Spooky enough that the hard-on Kelly had coaxed out of him was long gone.

It was for the best, really. He pulled Kelly close and they wrapped around each other, fitting together so well after so many months of being able to spend every night together. It didn't take too many minutes of Kelly's breath on Nick's neck, of Kelly's warm, lithe body against his to have him responding again. He groaned quietly, frustrated.

"Me too," Kelly whispered. He kissed Nick's collarbone, his cock growing harder against Nick's hip.

"Fuck," Nick growled. Kelly raised his head and Nick kissed him, rocking their hips together. "Why'd we think we could do this for a week?"

Kelly tossed his leg over Nick's hip and dove his fingers into Nick's hair, moaning into the kiss.

The music began again, blasting from Nick's phone, which was now even closer to them since he'd stuffed it under his pillow like he always did.

Kelly's hand tightened when he jumped, yanking Nick's hair and causing him to yelp.

"Fuck, I thought you turned it off," Kelly hissed.

"I did!"

"Fuck this," Kelly said, and he pushed Nick to his back and rolled, stretching across him to grab Nick's phone. Nick watched his face in the light of the screen as he did whatever he thought would keep the phone silent. Then he scowled as he turned it over to look at the buttons on the side and, Nick assumed, found that it was already on silent. He pushed the button that manually turned the volume down, then set it on the table carefully. "Okay, we're being haunted then."

Nick nodded.

"So. We can't fuck, because Sanchez is obviously watching us like a transparent creeper. And you and I both know we can't sleep in the same bed without . . . I mean . . . we'd probably fuck and not even be awake for it, it's just what we do."

Nick nodded again.

"Solutions?" Kelly demanded as he pushed himself up to sit. "I mean, I think maybe we need to not touch like we usually do. It's going to be torture if we keep petting each other but can't fuck."

"Okay," Nick said with a slow nod, even though the thought of not even being able to touch Kelly for the next week was almost physically painful. He found himself rubbing at the scar on his side, trying to make the throbbing stop. "If you think it'll be easier."

"I do. And you know what I think we need to do at night? If we're going to be celibate?"

"We . . . don't share a bed?" Nick winced as he said it.

Kelly's shoulders slumped. "It's just for six nights, right? We can do that. We'll just get double beds from here on out, sleep alone."

Nick nodded a third time.

"And for tonight, I mean, Ty and Zane are probably having the same problem, what do you want to bet?"

Nick sighed quietly. "I'll call Ty."

Kelly merely nodded, just like Nick had. He flopped to his back as Nick reached for the phone. It vibrated in his hand, nearly scaring him into dropping the damn thing. Ty's photo and name lit up the screen as it vibrated again.

"Hey," Nick answered with a laugh.

"So," Ty drew out.

"You want to switch sleep partners?"

Ty gave a relieved laugh. "How'd you know?"

"It's hard," Nick drawled, and Kelly started snickering at his side.

Minutes later, a very disgruntled Zane knocked at the door, and Nick let him in. He was about to give Kelly one last chaste kiss good-night, but Kelly stepped back and held up his fist instead. Nick stared at him, brow deeply furrowed in confusion, before he remembered their deal. He pressed his fist to Kelly's, feeling like an idiot as Zane watched with one eyebrow raised, and then he grudgingly headed for Ty and Zane's room, right next door.

Ty was sitting on one side of the queen-sized bed with his phone in his hand when Nick walked in.

"Hey," Ty grunted. He held up his phone. "My Pandora app is going nuts, do you know how to fix it?"

Nick stared at him, a shiver running up his spine. He shook his head. "Not really."

February 14, 2003

"Hey Red, did you know berries ain't a fruit?" Eli asked.

Nick glanced up from the poker chip he was rolling over his fingers, scowling. Eli was sitting at the other end of the table reading some sort of Valentine's Day special pamphlet. "What?"

Eli seemed troubled when he lowered the paper. "This says they're not a fruit."

"Berries?" Kelly asked.

Owen plunked four beers on the table and sat to Nick's left. "Berries have to be a fruit."

"This says they're not," Eli insisted.

"You're getting fruit facts off a casino bar menu?" Ty asked. He was lounging on the long bench against the wall, resting his feet on the bench beside him and using Digger as a backrest.

"It's not a menu, it's a pamphlet."

Ty made a gesture with his hand, as if asking what the difference was.

"What are they if they ain't fruit?" Digger asked.

"They're berries!" Eli told them. He waved the paper around.

Nick shook his head and looked back down at the chip, turning it over. It was a thousand-dollar chip he'd won at the blackjack table.

"But berries are a kind of fruit," Kelly insisted.

"No, this thing," Eli said as he handed the paper to Kelly. "It says 'avocados are not only a fruit, they are *also* a berry.' That means berries aren't fruit."

"No," Kelly grunted.

"Yes!" Eli shouted. "Look it!"

"Well no, berries *are* a fruit if it says an avocado is both, right?" Owen said.

Digger waved his drink around. "Ho ho. You can be both and not the same at the same time!"

"What?" Ty asked.

"A paper can be a menu and also a pamphlet, but pamphlets can't be menus," Eli explained.

Nick closed his eyes and ran the poker chip over the bridge of his nose. "I can't believe we're having this conversation. *Again.*"

"Did you know this?" Ty asked him.

"Why do you think they list it on menus and stuff as fruit *and* berries?" Nick asked.

"I just . . . I just thought they were being insistent."

"Oh Jesus!" Kelly cried. "Vegetables aren't real, guys!"

"Are they figments of your imagination?" Owen asked between sips of his beer. "Like . . . leprechauns and gnomes."

"Give me a leprechaun salad, hold the veggies," Nick drawled, and he and Owen tried desperately to avoid eye contact so they could maintain their stern expressions.

"Stop it! This says it's a culinary term, there's no such thing as vegetables!" Kelly shook the paper in Eli's face. "*Why would you hand this to me?*"

Eli laughed heartily.

"My mind!" Kelly cried.

Owen plucked the pamphlet from his fingers and frowned as he perused the page they'd been reading. "Although berries are fruits," he read, "There are many fruits which are considered berries by most people that may not actually be classified as berries."

"So wait, berries *are* fruits then," Ty said.

"But berries aren't berries," Nick added.

"Some berries are fruits but not all fruits are berries," Digger tried. "This is some philosophical shit, dog. What else does it say?"

"Oranges are berries," Owen announced.

"No," Kelly snarled. He slammed his hand on the table. "No!"

Owen was fighting a smile as he continued scanning the information. "There are also false berries."

"Fucking posers," Digger muttered.

Ty finally sat up and leaned against the table. "What the hell is a false berry?"

"Bananas. Cucumbers. Oh, and cranberries and blueberries aren't berries either."

"An orange is a berry but a blueberry isn't?" Eli asked.

Nick swallowed a large gulp of Guinness. "I thought cucumbers were vegetables."

"Vegetables don't exist," Owen drawled.

"That's some fucked-up menu," Digger said.

"It's not a menu, it's a pamphlet!" Eli shouted.

"That's a fucked-up pamphlet," Digger said with a sip of his drink.

"Berry fucked up," Eli added, almost giggling.

"Next person who says berry is getting hit," Kelly warned.

Owen put the paper down, trying not to smile.

Nick put a finger on it and slid it toward himself. It was some sort of fun facts of Valentine's Day gift-giving page that Eli had picked up at some weird café in Wyoming. Why he'd held on to it, Nick didn't know. He scanned it, shaking his head and grinning. "This says honeysuckle is a berry," he announced.

Kelly stood and threw his napkin at Nick. It didn't even make it to the end of the table, and they both watched it flutter onto Nick's plate.

"What the hell is honeysuckle?" Owen asked.

Digger gasped. "You don't know what honeysuckle is?"

"Goddamn Yankee," Ty muttered into his glass.

"It's a vine," Kelly explained. "Little flowers you can suck the juice out of."

Nick glanced up, grinning. "It's not a vine, it's a berry."

"No!" Kelly cried. "No, no, no! Oranges are fruit, honeysuckle is yummy, cranberries are berries, vegetables are real, and that's it!"

The table fell silent, all of them waiting for someone else to break the silence.

"So," Digger finally said. "Does this make guacamole a fruit dip?"

The table erupted yet again, and Nick sat back with a grin, watching them fondly. His friends . . . his brothers. A sense of melancholy swamped him as he realized that these moments were waning, that every night was bringing them closer to the end. Suddenly he needed air, and silence.

Nick set the pamphlet down and took a gulp of his Guinness as Digger waxed poetic about guacamole. When Nick put his glass down, it made a louder sound than he'd intended, and the table vibrated.

It drew the attention of the others, and they all watched him as he stood up. "Going to bed," he grunted.

"Hey Irish, you okay?" Ty asked him, and he was scowling when Nick looked back at him.

Nick gave him a curt nod and tried to smile. He flicked the thousand-dollar chip to Eli, who caught it deftly. "Just need some good sleep. Night."

He turned and headed for the door. Their hotel was just across the street from the casino, but Nick hesitated when he got to the sidewalk. It was freezing. Snow drifted in lazy flurries around him. But still, the urge to stroll under the moonlight was overwhelming. Deadwood, South Dakota, wasn't exactly a huge town; he could probably lap it before the others left the casino bar and had a chance to miss him.

He wasn't really paying much attention, so it startled him when Kelly appeared at his side. Kelly laughed at him when he jumped and cursed.

"What the hell, Doc?"

"You going for a walk?" Kelly asked.

Nick cleared his throat.

"You had that look." Kelly unzipped his coat and pulled the lapel, turning to show Nick a lighter and two blunts, hidden in the lining. "Mind if I join?"

Nick rolled his eyes and smirked, jutting his chin toward the street. "We'll probably freeze, you know."

"I'll keep you warm," Kelly crooned, and he slipped his arm into the crook of Nick's elbow.

They spent an hour wandering around Deadwood, looking at the historic markers without the crowds of the day, Nick barely keeping the excitement out of his voice when he started telling Kelly the bits and pieces of Deadwood's history he knew. Kelly let him ramble, actually listening and asking questions. They wandered out of the historic main street area and into the residential streets, climbing the steep, winding road that led to the cemetery.

They had to scale the gates to get in, but once they were inside, they had an incomparable view of the town and the mountains that surrounded the gulch the town had been built in.

They hunched together under the flagpole on the overlook, sharing the blunt Kelly had lit, the graves of Wild Bill Hickok, Seth Bullock, and Calamity Jane as their backdrop.

"I think, when this is over, I'm going back to Colorado," Kelly said. His words formed wisps in the cold, floating away with the snow.

"That little town we passed through?" Nick asked, and he wondered why his heart was sinking, why his chest felt tighter as they talked about it. Sidewinder was no more. There was no team to go back to, there was nothing left. Of course they'd each need to find somewhere to go, something to do. Of course they'd each be leaving to make a new home. And that little town with its friendly main street and its quirky shops and cottages nestled amongst the Rockies where Kelly could build himself a cabin in wide open spaces, that was the perfect place for Kelly.

"Yeah. It felt right," Kelly answered, his voice taking on that relaxed whisper Nick knew so well. "Felt like . . ."

"Home?" Nick provided, shocked when the word came out sounding sad.

Kelly turned his head, still smiling serenely. "Yeah. I never really had anywhere that felt like home, you know? Not since my mom and dad died. Closest thing I've ever had to that feeling is you, man."

Nick blinked rapidly and fought to swallow. Kelly's parents had died in a car crash when he was ten years old. He'd spent the next eight years of his life bouncing from his aging grandparents to foster homes to the Navy. Being with Sidewinder was the longest time he'd ever spent with one set of people. Nick stared at him as flakes landed on his shoulders, melted in his hair.

Kelly was laughing, his entire body shaking and his grin wide. "I mean, how fucking sad is that? Twenty-six years old and the closest thing I got to home is my best friend? It's time I found somewhere permanent."

He brought the blunt up to take a drag and then passed it to Nick. Nick took it with fingers that didn't feel and eyes that didn't see. He'd spent his entire life trying to be everything for the people he loved, trying to be what they needed. For a brief second just now, he thought he'd actually succeeded for Kelly. And he was trying not to linger on it, trying desperately not to let it bring him crashing down, but to hear

Kelly say that wasn't good enough . . . that he wasn't good enough to be called home . . .

Nick took the hit and stared down at the town, watching the snowstorm rolling in over the hills.

"Nicko?"

Nick heard him, but he couldn't tear his eyes away from the twinkling lights below. He didn't want to. He hummed to let Kelly know he was listening.

"What do you think?" Kelly asked.

Nick licked his lips, closing his eyes. "I think we should head back before that snow gets worse."

They were as silent as the falling snow on their trek back to the hotel. Nick could feel Kelly's eyes on him, but he just couldn't find the energy within himself any longer to fake it. Not for himself, not for Kelly, not for Ty. Not for any of them. He was tired, and now that they'd stripped the honor of being a Marine from him and taken everything he'd ever worked for, what was the fucking point of being strong for anyone? What was the point of trying to be *home* for anyone? What was the point of pretending anything was okay?

The elevator ride up to their floor was awkward as hell, and Nick closed his eyes with a sigh. For the first time in his life, he could feel life crumbling and he couldn't gather the pieces fast enough. He didn't have the glue to put it all back together.

He murmured a good-night to Kelly when they got to his room, and Nick trudged to the next door, struggling with the key and then shouldering his way in. Kelly stood at his own door, probably watching Nick with that confused frown he could sometimes get when he was trying to figure out a puzzle. Nick didn't look back at him, though. He closed the door and leaned against it, taking a deep breath when he heard the other door close out in the hall.

"Irish?" Ty said from the darkness of the room.

"Yeah, it's me."

"You okay?" Eli asked, accompanied by a rustle of sheets. "We were about to go looking for you."

"Yeah, I'm sorry. We wandered further away than we meant to," Nick said as he stripped out of his clothes and headed for the shower. He stayed in there just long enough to get the weed smell off, long enough for the others to fall asleep, then he fumbled around in his suitcase in the dark, hunting for some clean briefs to sleep in.

"Rico," Eli whispered from one of the beds.

Nick squinted through the darkness as he stepped into his briefs, almost tripping when he missed one of the leg holes. He struggled into them, pulling them up his hips.

"Come bunk with me, man," Eli whispered, and Nick heard him pat the mattress beside him.

Nick edged his way across the floor, leading with the side of his foot because he knew damn well it was a minefield for toes down there. He found the end of the bed and crawled into it, finding Eli's leg under the covers and following it up so he could settle in beside Eli without squishing him. He was still a little buzzed and floating, and usually he knew better than to grope his teammates when he got like that. Tonight it didn't matter, though. They weren't teammates anymore, and this was Eli so he could fucking grope him all he wanted.

They'd been rotating bedmates the entire trip. It was supposed to be Eli's night to get the bed to himself, but Nick didn't question him. He threw himself down next to him, facing him, and started struggling with the sheets. Eli helped him get settled, pulling the covers up around them.

"Doc's leaving," Nick murmured miserably.

"That little town we went through?" Eli asked.

Nick nodded.

"Damn. That was faster than I was expecting."

Nick was silent. His eyes were adjusting to the dim light, and he could see Eli clearly.

"That why you're upset?"

"Am I upset?" Nick countered. He wasn't trying to be a smart-ass, he was just seeking answers from one of the only men he trusted to give them.

Eli clucked his tongue and draped his arm over Nick. "Yeah, *papá*. You are."

Nick closed his eyes. Of course he was. The only family he'd ever known was breaking away piece by piece and there wasn't a damn thing he could do about it. "I'm not ready to lose everyone."

"*Vírate para que te pueda acurrucar, mijo*," Eli grumbled.

Nick snorted, hating to smile when he felt like such utter shit. But if he was translating that correctly, Eli was demanding a cuddle and Nick couldn't help but laugh. He rolled over obediently, letting Eli pull him close.

"I ain't ready neither," Eli finally said. He pushed his nose and mouth against the back of Nick's shoulder. "I thought you were wearing more clothes when I asked you for a cuddle."

"I just got out of the shower, dude, what did you expect?" They both snickered, trying to stay quiet. Eli held him tighter instead of pushing him away.

The bed opposite them squeaked, and Nick could just barely make out Ty raising his head. "Thought it was my night for cuddles," he grumbled.

"I pulled rank," Eli said, right in Nick's ear.

"You can't pull rank anymore," Ty pointed out, and he tossed his covers back and sat up. "What's going on?"

"Doc's decided to leave," Eli said, the smile gone from his voice.

"That little town in Colorado?" Ty asked.

Nick and Eli both grunted in answer.

"Team's breaking up on us," Eli muttered.

Ty sat on the edge of his bed, head cocked, shoulders slumped. Without another word between the three of them, Ty pushed to his feet and shuffled across the floor between the beds. Eli scooted back, pulling Nick with him like Nick was a rag doll, and Ty crawled into the bed and tugged the covers up around all three of them.

Nick closed his eyes and relaxed into the warmth of Eli's arms around him, of Ty's soft breaths on his face.

"Housekeeping going to find us in the morning and be all scandalized," Eli whispered. "Who wants to get naked?"

Nick bit his lip against a laugh. Ty began to snicker. "Nick's already naked," he said.

"Am not."

"You're also wet, dude, what the hell?" Ty said, sounding appalled as he looked at the hand he'd just put on Nick. He didn't back away from them, though, just tossed his arm over them both regardless.

"Rico can get it, I don't care," Eli crooned.

It took a few minutes for their laughter to settle again. It felt good, and Nick knew this easy camaraderie was exactly what he'd sought out when he'd come back to the room and left Kelly standing in the hallway.

"Other people have always come and gone," Ty finally whispered. "But you've always got us, Irish. It's always been us three."

Eli waited a few beats in the dense silence, then added a snickering, "Like the Three Amigos."

Nick smiled, relief flooding him and working to soothe the heartache he'd allowed himself to let in. "I love you both."

Ty patted his hip, and he could feel Eli's heart beating against his back when Eli squeezed him in a tight hug. They'd done this many times over the years, usually in the middle of a desert, trying to stay warm. Sometimes it wasn't the body that needed that shared warmth, though, it was the heart and mind and soul.

"We'll stick together from here on out," Ty said.

"Buy us one of those swank-ass yachts," Eli added. "Live on the water like we always talked about."

Nick was nodding, his eyes still closed.

Ty patted his face. "Three of us. No matter what. Deal?"

"Deal," Nick and Eli both whispered.

June 10, 2013

Kelly woke with a start, blinking away the remnants of the dream he'd been having. He rolled and reached for Nick, murmuring his name when his hand landed on hard muscle and warm skin.

"Doc," his bedmate whispered as he swatted at Kelly's hand. "No snuggles."

"Shit! Sorry," Kelly gasped, squinting at Zane in the early morning light. He'd forgotten about switching partners in the middle of the night. He sat up, shoving the blankets off his legs. "I need to talk to Nick."

"It's not even sunrise yet," Zane groaned.

"He'll be awake," Kelly said with certainty as he shoved out of the bed and jogged to the door.

"What's wrong?" Zane called after him, still trying to whisper. "Doc?"

Kelly ignored him, barreling out onto the walkway and using Zane's key to get into the room next door. He was quieter than he meant to be, because his unannounced entry didn't wake either Ty or Nick. He went to the side of the bed Nick always slept on and patted Nick's face to make sure, because odds were if it was Ty, his head would be under the pillow instead of on it.

Nick gasped and raised his head, striking out. Kelly had been ready for it, though, and he deflected Nick's hand with his forearm, ducking out of the way in case Nick followed with that devious right that almost always finished the job his left hook didn't.

He trapped Nick's arm between both of his and leaned closer to Nick's face so Nick could see him in the predawn light. "It's me, babe, just me."

"Kelly?" Nick grunted, his voice choked with sleep. "What's wrong?"

"I need to talk to you," Kelly whispered. "It's really important."

Nick pushed onto his elbow, reaching for Kelly's face, a concerned frown marring his handsome features.

"What?" the pillow behind Nick groaned. It shuddered and then flipped over, and Ty raised his head like a bear emerging from hibernation. "What?"

"Go back to sleep," Kelly urged. He crouched beside the bed, meeting Nick's eyes. "It's important," he repeated.

"Okay," Nick said, struggling to sit up.

Ty moaned and groaned and bitched and muttered as he struggled his way out of the cocoon of sheets he'd created during the night. He thumped out of bed, still grousing at them and scratching his bare belly as he shuffled around the end of the bed. "Switch places," he said to Kelly as he headed for the door and the other room, where Zane had probably gone back to sleep alone in his bed.

Through the wall, Kelly heard him speaking to Zane as soon as he entered the other room, probably diving into bed with him to get some time to themselves before the day started. Kelly returned his attention to Nick and took a shaky breath to calm himself. Nick sat up and started to scoot over to let Kelly into bed with him, but Kelly stopped him with a hand on his shoulder, and then crawled over Nick to aim for the warm spot Ty had left behind.

He intended to crawl over Nick, anyway. He got as far as straddling Nick's lap before he lost all self-control and took Nick's face in his hands to kiss him. Neither of them had brushed their teeth, but Kelly was pretty sure Nick cared just as little as he did.

Kelly sat in Nick's lap, his forehead pressed to Nick's as he held on to his face.

"Kelly?" Nick finally whispered.

"Sorry," Kelly grunted. He kissed Nick one more time and then crawled off him. The sheets had already cooled because both Ty and Nick loved to keep the temperature in a room at near freezing. Kelly hurried to get the covers back up over himself, then pulled closer to Nick so he could see Nick's face as they spoke.

"What's wrong?" Nick demanded.

"I had a dream."

Nick blinked at him. His lips parted, then he pressed them tight and scowled, obviously fighting to be patient and let Kelly explain. "Okay."

"Do you remember the night in Deadwood? When I decided to move to Colorado and I talked to you about it in that cemetery?"

Nick's expression didn't change, but Kelly could see the absolute pain in his eyes.

Kelly nodded before Nick could give him an answer. "You remember."

"Yeah. What about it?"

"I dreamed about it. It's the first time I've thought about that night in . . . years. Ten years. I remember you being upset after, and I could never quite figure out why. And I never really gave it all that much thought after, I just . . . I just carried on. But I dreamed about it and I figured it out."

"Kels, what are you talking about?" Nick asked, and he sounded exhausted.

Kelly licked his lips and scooted closer, placing a gentle palm against Nick's cheek. "What I said to you that night. It was fucking horrible, Nick. I told you that you were the closest thing to home I'd ever had. And then in the next breath, I told you it wasn't good enough."

Nick swallowed hard, blinking fast.

"I'm so sorry," Kelly breathed.

Nick's hand came to rest on Kelly's hip, his fingers digging in. "You woke me up to apologize for something you said more than ten years ago?"

Kelly winced, feeling sort of stupid when it was laid out like that. "I guess, I . . ."

"Kels," Nick hissed, bringing his hand up to cup Kelly's face. He kissed Kelly before either of them could say more, and when he pulled back, he brushed his nose against Kelly's. "Thank you."

Kelly puffed out a breath in relief. "I was so stupid," he said, pain lancing through him at the thought of what his careless words must have done to Nick. It must have broken his fucking heart to hear Kelly say he wasn't good enough. "You were always my beacon in a storm. You were always the light calling me to safety, and I was so fucking stupid to say that wasn't enough for me. To lose that."

"You never lost it," Nick broke in.

"Yes, I did. I did. Not only did I lose it, but I pushed it away. You never looked at me the same way after that night, you didn't treat me the same way. And I didn't deserve what you gave me either, because I hurt you so much more than I ever realized. I know now what I didn't then, that even if I built it from the ground up, I still couldn't make a home for myself without you in it. It was always you. I woke up and I couldn't go another minute without saying I'm sorry after I realized what I'd done."

Nick sighed, but he didn't say anything as they stared at each other. The sun was rising, and apparently neither Nick nor Ty had bothered to close the curtains the night before, so the light was already warming the room, already touching Nick's eyes with the most amazing green Kelly had ever been witness to.

"Nick," Kelly whispered, and he tried to scoot even closer. Nick's hand tightened on his hip, keeping him at bay. Kelly cleared his throat, thrown by the inability to touch Nick whenever he wanted. "You gave so much of yourself to all of us. So much. You were everything we needed. You . . . you were my beacon. When I was drifting and thought I'd drift all my life, you gave me a home. You were Ty's rock, you kept him grounded and sane and good when he could have gone tailspinning off into Bond villain territory. You were Eli's brother, you were Owen's sounding board, and hell, I'm sure you provided Digger with matches and then put the fire out for him after."

Nick snorted and closed his eyes.

Kelly was shocked to realize he was almost in tears. "You gave so much of yourself to each of us, and we never even realized it. And you never asked for anything in return. Did you?"

"I . . . don't—"

"You know you didn't," Kelly said forcefully. "You cut yourself into teeny tiny pieces and just kept giving them away, but you never got them back because once you gave them up, we cherished them so much we kept them. And you never asked for replacements and you wound up—"

Kelly blinked away the tears blurring his vision. Nick used his thumb to wipe them away from Kelly's cheeks.

"I've been so angry at you," Kelly admitted. "I couldn't figure out why you weren't putting yourself first, why you couldn't just be selfish, just once. But I get it now. If you had been selfish, none of us would be what we are now. You . . . Eli was right, you're the linchpin, Nicko. And I'm so sorry I've been giving you a hard time for protecting us. I'm so sorry."

"We both know that's not the only reason you've been angry with me," Nick said. "I deserved it."

"You did. But I'm over that, and I'm still angry. And I just figured out why, and I needed to come in here and . . ."

Nick's hand was gentle on Kelly's cheek as Kelly trailed off, his fingers sliding into Kelly's hair, his thumb at Kelly's cheekbone. "I'm glad you came in here," he finally said. "Thank you."

Kelly nodded and sighed. He rested his hand against Nick's chest, twirling the tips of his fingers through the soft hair there. "I know I made a new rule, but will you hold me anyway?" he finally asked, voice choked with laughter.

Nick snorted and rolled to his back, sliding his arm under Kelly's head. "Come on."

Kelly laid his head on Nick's chest, wrapping around him and closing his eyes in relief. "Zane's all built and stuff, but his cuddles aren't the same," he teased.

Nick squeezed him tighter, and he shoved his face in Kelly's hair. From somewhere above their heads came a tiny, muffled meow.

Kelly lifted his head to see Jiminy and Cricket struggling over the mountain of pillows piled against the headboard, all fuzz and whiskers and blue eyes.

"Hi, babies," Kelly whispered. Nick groaned as Kelly rested his head on his chest again, and the kittens joined him, curling up on Nick like he'd been sent to be their very own personal belly warmer.

Nick gave a harsh sigh as Jiminy burrowed under his chin. Kelly tried not to laugh, laying claim to his own space before it could be taken over. Cricket shoved her rear end against his face, vibrating his nose with her purrs.

Every time Sidewinder had come into possession of animals, whether they were rescuing a feral cat from a blizzard, dog-sitting a mutt for a friend, or dealing with Kelly's very poor impulse control while volunteering at the humane society and adopting two kittens who had reached the end of their allotted time, the animals had always gravitated toward Nick. And Nick fucking hated it.

Kelly's eyes began to grow heavy again as the purring lulled him back toward sleep. He fought against it, though, letting his thoughts wander back to that last road trip. As they'd traveled all over the country, each of them had found somewhere that spoke to them, called to them.

Kelly, then Owen, and then Digger had all left to go find their own place in the world, leaving Nick and Eli and Ty to make the trip back to DC alone. But Kelly had been the first to leave. He'd pined for that spot in Colorado, that little town that felt like home, that plot of land in the middle of nowhere with the for sale sign that had been the perfect place to build his cabin. Eventually the call of that place had been too much for a young man who'd had his fill of adventure, and he'd said good-bye to his boys and left.

Some nights, he'd lain awake and regretted it, lain awake and cried because he couldn't go back.

"Did you blame me?" Kelly blurted.

Nick jerked awake. "What?"

"After I left. You all kept going without me for a while. But then the others all left, too, because I had broken the seal. Did you blame me? For leaving? For killing the team?"

Nick was silent, his fingers digging into the skin of Kelly's arm, his heart racing under Kelly's hand, his breathing so hard that it woke the kittens and started them purring again. After several torturous moments of waiting for an answer, Nick nodded.

"Yeah," he croaked. "Yeah, I did."

February 17, 2003

"I don't get the Colorado state signs," Eli said as Nick was navigating through the twists and turns of yet another mountain range.

They'd left Grand Junction, Colorado, that morning at the ass crack of dawn, and they were still only halfway to Santa Fe. They'd kept passing in and out of Colorado the past couple days, and every time they passed back into the state, they made fun of the plain brown sign with white lettering that said, "Welcome to Colorful Colorado."

"What do you mean, you don't get them?" Nick asked.

"Colorado is not colorful," Eli insisted. "All we've seen is green in the mountains, brown in the plains. And white everywhere. They could fucking run the Mountain Leaders course up here, bro. It's that *un*colorful."

"I think it's a play on the name," Ty offered. He was in the backseat, taking a rest from his last turn driving. He was sitting backward, his shoulders wedged between the two front seats as they played cards in the back.

"What do you mean?" Eli asked as he turned to scowl at them.

"Colorado," Nick said, glancing at Eli quickly and then turning his attention back to the winding road. "It's a fucking Spanish word, dude. *Colorado*," he said again, except this time he said it with an accent, as if he were speaking Spanish.

Eli was silent, and Nick glanced at him again, raising both eyebrows when he found Eli staring at him. Ty turned and leaned his elbow on the console, and the sudden silence from the card game in the back told Nick that they'd drawn the attention of everyone.

Nick had to look away fast before Eli could see him smiling. He covered his mouth with his hand and focused everything he had on the road, frowning to compensate.

"Dude," Owen grunted. "Did that never occur to you before now?"

"You white people don't say it right, okay," Eli finally growled.

Ty and Owen burst out laughing, and Nick could see Digger in the far back, shaking his head as he shuffled the deck of cards they were playing with.

"Did you ever wonder why Montana has so many *mountains*?" Nick asked Eli, barely keeping the laughter out of his voice.

"*Tu madre*, bro."

Nick was laughing so hard he had to slow their progress so he didn't wreck the Bronco.

"Montana, that's fucked up. There weren't even mountains in Montana, man, they were just, like . . . like . . . lumpy plains."

"Lumpy plains?" Ty cried, and they were all rolling around in the back, no seat belts in sight, cards forgotten.

"You better stop fucking talking to me until your ass is bilingual inside your head, okay." Eli had to grip the handle above as Nick took a turn a little too hard. "Pay attention to the road, Rico! Jesus Christ!"

There was a chorus of complaints and laughter from the back, and Nick wiped his eyes and slowed the Bronco to a near crawl. If he laughed any harder, he'd have to pull over.

Eli was still grumbling, his foot on the dash and his knuckles turning white as he gripped the handle. Nick glanced into the rearview mirror at the others. They were laughing, grappling around for the seat belts to secure themselves, arguing over whether Digger would fit in the middle seat or if he had to stay in the back with the luggage.

The only thing missing was Kelly.

Nick's grin fell. The realization that Kelly was gone and wasn't coming back hit him just as hard as it had the last time it had confronted him. It was instantly sobering. He cleared his throat and focused on the road, fighting the melancholy he'd been trying to ignore since they'd left Kelly behind in the tiny town near Colorado Springs where he intended to start his new life.

"Irish?" Ty said, gripping Nick's arm and shaking him. "You awake?"

"Huh? Yeah. Why? What?"

"If you're tired we can switch up. You been driving all morning."

Nick glanced over his shoulder at Ty, damn near knocking his chin into Ty's nose because he was leaning so close to Nick's face. He shoved at Ty's chest with his elbow. "Calm yourself."

"Lumpy plains," Eli muttered, shaking his head in disgust as he watched the scenery pass by. "I'm too brown for this."

June 10, 2013

"Sometimes Eli would get mixed up, lose words," Owen said. He was sitting in the middle row of seats with Nick as Ty drove.

Zane was enjoying the stories they were sharing. He felt like he was finally getting to know not only Elias Sanchez, but also Owen, Digger, Nick, and Kelly better. It was the first time he could remember that they'd all been together when they weren't being chased or threatened or hurt or any number of other unsavory activities that often got in the way of small talk.

He was sitting sideways so he could see into the back as they talked. He wouldn't be able to do it long because it would make him sick as a dog, but watching the other men as they talked about Eli was compelling.

"He grew up speaking Spanish at home, English everywhere else. So he would just sort of weave them into each other without realizing he was doing it," Nick explained. His voice sounded distant and sad, and Zane's smile faded as he listened. "It made for some interesting conversations sometimes. He had a great sense of humor."

"Lumpy plains," Ty said under his breath, snickering. "He also called a bunch of bushes 'green rocks' one time. And on one of the recon missions we ran, he kept talking about 'the big blue blanket,' and then he finally got all angry at himself and shouted 'the sky! It's called the sky!'"

Zane barked a laugh. "I get it," he assured them before they could get defensive on Eli's behalf.

Zane hadn't grown up speaking both languages equally like Eli apparently had, but he had been taught both from an early age thanks to his mother's Spanish heritage. She'd insisted on teaching him the dialect of Spain, the language her great-great-great-great-grandfather had spoken. Needless to say, he'd had to teach himself the different local dialects when he'd gotten older. He sometimes hit words that had no equivalent in any of the languages he knew, and was left searching for a replacement. He could only imagine the difficulties Eli had faced with the language barriers.

"The gentlemen in the back have to pee," Digger announced.

Zane was watching Ty's profile as he drove, and the way Ty's eyes flicked up to check the rearview mirror when Digger spoke made Zane's stomach flip pleasantly.

They were only one day into the trip following Eli's rules, and Zane was already regretting the fact that no one had protested the no-sex clause. Nick and Kelly were having the same problems, Zane had learned that much from Kelly last night. Owen had a steady girlfriend in San Diego, so he had merely shrugged about the sexbargo, as Kelly had called it. And Digger didn't seem to care. Zane didn't know if he was in a relationship with someone, and no one had asked him. He just didn't seem bothered by the sudden lack of sex in his life.

Zane was bothered by it, though. He watched Ty with a smile, watched the way his hands moved on the steering wheel, the way the sunlight hit his hazel eyes and made him squint away from it as he kept his eyes on the road, the way his knee bounced since the Suburban was an automatic and he didn't have a clutch to deal with.

He flicked the turn signal with long, talented fingers, and Zane had to look away from him as they changed lanes. He just barely repressed a frustrated groan.

The song on the radio stuttered, skipping like an old record. Ty tapped the display.

"Dude, how does an iPhone skip?" Ty asked Nick.

"I don't know, the Pandora app was being weird last night." Nick stuck his hand up between Ty and Zane. "Let me have it."

Zane unplugged the phone and handed it back. The music abruptly quit when he disconnected the phone, which was exactly what it should have done. A few seconds later, though, the music blipped back on. The song wasn't the same classic rock tune it had been struggling to play, but rather old-school salsero that made every muscle in Zane's body want to dance.

"Dude," Kelly said from the back row. "How much of that salsa music do you have on your phone?"

"I don't have any of it on my phone," Nick insisted. "It's not even connected!"

Ty banged on the dash of the Suburban. "Get a hold of yourself, Helen!"

The music stopped again, leaving them with that odd static coming over the speakers that only a disconnected AUX accessory could make.

Nick groaned from the backseat. "He told me he would haunt me if we didn't follow directions, he said he'd haunt my Irish ass."

"Dude," Digger said quietly.

"But we *are* following directions," Owen said, and he took the phone from Nick as Nick started cussing at it.

"It started playing salsa music last night too," Nick admitted as he sat back and scowled, watching Owen tap at the screen of his phone.

Owen made a clucking sound without looking up. "And what rule were you two breaking?"

Kelly and Nick both muttered an answer, neither of them really audible. But Zane knew exactly what they were saying. He glanced at Ty, who met his eyes, biting his lip against a smile. They'd been preparing to break the same rule last night when Ty's phone had gone haywire. Ty shook his head, and Zane tossed him a wink before he looked away. They'd keep that to themselves.

"Must have been a rogue signal passing by," Owen decided. "A big rig with a satellite or CB or something sending off a burst. It's pretty common. And your Bluetooth is connecting to Helen right now, that's why it's doing weird things."

"Who is Helen?" Zane asked, turning to look back at them.

"The car," Owen said, as if that had already been discussed and decided and Zane should probably know that. "She's a Suburban."

Zane rolled his eyes and gave Ty a dirty look. He knew exactly whose twisted mind *that* had come from.

"The gentlemen in the back still need to pee!" Digger called.

Ty grunted. "The gentlemen in the back need to be fucking patient!"

"The gentlemen in the back are going to piss in your Wheaties if you don't find a fucking gas station," Kelly warned.

"We're in the middle of a national park," Ty growled. "There aren't any gas stations!"

"I think we need to redefine the word gentlemen," Owen said nonchalantly.

Nick thumped his bare feet onto the console and crossed his arms as he relaxed against the door panel. "Are we there yet?"

Once you reach Yellowstone, find a campground as far from the little villages as possible. You've probably already figured out what you're supposed to do for the next couple days, so here we go.

Two camps, no more than two miles apart. Two flags, made of whatever you can find. Two teams, Alpha and Bravo. These will be your teams for the rest of the trip. Split up by drawing straws. If you have an uneven number, or someone is too old and decrepit to play, make the uneven straw a rogue who can be bought, bribed, or blackmailed by either team. We're playing Jacksonville rules.

You start the game at midnight, and it doesn't end for the next 24 hours. Winning team will find out what their prize is in the next letter, which you will open only when one of the flags has been captured or the 24 hours are up.

We were once counted among the finest spec ops teams in any military. It's time you remembered what made us so special.

"What are Jacksonville rules?" Zane asked hesitantly after Owen had finished the letter.

They were sitting on several wet benches in front of Old Faithful, amid the crowds of people milling about with cameras and children and ponchos, waiting for the geyser to blow. The crowd was making Kelly anxious, and he wasn't sure quite why. He edged closer to Digger, and Digger put a hand around his shoulders, patting him like he knew Kelly wasn't comfortable.

"Jacksonville rules mean no weapons," Ty explained. "Use your environment and any resources you can, but no weaponry. Basically."

"There are more nuances to Jacksonville rules," Owen added. "But basically it boils down to, if you're bleeding or on fire, yell time-out."

Zane nodded, looking a little sick. "Okay then."

"I'll get something to use as straws," Owen said, and he handed the letter to Nick before strolling off to the manicured tree line toward the parking lot.

Kelly turned to the geyser. The last time they'd been here, they'd never caught the damn thing going off. One early morning they'd actually seen it from the road as they'd driven up, and that had been their last attempt; they'd left Yellowstone that morning, all grumbling variations of, "Old Faithful my ass."

"Hey," Nick said from behind him.

Kelly turned to find Nick just out of arm's reach, his head cocked, his brow deeply furrowed, and both hands stuffed in his pockets.

"You okay?" he asked Kelly.

"No, but I'm not sure why," Kelly admitted. "I think I'll be fine when we're out of this crowd."

Nick didn't respond, he merely continued to frown at Kelly. Kelly offered him a smile, wishing he could step closer and lean into him to ease the anxiety. He'd made the no-touching rule himself, though, and it was best to not even tempt either of them with that sort of contact. He found himself hoping that when they did split up into teams, he and Nick would be on opposite sides.

Owen returned with a handful of twigs. He'd cut them so that three of them were the same length. The others he'd left longer. He held them all in his fist, making sure the tips were even. "Alpha are the short ones," he decided, and he pulled the first stick and held it up.

One by one they chose, splitting themselves into Alpha and Bravo. Ty, Zane, and Kelly wound up with the Alpha sticks, and Nick, Owen, and Digger had the uneven Bravo sticks.

Kelly gripped his stick tighter and watched Nick as his heart pounded. Was he relieved or disappointed? He couldn't even tell.

There was a change in the atmosphere of the crowd, and a roaring, gushing sound behind them. Kelly stared at Nick, though, his heart pounding too hard for him to breathe, much less rip his eyes away and turn to see the spectacle. Nick's gaze drifted upward, his lips parting the higher he looked. The others all stood the same way, awestruck by the erupting geyser.

Nick reached out almost without seeming to realize he was doing it, without taking his eyes off the tower of water and steam, and he gripped Kelly's arm and turned him around, forcing him to watch. And suddenly Kelly could breathe again. He could feel his heart hammering at his chest, and he could feel the warmth of Nick's touch as it trailed down his arm and into his hand, tangling their fingers together. He was aware of Ty and Owen struggling to get Seymour out so they could take his picture in front of Old Faithful, but he didn't move to help them.

Minutes later, when the geyser seemed to be running of steam, Nick lowered his head and squeezed Kelly's hand, glancing sideways to meet Kelly's eyes. He seemed surprised, and his fingers loosened, releasing him. "Sorry," he whispered.

Kelly shook his head, but whatever he'd intended to say didn't come out. Nick offered a gentle smile as he turned away, and Kelly stood there, watching him as he joined Owen and Digger and they started off toward the parking lot together.

Kelly swallowed hard, blinking as if just remembering his eyes could do that. Were he and Nick okay? Was this normal, to feel despondent like this when nothing seemed to be amiss? For the first time since Nick had kissed him and lit that spark inside both of them, Kelly was worried. He could feel the air pressing tighter around him, feel the panic creeping closer. What if he and Nick just weren't meant to work? What the hell would he do if Nick was feeling this panic, too? What would he do if he was set adrift?

"Doc? You okay?" Ty said, and a hand on his shoulder finally knocked him out of his reverie.

Kelly glanced at him, taking a deep breath and trying to smile. "Yeah," he said, nodding and glancing at Ty and Zane. "Let's do this."

He could feel their eyes on him as he followed after the other three amidst the dispersing crowd. But he had bigger things to worry about now. Like how the hell the three of them were supposed to win a battle of wits and wiles against a team as fucking stacked as a bayou firebug, a devious asshole, and an Irish MacGyver.

CHAPTER NINE

Two days after entering Yellowstone National Park, the six of them were exhausted, dirty, bruised, and hungry as they climbed back into the Suburban.

Digger had tied Alpha Team's flag around his head, wearing it proudly as he claimed shotgun for the drive to their next destination.

"Who the hell knows that pinecones will explode?" Ty grumbled to Zane. They were both in the third row of seats, curled up together and squished into the back. Losers sat in the back. "Who knows that?"

Nick snickered and pressed his fist to Digger's. "Oohrah," he said with a grin as he started the car.

"Who's got the next letter?" Zane asked. He sounded exhausted, but then all of them were. Zane had held his own out there, and Nick was impressed. He'd actually been last man standing from Alpha team, but he hadn't been able to save their flag and Digger had managed to snag it with just minutes left to the twenty-four hour end of game time.

Despite being tired and sore and dirty, and enduring some arguing over whether Nick had broken the rules when he'd faked blowing out his knee to lure Kelly out and 'kill' him, none of them could stop grinning.

Kelly was digging in Nick's bag for the letters, so Nick waited before getting under way. Helen's air-conditioning felt amazing, so he closed his eyes and let it blast right in his face as they waited.

Kelly handed the next letter to Ty, who opened it up while still grumbling about pinecones. Nick watched him in the mirror as his eyes darted over it, no doubt scanning it to make sure he could read it out loud without crying. He finally cleared his throat and looked up. "Ready?" he asked.

The other answered with nods and murmurs. Nick turned a little in the driver's seat so he could see as Ty read.

"First of all, I want to congratulate whichever team had more devious assholes on it," he read, eyes flicking to Digger and narrowing. He hummed as Digger beamed at him. "The winning team doesn't get shit for winning, this ain't Little League. Climb back in your ride and start heading for Doc's cabin. Even if he doesn't own the cabin anymore, I want you to get as close to his property as you're legally able. I know that's a long drive, so stop somewhere along the way and have yourselves a nice bath, a nice dinner, and a good night's sleep. You've earned it since you each just spent the last two days trying to viciously fake kill your buddies."

Owen gave a relieved sigh. "Thank you, EZ."

"There's more," Ty told them. "Alpha Team and Bravo Team will room together from here on out, when the size of the rooms allows it. Be a team."

Ty snorted as he glanced around. "He also says we can open the next letter when we get to Doc's place."

"Why are we going home?" Kelly asked. He had turned so his back was resting against the door panel, and his bare feet were propped in Owen's lap.

Ty just shook his head, shrugging. He offered the letter for Kelly to read over, and Nick turned around and started them on their way.

"Any preferences for where we stay tonight?" Nick asked.

"Can we drive through Jackson Hole?" Zane asked. "I've always wanted to see it."

Nick nodded. "We can stop in Jackson for lunch, it's a weird little town. It's not far enough for halfway, though."

"Let's just go 'til you get tired," Owen suggested. "None of us are allowed to drive today anyway."

"Okay," Nick said, glancing in the rearview mirror out of habit. He found Kelly's storm-cloud eyes on him, and they stole his breath away.

Kelly gave him a sad smile, then looked away. Nick stared at his profile for as long as the road would allow, his chest aching so much he had to put a hand over the scar on his side to keep himself from wincing. He could feel Kelly slipping away, and he didn't know why.

The music skipped and stuttered, and Nick banged on the dash. "Helen!"

The music stopped, leaving them with the sound of the tires on the road and nothing more. When it started again, the song was in Spanish, the Pandora app playing away happily even though Nick had made a point to have one of his iTunes playlists going instead.

Digger picked up the phone, pursing his lips. "I can fix this, you know."

Nick snatched it out of his hands. "You set fire to my phone, I set fire to *you*."

Digger was nodding, his lips still pursed, considering. "That's fair."

Nick was fighting sleep when he pulled over on the side of the road and got out of the car to walk around. The others took the opportunity to stretch, and Ty let the kitties out to use a patch of grass. Nick was pacing back and forth along the pavement, his head down, when he saw a coin on the ground. He stopped and frowned down at it for a few seconds before picking it up.

"What'd you find?" Ty called to him.

"It's a dime."

Ty threw both hands up. "We're rich!"

"Shut up and get your damn cats in the car," Nick grumbled as he trudged back to the driver's side. He dropped the dime in the cup holder, waiting until Ty had the kittens in the Suburban before he turned it on and got them back on the road. Whoever sat in the passenger seat had to talk to Nick to keep him awake after that. It was hard not to notice that Kelly stayed in the back.

They stopped for the night at the first large town they saw, which happened to be Rock Springs, Wyoming. Again. This time Kelly was grateful for the hotel Owen made them find, because the beds were soft and the shower had excellent water pressure and there was a bar in the lobby that was open until midnight.

Kelly spent his entire time in the shower trying to decide why he felt off. He knew the lack of contact was one thing causing him problems. He'd been relieved by Eli's instructions separating the teams, at first. The rules he and Nick had set for themselves—no touching, no sharing a bed—were all being made official by Sanchez. It eased some of his guilt, because he couldn't remember a time when he and Nick hadn't touched. He just couldn't put his finger on the rest of it, other than knowing that it was getting harder for him to work up the nerve to talk to Nick, and he decided he needed to nut up and talk to Nick about it before it became something too big for them to deal with together.

When he got out of the shower, there was a note from Ty on the desk saying they'd gone down there, and when Kelly joined them, they'd find dinner.

He got dressed quickly and headed down to the bar. It was surprisingly crowded, and Kelly stood at the entrance, scanning for his boys. He found them in a round booth in the far corner. All of them but Nick. Maybe Nick had taken the last shower as well and just wasn't down yet.

As he threaded his way through the diners, he happened to glance toward the bar, and he stumbled against a vacant chair when he saw Nick standing there. He would recognize those broad shoulders and auburn hair anywhere. He seemed to be waiting for a drink order, both elbows on the bar, leaning his weight on one leg to give him that insolent hitch to his stature that always seemed to hit Kelly deep in his gut.

As Kelly stared at him, Nick took a sip from a beer mug and nodded to something the man beside him was saying. The guy was maybe in his late twenties, light hair, a ragged Boston Red Sox hat on. Whatever he was saying had him excited, and he was using his hands as he talked, patting Nick's arm and back, grabbing his shirt and shaking him as he said something that made Nick chuckle.

Kelly smiled when he saw the laugh lines on Nick's profile. But then, against his will and against every instinct Kelly had in him, his mind flashed to that video he had found on the *Fiddler*, the one of Nick and a fireman from Boston named Aidan.

It was like a lance to his heart, and he had to turn away before the images in his memory could blend any further with Nick standing at the bar. He staggered through the dining area, shaking it off as he got to the table where the others all were.

"Hey, Doc," Zane greeted with a smile. He slid over, shoving his shoulder into Ty's as he made room for Kelly. "You okay? You look a little . . ."

"Rough," Ty said when Zane couldn't seem to find an appropriately sensitive word for it.

"Eh," Kelly offered as he threw himself into the booth. He glanced off toward the bar, but thankfully he couldn't see Nick or the kid he'd been talking to. There was no way in hell he was going to allow himself to become a jealous person. It just wasn't going to fucking happen.

A few minutes later, Nick returned to the booth with an armful of glasses. Owen stood and helped him unload them, laughing at Nick as he put his lips to one of the overfull drinks and tried to sip enough out of it so it wouldn't spill.

By some miracle they managed the feat without a drop being wasted, and Nick was grinning at Kelly when he finally sat. Kelly couldn't help but return it.

"What the hell took you so long?" Ty asked, sliding his drink closer to him.

"Kid at the bar," Nick said with a jerk of his thumb over his shoulder. "He heard me order and lost his shit, said I was the first person from home he'd met on his trip. He wouldn't stop talking, Jesus." He took another careful sip of his drink. "Fuck, this is wicked strong."

"Mine too," Digger said gleefully. He leaned as far as he could, pushing on Owen's shoulder to give him some leverage. "Which bartender made these?"

They laughed their way through dinner, and then dessert, sharing stories about Sidewinder and Eli. Kelly was glad Zane had tagged along; it gave them ample excuses to reminisce, and they'd been taking advantage of it.

Despite the fact that Zane was a recovering alcoholic, he'd insisted that he didn't mind them drinking, and though Ty stopped after one drink, the others didn't.

Kelly had intended to. But he was trying to wipe his mind clean, and he and Nick went round for round, drink for drink. Something that wasn't usually advisable for anyone, considering how well Nick could handle alcohol.

By the time midnight rolled around, the bar area had cleared out, and the lone bartender remained, waiting for them to pack it up so she could go home. Kelly noticed all of this only peripherally, of course, because he was hammered. *Hammered.*

Zane had kept a hand on his elbow because when he laughed he leaned to the side and almost fell out of the booth. Finally, Zane had just thrown his arm around Kelly's shoulders to keep him upright, and Kelly appreciated the contact.

As he thought about it, he remembered his decision to talk to Nick about the no-touching clause they'd created, and about the feeling of impending doom he'd been suffering. What better time than right now?

He reached across the table and tapped Nick's empty glass while Digger and Owen shared a story with Zane.

Nick blinked at the glass, then up at Kelly with a raised eyebrow.

"I need to talk to you," Kelly told him, his voice a little louder than he'd intended.

Nick just nodded, but he didn't move. He had his arms crossed, leaning back in the padded bench seat. Occasionally his feet had snaked their way across the table when he'd been stretching them out, and Kelly had fought hard not tap back with his toes.

"I mean like, now."

Nick's lips parted and his eyes widened. "Oh. Okay."

Kelly managed to get out of the seat without falling over, or even swaying too much, and he pulled Nick out of the booth, knowing his knee would be stiff and sore by now. Nick held on to his forearm after he found his feet, and Kelly realized how close they were as he gazed up into Nick's eyes. He blinked and shook away the desire to pull him closer for a kiss, and instead jerked his head toward the other side of the restaurant. Nick followed obediently.

They slid into another booth since all the tables already had their chairs stacked on top of them. Nick was frowning toward the bar when he scooted over on the seat to let Kelly sit beside him.

"We should let her close up," he said.

Kelly glanced at the bartender, who was wiping down her bar. As they watched her, the other guys called to her and she headed over there, talking with them for a few seconds before sitting with them. Kelly snorted. "Owen could talk his way out of a mortuary."

Nick made a humming sound of agreement. He turned a little, resting his arm on the back of the bench behind Kelly and leaning his other elbow against the table. "What's going on, babe?" he asked gently.

Kelly shrugged and winced. "Something's not right," he blurted, and he forced himself to meet Nick's eyes. "I don't feel right. *We* don't feel right. And I can't figure out why."

Nick nodded. "I know," he said softly.

"Do you know why?" Kelly demanded.

Nick was chewing on his lip, staring at Kelly almost like he didn't see him. "We can't fill the silence like this," he said finally.

Kelly's frown deepened as he watched Nick. He was definitely not sober, maybe less sober than Kelly right now. Maybe this hadn't been the best time to do this.

Nick's gaze seemed to focus a little as he looked into Kelly's eyes. "We've always touched. We've always talked. Now we can't do either."

"We can talk," Kelly argued. "We just aren't."

Nick nodded, as if Kelly had just agreed with his point.

Kelly sat back, leaning against Nick's arm.

"When we hit a silence we can't deal with, what do we do?"

Kelly scowled and shrugged. He had no idea what Nick was talking about.

"We fuck," Nick answered. "If we can't talk about something hard, we just fall into bed and ignore it. And ignore it." He was staring past Kelly now, his eyes glazed over. "We've forgotten how to talk to each other."

And suddenly Nick's words made sense. Kelly gasped a little when he took in a shaky breath. "And since we can't touch, we can't communicate at all now."

Nick was nodding almost as if he didn't know he was doing it, still staring past Kelly at nothing.

"Wow," Kelly whispered. "Okay. Okay."

Nick finally looked back at him, his eyes soft and sad.

"Okay," Kelly said again, and he turned to meet Nick head-on. "Let's talk then. I feel like we're not working. And I don't know why."

Nick didn't say anything, just met Kelly's eyes unflinchingly.

"And I feel guilty," Kelly continued. "I feel like I'm the reason Sidewinder died. And all this, it's Eli trying to fix the mess *I* made of us. And it's just making it worse, it's making me realize more and more what I ruined by leaving. And I think . . . I think I blame you for being here and realizing all this."

Nick was still silent, but now he was nodding almost imperceptibly.

"And I'm scared," Kelly whispered. "Because I almost lost you in Miami. And I can tell that I'm pushing you away, and I don't know why, and I don't know how to stop me from doing it." He held his breath, waiting for Nick to respond, for him to break this torturous silence somehow. He gritted his teeth and closed his eyes. "Say something."

"I don't know if I can," Nick said softly.

Kelly could feel the anger bubbling up inside him. He was laying his heart open here, and Nick couldn't think of a damn thing to say to him? He'd just admitted he was afraid they couldn't make this work, and Nick didn't have a word to say in their defense?

"What's so fucking hard about it?" Kelly growled. "You know what's hard for me? Seeing you innocently talking to some stranger in a bar and not being able to get the thought of you and Aidan on that video out of my head."

Nick blinked and jerked his head back, lips parted.

"See?" Kelly practically shouted. "You've got to fucking talk to me! You've got to defend yourself before my mind is allowed to run rampant!"

"I can't stop your mind from doing *anything*, Kelly, you and I both know that too damn well," Nick finally blurted.

"I'm being serious!"

"So am I!"

Kelly shoved out of the booth, stalking away from Nick. He gritted his teeth and ran his hands through his hair, growling wordlessly.

"Kelly," Nick called, and he sounded irritated and impatient. He sounded almost angry, and it pissed Kelly off even more. What the hell right did *Nick* have to be angry with *him*? Kelly was the one being haunted by the sight of Nick and that fucking fireman in their bed, haunted by guilt. Kelly was the one losing sleep!

Kelly whirled on him, pointing a finger and waving it in utter frustration. "I can't get it out of my head, okay! Any of it! I can't stop seeing your face when I told you I was leaving the team! I can't stop it! And I can't make myself not think about you being with someone else, someone who's never hurt you!"

Nick stood, still looking confused as he shook his head.

It made Kelly even angrier. "All I can see is you and this other guy that I know damn well you were serious about, okay? And I know . . . I know you were thinking about trying something serious with him. And then I came along, skipping right back into your path and ruining it! I can't get it out of my head, okay! I can't help it!"

"Neither can I!" Nick shouted. He had his fists balled at his sides, and his eyes were blazing. He'd squared his broad shoulders, too, making him look even more hulking than he usually did.

Kelly had to stop short, taken aback by the anger and fire in his lover. He hadn't seen that in a long time, and it brought everything reeling in Kelly's mind to a screeching halt.

"It happened! It happened before you and me. It happened in the past, and there's nothing I can do about that! I can't change it, I can't defend it! Everything you've said, everything you're lingering over, it's done and gone, there's nothing I can do about it now!" He was shouting at full volume now as everyone in the room watched him with wide eyes, and he turned his back on Kelly and stalked away. Kelly could feel the others moving, getting to their feet in case there was a fight. "I can't go back and fix my mistakes, I can't go back and make my decisions over again! Just like you can't go back and change yours! If I could, do you really think I'd be here now? Do you think I'd be stuck in this hamster wheel of guilt and regret, just *stuck* here trying desperately to earn forgiveness?"

"Nick," Kelly breathed, unnoticed by anyone else as Nick paced and ranted to himself.

"Do you think there isn't a second of my life that I wouldn't go back and change if I could?" Nick grabbed up a beer bottle from the table he was stalking past. He put his other hand to his chest and rounded on Kelly, looking pained and seeming to implore Kelly to just *listen* to him. "You think I wouldn't go back? You think I don't remember every moment of our past together, every time you've looked at me like that? Every time someone has looked at me like *that*!" He waved the beer bottle in his hand at the expression on Kelly's face and then spun on his heel and hurled the bottle at the wall.

Ty and Owen both flinched and then moved, Ty going to the doors of the bar and closing them, and Owen taking the bartender and escorting her out with murmured assurances that they'd take care of this. She left with little protest, and Ty latched the doors behind her so no one else could come in.

Kelly stood, slack-jawed, staring at Nick's back. He had both hands on his hips, his head lowered, breaths heaving. He finally turned, glancing around the room as if just realizing that they were in the hotel lobby bar and he might have just terrified everyone in the vicinity.

He was calm and silent as he went to the bar and gracefully hopped over it. He was light on his feet when he hit, no sign that his knee or anything else was bothering him. He grabbed himself another beer, and the sound of the bottle opening in the dead-silent aftermath of his outburst was as loud as a gunshot. Nick met Kelly's eyes as he leaned against the back of the bar and took a gulp of the new beer.

"Irish," Ty whispered carefully as he approached the bar.

"First time he looked at me like that," Nick said with a tip of his bottle toward Kelly, "was when I shot that kid in Kyrgyzstan. You remember?" he asked, turning to Ty.

"I remember," Ty assured him with a curt nod, speaking like he was trying to soothe a wild animal.

Kelly's heart skipped a bit. He knew exactly what incident Nick was talking about. He remembered seeing the kid pop up out of nowhere, a gun in hand. He remembered screaming at his team to stand down, it was just a boy. And he remembered the thump of the bullet hitting the child's chest, the horror and anguish as he'd watched the boy fall away. Nick hadn't blinked. Hadn't flinched. Kelly hadn't even been able to find a hint of regret in Nick's eyes as he'd screamed at him. He remembered the harsh words he'd spat out after Nick had pulled the trigger and the others were securing the body.

"How can you even have a soul if you pulled that trigger without hesitating," Nick recited, echoing the words in Kelly's memories. His voice dropped to a pained whisper. "Heartless bastard."

Kelly swallowed hard, shaking his head and desperately trying to find something to say. He watched helplessly as Nick rested his back against the refrigerator behind the bar and sank down to sit on his ass, out of sight behind the bar. Ty climbed over the bar and thumped out of sight after him. Kelly took a hesitant step forward as he glanced at Zane and Digger, neither of whom had moved or made a sound. Digger was scowling heavily, and Zane merely looked like he wanted to fade through a crack in the wall.

Kelly approached the bar, Owen and Digger joining him as they peered over at Ty and Nick, huddled on the floor together. Ty had taken possession of the beer bottle and set it far enough away that Nick couldn't reach it, and Nick had his knees pulled up, his elbows resting on them, his chin on his arms as he stared at the floor without blinking.

"You never told him why you pulled that trigger, Irish," Ty was saying softly. "You should have told him, he would have understood so much more."

Kelly's heart was hammering, he could feel it in his throat and in his ears. He hadn't spoken to Nick for weeks after he'd shot that boy. Yes, they'd found weapons on him. And yes, he'd probably been about to open fire on them. But Kelly hadn't been able to reconcile the killing with the man he knew Nick was, he hadn't been able to look into Nick's eyes without seeing that flat absence of emotion. Truth be told, he'd never really looked at Nick the same way again, even after they'd both apologized and forgiven each other.

Kelly eased around the end of the bar and approached Nick and Ty carefully, crouching a few feet away from them. "What don't I understand?"

Nick didn't move. As far as Kelly could tell, he hadn't even blinked.

"You say you can't change the past," Kelly said, trying not to let his frustration bleed through again. "You can't change it, but you can change what I think of it, right?"

"Can I?" Nick said as he turned his head to stare at Kelly. The look in his eyes chilled Kelly to his very bones and stole his breath away. There was nothing behind those eyes that were usually full of warmth and light, that usually danced like waves on the shore. They were empty. And they were terrifying. "You can't change the way you see the past, so why should I try?"

"Nicko," Kelly whispered.

"There was a kid," Nick said as he glanced up at the others and then down again. "When Ty and I were on our first tour. We were on the gate, and he wouldn't halt. He just kept walking, coming toward us. Had his hands raised. He stepped over the dead man's line, and I . . ."

Kelly inched closer as Nick trailed off. His eyes had gone distant, and Kelly realized with a sinking feeling where he was going with this.

Ty slipped his arm around Nick's shoulders protectively, and Kelly almost glared at him. Ty didn't have to fucking protect Nick from *him*.

"Irish tried to save the kid's life," Ty practically snarled. "He didn't shoot when he should have, and when the bomb strapped to that fucking child's back went off, we got caught in the blowback."

"That's where the shrapnel in your femur is from," Kelly realized out loud, breathless from the revelation. Nick just closed his eyes. "Is it? Nick?"

"When I hit my back, I still had my finger on the trigger," Nick whispered, his eyes unfocused, his voice distant. "My weapon discharged. And when I came to, I found Ty beside me, bleeding out from a bullet I'd put in him. Shrapnel in my thigh so I couldn't get to him. It was my worst nightmare, come to life."

Ty pulled Nick tighter, his jaw jumping as he looked around at each of them defiantly, like he was challenging them to blame Nick for those injuries. Kelly glanced up at the others, who were still leaning over the bar and watching. Zane had joined them, and his mouth was ajar as he listened.

"I almost killed my best friend because I didn't pull the trigger," Nick hissed. "And I'm the reason Ty . . . can never have kids. Because I shot him."

Kelly stared at them both, huddled together, Ty glaring at anyone who dared to say a word and Nick simply drunk and shell-shocked, unseeing as he lost himself to the past.

"I shot him."

Kelly crawled closer, reaching for Nick's arm to squeeze it, trying to get Nick to come back to them. When Nick met his eyes, Kelly slid himself closer so he could sit next to Nick. He kept his hand on Nick's arm.

It flashed through Kelly's mind again, the bullet hitting, the kid falling out of sight, Nick with his gun against his cheek, his eyes hard and deadly. Kelly closed his eyes and licked his lips. He should have known. The only thing that could kill that light in Nick's eyes was a ghost from his past, he should have known before he'd torn into him, before he called him a heartless bastard with no soul. Jesus.

"That was the first time you looked at me like that, like I was a monster," Nick said. Sitting next to him now, sobered from the shock of the argument, it was easy to hear the slur to Nick's words. The alcohol had hit him faster than it used to, and neither Kelly nor Nick had expected that. He made a mental note to keep an eye on that from now on, to remember that Nick's tolerance was no longer superhuman. Nick would have to relearn his limits. So would Kelly. Kelly glanced carefully to his side. When Nick spoke again, Kelly wasn't even sure he would have heard the words had he not been looking at Nick's lips moving. "It wasn't the last time. It won't be the last."

"I'm sorry," Kelly managed. "Nick. You know that's not how I see you. You know that."

"You see a video of me and another guy," Nick drawled, eyes still staring at nothing, "and it crosses your mind that I would hurt you like that. On purpose. That I could lie to you so easily without a gun to your head as a consequence."

He rested his back against the refrigerator, letting his legs slide out in front of him, his body going limp as he lowered his head.

"Nick," Kelly tried again.

"You tell me you think it's your fault the team died," Nick mumbled to Kelly. "And then tell me to change your mind. I can't change the past." Nick shook his head and lurched forward, struggling out of Ty's grasp and getting to his hands and knees before he was able to push himself to stand. He wavered, shaking his head as he went to the end of the bar, where a broom and dustpan were propped against the wall.

Digger shoved away from the bar and went to him, trying to convince Nick to let them clean up the mess. Kelly got to his feet, but then he realized he was stuck there, staring at Nick, lost in a sea of emotions he couldn't begin to navigate.

"I'll take him to bed," Ty whispered to him as he squeezed past Kelly. He patted his shoulder, nodding encouragingly. "You two can do this better when he's sober tomorrow, right?"

Kelly didn't respond as Ty moved away. He just watched as Ty took Nick's arm and convinced him to let Digger have the broom, then pulled him toward the door. They were almost at the end of the bar when Nick stopped and turned around, and he locked eyes with Kelly as Kelly held his breath, waiting.

"I've spent so much of my life trying to keep that look off your face," Nick said, waving a hand unsteadily at Kelly. "But I can't change the past."

Kelly breathed out his name, but Nick was turning away from him before Kelly could speak more, letting Ty lead him out. Kelly grasped at the bar in front of him, trying to steady his head and his heart and his body. Jesus, he felt like he'd been hit by a truck.

"Doc," Zane said, and Kelly's head shot up. Zane was looking at him as if he'd called him several times before Kelly heard him. "Come with me. Get some rest. It'll be okay in the morning."

Kelly glanced at Owen and Digger, and they both nodded for him to go. "I'll get us another room, give him some space," Owen told them.

"Ain't the first time you two gone 'round," Digger told Kelly as he swept up the bottle Nick had broken. "You'll be all right, Doc."

"Is he right?" Kelly asked them without moving. He was met with uncomfortable silence.

Kelly's stomach churned the entire way to the room, going over every word they'd said to each other, and every word they hadn't.

When Zane got the door unlocked and pushed it open, Kelly grabbed for his arm, stopping him from entering. "Was he right?"

Zane winced and looked into the darkened room like he just wanted to slink into it and disappear. He sighed and met Kelly's eyes again. "I think you both are."

He turned and headed into the room, and Kelly followed him, scowling as Zane flipped the lamps on. Zane shrugged out of his jacket and tossed it at a chair in the corner.

"I don't know the whole story. I mean, you two, you've got twenty years behind you, I'll never know the whole story. That's just you and him."

Kelly glanced up, meeting Zane's eyes with a little bit of difficulty.

"You think Nick's a monster?" Zane asked neutrally.

Kelly's response got stuck in his throat. He had to struggle to find it again as Zane watched him. "I don't know. The thing is, I don't care."

Zane raised an eyebrow, crossing his arms.

"I don't care if he is," Kelly said again, voice stronger this time. "Monster or not. All I know is he's mine."

Zane nodded minutely, chewing on his lip. "I'd bet he feels the same way about you. No matter what you think of yourself. And if I were him? I'd want to hear *that* tonight."

Nick sprawled on the king-sized bed, a hand tossed over his eyes. The room was spinning on him, and he was afraid to open his eyes in case it wasn't just him going in circles.

"Irish?"

"I'm okay," Nick grunted.

Ty sat on the edge of the bed, the covers rustling as he moved next to Nick. "Not used to your tolerance being so low. You still on those painkillers?"

"Yeah," Nick answered, knowing Ty would be giving him that disapproving scowl of his and not caring.

"Maybe we avoid the bars until you're off 'em, huh?"

"Don't mother me, Tyler, you're not very good at it." A tiny mew answered Nick's words. He raised his head, scowling. "The hell was that?"

"Kittens," Ty answered, and then he was murmuring under his breath, which started more excited meowing.

Nick groaned. "I forgot you had them with you. What'd you do with them at Yellowstone?"

"Kept them locked in the tent until Johns killed me."

Four tiny paws landed on Nick's belly, complete with needle-sharp claws. The kitten balanced on Nick's abdominal muscles, using its claws as it got its footing. Nick groaned louder.

Ty stretched out on the bed beside him, and Nick finally risked a peek at the ceiling. It wasn't going quite as fast as he thought it would be. He took in a deep breath. At least he didn't feel sick. That was the last thing he needed tonight, to spend the rest of it with his head in the toilet and a curious kitten on his shoulder.

"That's Jiminy," Ty told him.

Nick groped around and patted the kitten distractedly. "Bad kitty." He meowed in response, and the purring that started up was like a damn tractor engine as it vibrated Nick's belly. "No."

"He likes you."

"No," Nick drew out with more feeling. The kitten began stalking its way up his body and plopped its tiny butt down on his chest, purring delightedly. The other one, Cricket, joined her brother on Nick's chest, kneading him with claws so tiny and sharp they had to belong to something evil. "I hate you," Nick claimed, not sure if he was talking to Ty or the kittens that were happily making their beds on Nick's body.

Ty plucked them off Nick's chest, and Nick could still hear them purring as they settled wherever Ty had relocated them.

"I'd be kind of upset too," Ty said after a while. Nick sighed as he draped his arm over his eyes. "I wouldn't even want to *think* about Zane with someone else, much less *see* it. You got to know that, dude. Where he's coming from."

"I know," Nick murmured. "It's not that he's upset. It's . . . he thinks it was his fault that the team split up. He asked me if I blamed it when it happened, and I said yes. He's got to know I don't blame him now. He has to know that. And to use that as an excuse to push me away, to tie it into that fucking video he found, I just . . . it's cruel. I've never seen him cruel before."

"Maybe just give it time. It's a knee-jerk, you know? He'll figure it out soon enough."

Nick nodded, his eyes losing focus as he stared at the wall behind Ty. "When he found that video, and he told me he thought I might have cheated on him? I didn't want him to know it hurt me," he admitted. "I knew he had the right to be upset, I didn't want him to feel bad about his reaction. But it just hurt more and more. I kept dreaming about that kid, about Kelly's face after I took the shot. Same face I saw when I walked in on him watching that video. And I started realizing, some part of him still thinks I'm a monster."

Ty turned onto his side so he was facing Nick, and reached for Nick's hand, holding it in both of his. There was sorrow in his eyes, and his brow was furrowed as he met Nick's eyes.

Nick turned onto his side to mirror his friend, clutching to his fingers. "What are we, Ty?"

Ty shrugged one shoulder. Two tiny orange ears popped up from behind Ty's neck, the purring getting louder. Ty was obviously fighting a smile, but before he spoke he was solemn again, his brow furrowed. "We might be monsters," he said. "But that don't make us bad."

Nick fought to swallow against the tightness in his throat. He closed his eyes as Ty scooted closer to him and pressed their foreheads together. Just as Nick had known would happen, warm paws landed on his face, and Jiminy circled around and around until he settled in Nick's hair.

"Why do they always like me," Nick groaned.

"Same reason I do," Ty whispered fondly. "Sleep. What was it you used to tell me? When I was losing hope? About the sun rising on a new day?"

Nick squeezed his eyes tighter, his heart hammering and Ty's breath warm on his face. He pulled their hands up between them, clasping them between their chests as if they were at prayer. "Only thing I ever told you was to shut the fuck up and go to sleep," he said. "Don't fucking wake me until the sun's up."

Ty was chuckling softly, and Nick found himself smiling along with him.

"I must have heard it wrong," Ty teased. "I remember you more eloquent."

"Shut up, Tyler."

Nick wasn't sure how long he'd been asleep when the knocking at the door woke him. He was instantly tense and alert, his eyes wide in the darkness. He could feel Ty close to him, his breaths hard against Nick's face. The kittens both complained when he moved.

"It's okay," Ty whispered. "I got it."

Nick rolled to his back as Ty got out of bed, rubbing the heels of his palms against his eyes until he saw stars.

"Hey, Doc," he heard Ty greet when the door opened.

Nick's stomach flipped. He lay there another moment, trying to get his nerves under control before sitting up in bed. Light streamed into the hotel room from the hallway, and he squinted against it as a shadow fell across the end of the bed.

Nick raised his head.

"I can't sleep," Kelly said when their eyes met. The door closed with a quiet snick as Ty left the room, throwing them into darkness once more.

Nick stared until his eyes had adjusted, until he could almost make out Kelly's features. Nick glanced back at the bed. He and Ty had been sleeping on top of the comforter. He reached back and tugged the blanket down, exposing the sheets and pillows next to him.

"Some things are easier to say in the dark," he mumbled as he looked back at Kelly.

Kelly waited a few heartbeats before crawling into the bed. He laid himself out next to Nick, sliding under the covers and resting his head on his arm. Nick shoved the blanket down further, trying to get under it and stretch back out on his side. He stared at Kelly across the expanse of the bed, his heartbeat thundering in his ears.

"I lost my temper," he said when he finally decided Kelly wasn't going to speak first.

"Me too."

Nick shook his head. Kelly's hand found his, grasping through the dark. Nick gripped him hard, tugging at him to come closer.

"Can't fix it overnight," Kelly said with a sigh. "Any of it. But it can be fixed. I was wrong, I was . . . so wrong, babe. It's not *us* that's falling apart, it's *me*. But I'm with you. And I don't think you're a monster, but I wouldn't care even if you were. I love you. And I'm with you. You just have to stay with me."

Nick pulled Kelly's hand up to his mouth, pressing his lips to Kelly's fingers. Kelly scooted closer, bringing the warmth of his body to Nick's as he wrapped around him. He took his hand back, sliding it over Nick to hold him.

"I love you, Nicko," he whispered against Nick's lips.

Nick couldn't answer. He just dug his fingers into Kelly's shirt as Kelly pulled him closer. He rested his head against Kelly's chest, clinging to him. Kelly kissed his temple, squeezing him.

"God, I love you." Kelly said quietly. "Just stay with me."

Nick pressed his face against Kelly, like he could burrow into him. He held on to him gratefully, just breathing in his scent.

"What the fuck is touching my foot?" Kelly demanded in a panicked whisper.

Nick raised his head, snorting. "Ty's kittens."

"You've been in here cuddling with sweet, fuzzy little kitties?" Kelly asked, his voice going higher. "How is *that* fair?"

Nick rested his head against Kelly's chest again and made a sound like air being let out of a tire. Both kittens responded happily, clambering up his and Kelly's bodies to nudge at Nick's face and under his chin. Kelly was laughing softly, jostling Nick's head as the kittens tried to snuggle between them.

Nick hid his face in Kelly's neck so he wouldn't get another cold nose shoved against his cheek, and he sighed in relief as he was surrounded by Kelly's warmth. Even the high-pitched purring of the kittens as Kelly rubbed them both was comforting.

"Can we get a boat cat?" Kelly asked after a few minutes of snuggling with the beasts, his voice wavering with laughter.

"Absolutely not."

They drove for about four hours before they stopped for a rest and to let the kittens get out of the car. The others walked around and stretched, but Kelly couldn't resist when Ty got down onto the grass to let the kittens romp over him; he joined them.

They were still little enough that they had a hard time running full throttle without tripping over themselves, and watching them play, watching them enjoy the hell out of a tiny patch of grass at a rest stop off the highway, started clarifying things in Kelly's mind.

Life wasn't complicated. Life was a patch of grass and a butterfly to chase.

He hefted himself to his feet and searched around for Nick, but he wasn't nearby. He picked up Cricket instead, carrying her over to the picnic tables to sit and wait. She purred so hard she was vibrating as she curled up in his arms, and Kelly grinned as he cradled her.

He sat staring off at the Rockies in the distance. They weren't far from where he'd grown up, in a tiny town perched on the edge of the state. It was just as flat as the prairies to the east, but in the distance Kelly had always been able to see those mountains' peaks touching the sky. He'd grown up in the shadow of those peaks, and he'd always sworn he would live among them one day.

He'd been ten years old when his parents had died in a car crash one stormy night, and he'd been sent to live with his grandparents in Colorado Springs. Those mountain trails had been everything he'd always hoped they'd be, and they'd helped begin to heal the broken heart of a ten-year-old boy. At the age of twelve, when his grandparents had become too old and ill to care for him, he'd been put into the foster system. But he'd been lucky. He'd known even when he was a kid that he was lucky. His foster family had been good and kind, and he'd been able to stay near the last members of his family until they both had passed when he was seventeen. A year later, he'd joined the Navy, searching for adventure and purpose. Searching for home.

He'd found it, and realizing that made all the turmoil in his mind the last few months seem petty and useless.

Sitting here, though, on the border of Colorado and Wyoming, Kelly remembered the hope and longing he'd always felt when he'd looked out the windows of his parents' home and gazed at those mountain peaks.

"Hey," Nick whispered, yanking Kelly's mind back from the past and making him jump. Kelly turned to blink at him. "You want to go see them?"

"What?" Kelly asked, dumbfounded. How the hell could Nick have possibly known what he'd been thinking about?

"Your parents. We're no more than an hour away. We can take the time if you want to go see them," Nick said gently.

Kelly's mind swirled, cycling through a myriad of emotions as he stared into Nick's eyes. He slowly became aware of a tickle at his kneecap, of warmth just above his calf. He looked down with a frown to find Nick's hands both there, one on each of Kelly's legs as Nick sat opposite him at another table, his fingers curled behind Kelly's legs, his thumbs rubbing gentle circles against Kelly's knees.

Nick glanced down with a frown, and his thumbs stopped moving. He raised his gaze to meet Kelly's, and his eyes were wide. "Sorry," he whispered, spreading his fingers as he lifted them. "Had no idea I was doing that."

Kelly grabbed for one of his hands, keeping it where it had been. "You've always done that," he told Nick, squeezing his hand harder. "Even before you and me started. We've sat like this before."

Nick was silent, the pads of his fingers pressing into Kelly's skin, their knees almost touching as he bent close enough to speak quietly. "We have," he said.

"I think we fucked up," Kelly whispered harshly.

Nick looked up quickly, his eyes wide.

"Saying we shouldn't touch," Kelly added quickly. "That's our language. It's always been our language. Like you said last night. Years and years before I ever asked you to kiss me, touching was the way we talked."

Nick's hands were gentle as he leaned closer, his fingers gliding behind Kelly's knees. "Maybe that's why I've felt like we can't hear each other this trip," he said, wincing as he met Kelly's eyes again.

Kelly's shoulders slumped in relief. "You too?"

Nick's grip tightened and he inadvertently pulled Kelly closer. Kelly licked his lips, his body flushing with heat. They stared at each other, neither of them even breathing.

"Do we need the bad-kitty spritzer?" Digger asked, jerking both Nick and Kelly out of their trance. They broke eye contact, and Nick cleared his throat, glaring at Digger. "Hey, you told me no touchy,"

Digger said with an unapologetic shrug before turning away. "We're gearing up."

Nick glared after him for a few seconds as Kelly stared at Nick. "Babe," Kelly grunted. Nick looked back at him with a sigh and a tired smile. "We can still follow the rules and end the moratorium on touching."

Nick was nodding as he gazed raptly into Kelly's eyes. "Good."

Kelly slid one hand up Nick's forearm, squeezing his biceps. "Maybe even give me a snuggle tonight instead of sneaking off to sleep with Ty's kittens?"

Cricket complained in Kelly's lap, as if she knew she was about to be denied her second-favorite sleep buddy.

Nick chuckled and pushed out of his seat to press his lips to Kelly's. Kelly grinned through the kiss, and then another one.

"Oh my God, stop!" Ty called from the parking lot of the rest area.

Nick and Kelly both snickered, taking one last, longer kiss before Nick pulled Kelly to his feet.

"You never answered me," Nick said as they turned to head toward the car. He slid his hand into Kelly's.

"Remind me what the question was."

"Do you want to see your parents?"

Kelly's eyes focused on the mountains in the distance beyond Nick, and he smiled serenely. "I already did," he said quietly.

Nick was scowling when Kelly turned his attention back on him. "We talking symbolically, or like Eli in my iPhone type of seeing them?"

Kelly barked a laugh and shook his head, letting Nick continue to grumble as they joined the others.

I hope you're standing in Doc's front yard. If not, then you better be as close as your Marine asses can get.

This is where we dropped Kelly off when he said it was time to go home. This is the moment where Sidewinder officially breathed its last breath as a team of Marines. But Doc, this ain't where Sidewinder

died. I know you think you killed the team, you been carrying that with
you since you got married. But we ain't dead, son. I guess I am if you're
reading this, but that's semantics. The team, the team we made, it can't
die. They didn't take that away from us when we were discharged.

So I want you start here and go on an adventure. Go see all those
places we couldn't find the first time. Take Seymour to the Grand Canyon.
And then go to each place where we dropped someone off on that road
trip, and I want each of you to tell the man we left there why he didn't
actually leave us.

And before you start bitching, yes, after you're done in Las Vegas, you
can fly to the other locations. You got lives to get back to.

Nick lowered the letter after reading it, and glanced around at
the others. Kelly stood facing his cabin, his shoulders slumped and his
head bowed.

"Kelly?" Nick said softly.

"How'd he know that?" Kelly asked as he turned toward them.
His eyes were almost watering, but he was also smiling. "How the hell
did he know that?"

"You didn't exactly hide it well," Owen offered under his breath.

Nick gently folded the letter. He moved toward Kelly and took a
hold of his shirt, meeting his eyes as he slid the letter into his breast
pocket and patted Kelly's chest. "We should have told you it was
okay," he said. "We all knew you blamed yourself. After your wedding.
After you settled here. We should have done something more to let
you know it wasn't true."

Kelly frowned as he fought to swallow. "You told me you blamed
me," he whispered.

"I did. I did, at the time. I blamed everything under the sun,
including you." Nick stepped closer and took Kelly's face in both
hands. "I was wrong. Kels, look at this place."

He forced Kelly to turn his head and look behind them at his
cabin. It was on the smaller side, less than a thousand square feet total.
The sloped roof hid the little loft bedroom, and the balcony over the
wide deck sat nestled amongst flower pots and rustic greenery.

The deck and its rockers were weathered by nearly ten years of living, and the old Jeep sitting under a little carport off to the side had hosted many of their forays into the mountains.

Kelly stared at the cabin, and Nick wrapped his arm around Kelly's shoulder. "This is home," Nick whispered. "You found it. We all did, and none of us would have been able to do that if you hadn't been brave enough to try it first."

Kelly lowered his head, then glanced sideways at Nick and over his shoulder at the others. Nick couldn't see the way they were reacting, but judging by the light in Kelly's eyes, they were all backing Nick up.

"Doc," Owen said slowly, almost like he wasn't sure if he should interject in the moment. Nick and Kelly both turned to him. "I wouldn't have stayed in San Diego if you hadn't stopped here. If we'd all still been together? I . . . I wouldn't have had the nerve. And I've found my life there. That's because of you."

Digger hummed and nodded. "I'd never have gone back. I'd have stuck with y'all. I still would, if you needed me. But I never would have gone back to Louisiana, and I'm happy there. I'm with Ozone— that's only 'cause you had the balls to do it first."

Kelly snorted, and when Nick glanced at him he was smiling.

"I blamed you too," Ty admitted. "For a while, after you left. But it was always me. We all know it was me."

"That's not true either," Kelly practically snarled. "Six, you been blaming yourself way too long for all that. You did the best you could. The NIA wanted us, and you didn't let them have us. What they did to Nick, that would have been all of us. You were looking out for us, you saved us all."

Nick watched wistfully as Ty's shoulders seemed to square a little, like he was shaking off a weight he'd been carrying for too long. Nick leaned closer to Kelly and touched his hand to the small of Kelly's back, then pressed his lips to Kelly's cheek so his words would be for Kelly's ears only. "That's why we need you," he said with a tilt of his head toward Ty. "That's why Sidewinder never died. 'Cause you're the heart of it."

He pulled back and cocked his head at Kelly, meeting his eyes and nodding. Kelly was chewing on his lip as he met Nick's eyes, and then he began to smile when he looked back at Ty.

"Okay," he said with a curt nod. He smiled a little wider, that sparkle coming back into his eyes as he glanced around at them all. "Okay."

Nick couldn't help himself as Kelly seemed to simply blossom right in front of his eyes. He grabbed Kelly by his shirtfront and pulled him closer to kiss him. They were met with a variety of groans, teasing whistles, and threats about getting the bad-kitty spritzer from the car.

Nick could feel Kelly smiling against his lips, and he hummed when he forced himself to step away. His hand was still cradling Kelly's face, though, and Kelly was still grinning.

"Who wants a meal that didn't come out of a gas station?" Nick asked the others without looking away from Kelly's eyes.

"I'll get the kitties," Ty said, heading for the car.

Digger grunted and stomped after him. "I ain't eatin' those cats, Grady!"

CHAPTER TEN

Over the next few days, they put Eli's letters aside and turned instead to another higher power to dictate their travel choices. The dime Nick had found on the side of the road was deemed the Dime of Fate, and whenever they came to a proverbial fork in their road, they would flip it to decide which way they would follow. The dime saved their lives in the desert of Arizona, preventing them from getting even more lost while they were looking for a cliff that didn't exist. The dime was how they wound up with mild cases of food poisoning at a restaurant in New Mexico, and also how they almost lost Seymour *and* Digger over the edge of the Grand Canyon.

Ten days after they left Kelly's cabin, the Dime of Fate delivered them relatively safely to Las Vegas, where they turned in Helen to the rental car agency, and then continued on to San Diego. There they got to meet Riley Williams, the woman who'd stolen Owen's heart instead of his security clearance like he'd suspected of her when they'd first met. Kelly was surprised to realize that Owen seemed very serious about her. They spent the night at Owen's penthouse loft in the building owned by Caliburn Technologies, and Owen finally got a taste of the agony Nick, Kelly, Ty, and Zane had been suffering under Eli's sexbargo. They left with promises to return soon, when they weren't under orders from a higher and more insistent power, to get to know Riley better.

In New Orleans they were met at the airport by one of Digger's cousins with a pickup truck that smelled like fish, and they rode in the back out to the little backwater town Digger had grown up in. They were welcomed in by his mother and force-fed something that Kelly knew they would all regret eating later, and then Digger took them to his new home, an adorable little bungalow in the Garden District.

He'd grown tired of the paranoia, he claimed, and dug up his share of the money they'd all received and finally bought a house. A home.

It was a really nice place, too. It was a duplex, but Digger had purchased the entire structure with plans for renovating it. The only thing he'd done so far, though, was blow a hole in the wall that separated the two units. Nick kept going on and on about the historic details while Digger showed them around, and Digger lit up like a Christmas tree when he started in on the history of the more than hundred-year-old house.

They were still sitting in the living room, drinking and talking about molding and original wood floors when Kelly gave up and told them good-night. He headed for the shower, a last-ditch attempt to ease the kink in his back he'd been suffering from the last couple nights.

Half an hour later, he was moving stiffly when he came out of the bathroom. He'd hoped the steamy shower would loosen up his back, but it didn't seem to have done much for him. He was going to have to give in and ask Nick for one of his pain pills. He turned and twisted as he patted at his dripping hair with a towel, grimacing as his back teased him with the promise of a few nice pops but never delivered.

"You okay?" Nick asked.

Kelly glanced up, surprised to find Nick there. "Hey," he said, feeling stupid almost immediately. "I thought you'd still be out there with Digger."

"We called it a night." Nick was lurking near the end of the bed, fiddling with the buttons of his shirt. He didn't raise his head again before adding, "You look like you're in pain."

Kelly cleared his throat, hating that he felt awkward with Nick in the room. He had to look back through nearly fifteen years of knowing the man to remember a single time he'd felt awkward being alone with Nick. They'd been in a tiny back room of a church in Jacksonville, North Carolina. And Nick had been removing a dainty golden ring from his pocket to assure Kelly one last time that he knew where it was. Kelly's heart had stuttered through the moment, and he'd chalked it up to prenuptial nerves.

He remembered the look in Nick's eyes that day, though. Melancholy with a touch of fear. The day Kelly had said "I do" to a woman he'd convinced himself he loved was the day Sidewinder had begun to unravel. They'd been unraveling ever since. Kelly was beginning to accept that it wasn't his fault, that things change no matter how much you pray they'll stay the same. It still hurt him looking back, though.

This trip had been a balm on that old wound, with the entire group back together and enjoying antics like old times. They went hard from sunup until they collapsed in bed, exhausted, with no energy or time to be awkward with each other. Now, Kelly could feel the spaces around them opening up to give them room to breathe. And it was . . . uncomfortable.

When Kelly realized his mind had wandered, he blinked at Nick, and his body flushed with heat. "My back's all torqued up," he managed to answer.

Nick watched him from under lowered brows, but remained silent. A shiver ran across Kelly's damp neck. The longer they went without being intimate, the more hellish it was to be alone with Nick.

Somewhere in the afterlife, Eli was laughing at them.

Kelly sniffed and tucked his towel in at his hip a little more securely. "You remember how you used to pop Sanchez's back for him? You'd pick him up and it would crack and shit."

Nick nodded. "Your back's that bad? You want me to try cracking it?"

"Yeah," Kelly said, breathing out in relief. He was thankful Nick hadn't outright refused to do it. From what he remembered when Eli used to have Nick pop his back, it required some pretty intimate contact. And at this point in Eli's sexbargo, any contact at all was torture. That was the main reason Kelly hadn't asked Nick to rub his back down with emu oil yet.

He checked the towel one last time to make sure it wouldn't pull a porno trick and flutter to the ground as soon as Nick touched him, and then moved closer to Nick as his heart hammered. He made the mistake of meeting Nick's eyes before turning his back to him. There was just as much longing in Nick as Kelly felt in himself. Longing, frustration, lust, and a hint of sadness that Kelly didn't quite understand. But then, a hint of sadness pretty much described Nick these days, didn't it?

Nick stepped up behind him, moving the cool air around Kelly, pushing his familiar scent into Kelly's space. Kelly shivered harder and squeezed his eyes closed. When he spoke, he kept it at a whisper so Nick wouldn't hear the tremor in his voice. "How do you do it?"

"Cross your arms, hands to shoulders," Nick murmured, just behind Kelly's ear. It may have been the nerves coursing through Kelly's body, but he thought Nick sounded shaky as well.

Kelly swallowed past a sudden tightness in his throat and brought both hands up, placing them on his shoulders. Nick edged closer, his fingers gentle on Kelly's overheated skin, sliding down his forearms, wrapping around Kelly. He nudged Kelly's neck with his chin as he settled his body against Kelly's. He locked his fingers around Kelly's wrists, squeezing him against his chest. Kelly felt him inhale deeply, and he knew without a doubt that Nick was taking in his scent. It was one of the little things Nick often did when they were close, when they were fooling around, when they were having sex. Kelly loved it, and he realized that he missed it when Nick failed to do it. Kelly smiled as butterflies danced in his chest.

"I'm going to bend backward and lift you off your feet," Nick said against Kelly's ear, and if Kelly didn't know better he would have said the tremor in Nick's voice was more pronounced now. "When I do, just relax and go limp, let your weight do the work."

Kelly turned his head a little, his cheek brushing against Nick's. Nick was still for a moment, not even breathing as he rubbed the very tip of his nose against Kelly's cheek.

"Okay," Kelly said shakily.

"Take a deep breath in, hold in for a few seconds, then let it out slowly. At the end of that breath, I lift you. Got it?"

"Got it."

Kelly leaned into Nick's body, resting his head on Nick's shoulder and staring at the ceiling. He hadn't realized how hard it would be to go so long without Nick's arms around him, without these special, quiet, intimate moments they shared. He wanted this innocent encounter to last as long as he could make it, because they still had two days left to go with Eli's rules.

He breathed in, closing his eyes as he tried to clear his mind of everything but the man holding him. The strength in his arms, the familiarity of his scent, the warmth in his voice. Good God, Kelly loved the man. How long had Nick been his beacon before Kelly had even realized it? And how long had Kelly been pushing that away, intent on some mirage in the distance?

When he blew out the last of his breath, Nick's hold on him tightened. Kelly grunted as Nick squeezed him and bowed his back, lifting Kelly's feet off the floor a little more forcefully than he had expected. As Kelly let his body go limp, let Nick take all of his weight both physically and mentally, he felt his spine popping all the way down to the small of his back, and the tension he'd been battling for days simply melted away.

Nick held him like that for a few seconds, then slowly straightened, setting Kelly on the floor again in the process. His grip didn't loosen, though. "Again?"

"No, it's good," Kelly answered, his eyes still closed, still leaning his troubles into Nick's embrace. He could almost imagine this was a touch intended for more than just popping his back. He turned his head when he felt Nick's arms loosening, and he was disappointed when he couldn't make eye contact. "Thanks."

Nick had his head down, and at first glance it appeared his eyes were closed. They weren't, Kelly realized. He was watching his own fingers as they drifted over Kelly's wrist and up his forearm, his lashes nearly concealing the fact. He hummed as he let go, meeting Kelly's eyes even though they were so close they almost had to go cross-eyed to do it.

"Anytime."

He inched closer and carefully nuzzled against Kelly's neck, his fingers still agonizingly gentle on Kelly's skin and the barest of trembles giving away his nerves. He had his eyes closed when he lifted his head, and Kelly's drifted shut as well as Nick rubbed the tip of his nose against Kelly's cheek and then released him.

Kelly cursed under his breath as the warmth of Nick's body against his back threatened to move away, as the breaths on his face faded. He grasped at Nick's wrists, trapping him in the embrace.

"One kiss," he gasped, despite the fact that straining his neck for that one kiss put them both in a difficult position.

It sounded like Nick was sucking air through clenched teeth.

"Just one," Kelly begged before stealing the kiss he'd requested. Nick's response was subdued, at first, as if he thought they could stop at just one kiss if it was simple and bland. When their lips parted, though, Kelly could feel his heart pounding away at his chest and his blood rushing through his body so fast it made him dizzy. Nick's shaky breath on his lips and his iron grip on Kelly's forearm told Kelly that Nick was having the same violent, visceral reaction to their one, tiny, innocent, isolated, vanilla kiss.

Kelly wasn't sure how long they stood like that. He had no concept of time. Time was something that would pester a man who wasn't being held in the arms of the love of his life; it could find no foothold in Kelly's awareness.

His eyes fluttered shut again as Nick's breaths on his lips sent jolts through his body. "Irish. Will you kiss me?" he pleaded, his voice barely there and his breath stolen.

"Kels," Nick practically whimpered, but before his weak protest could go one more word, he indulged Kelly in the kiss. Fervently. One hand came up to cup Kelly's face, the other hand found a hold on Kelly's hip just above his towel, and he kissed Kelly like he hadn't tasted him in years.

Kelly's body flooded with the tingling excitement that seemed to be Nick's specialty, and he could feel Nick growing hard against his ass as his bit and sucked on Kelly's lip and tongue. Nick's hand delved under the towel, upsetting the precarious fold Kelly had been fussing with just minutes ago, and he dropped it to the ground with a judgmental *fwump*.

Kelly moaned into the kiss and turned in Nick's arms. They dropped all pretense of it being a simple kiss, just like Nick had dropped that towel, and Kelly wrapped his arms around Nick's neck, hand going into Nick's hair, fingers dragging at the collar of his shirt.

"We're breaking the rules," Kelly managed to growl once he'd regained enough self-control to end the kiss.

Nick's fingers dug into Kelly's back, pulling him flush and dragging his teeth over Nick's chin.

"You're right," Kelly said. "Fuck the rules."

Nick dragged him the two or three steps toward the bed, kissing him hungrily, strong hands roaming over Kelly's still-damp skin. The backs of Kelly's legs hit the edge of the mattress, and Nick shoved him. He was still bouncing on the mattress when Nick crawled over him, using his knees and hips to force Kelly's legs apart.

Kelly wrapped around him, his fingers in Nick's hair again, his heels finding his favorite spot to rest at the small of Nick's back. Their kisses were getting noisy, messy, and a little obscene.

Kelly realized in the back of his mind he was expecting Eli's music to start playing any second now, and he grunted plaintively. Nick growled and shoved away from him, hanging his head and closing his eyes as Kelly blinked up at him.

"Babe?" Kelly whispered.

"I told myself we'd learn what we were on this trip," Nick told him, his voice grave.

Kelly cupped his face, his body relaxing under Nick's, his heartbeat slowing. "We know what we are."

Nick was nodding. He pushed up so he was kneeling between Kelly's legs, head bowed, fingers digging into Kelly's thigh. "You know what you are. And I know what I am. But we don't know what *we* are. And this isn't helping us figure it out."

Kelly deflated, resting his head against the mattress and closing his eyes. He felt Nick moving, felt him getting up and moving away. "Have we ever known what *we* were?" Kelly demanded. He hated that he was getting angry, but he had been angry for a long time, and he was tired of repressing it.

Nick stood with his back to Kelly, his shoulders hunched and his head down. He shook his head in answer.

"I've always been . . . confused as hell about the way you make me feel." Kelly struggled to sit up, wincing as his back complained. "And you? You've always been in love with your best friend."

Nick turned, his expression a mixture of wounded and confused. "You're holding that against me?"

Kelly shrugged sadly. "I'm running out of reasons why you'd possibly still be pushing me away, Nick."

"That's not one of them," Nick snarled.

"Then tell me one of them. Tell me *all* of them."

Nick closed his eyes, shaking his head as he ran his fingers through his hair. "There are no reasons, Kels. I'm not pushing you away."

"That's funny. 'Cause I sure do feel pushed."

Nick stared at him for a few seconds, his jaw tight and his eyes narrowed, before his shoulders relaxed a little and he appeared to be coming to a realization. His mouth parted, and his eyes went distant for a brief moment before focusing back on Kelly. "Wow," he whispered.

"What?" Kelly snapped.

Nick was almost smiling when he took a step toward Kelly and dropped his voice lower. "You haven't pulled this shit in a long time, Doc."

Kelly didn't speak. His brow furrowed and he tilted his head carefully, not sure what Nick was getting at.

"You have no idea why you're angry, do you?" Nick asked him.

Kelly huffed, but he couldn't think of anything to say. He snorted instead, waving his hand at Nick. Wasn't it obvious why?

Nick moved closer, ducking his head. "You've been angry with me, but you couldn't bring it up, and you couldn't call me on it. So you saved it until you had a good reason to use it."

"What the fuck are you talking about?"

"Kelly. I asked you to marry me," Nick whispered. "I meant it . . . I meant it with everything I have in me. And then I had to hide it."

Kelly blinked a couple times, his breath gone and his heart seeming to race as they stared at each other. His world was swirling, spinning, diluting down to just one pinpoint of light.

Nick.

"You thought I'd forgotten doing it, so you couldn't be mad about it, isn't that right?"

Kelly swallowed hard, shaking his head.

"A lot's changed between us since then, Kelly. But the way I feel about you hasn't," Nick continued, his voice deceptively calm as he moved closer to where Kelly sat on the edge of the bed. He met Kelly's eyes earnestly for a moment, then dropped slowly to his knees at Kelly's feet. His hands snaked around Kelly's calves, gripping him hard. "I still mean it."

"Babe," Kelly breathed. Both of his hands were on Nick's shoulders before he knew he was moving, and he slid them up toward his neck, cupping Nick's face. "I think . . . I think we've both realized this week that we deserve to be happy, but we're fighting it for some reason and I . . ."

Nick finally managed to blink away the moisture shimmering in his eyes, and his hand dragged up the side of Kelly's leg. "I've been trying so hard to make you happy," he said in a rush of fear and hope. "I hated myself for lying to you. You said yes to me and it was the best moment of my life, Kels, it was like goddamn angels singing in your voice."

Kelly gave a weak laugh and closed his eyes.

"And then I failed you. I'm so sorry I took your trust in me and stomped it out. I swear to God I'll do everything I can to earn it back."

"See that's the problem, Nick," Kelly said with a wince. "You don't have to earn anything from me. You've spent twenty years earning a second chance from me."

"Kelly."

"I said yes, Nick. And I meant yes."

Nick tried to suck in a breath and failed.

"With everything I have in me," Kelly said forcefully. "I still mean it. I love you."

"Marry me, Kelly," Nick whispered. He seemed to resist the urge to pull Kelly closer. Not wanting to pressure him in any way to answer. It was so like Nick. "I don't care when. Or how. You don't have to answer me now. But I mean it with all my heart and what little of my soul I have left. And I just . . ." He stared into Kelly's shocked eyes, his words drowning as nerves finally seemed to swamp him. He managed to force out one last whisper. "I just needed to say it. I've needed to say it since . . ."

"Stop," Kelly said shakily. Nick pressed his lips tightly together, gazing up into Kelly's eyes, waiting for his next orders. Kelly slid his thumb across Nick's cheek. "Don't hedge your bets. Try it again."

Nick sucked it a sharp breath and held it for a second, then let it out with a huff. He took Kelly's hand in his and ran his thumb over Kelly's knuckles. "Kelly Abbott. Marry me."

Kelly blinked rapidly, already nodding as his eyes darted back and forth, like he was trying to decide which of Nick's eyes to stare into as the words hit him hard enough to steal his breath away. "Yeah. Babe. Of course, yes."

Nick patted the side of his face, grinning widely as relief visibly washed through him, making his face flush.

Kelly's expression softened and he gave a curt nod. "Yeah," he whispered again. "Let's do it."

"Yeah?" Nick asked, that tremor of stark fear still hiding in his voice.

Kelly breathed out unevenly. He realized he'd been bundling up all his anger and resentment and tossing it at Nick like a softball, for months. And Nick had finally sniffed out the reason why; that proposal, the one Kelly had so desperately wanted to be real, left neglected in his memory and pushed to the wayside.

"I don't have a ring," Nick admitted.

"It's okay," Kelly told him, shaking his head.

Nick scowled. It obviously didn't sit right with him, and Kelly understood why. It did feel a little like the last time, unplanned and unprepared and . . . before Kelly could finish the thought, Nick was twisting the claddagh ring off his own finger, working it loose with a frown. He finally got it off and held it up. "Until we find one you love."

Kelly nodded, and Nick slipped the ring onto his finger, heart facing outward. "Means you're engaged," Nick told him with a gentle smile.

Kelly looked at it for a few seconds, then took Nick's face in both hands and kissed him. Nick clutched at him, wincing as he tried to get closer.

"Fuck you, dude," Kelly grunted as he tugged at Nick. "Get off your fucking ass, Jesus. Come kiss me for real."

Nick chuckled, and his smile was so wide it had to hurt his face. He shook his head. "I can't. I'm stuck."

Kelly rolled his eyes and slid to the edge of the bed, then gracefully to the floor, almost perfectly landing in Nick's lap and shoving him back. Nick fell on his ass, but he wrapped his arms around Kelly, positioning them so Kelly was straddling him.

"I love you," Kelly said solemnly. "God help us both." He pressed himself against Nick, hands warm under Nick's shirt, chest hard and comforting against Nick's. He kissed Nick languidly, and Nick could feel his contagious smile as Kelly wrapped around him. Nick's breath was warm on Kelly's face when he breathed out. Kelly stared at him, heart pounding, ears buzzing. They were engaged.

He and Nick were engaged. This was real. This was as real as it got.

"No taking it back this time," Kelly warned, pointing his finger in Nick's face.

Nick shook his head, and Kelly kissed him again, wrapping his legs around Nick's waist and burying his fingers in Nick's hair.

"Can't believe you proposed to me while I was naked."

Nick chuckled as he kissed his way down Kelly's neck and back up to his mouth again.

"Surely to God Sanchez would let us fuck to celebrate getting engaged," Kelly said against Nick's lips.

"We can make it," Nick insisted. "We can make it until we're back on the *Fiddler* and it's right."

Kelly laughed and tried to wriggle his hips a little to weaken Nick's resolve. "Fine, but when we get there I'm going to climb you like a fucking ladder."

Nick grabbed for him and rolled them, a cat trying to trap a mouse so he could eat it later. Kelly writhed under him, and Nick groaned.

"Bring out the tow truck, babe, 'cause someone needs to be wrecked," Kelly taunted.

"That doesn't even make any sense," Nick grunted as he pushed to his hands and knees.

"Call in the plow—"

Nick laughed. "Stop!"

Kelly cackled and rested his heels on the small of Nick's back. Nick was hard against him, and Kelly's own erection was almost painful. Nick shook his head fondly, and Kelly's laughter ebbed as he rested his head on the floor, his hands on Nick's chest.

"I really want you right now," he said, voice nearly somber compared to his previous tone.

Nick kissed him, seemingly unable to help himself.

"Let me get you off the floor," Kelly murmured against the shell of his ear. It sent a shiver down Nick's spine that Kelly felt under his fingertips. Kelly nipped at him. "You're going to be so turned on after you see this display of muscles, baby."

Nick was still laughing when Kelly managed to get him to his feet, muscles straining, eyes glittering. Nick took a moment to stare at him, then picked him up and tossed him onto the bed. "You were right," he growled as he climbed on top of Kelly and kissed from his belly up to his chest. "As soon as we get home, I'm going to fucking wreck you."

"Call in the wrecker?" Kelly suggested.

Nick kissed him to make sure he wouldn't keep talking, then with a growl he shoved himself off the bed and paced away. "Just a few more nights," he told Kelly determinedly. "We can do it. Right?"

Kelly nodded, grinning at the sparkle in Nick's green eyes. "Right."

"Who broke the rules last night?" Digger demanded as they waited in line to board the plane that would take them to DC.

Zane raised his hand, glancing at the others ashamedly. Ty rolled his eyes and raised his hand, too. Zane was a little surprised to see Nick and Kelly both raise their hands as well, looking at each other sideways.

"It was only a little, though," Kelly insisted.

Zane almost laughed when Owen turned around from the front of the line, sighed heavily, and raised his hand.

"If they're copping to it, I might as well too."

"You better be talking about San Diego and not last night," Digger said as he shoved an elbow into Owen's back. He seemed truly offended as he looked at all the hands in the air. "Am I the only man a brother can trust around here?"

Owen, Nick, and Kelly all mumbled apologies. Zane just bit his lip, shrugging. He wasn't about to apologize for what he'd done to Ty last night.

The flight to DC was uneventful. Ty mostly stayed in his seat beside Zane, the kittens in their carrier on his lap, his fingers threaded through Zane's.

"Nick and Kelly seem better," Zane commented after they'd been in the air for ten or fifteen minutes.

Ty winced in reply. "Something still feels like it's heading their way."

"Why do you say that?"

Ty was shaking his head, his eyes on the men a row up and over. "Just a feeling, I guess."

When they landed in DC, they retrieved Ty's Mustang from the long-term parking lot and rented another car for the day. Ty sat rubbing the steering wheel and cooing to the Mustang long enough that Zane threatened to get out and ride in the other vehicle, and then they were on their way to a little restaurant on the outskirts of the city. It was closed and boarded up when they found the place, and it looked to Zane like it had been that way for quite a few years.

That didn't stop Sidewinder, of course. Within about five minutes they'd found their way in, and they were picking their way through the dusty debris of a long-forgotten roadside diner.

Ty led the way to a booth near the end of the long counter, and he slid into it, heedless of the dirt. Nick hesitated as he watched, and then he gave the others an uncomfortable glance and sat himself on the opposite bench. He had his fingers clasped together, and his shoulders were hunched defensively.

Ty looked around the booth, sighing heavily. "This was where we sat and talked about Burns's offer to join the FBI." He took another deep breath and turned his attention to Nick. He stared at his hands for a few seconds, then seemed to force himself to meet Nick's eyes.

Nick was chewing on his lower lip, so obviously uncomfortable that even Zane kind of wanted to call a halt to all this.

Nick took a deep breath. "I—"

"No," Ty said quickly, the word coming out angry and a little more forceful than he appeared to have intended, judging by the look on his face. He reached across the table and laid his hand over both of Nick's. "You already done this, bud. You told me and Sanchez all the reasons we should stay the day we sat here ten years ago. You told us. But we didn't listen. So it's my turn."

Nick shifted his shoulders, cocking his head as he listened. He looked like he wanted to slide beneath the table and disappear. Nick was great at propping up someone grasping for support, but when he was stumbling himself, he didn't seem to know support when he saw it.

Ty wouldn't let him look away, though. He ducked his head to make sure Nick was meeting his eyes before he began speaking. "You're the reason we're a team. We were each lost and drifting when you found us. And you pulled each of us in like a moth to a flame. A lighthouse on the shore, bringing us in to safety. That's what you are, Irish. Eli was right in his first letter. Without you, none of us would be here. None of us would have ever known what home really felt like."

They sat in silence, and eventually Kelly slid into the seat beside Nick. The others pushed Ty aside and crowded into the little booth.

"You need us to keep talking, bud?" Owen asked Nick gently. "Because we can."

Nick shook his head. His lips were pressed tight together, and his eyes darted between them.

Kelly shoved his shoulder into Nick. "We all left you, thinking you were strong enough because you made each of us so much stronger. I don't think any of us realized that your strength came from what you were doing for us."

"What's a lighthouse without any ships to signal?" Zane blurted. He'd once thought to himself that Nick was a rocky seashore, calling a drifting Ty home. When they called him a light drawing them to safety, a beacon, Zane was on board the analogy one thousand percent.

"Nicko," Kelly whispered.

Nick answered with a deep inhalation, and he wrapped his arm around Kelly and hugged him. "Okay," he said, and sounded relieved. Infinitely relieved. "Let's open that next letter."

Ty cleared his throat and pulled the letter out of his pocket. "There's, um . . . there's one more thing on the last letter that I didn't read out. I wanted to wait until we were here."

Everyone seemed to tense a little, realizing the task they'd thought was completed still might have more to it.

Ty licked his lips and ran his thumb over the paper. "He says to add up all the mileage we drove on the trip. I looked when we dropped the rental off, and it was two thousand, one hundred, and fifty-nine miles."

Zane whistled, impressed, and the others all shifted around and nodded.

Ty cleared his throat again. "And then he says to figure out how many of those miles we went that Nick carried us."

The table fell silent. Zane could hear the squeaking of the old, dried-out pleather seats. He could see Nick vibrating a little, like he might have been bouncing his knee under the table.

"I did the math on that, too," Ty said solemnly. "Nick carried us one thousand, six hundred, and thirty-eight of those miles."

"Wow," Nick whispered after a few moments of silence.

"I think it's pretty clear what EZ was trying to say with that one," Owen croaked.

Digger gave Nick a nod and a wink. "Respect, brother. That's one hell of an analogy he's tossing out there."

Nick closed his eyes, taking a deep, steadying breath. "You're right," he whispered to no one in particular. "I'm not me unless I've got someone who needs me. You're right. That's where I lost myself the past few months. I convinced myself no one did."

"Babe," Kelly whispered. "We'll always need you. If you knew what state we were all in when we thought you'd died in that street . . ."

"We had to hold Kelly back. Took three of us," Owen told him.

Nick was shaking his head quickly, his eyes closed. "I don't want to know."

Kelly pulled his head over and kissed his temple. "Maybe you should, you know?" he suggested quietly.

"You're not useless, Irish," Ty whispered. "We all still need you. Eli knew that, that's why he sent these letters to you, why he charged you with this mission. He knew how much we all still need you."

Nick was just barely keeping it together, and he finally exhaled a puff of air that disturbed the dust around them. "I love you all," he said, making a point of including Zane when he met the eyes of each man present. "Thank you."

Owen clapped his hands, and the sound echoed off the abandoned chrome and stainless steel. "Let's go find a fancy fucking hotel, get a good night's sleep, and open that next letter over a steak!"

They found a fancy fucking hotel that fit even Owen's standards, and went their separate ways to rest up for several hours before dinner, where their next task would be read. Kelly was restless and just wanted to get these last two letters done so they could head home and start living like they were supposed to be: happy and free. But they had these last few hurdles left, and Kelly was determined to get through them unscathed, with Nick right there by his side.

He sat in the bed of their hotel room and gazed at Nick, a soft smile on his face. He realized that he was grinning whenever Nick grinned. Cocking his head to mirror his lover—his *fiancé*—whenever Nick did it. Even his hands were following Nick's lead, fingers fidgeting, running over his lips, grazing his hair in time with Nick's gestures.

"Are you even listening to me?" Nick demanded after about ten minutes.

Kelly shook his head.

Nick rolled his eyes and stood up from the desk chair. He strolled toward Kelly and put one knee on the foot of the bed. "What's so important that you can't bother to listen to my funny fucking story?"

Kelly licked his lips. He'd been losing himself in Nick for ten minutes or more. He sat up straighter, leaning against the padded headboard and taking a deep breath to steady his nerves. He cleared his throat, but he didn't tear his eyes away from Nick. He had no idea what Nick had been saying, he only knew that Nick had been laughing at his own words, laughing so hard he kept having to start his sentences over. But Kelly hadn't been listening. His mind had been screaming the same thing, over and over, for hours. For days. Weeks. It seemed like he'd been hearing it for years:

Marry me.

Marry me. *Marry me.* God, Nick'd actually done it!

Nick crawled onto the bed, and the roll of his shoulders and that mischievous smirk of his made Kelly's gut cramp, made his heart flutter and his mouth go dry, made his mental wheels stop spinning and screech to a halt in order to concentrate on the piece of artwork that was Nick's smile.

"Trip's almost over," Nick said, his words rumbling across Kelly's skin and raising the hair on his arms and the back of his neck.

Kelly's breath caught in his throat, and he pressed his shoulders against the headboard, sprawling a little more. Nick crawled up his lap, his fingers grazing Kelly's bare thighs, his shadow feeling heavy over Kelly's knees. He bumped his nose against Kelly's chin, grinning when his lips met Kelly's.

"Nick," Kelly breathed as his eyes fluttered shut.

Nick's hands slid up under Kelly's shorts, squeezing his thighs possessively as he kissed him again. "I'm not sure I can go another night without you."

"I know," Kelly groaned. He bunched his fingers in the sheets, trying desperately to follow the rules. They hadn't broken them once, but Ty and Zane had and their fucking iPhones wouldn't stop playing sad Spanish music! He knew if he got his hands on Nick's body right now, those rules would go flying out the window, and he had no desire to find out what sort of hell the sulking, indignant ghost of Eli Sanchez would wreak on him and Nick if that happened.

Nick nipped at his lips. "There has to be a loophole."

"Has to be," Kelly gasped. He gripped Nick's hips, his fingers digging in, pulling Nick into his lap. They both moaned pitifully as Nick's weight settled on Kelly's half-hard cock.

"Fuck, babe." Kelly took Nick's face in his hands and kissed him, and Nick grabbed a handful of Kelly's hair, holding on as the kiss grew more desperate and raunchy.

Kelly bit Nick's lip and held it between his teeth as he said, "Don't squirm or I'll fucking come all over both of us."

Nick stilled his hips, his breaths harsh against Kelly's face, his heartbeat thumping against Kelly's chest. Kelly released his lip and Nick took advantage to steal another kiss. He started to roll his hips again, either completely unaware that he was doing it, or reaching a new level of evil.

Kelly squeezed his eyes closed and pushed his head against the padding, trying to focus on *not* coming all over Nick's ass as he writhed.

"Okay, stop, stop," Kelly hissed as Nick kissed along his jawline and licked Kelly's neck. "I have to ask you something that might effectively kill the mood here."

Nick cleared his throat and sat back, meeting Kelly's eyes for a moment before moving so he was no longer straddling Kelly's lap.

Kelly realized belatedly that it must have been hurting Nick's knee. He watched the wince flash across Nick's face when he settled onto the mattress and straightened his leg out.

Kelly licked his lips and waited until he had Nick's full attention. "When you asked me to top you," Kelly said, shocked by how hoarse and nervous his voice was.

Nick shifted, inhaling noisily. He nodded for Kelly to go on.

"Was it . . . was it just you trying to gain forgiveness?"

Nick blinked at him, his lips parting. "Babe," he said in shock. He brought a hand up to his mouth and swiped it across his chin, then glanced around the room and shifted back to his knees, crawling into Kelly's lap again. He took Kelly's face in both hands. "I'm sorry," he whispered. "That's not why I asked for that. I'm sorry I made you think it was anything other than me wanting that from you."

Relief flooded Kelly so fast he was almost light-headed. "You're sure?"

Nick nodded. He ran his fingers down the side of Kelly's face, and his expression morphed from one of sympathy to a hint of mischief. "You want it again?" he asked, voice lowered.

Kelly breathed out unsteadily. "Yeah," he admitted. He gripped Nick's elbow hard. "But not now. Right now I want you."

Nick exhaled hard, like the words had physically made an impact. He closed his eyes and raised his face toward the ceiling. Kelly reached for him, and Nick reciprocated, somehow wrapping his arms and one leg around Kelly and flipping him. Kelly hit his back with a grunt, and the mattress complained as Nick stretched out over him. Kelly grabbed for him, kissing him urgently, grappling with him as they positioned themselves.

"I thought it'd be so fucking easy to get through the week," Kelly said as Nick kissed at his jaw and neck. Nick's hands were rough on his skin, and it felt like Kelly was on fire as he sought out more contact. He pulled at the back of Nick's shirt, bunching it up around his neck, dragging his blunt fingernails up and down Nick's back.

"Do you want me to stop?" Nick asked, and though he was obviously trying to sound like he was still in control, that tremble to his breathless voice gave him away. He pushed up to meet Kelly's eyes, and Kelly stared, enchanted. There was passion and longing in them, and some pain, frustration, and melancholy as well. But there was also something Kelly had been longing to see return, something he'd begun to fear might have died inside Nick when Nick was too busy fighting for his life to save it: delight. Delight and amusement and glee and *fun* sparkling in those ivy-green depths, trying to rise to the surface like they used to so easily.

"Oh my God, Nicko," Kelly whispered before he could stop himself. "You're back in there."

Nick cocked his head, brow furrowing in an almost painfully confused expression. "Not yet, but I could be," he said, voice wavering with laughter.

Kelly grabbed his face in both hands, his excitement nearly overriding his lust. "I didn't think I'd ever see that color again!"

Nick shook his head, looking even more confused than before. "Babe, you lost me."

"Almost, yeah." Kelly kissed him, scrabbling at his back with both hands to get him closer.

Nick groaned in a mixture of delight and lingering confusion, but he obviously intended to use Kelly's giddiness to his advantage for as long as he could. He lapped at Kelly's tongue, bit at his lips, kissed him from every angle he could manage as his fingers delved into Kelly's hair and then tightened, holding his head in place.

Kelly couldn't seem to get close enough, couldn't manage to make his knees squeeze Nick's hips hard enough, just couldn't get a tight enough hold on Nick to satisfy the need to have him in his arms. He finally took a deep, shuddering breath when Nick raised his head for air, and he placed both hands on Nick's chest to keep him from continuing. "We should stop," he managed, blinking in astonishment at the fire in Nick's eyes. "We've worked so fucking hard on these rules."

Nick was resting on his elbows, close enough that his breaths were harsh against Kelly's face, and with every heaving attempt for air his chest and belly pressed down into Kelly's, stirring the need, fanning the flames Kelly didn't really want to douse.

Nick's phone, somewhere on the other side of the room, began to play a song, one Kelly recognized very well. He grinned as Nick cursed the phone up and down, and then grabbed Nick's face to keep him from getting up. "I roomed with Sanchez for five years, babe. I know that song."

Nick raised an eyebrow.

"That's the song he played whenever I got kicked out of the room."

"You saying that's Eli's favorite sex song," Nick asked, his voice trembling with laughter.

Kelly bit his lip, pulling Nick as close as he could get him.

"I'll follow your lead," Nick promised, breathless and sincere. His thumb grazed over Kelly's cheekbone as he cradled the side of Kelly's head in one hand.

Kelly stared at him for several seconds, basking in the light of those green eyes, reveling in the discovery that Nick was finding his way home again, that the man Kelly so adored was still in there, still battling his way back to him. He shook his head, his fingers curling in the fine hair on Nick's chest. "We've lost so much time, Nick. Wasted so much of the time we've been given. I don't want to lose another second with you."

"Neither do I."

Kelly was silent, holding his breath, waiting.

"It's worth breaking the rules?" Nick finally whispered.

Kelly grinned, and Nick mimicked the expression, the shadows playing off his laugh lines, making his smirk and sparkling eyes nearly sinister. Kelly heart thumped happily against his chest. The rest of his body responded to that menacing smile, too, and he shimmied his hips under Nick's weight to show Nick exactly how worth it breaking the rules was to him tonight. He dragged his hands down Nick's sides, shoving at Nick's belt even though he knew damn well those pants weren't coming off until he unwrapped his legs from Nick's waist.

"Kels," Nick breathed.

"Fuck the rules," Kelly practically snarled, and Nick kissed him again as they started working together to try to get Nick's jeans off him. "Hell, I think we can take that music as permission from Eli's pervert voyeur ghost."

"Agreed," Nick growled as he pushed off the bed to disrobe. He went to his phone, turning the music off as he headed for the door. Kelly undressed as he watched Nick in confusion. Nick opened the hotel door as the phone happily started playing its music again, and he tossed the phone out into the hallway. The music was still playing when Nick let the door slam shut and turned back to Kelly. "I'm not letting him watch, though."

Kelly laughed delightedly as they got rid of the remnants of their clothing. Just minutes later, Nick was using his bulky muscles to keep Kelly's shoulders pinned but his hips held off the mattress as he rocked into him. Kelly was loath to move his heels from the choice real estate at the base of Nick's spine, but he couldn't help himself, and he tossed one leg up onto Nick's shoulder because he knew exactly what it would feel like when Nick hit his prostate in the position Nick was about to put him in. Nick grunted happily as he wrapped his arm around Kelly's thigh, then straightened up, kneeling and pulling at Kelly's hips until his ass was in Nick's lap. Nick found a handle around Kelly's other leg, hitching it up tight against his hip, and he kissed Kelly's knee as it rested on his shoulder. It made Kelly grin.

"Like this?" Nick asked as he rolled his hips.

Kelly nodded. He had his head tossed back, his arms spread out to either side, his fingers bunching in the covers. His back was bowed, not from the position Nick had dragged him into, but from the sheer pleasure of having Nick inside him, of Nick's hands on his body, of the smell of sex mixing with the scent of the hotel bath products Kelly had used in his shower.

Nick's thrusts were smooth and rhythmic. He couldn't go particularly hard or fast in this position, and that was one of the reasons they both favored it. They could take the time to feel each other, to *see* each other.

Nick could wrap his arm around Kelly's thigh and jerk him off as he fucked him, and Kelly would writhe and buck his hips, plaintively grit out Nick's name when Nick changed up the rhythm on him.

Kelly could watch Nick's sinuous hips moving between his thighs. He could lock eyes with him and see what it did to his lover when he squeezed his muscles around him. He could urge him to change the speed of his thrusts with just a nudge from the heel of his foot or a gasp of breath that told Nick exactly what he wanted.

Nick could lean over Kelly—slowly, carefully—bending Kelly's pliant body under him. He could open Kelly up like that, expose his most defenseless position, render him so vulnerable that in any other situation, with any other person, Kelly would have been ready to fight. Nick could do that to him, only to steal a languid kiss as his thrusts slowed and his wandering fingers gripped Kelly's hip.

Kelly's tossed his head to the side as the most recent stolen kiss ended, moaning as he caught sight of the clock by the bed. He'd trudged out of the shower just an hour ago. It felt like a lifetime had passed since then, like they'd had a thousand conversations and shared hundreds of kisses. It felt like a different, sallow life he'd been living, one devoid of the color green and growing more and more hopeless as the minutes ticked by.

"Okay?" Nick gasped. His head was still hanging, his hips rolling in a way he knew damn well would make Kelly scream in mere minutes if he continued

"Yes," Kelly hissed. He repeated the word a few times, a whispered prayer from his lips to Nick's as Nick kissed him once more. His hips were still moving, rolling expertly, his hard cock filling Kelly, spreading him, teasing at his prostate with promises of an amazing climax just minutes away.

Nick pushed off the mattress and knelt again, tilting his head back. His mouth fell open and he sighed desperately as his hands tightened on Kelly's hips. He was close to coming, and he was struggling to stave it off, trying to make their indiscretion last, trying to make breaking the rules something that would leave them both sore and walking funny the next day. Kelly moved his hips to match Nick's movements, and he watched Nick raptly.

Nick and Kelly had both had plenty of sex partners to help them hone their craft separately, and it hadn't taken them long to figure each other's bodies out when they'd started fucking. But Kelly had never seen anything like Nick when it came to timing. Nick swore it was more of a hit-or-miss type of thing, that hearing or seeing Kelly shoot off often helped him come too—and probably vice versa—but Kelly was of the opinion that Nick managed to hit more than he missed when he tried to time their orgasms so they both came within a minute of each other. Sometimes it was mere seconds. A handful of truly memorable times, Kelly *knew* that Nick had been filling him full of cum in the same seconds that Kelly had been in the throes of his own orgasm.

And in Kelly's vast experience, that wasn't something that happened regularly. Still, Kelly hadn't really appreciated it until he himself had been fucking Nick, and he'd realized just how fucking hard it was not to shoot a load early when you were inside someone that tight.

Kelly squeezed his eyes shut, his memory offering up a flash of that night, of their positions reversed and Nick's legs spread wide as Kelly's cock disappeared into his ass.

"Oh God, babe," Kelly gasped. He reached blindly for Nick, afraid to open his eyes for the next few seconds because seeing Nick there between his thighs, seeing the look on his face as he tried to fight off his orgasm, it would be too much. Kelly would shoot his load all over both of them.

His hand hit Nick's belly, and a second later Nick's fingers were grasping for his wrist.

"Will you ride me?" Nick hissed.

Kelly's eyes popped open, and he was nodding before Nick had even finished the question.

"Come on." Nick grunted as he moved them, sliding Kelly's ass sideways. They took the bed covers with them, but neither of them were really concerned with the fact that their mussed bed would give them away. Their mussed *bodies* would do that.

Nick was still on the floor, and Kelly spared a thought for his sore knee, but Nick was a big boy; he wouldn't put himself in a position that would hurt him for very long. Kelly pulled himself upright, getting one knee under him as Nick moved to support the new position, but as Nick sat up with his legs stretched out under Kelly, Kelly's other leg was still propped over Nick's shoulder, trapped by Nick's grip.

Kelly grunted in exasperation, realizing the position Nick had lured him into. He pressed his tongue to the back of his teeth, shaking his head at Nick's grin. Nick leaned on one elbow, putting Kelly's free leg in the perfect position to provide the leverage to move. Nick was keeping Kelly's other leg over his shoulder, though, that much was crystal clear.

Nick's eyes were sparkling, promising a future full of mayhem and more yoga. "I want your cum all over me."

Kelly's cock twitched against Nick's belly, and he groaned as he rolled his hips experimentally. "Christ, this might actually work."

"It does," Nick assured him, and he held up one hand as he propped himself up with the other one. Kelly threaded his fingers with Nick's, squeezing them, palm to palm as he put his weight onto that hand.

Nick's cock pushed deeper into him and he moaned, surprised at how loud and desperate the sound was.

"That's it," Nick whispered.

Kelly found his rhythm, and every sound he made turned into a desperate whimper, whereas every one of Nick's moans seemed to be followed by increasingly lusty grunts.

Nick turned his head and sank his teeth into the inside of Kelly's thigh, and Kelly howled. He bucked his hips, continuing to cry out because it felt so damn good to vocally let Nick know how much he loved this. Nick continued to suck on the inside of his thigh, and Kelly realized that Nick was marking him.

"Oh, God, yes," he cried out, possibly louder than he needed to. He grasped for Nick's hair, giving up on one of his two supports in order to get more of Nick in his hands. The only things keeping their precarious balance now were their twined fingers, Kelly's leg hooked over Nick's shoulder, and a few heroic muscles and tendons that would probably give out right before the orgasms for maximum frustration.

"Babe," Kelly gasped. "Baby. Oh, fuck!"

"God, you're so fucking beautiful." Nick's voice was low and hungry. "Come on me, Kels. Please!"

Kelly tried to hold out just so he could hear Nick's voice for a little longer, just so he could hear that rumble of lust and possessiveness and know that it was *his* for the rest of their lives.

"Kelly!" Nick cried, his voice cracking as he bucked his hips.

Kelly squeezed every muscle in his body, and Nick's cock pulsed inside him. Nick shouted again, but he couldn't seem to get any sound out this time. He pushed his ass off the bed, shoving up into Kelly as he came. Kelly held on, his breaths ragged, his imagination running wild, thinking back over every video they'd ever taken of themselves fucking, trying to remember what it looked like when Nick was emptying himself inside Kelly.

"That's it, that's it," Nick was saying over and over, his hands on Kelly's body, his hips still moving, his cock almost still hard in Kelly's ass.

Kelly was shooting cum all over his chest and belly. Neither of them had touched him yet. He watched greedily as he covered Nick's skin, and finally Nick reached around Kelly's thigh to swipe a hand through the mess on his chest, then gripped Kelly's cock to pump the last spurts of cum out of him.

Kelly threw his head back, gasping, moaning, and it tossed their precarious balance off and sent them both sprawling.

Kelly sprawled on top of Nick's legs, staring dazedly at the ceiling, gasping for breath, his cock pulsing in the aftermath of his orgasm. One leg was caught under him, and the other was draped over Nick's shoulder beside his head. Nick was groaning, spread-eagled under him. After a few seconds of what appeared to be post-orgasmic coma, Nick turned his head and kissed the inside of Kelly's knee.

Kelly raised up to see where Nick's head was. "Prepare yourself," he warned. "Only way to get out of this is my ass in your face."

Nick chuckled darkly. "Give me about thirty minutes and I can work with that."

CHAPTER ELEVEN

Once again, Sidewinder was sitting around a table in a bar, but this time they were enjoying rounds of anything but alcohol. Zane was relieved. He'd been holding steady with tea. Coffee. Water. Soda. Some of the best onion rings he'd ever eaten. But being around a bunch of men drinking each night had sorely tested him, and he was happy to see an array of waters and sodas at the table tonight.

They had two more envelopes to open. It had been a harrowing week, and Zane couldn't decide if he loved Elias Sanchez or hated the bastard. Only a man who knew he'd be dead when all this was going on would make the demands he'd made. They'd covered so many miles and had so many heart-to-hearts. Zane was exhausted, he couldn't imagine how the others felt.

Ty held the second to last envelope up, offering to let anyone else open it. When no one asked for it, Ty slid his fingers under the seal and ripped it open. He cleared his throat before beginning to read.

"The team has always been something we all held sacred," he read, Eli's words filtering to them from the past. "Almost to a fault, we've been honest with each other, brutally and maliciously sometimes. But whenever I told Doc he was a fucking slob and to make his bed, it was out of love."

Ty smiled sadly and cocked his head. At the other end of the table, Kelly lowered his head, sniffing. Nick slid a hand across the table, grasping Kelly's fingers.

"We did something else out of love, something we had to back then. But now, so many years later, it's time to . . . it's time to let go, boys." Ty's words hitched and he had to pause, rubbing a finger over his lips.

"Want me to read it?" Zane offered quietly.

Ty's eyes were welling, and he nodded and handed the letter over, looked away and ran his hand through his hair.

"Anyone object?" Zane asked the others as he held the paper up almost reverently. He hadn't realized it before, but the letters were handwritten, Eli's sweeping words coming to life in all their glory, with some crossed out and some misspelled and others squeezed onto the ends of the line to make them fit. Zane smiled fondly. He hadn't known Eli, but after this trip, he felt like he did. The others all gave him the go-ahead to read the letter for them, and he scanned to find where Ty had left off.

"But now, so many years later, it's time to let go, boys," he read, glancing up at the others. "We all kept secrets, things close to our hearts that we couldn't tell each other for so many reasons. Secrets that hurt us to keep. Secrets that kept us up at night. It's time to take that weight off our shoulders, and share something with each other that we've kept to ourselves all these years. So your penultimate task is to tell the others something they've never known about you. I'll go first."

Zane paused and looked at each man in turn. They were all trying to be stoic, lips pressed tightly, eyes either glistening or closed. Nick and Kelly clutched each other's hands, their heads bowed like they were praying.

"Y'all want me to keep going?" Zane asked.

Owen and Digger both nodded. Ty had given up on being stoic, and his eyes were welling. He swiped at one and smiled at Zane. "Go for it."

Zane found his place again, almost as nervous as he imagined Eli had been when he'd penned this letter. He cleared his throat. "From the day I met Ty and Nick, I kept something from them. And the rest of you, when I met you. So many times I almost confessed this. When we'd go out drinking and Digger would get sad about his lost love from high school, I wanted to share it with him. When Rico and I were on patrol in the middle of the night and he talked about his dad, I wanted to confess this. You see, I told myself it wasn't really my secret to share. But it was. I was just scared. A coward. And now, since you're all reading this and I'm dead and buried, I know I died a coward. It will forever be my biggest failure and shame."

From the opposite end of the table, Zane caught movement. He looked up to find that Nick had covered his face with both hands. Ty had his hand on Nick's shoulder.

Zane pushed on, trying not to draw out the pain. "I had a son."

There were gasps and murmurs from the others, but Zane kept reading.

"I had a son with a girl I knew in San Diego when I was stationed there. We were both still teenagers, and I didn't know about it until I'd been given new orders and moved away. When I tried to make it right, she told me he was better off not knowing who I was, what I was, that he was better off where she had family, and it wouldn't be fair to me or her to get married when we didn't love each other. And I let her think I agreed, that I thought my son was better off without me in his life. I was scared and relieved not to have that responsibility. I took the out she gave me and I ran from that baby boy. And I've regretted it ever since. I have a son out there, and I never met him. I hope one day, you boys can find him. And maybe you can tell him how sorry I am that his daddy was afraid."

Zane pressed his lips together, looking over the top of the letter. The Sidewinders weren't handling this well. Zane felt how shaken they must be. It was obviously a Sidewinder trait to be hard on themselves when they judged internally, because Eli's letter wasn't the first time Zane had heard one of them call himself a coward. "He's wrong, you guys know that, right?"

Ty wiped his face with his sleeve, nodding. He'd snaked his arm around Nick's shoulders and pulled him closer on the bench they shared. Nick was still hiding his face behind his hands, leaning against Ty like he was used to being cuddled when he was upset. Digger and Kelly were both staring at the tabletop, tears tracking silently down their faces.

"Does he leave any information about this kid?" Owen asked shakily. "His name, what year he was born so we can find him?"

Zane nodded, rubbing his thumb over the scrawled words in the bottom corner of the letter. "It's here, yeah."

Owen nodded. Whatever happened from here on out, Zane knew without a doubt that Owen was going to find Elias Sanchez's son. He held his hand out for the letter, and Zane gave it to him with a nod.

Owen cleared his throat, scanning the paper before reading off the last lines with a tremor in his voice that seemed to give it so much more poignancy than Zane's reading ever could have managed. "Now that I've confessed," he said softly. "It's time for each of you to let the rest of us help you carry that weight. We're your brothers. And no matter what's said tonight, we will always love you."

Owen put the paper down and lowered his head, ending the last word on a sob. He took a moment to compose himself, then looked around the table at all of them. He took a deep, shuddering breath before speaking again. "I never should have left that night in the bar, when you came out to us," he told Ty. "I never should have walked away. What I did . . . I'm so sorry, Six."

Ty nodded, attempting to speak but unable to. He closed his eyes to try again. Owen got up and rounded the table behind Zane, sliding onto the bench next to Ty.

Ty raised his arm and pulled Owen into the huddle he was still sharing with Nick, then he sniffed and glanced at the others. "Well you all know what my secrets were. I should have trusted you with them earlier." He met Zane's eyes. "You too, Lone Star. So much earlier."

"What's past is past, right?" Zane tried.

Ty shook his head. "Past is past, but it can still hurt like an open wound. I never understood that before you. I . . ."

Zane realized he was fighting tightness in his throat, influenced by all the waterworks going around the table from normally unflappable men. He swallowed hard and nodded, hoping to keep his composure until the end of the session.

Digger reached for Owen's glass of water and downed it, setting it down with a clank. "I can't think of any secrets," he admitted, sounding forlorn over the news. He lowered his head, twisting his fingers together like he was ashamed of not having a deep dark secret to share like the others did.

Kelly placed a hand on his shoulder, shaking him gently. "You like fire, bud. You just can't hide it anymore," he suggested, a gentle smile accompanying the tease. He and Digger chuckled, and Digger was nodding, a gleam in his eyes that was quite frankly terrifying.

"Wait," Digger said suddenly, the gleam morphing into a light of understanding as he glanced around at everyone. "No, wait, I got something."

Kelly leaned back, his hand still on Digger's shoulder and his head cocked, probably so he could see Digger's face better.

"I guess it ain't really a secret 'cause I wasn't keeping it on purpose. But still . . ." He frowned briefly, his focus on the tabletop now. He seemed more confused than nervous. "I don't really like sex."

Ty and Nick both tilted their heads in a perfectly timed motion that almost made Zane laugh. Digger glanced around, and for the first time in Zane's memory, he seemed self-conscious.

"Are you asexual?" Kelly asked carefully.

"That mean I don't really like having sex?" Digger asked, and Kelly shrugged and nodded. "Then I guess so."

"But . . . all those women?" Owen said.

"Seemed like what I was supposed to do," Digger answered, pursing his lips and then chewing on the inside of his cheek. "Sometimes I'd go home with a girl, and we'd watch a movie. Or play card games. I never really enjoyed it, thought there was something wrong with me." He glanced at Kelly with a weak smile. "Never knew there was a word for it."

Kelly scooted closer and hugged Digger, patting his back and murmuring to him under his breath. Zane could see the relief in Digger's body language, and he understood. All those years of wondering if he was broken, faking it because he thought that was what he should be doing. Zane suddenly wished he'd spent more time trying to get to know Digger, rather than writing him off as batshit crazy. He'd work harder at it from now on, and that went for every member of Sidewinder.

Kelly finally kissed Digger's forehead and squeezed him one more time, then he straightened and took a deep breath, wincing as looked at Nick. "Whenever we went out, when we were all rooming together, and I saw Ty picking up a girl? I'd wingman Eli so he'd hook up with someone and kick me out of my room, and then cockblock Nick so he'd end up alone that night and either have to share the couch with me, or offer to let me bunk with him."

Nick finally looked up over his fingers, still covering the lower part of his face with his hands. He stared at Kelly for a long time before he began to laugh. The chuckles infected the others, and Zane grinned across the table.

"How did you two not fuck ten years before?" he finally asked them.

Kelly shook his head. "I just didn't understand what I was feeling. I knew it felt right being with him, but I didn't really register the difference between friendship that was comfortable and right, and something more." He bit his lip, pushing a coaster across the table and giving Nick a sideways glance. Nick smiled gently at him, and Kelly returned it.

"It wasn't until Ty and Nick both started talking about being bi that I started thinking that there were different . . . I don't know. I started self-analyzing a little. And after you all were sent back, after I asked Nick to kiss me that first time and realized it felt *right*, I started looking around for some answers, trying to understand. There's a term called demisexual that . . . it means you're only sexually attracted to someone you have a deep emotional connection with, and I think maybe that sounds a little like me. I mean, it doesn't fit entirely, but it's a start. And I think maybe that's one of the reasons I sucked at being married." He stopped and blinked hard at Nick, a blush coming over him as the silence caught up to him. His thumb was pushing furiously at the ring on his finger, spinning it around and around. "Married to the wrong person, anyway."

Zane wasn't the only one who noticed Kelly fiddling with that claddagh ring on his finger. "Are you two engaged?" Ty blurted.

Kelly didn't take his eyes off Nick, but he was grinning when he ran his teeth over his bottom lip and nodded.

Zane found himself grinning widely as the others all reacted. Ty tightened his grip around Owen's and Nick's necks, pulling them both closer to him to hug them. Possibly against their will, considering the way they both struggled for air. And Digger got a hold of Kelly's shoulders and shook him happily.

"Why the hell didn't you say so earlier?" Owen asked once he freed himself of Ty's grasp.

"We didn't want to overshadow Eli's finale with anything," Kelly answered, practically beaming. "We were going to tell you guys after the last letter."

"Congratulations," Zane told them both, looking from Kelly's smiling face to Nick. Nick's smile was melancholy at best, though, and he was still looking devotedly at the table. Kelly leaned closer to him, whispering in his ear and then kissing his forehead before relaxing back in his chair.

The group grew silent, and Zane could feel the awkwardness settling in. He wasn't sure if it was coming from the public display of affection that was still sort of new to Sidewinder, or from the silent wait for the last secret.

Nick sat up straighter, shaking off Ty's arm around his shoulders and putting both hands on the table. He seemed to be bracing himself, and his nerves made even Zane edgy. He glanced around the table, looking unsteady and sort of ill. "I have . . . a couple things I kept from everyone. You all know the one, now. But . . ." His eyes went distant, and he lowered his head again, speaking quietly. "The other is not completely mine to tell."

"You don't have to tell us, Irish," Ty whispered. "You've been through enough this year."

Nick shook his head and looked up at Kelly, licking his lips. "I need to. I'm sorry. I can't . . ." He lowered his head again, closing his eyes.

Kelly moved, sliding his chair closer to Nick's so he could put his hand on Nick's back. "Let us help."

Nick turned a little in his chair, facing Kelly. They stared at each other, silent, still, neither man even appearing to breathe. Zane tore his eyes away from them to meet Ty's. He was scowling, giving Zane a concerned glance before he returned his attention to Nick, sitting alone in a sea of turmoil like the craggy seashore Zane associated with him, like an embattled lighthouse in a hurricane. Zane got the impression that whatever this secret was, it wouldn't end in a hug or a laugh like the others.

Nick picked up a stirring stick from the table, and he seemed to be unconsciously fiddling with it as he glanced around at the others. Then he looked back at Kelly, and the fear in Nick's expression damn near broke Zane's heart. After all Nick and Kelly had been through, did Nick really think anything he could say to Kelly would make the man think less of him?

"Should we leave?" Zane whispered.

No one answered him, so he stayed put.

"Okay," Nick finally said with a nod. Zane had no idea what he'd seen in Kelly's eyes as he'd searched for an answer. He had no idea what was going on.

Nick turned to square up to the table again, straightening his spine, taking a deep breath. "You all know about my dad," he said in a rush that made it seem like he was relieved to be speaking. "How he knocked me around. What he did."

Owen and Digger shared an uneasy, confused glance. Kelly and Ty were both still watching Nick avidly, waiting for him to continue.

Nick had his fingers clasped together, eyes down. "I found out when I was a teenager that he wasn't my biological father."

No one at the table moved. Ty and Kelly were still staring at Nick, like they were overcompensating and trying desperately not to react. Owen finally eased back on the bench and slumped against the wall, huffing.

"But," Zane found himself saying. "You donated a piece of your liver to him."

Nick nodded, pursing his lips and narrowing his eyes. "I'm a universal donor. I wasn't an exact match, but my height and weight and blood type, they said I was close enough to be viable." His voice was so low and cold when he answered that it gave even Zane the shivers. "Turns out they were wrong."

"So . . . did *he* know?" Kelly asked. "That you weren't . . ."

"I can only assume," Nick answered as he reached for Ty's water and took a gulp of it.

"That rat bastard," Ty muttered, and he stood up and took a step away. He put a hand on Nick's shoulder, squeezing it as he stood behind him, obviously trying to get control of his temper. "I'm fucking glad he's dead, fuck him."

"Ty," Zane said in shock.

Ty shrugged as he met Zane's eyes. Nick didn't seem to mind Ty's anger. In fact, Zane thought he saw a smile flit over Nick's lips as Ty squeezed his shoulder tighter.

"So . . . I'm confused," Kelly said. "Why were you so afraid to tell us this?"

Nick shook his head, running his hand over his face. His shoved his hand into his hair, his fingers tangling in his curls as he closed his eyes. He wouldn't look at any of them as he spoke. "You remember Paddy Whelan?"

Kelly's brow knitted further. "Guy we met with last summer?"

"Paddy Whelan?" Owen blurted.

Nick nodded silently.

Ty was frowning so hard he struck Zane as a confused puppy trying to follow a laser pointer light. "Who's Paddy Whelan? Why does that name sound familiar?"

"The Boston mob boss?" Owen cried, and the others shushed him before his voice could carry. No one in the restaurant was paying them any attention, though.

Nick brought up his other hand, covering his face with both palms.

"This guy your real dad, Irish?" Digger asked quietly.

Nick raised his head, sighing as he tried to smile at Digger. "Yeah. Yeah he is."

"The . . . the mob boss?" Ty stuttered.

Nick straightened again, putting both hands on his knees as he looked up at the ceiling.

Ty had a hand on the top of his head, staring at Zane. "I finally get it," he whispered.

"What?" Owen asked him.

"Irish was always talking about evil running in his family, and I never fucking understood until just now."

Nick cleared his throat, nodding.

"When did you figure this out?" Kelly asked Nick, voice still gentle even though Zane could tell he was distraught.

"When I was sixteen. He took me in like I was his own. It's because I *was*. Took me a few months to get up the nerve to ask him, but when I did he told me the truth. Said I deserved to know *why* my dad hated me."

Kelly scowled and looked down at the ring he was wearing on his left hand.

"You said he gave this ring to you when you were sixteen. You wore it every day of your life; I've only seen you take this thing off a couple times."

Nick was watching him, eyes darting to the ring and then back to Kelly's face. "Yeah. It was . . . it was a family heirloom. Only thing I have of it, I don't even have his name."

Kelly nodded, frowning harder.

Zane pushed his chair back and stood, drawing everyone's attention. He shrugged unapologetically. "I can't hear," he said as he edged around the table and plopped himself in Ty's vacated seat between Owen and Nick.

"Okay," Owen grunted, and he slapped his hand against the table. "This is a surprise. But it's not awful. Hell, I'd rather Paddy Whelan be your real father than the asshole you grew up with, dude. At least Whelan cared enough about you to do something for you."

Nick snorted, and he almost smiled. But he still looked sick and worried, and Zane knew they'd only heard half of the story.

"Irish?" Ty asked softly, and he sat on the end of the bench seat, his back pressed to Zane's side. "What does he have you doing for him?"

"Nothing," Nick answered immediately. "Nothing . . . *active.*"

Zane felt Ty tense against him.

"That's . . ." Ty wasn't able to finish whatever he'd been trying to say. He just nodded like he understood, lowering his head to scowl at his hands.

"Are you saying you're on the payroll of the Irish mob in Boston?" Zane asked, trying to keep his voice as even as possible.

"Yeah," Nick whispered.

"When did this start?" Ty asked quietly.

"As soon as I got home to Boston. After I left you and Eli on your way to Quantico," Nick said. He winced away from them, turning his gaze to Kelly instead. Kelly hadn't taken his eyes off Nick, though, and they sat staring at each other for a few long moments.

"You've been getting paid under the table by an Irish mob family in Boston for the last ten years," Kelly said.

Nick gave a sharp nod.

"*Your* Irish mob family," Kelly clarified, speaking slowly like he was dazed by the words.

Nick either wasn't willing or wasn't able to answer. His lips were parted like he wanted to, but the words seemed to have struck him dumb.

"You're the only living son of a Boston mob boss," Kelly said. He lowered his head, and he nodded as if he was talking to himself internally. "Okay. Well, that won't get you killed, will it?" he asked softly, then he stood before Nick could respond and walked away.

Nick sat in the dark, coat wrapped around him to ward off the chill, staring sightlessly off into the lights of the city. He'd come to the roof of the hotel partly because the sea was calling to him and he was tired of being cooped up inside, but also because he didn't feel like getting a pep talk from Ty, and only the direst of pep talks could lure Ty onto the roof of a high-rise.

He just needed the silence. The peace that would come from the distant sounds of the city below.

He tore his eyes away from the sky, where he'd been seeking the stars, when he heard faint footfalls behind him. He knew without turning around that it was Kelly, and just the thought of the man made his chest ache and his heart pound a little faster.

How the hell could he love someone so much, and yet still keep fucking up like this?

Kelly didn't say a word as he shuffled up to the roof's edge and sank down beside Nick. He settled on the cold concrete, then scooted closer, pressing his shoulder to Nick's. A moment later he wrapped a blanket around both of them, and Nick shivered violently. He hadn't realized how cold he'd been until the warmth surrounded him.

"You been up here a long time," Kelly said, keeping his voice neutral.

"I'm . . . I needed time to . . ."

"You're scared to come inside because then you'll have to look me in the eye," Kelly stated. "And you're afraid of what you'll see. Right?"

Nick jerked and glanced at him, but Kelly was gazing out into the sea of humanity, his expression serene, his body relaxed. He slowly turned his head to meet Nick's eyes, and his fingers snaked over Nick's thigh to take hold of Nick's hand. He squeezed it, pulling it out of Nick's lap and into his, his thumb running over Nick's knuckles.

Nick couldn't catch his breath as he stared into Kelly's eyes, no matter how many shuddering gasps he attempted.

"You walked away," Nick found himself saying. "I didn't think you'd want to talk."

Kelly lowered his head. "I know. I'm not going to say I'm sorry, because I'm not."

Nick winced and had to tear his eyes away from Kelly, concentrating on the moonlight instead. He swallowed hard, wondering if he had the strength to weather yet another storm the size of this heartache. He didn't think he could.

Kelly sighed loudly. "I've found out that my temper sometimes gets away from me. Especially when it's you. When it's us." He stopped, and Nick had to glance at him again to see what the heavy silence contained. Kelly was looking at him again, his brow furrowed, his mouth turned down in frustration. "We don't fight much. We don't even disagree much. But the few times we have and I've gotten angry, I do and say things I regret. I hit you when you came clean last time."

Nick had to swallow again to fight the tightness in his throat. He merely nodded, staring into Kelly's eyes.

Kelly leaned closer to him, his expression still grim. "That's the kind of thing I can't take back. It's the kind of thing you remember, even if it's not . . . I know our friendship was a physical one, and we both threw a few punches over the years. But it's different now. And I don't want to ever do that to you again."

"Kels—"

"Don't," Kelly grunted. "Don't tell me you don't care, because even if you don't, you should. We both know my temper. We both know I act first and think later. And because it's the way we've always communicated, it's the way I go first. And it's bad. And I'm breaking myself of it. But that means I need to walk away sometimes before I say or . . . *do* something I'll regret."

Nick scowled. It sounded like Kelly had been thinking about this for a long time, that he'd been working through it on his own without mentioning it. That was such a foreign concept to Nick that he wasn't even sure he could name another internal conflict of Kelly's that he hadn't been privy to from beginning to end.

"So," Kelly said, and he rested his elbow against Nick's hip, looking back out over the city. "What now?"

"Kelly . . ."

"I get why you kept it from us. From me. You're the fucking long-lost prince of a Boston mob family. That's something that literally could get you killed if the wrong person found out. I know you hate secrets and you think keeping them is some horrible sin, but . . . some secrets are kept for a reason. I sure as hell chalk this one up to that category."

"And being on his payroll? That doesn't bother you?"

Kelly shrugged. "Honestly? No. That's your biological dad taking care of his son. Hell, makes me like the man a little more. And fuck it, you know what? If you want to go work for him and then take over the family business? I'm in. Just take me with you so I can watch your back."

"Jesus, Kels."

"What?" Kelly snapped. "I do not care. You're a hell of a better person than I am for actually giving a damn, because if it makes me happy and it only hurts the people who deserve it? I'm in. Paddy Whelan wants you to take over for him and we have to run the underbelly of Boston together? I'm in. Fuck it. Maybe we could even do some good in Boston. Can you imagine the kind of impact a man like you, with morals, could have in that position? I'm in. I am one thousand percent in. I'm tired of you torturing yourself trying to live up to this standard of human that just does not fucking exist."

"Trying to *not* become a mob boss is a pretty low standard, all things considered."

"Fuck you, dude, you know what I'm trying to say."

Nick huffed. He took in a deep breath and shook his head. "Okay. Will you answer me honestly if I ask you a hard question?"

When he glanced at Kelly, he got a nod in answer. He turned a little more, his grip on Kelly's hand tightening.

"Since that first kiss, have you spent more time being happy? Or more time being sad, angry, and worried?"

Kelly ran his teeth over his bottom lip, his fingers fidgeting with Nick's as his eyes searched Nick's face. When he spoke, the sadness in his voice made Nick want to pull him closer and just hold him. *Just hold on to him.* "Why do I get the feeling you're about to make a decision based on the answer I give you?"

"You said you'd answer honestly," Nick managed to respond.

Kelly rolled his eyes and looked away. He shook his head, his jaw jumping and his body growing tense. "You know what, fuck you, Irish," he snarled, glancing back at Nick. His eyes sparked in the moonlight. "If we had never kissed that night, if you had laughed it off and gone on your way, the last three years would *still* have been hard! I still would have spent six months agonizing over the fact that my brothers were off fighting while I was stuck at home. I still would have been worried sick and pissed off that you and Liam Bell were working together without ever asking one of us for our help! And I still would have been a fucking wreck at your bedside in Miami waiting for you to fucking wake up! Yeah, maybe I wouldn't have spent so many nights in bed, lonely, waiting until I could be with you again, but you know what? At least I fucking had you to look forward to! Without you, without what we have, life would have been the same old stupid nothing, just day in and day out, and at least now I know what it's like to have someone I want a future with. That sure as shit offsets anything you could possibly tell me is wrong with us."

Nick was struggling to keep his eyes on Kelly as he ranted. He was so goddamn beautiful when he got worked up, he was like a storm on the horizon, filled with lightning and thunder and whitecaps and threatening to take your vessel down with him when he swept onto your decks.

Kelly began to fight with the blanket around his shoulders, still spitting out words as he tried to get the material off him. "You want to fucking push me away because you think you're hurting me, you go ahead and do it. See how fucking much better it makes you feel when you go off trying to be a fucking island on your own. But know one thing. If you do that, if you send me away to save me, then *you* will be my life's biggest heartbreak. You won't be saving me from anything. Just saving yourself."

He finally managed to get the blanket off, and he rolled back and away from Nick, going over one shoulder to get to his knees. He knelt there, eyes flashing, teeth gritted as he stared.

Nick reached for him and snagged him by his shirt collar. Kelly tried to push his hand away, but Nick tightened his grip and gave Kelly a tug instead.

"What?" Kelly shouted.

"Don't go," Nick breathed. "I don't want to be your heartbreak."

Kelly studied him for a few seconds, and slowly his body relaxed, his eyes softening. He got to his hands and knees and crawled closer to Nick, and Nick pulled harder at his shirt to urge him the last few inches. Kelly's lips met his a little more violently than he'd expected, and his balance wavered. Kelly grabbed him by both arms and dragged him backward.

Nick didn't struggle, just let Kelly pull him away and lay him out on the wet concrete and sparse gravel when they got far enough away from the edge to be safe. Kelly snagged the blanket and threw it around his shoulders like a cape, then stretched out over Nick and kissed him again. The blanket fluttered to the rooftop as Nick clutched at Kelly and returned the kiss with everything he had to give to it.

"This is the last time we have this conversation," Kelly growled.

Nick recognized his tone of voice, and it sent a shiver down his spine. He nodded jerkily, his breath stuttering. "As long as you don't walk away from me again."

Kelly cocked his head, looking like he was about to argue.

Nick dug his fingers into Kelly's ribs. "I'd rather you lose your temper and get it out the same way we always have than watch you walk away. It hurts too fucking much," he admitted. "We've had our language too many years to change it now."

"Okay," Kelly whispered.

"Promise me."

Kelly pulled the blanket up over their heads and kissed him again. "I promise," he murmured between kisses, and Nick wrapped his arms around him, finally feeling his heart unclench.

If another storm came through, at least Nick had Kelly to weather it with him.

CHAPTER TWELVE

Sidewinder stood amongst the neat rows of white marble that stretched as far as the eye could see. They stretched too far, there were too many, so many lives lost and remembered on the sacred ground of Arlington Cemetery.

Nick held Elias Sanchez's last letter in both hands. The paper trembled in the breeze. It certainly wasn't Nick's hands trembling. It certainly wasn't that.

Zane stood to the side, watching solemnly. He didn't feel as if he belonged on this last task. It was too personal. Too hard.

"Who wants to go first?" Kelly finally asked. They all stood staring down at the headstone. No one answered him. No one moved.

After a solid minute of silence, the crinkling of the paper in Nick's hands finally urged Kelly into action. He stepped forward, twisting his hands together, and cocked his head at Eli's grave.

"The last words we had were over the phone," he began. He closed his eyes and swallowed hard.

Zane had to strain to hear what he was saying, and he edged a little closer and placed his hand on the small of Ty's back under the guise of offering silent support.

"We were talking about going hiking. He wanted to come to Colorado and spend a week at the camp." Kelly snorted and smiled, glancing over his shoulders at the others. "He had a plan for an adventure trek. And he couldn't even get it out because he was laughing so hard halfway through. You know that laugh he had, where his whole body shook and he started wheezing?"

The others chuckled and nodded. Digger wiped a hand over face, hiding his eyes behind his palm.

"He told me he'd email me his idea because he kept giggling," Kelly said, gazing at the headstone and shaking his head fondly. "The last words I said to him were, 'See you soon, babe.' And his last words to me were . . ." Kelly seemed to stumble over them, swallowing hard a few times. "He said, 'Be good, Doc.' And he hung up."

He wiped a hand across his mouth, his head lowered, and then he knelt on one knee and put his palm on the top of the headstone. "See you soon, brother," he whispered, and after another few seconds with his head bowed, the wind ruffling his hair, he pushed to stand again and stepped back. He leaned into Nick briefly like he needed the contact to comfort himself, then stood straight again, chin up and eyes on the marble.

"He was laughing last time I talked to him, too," Digger said without preamble. He glanced around almost self-consciously and stepped toward the headstone, getting down on both knees, shoulders slumping as he sat back on his feet. "He called me, said he needed one of my mama's recipes. The hotter the better, he said he wanted it to hurt coming out the other end. I told him he'd have to barter with her for it, so he sent her a basket of avocados over the internet. Fucking avocados. I called him to cuss his ass out, and he just laughed. Same kind of laugh he gave Doc, I bet. He told me to enjoy my fruit dip, then he said, 'Love you, sweetcheeks.'"

Digger laughed, grinning wide as he touched his fingers to the top of the headstone. "And the last words I ever said to him were, 'Love you too, pookie.' And we hung up. And the next call I got was from Rico telling me he was gone."

The group was silent as Digger's fingers slid off the headstone. "Love you too," he whispered. He didn't get up like Kelly had, he just remained slumped on the ground.

Soon enough, Owen got to his knees beside Digger, their shoulders pressed together, both of them hanging their heads. Zane glanced at the others to find Ty standing with his eyes closed, his face raised to the breeze.

"He called me to tell me he was coming to San Diego when he finished the case he was working on," Owen announced. "Said he wanted my help tracking down someone. He'd explain it when he came into town. I think he was planning to hunt down his son."

Owen knocked on the ground in front of the grave with his fist. "I'll find him for you, bud."

Zane glanced at the others again to see Ty watching Owen sympathetically, and Nick and Kelly both standing together, their heads lowered, their hands clasped together so hard Kelly's knuckles were turning white.

"Last words I said to him," Owen continued, his voice going hoarse and wavering. "I said, 'Stay out of trouble, chief.' And he told me, 'No promises.' Then he laughed and hung up. He laughed."

Owen nodded as his hand clutched at the manicured grass over the grave. He brought his fingers to his lips and kissed them, then pressed them to the letters engraved on Eli's headstone. "Stay out of trouble."

Ty leaned back into Zane's hand, sniffing. "I didn't answer his last call to me. I was busy," he admitted, his voice cracking. "He left me a message. Last time I talked to him was in person, I saw him when I was passing through New York. We met for a drink. He gave me a hug before I got in a cab to head for the airport. Tight hug, you know? Like he did. Patted me on the back and messed up my hair. I told him, 'I'll see you around.' And the last thing I heard him say was, 'Safe trip, bro.'" Ty closed his eyes, a smile playing at his lips. He breathed out shakily and stepped around Nick and Kelly to kneel beside the headstone. He placed his hand over the top, patting it with his fingers. "I'll see you around," Zane heard him whisper.

He stood up almost immediately, stepping away and glancing at Zane with glistening eyes. Zane gave him an encouraging nod. He knew how much Ty had tortured himself in the years following Eli's death, how often he had wondered if answering that last call would have saved his friend. Ty stepped closer, and Zane pulled him under his arm, hugging him silently.

The paper in Nick's hands rustled in the breeze. Kelly turned to face Nick, leaning forward like he was trying to get a good look at him. "Nick," he whispered, bringing his hand up to Nick's shoulder.

Zane scowled, wondering why in the hell Kelly would push Nick into taking his turn when this had to be hard for everyone. But then Kelly stepped closer and wrapped his arm over Nick's shoulder, and Ty broke away from Zane's grasp to go to Nick's other side like he sensed something wrong.

Zane realized, with a sickening twist in his stomach, that Nick was slowly sinking to his knees. A rock, finally crumbling to pieces. Ty and Kelly couldn't keep him on his feet, and he hit the ground hard, his head hanging, the letter crumpled against his belly as he clutched at it. Zane heard a quiet sob as he moved to help, and when he caught sight of Nick's face, he saw tears trailing down his cheeks. He took a step back, knowing there was nothing he could do to help. He didn't belong in this moment.

"It's okay, babe," Kelly whispered as the others silently watched Nick, seeming to be at just as much of a loss as Zane was.

"I can't remember," Nick managed to say as he raised his head. His eyes welled, and he tried to take a breath, but it turned into a wavering, distraught gasp. He stared at the headstone, another tear breaking free and trailing down his cheek. "Why can't I remember?"

No one moved. No one even seemed to be breathing, and the breeze picked up as if it was trying to cover the sound of Nick's words. He stared at the headstone, gritting his teeth. Then he lowered his head again and covered his face with one trembling hand. His shoulders shook, but he made no sound as Ty and Kelly both wrapped their arms around him, trying to comfort the kind of pain that Zane knew no one could soothe away.

Nick raised his head again, and Zane found his throat tightening sympathetically as he watched the man fall to pieces. He'd never fully realized what these men meant when they said *brother*, but watching them, he was beginning to understand now. Nick reached into his coat pocket and pulled something out, looking at it as it sat in his palm. It was a dime, probably the same stupid dime he'd found on the ground that they'd been using to toss when they made decisions. The Dime of Fate, they'd called it.

Nick smacked the dime onto the top of the headstone, lowering his head as he held on to the marble for dear life. He was crying again, his shoulders trembling, trying and noisily failing to catch his breath.

"It's okay," Ty whispered into Nick's ear, tugging at his arm. When Kelly and Ty struggled to their feet to pull Nick off the ground, Zane looked away. It didn't feel right to be privy to the pain on Nick's face.

Digger and Owen moved with them, each of them edging in to hug Nick, murmuring to him, pulling him away from Eli's grave.

Zane stood alone, hands stuffed in his pockets, the breeze tugging at his hair as he watched Sidewinder stagger away. He glanced down at the grave, at the dime reflecting in the sunshine.

"They still need you," he whispered to Eli. He was shocked to find his own voice wavering, and he cleared his throat, feeling sort of stupid. He swiped his hand over his mouth, leaving one last request before walking away. "Don't leave them yet."

The morning after Nick and Kelly returned home to Boston, they allowed themselves to sleep in. It was glorious, and even when Nick rolled himself out of bed and mumbled something about breakfast, Kelly remained happily tangled in the sheets. He wasn't sure how long he stayed there, catching up on all the sleep he'd lost the last couple weeks, but when he finally did drag himself up the steps to the galley, he was surprised to find the *Fiddler* empty, the stove cold.

"Nick?" he called, even poking his head through the hatch to check the flybridge when he searched the yacht. But Nick was nowhere to be found. When he returned to the galley, he found a slip of paper he'd overlooked on his first glance around.

It was a note telling him Nick had gone for groceries, since the *Fiddler*'s galley was barren.

Kelly wound up out on the foredeck, face turned to the sun, book forgotten on the table next to him. He heard Nick when he boarded the yacht, but he remained where he was. Nick would find him soon enough, and most likely join him. They might have been on a vacation last week, but it had been anything but relaxing. They deserved to lounge around on the boat for a couple years.

"Thought you'd be out here," Nick said softly when Kelly heard his footsteps approaching.

He turned his head, shielding his eyes against the sun as he squinted up at Nick.

Nick sat on the lounger next to him, elbows on his knees, hands clasped together. His expression was solemn, his forehead deeply lined and his mouth turned down in a thoughtful frown.

"You okay?" Kelly asked.

"Yeah."

Somehow, Kelly didn't believe him.

"I got some supplies," Nick went on, either ignoring Kelly's trepidation or oblivious to it.

"Supplies for what?"

Nick took a deep breath, and when he blew it out, he seemed relieved somehow. He tore his eyes away from the horizon, and met Kelly's with a wistful smile. "It's time to put the *Fiddler* back together. She served her time. She deserves to be made whole."

Kelly sat up and swung his feet to the warm deck, reaching for Nick's hand. It trembled in Kelly's fingers, and Kelly squeezed it gently. Either Nick hadn't taken his medication . . . or he was taking too much.

"Will you help me?" Nick asked him.

Kelly nodded. "Of course."

They spent the next weeks taking their time with the *Fiddler*, putting back every piece of her that had been torn apart over the last few years of gun battles, fighting, and physical and emotional turmoil. There was one bullet hole that Nick wouldn't let Kelly fill, though. Nick didn't seem to know why, but he said he needed it to stay there.

So Kelly left the bullet hole as it was, and slowly but surely the rest of the yacht was put back together. The door and the salon walls that had been shot apart by CIA agents and Nick's shotgun were replaced with decorative teak pieces that fit seamlessly into the original panels.

The doors to both cabins—the guest cabin that Zane Garrett had practically ripped off its hinges, and the main cabin that he'd obliterated with that same shotgun—were both replaced with doors straight from the shipbuilders. Kelly was relieved to be able to shut the door to their cabin again; it meant feeling safer as he slept, and not having to quiet themselves when guests stayed on the yacht.

And finally the bunk room, which had originally hosted two oversized single bunks and a small closet space, was made whole again. At first Nick had suggested making it a space for Kelly. But after some thought, Kelly realized that having the two bunks there meant space for the other Sidewinder boys when they set sail, and that was all Kelly could ask of the *Fiddler*.

Kelly and Nick sank into a glorious rhythm, almost the same level of comfort they'd enjoyed before they'd become a couple. Kelly knew the peace wouldn't hold, but he was willing to take it as it came. The only thing bothering him, three weeks after they returned to Boston from their Great Sanchez Trek of 2013, was that Nick disappeared once every day for about half an hour.

Kelly hadn't noticed it at first because Nick was pretty good about casually going off on errands and returning without being suspicious. But Kelly soon picked up on it, mostly because Nick grew increasingly anxious as the weeks marched on. It was the first week of July when they finished the *Fiddler*'s rehabilitation, and they were sitting on the deck enjoying the feeling of accomplishment when Nick announced that he was going to head out for more beer before the stores all closed for the Fourth of July holiday.

"You have to go now?" Kelly asked him, too tired and buzzed and sunburnt to get up.

"The packie's going to close, we'll go the Fourth without beer!"

Kelly narrowed his eyes.

"I'll be right back," Nick insisted, and he headed inside before Kelly could protest more.

Kelly scowled as he watched him go. What the hell was Nick doing every day that he had to hide it from him?

He lounged on the deck, worrying about it for the next twenty minutes, but true to his word, Nick was back with an armload full of alcohol and groceries. He came out to the deck and sat on the lounger next to Kelly, his expression unusually solemn.

Kelly raised his head when Nick rested his elbows on his knees and frowned at him. "You okay?" Kelly asked. A feeling of dread settled in his belly. He couldn't make himself sit up, though. Somehow fighting against the sun made it seem easier to face what had to have been bad news, if Nick was making that face.

Nick's fingertips played over his bare finger, where the tan line left behind by his absent claddagh ring was beginning to fade. He chewed on his lip for a second, then nodded in answer. "Kels," he started, and he took a deep breath, like he was steadying himself. "I need the ring back."

Kelly blinked at him, and Nick must have taken it as confusion, because he held his hand up and wagged the ring finger where his claddagh ring usually sat. "Oh," Kelly managed to get out. His mouth was dry as he twisted the ring off his finger. He was proud of himself for keeping his hand steady when he wordlessly handed the ring to Nick.

Nick plucked the ring out of his palm. "Thank you," he whispered. He smiled gently as he reached in his pocket, and when he held his hand out again, a little ring box was in his palm. "It finally came in the mail."

Kelly stared at it.

Nick's grin widened. "I thought it was time you had your own to wear."

"Really?" Kelly blurted, his voice breaking as he sat up and swung his legs over, bumping Nick's knee. "Is that where you've been disappearing to? The post office?"

Nick nodded. "I hope you don't mind I picked it out. If you don't like it, we can find something else. But this just . . . it felt like you."

Kelly took the box and narrowed his eyes at Nick. "Where'd you find this?"

"Saw it in Colorado, had one made for you and shipped back here."

Kelly gazed at him for a few seconds longer, then lifted the lid of the box carefully as his nerves tumbled. It was hitting him that this was real, that they'd done this and it was sticking this time. That this was an honest-to-God engagement ring.

Inside the felt box, he found a simple tricolor band with a metal interior, and an exterior ringed with white, turquoise, and brown. He immediately loved the colors, and he grinned when he pulled it out of its cradle.

"It's made of turquoise, wood, and antler, with a titanium inner ring to make it strong," Nick explained. "The artist assured me he finds all his materials, none of it is harvested."

Kelly ran his thumb over the smooth surface.

"I don't know much about the Ute tribe," Nick continued. "I was going to research them, see what their customs were. I know that part of your family is important to you. But when I saw this, I just . . ."

"It's perfect," Kelly said, grinning at Nick. He slid it onto his finger, holding it out so Nick could see.

Nick's thumb ran over the ring, sliding down Kelly's finger until he got to the tip, where he gripped him harder and tugged. Kelly scooted closer and kissed him.

"Can't believe you managed to do this right under my nose," Kelly said. "Again."

Nick actually smiled and kissed him harder, pulling him closer. A month ago, that joke would have had Nick averting his eyes in shame. They were taking baby steps, but they were definitely getting there.

Kelly grabbed his face and returned the kiss enthusiastically. "I have a question," he asked between kisses. Nick hummed and pulled Kelly even closer, forcing him to climb into Nick's lap. "If you're the son of an Irish mobster, does that mean we have to invite him to the wedding? What's the protocol on that?"

"You're fucking ridiculous." Nick kissed him again anyway.

Kelly finally pulled away from him and stared at Nick wistfully, the weight of the new ring on his finger a conscious thing. "There's some things we need to do before we settle down."

Nick grunted in agreement. "Should we make a list?"

"A list isn't a bad idea."

Nick tugged at Kelly's hand, brushing his nose against Kelly's, his lips against Kelly's. "Where do we start?"

Kelly shoved off the lounger so he was hovering over Nick, his head tilted sideways so he could kiss him. Then he backed away just enough that they could meet each other's eyes. "I say we figure out what's first the way Sidewinder always has."

Nick's grin was suddenly terrifying, and Kelly kissed him hungrily. When they parted for air, Nick was humming delightedly. "I'll go get the dartboard."

Explore more of the *Sidewinder* series at:
riptidepublishing.com/titles/series/sidewinder

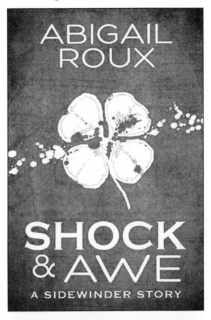

Dear Reader,

Thank you for reading Abigail Roux's *Part & Parcel*!

We know your time is precious and you have many, many entertainment options, so it means a lot that you've chosen to spend your time reading. We really hope you enjoyed it.

We'd be honored if you'd consider posting a review—good or bad—on sites like **Amazon, Barnes & Noble, Kobo, Goodreads, Twitter, Facebook, Tumblr,** and your blog or website. We'd also be honored if you told your friends and family about this book. Word of mouth is a book's lifeblood!

For more information on upcoming releases, author interviews, blog tours, contests, giveaways, and more, please sign up for our weekly, spam-free newsletter and visit us around the web:

Newsletter: tinyurl.com/RiptideSignup
Twitter: twitter.com/RiptideBooks
Facebook: facebook.com/RiptidePublishing
Goodreads: tinyurl.com/RiptideOnGoodreads
Tumblr: riptidepublishing.tumblr.com

Thank you so much for Reading the Rainbow!

RiptidePublishing.com

ALSO BY ABIGAIL ROUX

ABOUT THE AUTHOR

Abigail Roux was born and raised in North Carolina. A past volleyball star who specializes in sarcasm and painful historical accuracy, she currently spends her time coaching high school volleyball and investigating the mysteries of single motherhood. Any spare time is spent living and dying with every Atlanta Braves and Carolina Panthers game of the year. Abigail has a daughter, Little Roux, who is the light of her life, a boxer, four rescued cats who play an ongoing live-action variation of *Call of Duty* throughout the house, one evil Ragdoll, a certifiable extended family down the road, and a cast of thousands in her head.

To learn more about Abigail, please visit abigailroux.com.

Enjoy more stories like
Part & Parcel
at RiptidePublishing.com!

Catch a Ghost
ISBN: 978-1-62649-039-0

Peripheral People
ISBN: 978-1-62649-269-1

Earn Bonus Bucks!

Earn 1 Bonus Buck for each dollar you spend. Find out how at
RiptidePublishing.com/news/bonus-bucks.

Win Free Ebooks for a Year!

Pre-order coming soon titles directly through our site and you'll
receive one entry into a drawing for a chance to win free books for
a year! Get the details at RiptidePublishing.com/contests.

BRICK & MORTAR
books

Brady Wade ducked into the shadows of an old brick building near the water, his hair dripping and his arm bleeding. Kind of profusely. His arm probably wasn't the only thing bleeding, actually, but the water had been so cold he'd lost most of the feeling in his body by the time he'd dragged himself out of the harbor.

He'd lost every last bit of his gear when his boat had gone into the drink, but he was certain the safe house was here. He'd memorized the locations of all three in Baltimore, and this was definitely the only one he'd be able to reach before he lost consciousness. He'd been observing it since roughly three in the morning, and he'd seen nothing in the predawn hours. The front appeared to be a bookstore, information which hadn't been in the files, and that was the main reason he'd held back even while losing blood. The back door was where he was supposed to make contact, and it was unobstructed . . . but was it the right fucking place?

He closed his eyes to clear his head, and long minutes later he jerked when he began to slump forward. He snapped his chin back, blinking hard. He was going to pass out in the street if he didn't move now.

He was about to lurch to his feet when he caught movement down the street. Despite all his training, despite all the situations just like this one he'd found himself in during his career, his heart hammered faster as he watched the deadly woman slip through the shadows. She was moving deliberately; hunting. He breathed a sigh of relief when he determined she hadn't picked up his trail yet, but the relief was temporary. She was relentless, and he wouldn't last another minute going toe-to-toe with her.

He watched her, blinking away the darkness on the edges of his vision, trying to figure out a way to signal that safe house for help without getting himself killed. A few seconds later, she slipped into the shadows and was gone, her presence on the dark street replaced by the single headlight of a motorcycle piercing through the morning fog.

Wade watched it, pressing his fingers to his side and wincing at the cracked ribs under his body armor. Good God, that woman had kicked his ass.

The motorcycle roared to a stop behind the bookstore, and the rider took a moment to secure it before straightening to his full height. Okay, so this guy was a fucking giant, but Wade was pretty sure he could take him if he needed to. He pressed his knuckles into the cement, pushing up. A hand on his shoulder stopped him, though, shoving him back to his knees.

"Motherfu—"

"I ain't your mama, son," the man behind him said in a soft Appalachian drawl. A gun cocked. "Get up."

Wade blinked at the ground. Shadows were beginning to appear on the street as sunrise threatened. He shook his head. "I can't."

Even as he spoke, Wade toppled over and sprawled on his back. As the darkness crept in on his vision, he saw the silhouette of the man against the dawn, shaking his head in disgust and holstering his weapon.

"I told you no more strays," a voice was saying as Wade fought to consciousness.

"I don't want to *keep* him," another man insisted. Wade recognized that second voice as the one of the man who had sniffed out his hiding place. He'd never even seen the guy coming.

"Did you check the computer?"

"Last time I checked the computer, you told me never to touch the computer again."

"Fine. Start the coffee and I'll contact the home office."

Wade's head swam, and he went in and out of consciousness for a while. He didn't know how long he'd been out when he woke the next time. It was still and quiet, and so Wade was too, keeping his breathing under control as he listened.

He heard what sounded like sparse foot traffic and whispered conversations. The occasional ding of a bell over a door. Steps shuffling on hardwood floors. Every now and then there was a boisterous laugh. And he knew eyes were on him, he could feel them with a sixth sense that had been honed by a life of flitting through the shadows.

And then something sharp latched onto his toe.

It took every ounce of Wade's training to keep from reacting. He flinched, but after that he managed to remain still, biting back a pained cry. A moment later, whatever had been stuck into his toe was disengaged, and then he felt four tiny paws on his shin.

Paws?

Had he just been bitten by a kitten?

The animal crawled up his body and onto his face, sitting down on his mouth. It was long-haired, Wade knew that much from the fur going up his nose and tickling his eyelashes. He remained still, faking sleep, for as long as he possibly could. But breathing was harder with the warm, vibrating little ball of fluff blocking all his airholes, and he gave a false moan and tossed his head like he was sleeping restlessly.

The kitten slid down the side of his face, still purring as it went, until it rolled onto the mattress away from him. It mewed plaintively.

"Oh no, bubba," a quiet voice whispered, almost causing Wade to jump. He'd been so sure he was alone in the room, and he hadn't heard the man approach.

Who the hell were these guys?

The kitten meowed again in response to the whisper, and Wade felt the guy pluck the kitten off the bed. "Leave him alone, he's trying to pretend to sleep."

Wade didn't react. He continued his steady breathing, remaining still and faking sleep. Now that he knew where the guy was, he could feel him moving around. After a few more seconds of the guy lingering in the room, he left with the kitten, murmuring to it quietly before closing the door with a click.

Wade waited. He drifted in and out some more, letting himself do it so he could sell it better, and so he could regain some strength. When he woke for the last time, he listened for movement but heard none. Every one of his senses was straining, making sure he couldn't feel a presence near him. Finally, he cracked one eye open, his lashes masking it.

He was laid out on a single bed, his arms and legs tied to the iron bed frame. As soon as he was certain he was alone, he could easily slip these knots and be on his way.

The room was quiet, but he gave it another sixty seconds. When he still couldn't feel another presence in the room, he opened his eye a little wider.

A man was standing over him, arms crossed against his chest, a smirk on his full lips. "Hi there, kitten," the man said. It was the same mountain drawl Wade had heard on the street.

Wade said nothing, staring at the man.

The guy cocked his head, his brow furrowing as he looked Wade up and down. "How old are you?"

Wade gritted his teeth, staring at the wooden ceiling instead. He noticed writing in white chalk above him: a set of rules written on the dark wood slats above his bed.

1. No weapons.
2. No trying to kill us.
3. Don't make any noise during business hours.
4. No more bleeding on the goddamned hardwood floors.
5. Don't touch the kitties.

Wade scowled at the writing. He heard footsteps on creaky stairs, and steeled himself for whatever was coming.

"He awake?" the man asked as he came into the room. It was the giant from before, the one on the motorcycle. He had curly hair that was turning silver at the temples, black eyes that were hard and piercing, and the muscle mass of a large horse.

"We're in luck, he's a mute!" the guy with the hazel eyes responded. "What about the girl?"

Wade jerked at the words, his eyes darting to the guy.

"She's not mute. But she might as well be, since she's speaking in nothing but what I can only assume are Russian curses," the giant answered as he moved to look down at Wade. He scowled, the laugh lines around his eyes and mouth softening his appearance and making him look almost kind. "How old are you?" he asked Wade.

Wade rolled his eyes and looked back at the rules on the ceiling. Both men stood over him, watching him.

"Listen, I'm Ty, this is Zane," the shorter one said with a jerk of his thumb. "You have three words to convince us not to kill you."

Wade glanced at them again, taking a deep breath. Stitches pulled on the skin of his arm, and he could feel wrappings around his ribs. These guys had patched him up. They had to be the caretakers, and even if they weren't, Wade didn't have much choice, did he?

"Black market orchids," he told them quietly.

Ty and Zane shared a glance, and the one called Ty grinned triumphantly. "Told you."

"You keep plucking lurkers off the street and dragging them to the back stoop, they're going to change your call sign to Alley Cat," Zane threatened. A bell rang downstairs, and Zane glanced at the door. "Untie this kid, I'll be back."

His steps were heavy as he left his partner standing over Wade's bed, arms crossed, lips pursed. Wade met his eyes carefully.

Ty finally shook his head. "My call sign is stupid anyway, they can change it all they want," he said as he pulled a knife from holster at his thigh. He cut Wade loose, and Wade rolled and kicked out at him with a grunt. He wrapped a leg around Ty's knee and jerked, pulling him off-balance and sending them both crashing to the floor. They rolled, grappling for the knife, and slammed into the nearest wall with a rattle of glass and a thump.

Before Wade knew what had happened, his face was pressed into the hardwood floor, his hands held behind his back, and a knee pushed into his spine. He gasped for air against his cracked ribs, peering over his shoulder at the man who had easily dismantled his attack.

The guy was still grinning as he rolled Wade over to his back and cocked his head. He was handsome, with light-brown hair that was graying a little, and laugh lines that highlighted his shining hazel eyes.

His arms and hands were covered in scars, and his body was hard and lean.

Wade blinked up at him. "How old are *you*?" Wade finally blurted.

Ty clucked his tongue, still grinning. "Older than you'll ever be, if that was your best move."

He grabbed Wade by both arms and hefted him to his feet, then brushed him off like he was getting him ready for a prom photo.

Steps thundered on the stairs, but by the time Zane came through the door, gun raised and dark eyes no longer kind, Ty had Wade untied and straightened up, and was presenting him like a prize.

"What?" Ty said innocently.

Zane narrowed his eyes, gun still raised. "What happened?"

"Nothing. What happened to you?" Ty asked him.

Zane holstered the gun, eyes on Wade. "Stop fucking around. Get him debriefed so we can get rid of him."

Ty muttered unintelligibly and jammed his knife back into its sheath.

"You have the girl?" Wade asked them.

"Who is she?" Zane demanded.

Wade straightened his shoulders, shrugging Ty's hand off him. "That's classified."

Ty hummed, shoving his hands into the pockets of his jeans and glancing at Zane from under lowered brows as he strolled away a few steps. They shared a look, and they seemed to be communicating silently. It put Wade on alert, and he shifted his weight, preparing to defend himself.

"You haven't interrogated anyone lately," Ty finally said, his voice dropping to a teasing murmur as he moved toward Zane and the door.

Zane's stern expression finally broke as Ty moved closer, and the smile changed the big man's entire demeanor.

Wade suddenly feared for his life. Quite acutely. "You were checking the computer," he blurted.

Both men turned to look at him, and their smirks told him that they were once again one step ahead of him.

He sighed. "Check it."

"Already did," Zane said. "Brady Wade, twenty-five. This isn't your first rodeo, but it always hurts to get bucked, huh?"

Wade's cheeks warmed in embarrassment. He wasn't sure why, but part of him deep down wanted to impress these two men. They weren't like other caretakers he'd encountered, though they were always crafty and tough. These two looked like they could still be in the field doing the job he'd nearly failed at last night.

"Twenty-five?" Ty asked. He looked Wade up and down, obviously not approving of what he saw. "I was banking late teens. Purely on skill level, though. Don't make them like they used to, huh?"

"Maybe he looks older with his shoes on," Zane offered. Ty hummed and pursed his lips.

Wade gave an insulted grunt as Ty left the room, and Zane stood smiling and shaking his head.

"I need the girl," Wade insisted. "I have to take her in."

Zane made a negative noise. "From the looks of it, she won your little game of cat and mouse. We're calling in the big dogs to end it."

Wade took a quick step forward, and found himself staring down the barrel of Zane's gun before he could raise both hands. He stood still, gritting his teeth. "If you turn her over, I'm done. Please. I need this win."

Zane cocked his head. He didn't look very sympathetic.

Wade closed his eyes, keeping both hands up. "I've been chasing her for two years. Please."

Zane considered him for several long seconds, then holstered his gun. "You drink coffee?"

Wade nodded. "Are there people who don't drink coffee?"

Zane rolled his eyes. "Come with me."

Wade hesitated, but he followed the man through the narrow hallway and down three winding flights of stairs. Each level below the one he'd been held on, which was locked up tight from what he saw as they passed through the doors, was a warren of bookshelves, books stacked three and four high in some places.

The main level was more organized, with heavy wooden shelving and cushy chairs scattered throughout. Ty was flipping a closed sign on the antique glass door and locking up.

"Your call, Wildcat," Zane said to him, and Ty turned to them. "Let him talk to her or not?"

Ty narrowed his eyes as he met Wade's. "Let me guess. You don't bring her down, your career is over, right?"

Wade swallowed hard. He hated himself for answering, but he nodded.

Ty strolled up to him, standing a foot or two away, his eyes piercing right into Wade's soul. Wade flashed back to his childhood and standing in the kitchen as his father asked if he'd done his homework.

"And why do you think we give a shit about saving your career?" Ty asked him, voice low and cold.

Wade blinked, swallowing hard.

But then Ty snorted and grinned, smacking Wade on the shoulder so hard that he stumbled sideways. Zane caught him and righted him with two strong hands. "Jesus kid, lighten up," Ty said with a laugh. "Better lucky than good any day, am I right?"

"Tyler, quit playing with your food."

Ty shrugged and walked away.

Wade watched them both uneasily. "How'd you bag her?" he found himself asking.

Ty hummed as he took a gun from under his flannel shirt and set it behind the counter along one wall of the store. "Well, *you* were my mark. You'll have to ask Lone Star how he brought her in."

Wade glanced at Zane, who was sipping at a dainty cup of cappuccino and ignoring them as he settled onto a stool behind the counter and brought out a book. Wade shook his head. He didn't know which agent he was more wary of at this point.

"Okay, come on, you can talk to the girl," Ty said as he pulled another hidden gun from somewhere and handed it over to Zane. Then he took Wade's elbow and led him toward the back of the store. Wade glanced at Zane, scowling in confusion.

Behind a set of blue French doors near the stairwell, the quaint little bookstore transformed into a sleek, modern kitchen. It was a little disorienting, but Wade followed Ty to the far side of the kitchen, where a large refrigerator stood.

"You hungry?" Ty asked. He handed Wade an orange Gatorade before Wade could answer. "You lost a lot of blood, drink that."

"Please," he said through gritted teeth, losing his patience. He set the Gatorade down on a nearby counter. "I need information from her before they process her, and I need it now. I don't have time for a fucking snack."

Ty nodded and picked the Gatorade up again, shoving it into Wade's hands. Then he opened up the fridge, gesturing inside. Wade peered in, and then Ty pushed him from behind into a small elevator car, stepping in with him and closing the cage up. The space was so small that they stood nose to nose. Or, they would have, if Wade had been about three inches taller. He stood blinking up at the man, not even breathing because he couldn't tell that Ty was breathing, and he would be damned if he made more noise in a silent space than this fucking guy . . .

"Been doing this long?" Wade asked. When he did finally breathe, his chest touched Ty's.

Ty cocked his head, smirking. "Long enough."

The elevator car came to a gentle stop, and Ty was still smiling as he pushed the door open. "After you."

Wade blinked hard, then got out, eyes still on Ty. He finally tore his eyes off Ty and looked around. The basement was lined in stone, with metal shelving full of supplies covering the walls and brand-new wooden floors that seemed at odds with the burns and pitting on the stone.

"Your girl's in there," Ty told Wade, pointing to a jail cell door in the corner. "Only way out of here is through that elevator, you understand?"

Wade glanced at the elevator car and nodded.

"You got five minutes to get what you need. Your ride's incoming." Ty turned and closed the elevator gate, waving his fingers daintily in farewell as the car rose out of sight.

Wade stood with his mouth hanging open.

"Wade?" an accented voice called from the cage behind him. "These men are insane. Wade. Wade? Don't leave me here."

Wade snorted, still staring at the elevator shaft. Who were these guys?

Zane sipped his coffee and watched Ty stroll back in from the kitchen. "You left him down there?"

"I'm not a babysitter, dude," Ty grunted, pressing against Zane's back and resting his forearm on Zane's shoulder as they both watched the monitor built into the counter. The agent kid stood in front of the cell, discussing the terms of the female agent's surrender.

"Do you speak any Russian when you're not asleep?" Zane asked.

Ty rested his chin on Zane's other shoulder, humming. "No."

Zane turned his head, and Ty caught him with a kiss. He was grinning when he pulled back. "I'm glad he woke up, thought we were going to have to stay here through the night again."

"Last time we did that was pretty fun," Zane reminded him.

Ty made a sound that was something between a hum and a growl, and kissed Zane again.

"Home office is coming to pick this guy and his girlfriend up any second," Zane told him, turning on his stool and grabbing Ty's belt loops.

"Hope he gets what he needs before then." Ty grinned and raised an eyebrow.

Zane snorted. "You miss being out in the field like him?"

"Like him?" Ty pointed to the video monitor. "Not one bit."

Zane nodded. Ty grabbed his face and kissed him messily. "Out in the field like *us*, though?" he growled.

Zane wrapped his arms around him, smiling as Ty kissed him again.

"I miss that a little. Sometimes." Ty looked over Zane's shoulder wistfully. "When it's too quiet."

Zane stood and picked Ty up, setting him on the counter. He tilted his head one way, then the other, running his nose against Ty's. "It's never too quiet. Not with you around."

Made in the USA
Las Vegas, NV
12 January 2021